Dedication

For PH
May their watering cans turn to fire hoses, and then to waterfalls.

Published 2004 by Medallion Press, Inc.
225 Seabreeze Ave.
Palm Beach, FL 33480

Printed in the United States of America

Acknowledgments

Kurt R.A. Giambastiani and Karen Templeton for not laughing at me too heinously when I stumbled, and for helping me up

The real Vince Gainey
Looks like the Spinster of Lodwar finally made good.
"Raise high the makuti, fundi."

Jool
Thank you for being the foundation of all of my humor...Oh yes, and saving my life, without which I never would have annoyed as many people.
"Hospital? What is it?"
"It's a big building with patients, but that's not important."
The Big Trip still RULES!

Helen, Leslie, Pam, and Connie
The Visionary Goddesses of Medallion for physically restraining me from writing about The Most Notorious Rake in All of London

and
Leopold

THE HINTERLANDS

PRESS

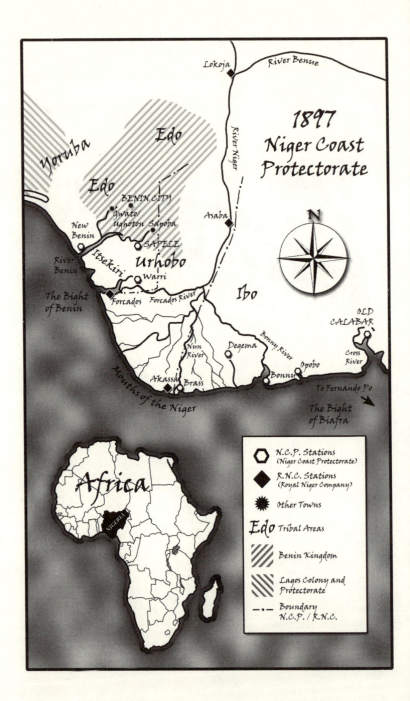

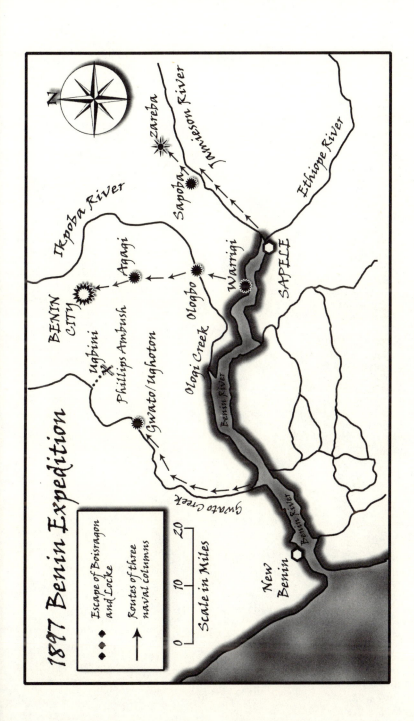

1897 Benin Expedition

N

Ikpoba River

Jamieson River

ZAREBA

Ethiope River

Sapoba

Warrigi

SAPELE

Agagi

BENIN CITY

Ologbo

Ologi Creek

Ugbini

Phillips Ambush

Gwato/Ughoton

Benin River

Gwato Creek

New Benin

Benin River

Escape of Boisragon and Locke

Routes of three naval columns

Scale in Miles

0   10   20

CHAPTER

1

September 2, 1896
Old Calabar, Niger Coast Protectorate

Perhaps she shouldn't have said it quite that way. She should have been more circumspect.

"I'm here to study clitoridectomy."

Ralph Moor stared as if Elle were wearing her drawers on the outside of her skirt. The nose on his marsupial face twitched. "I . . . see. Well, Mrs. Bowie. I am sure that to a young anthropologist this godforsaken coast seems an inviting opportunity. I feel compelled to tell you, however, that these people are extremely barbaric and vicious in their dealings."

Elle leaned forward in the chair. "I had heard something to that effect, Consul. And it only served to incite my curiosity even more. I wish to learn about the most far-flung aboriginal peoples of the world. Why, last year, I was in Australia studying the bush people." That was an exaggeration. The closest she had come to bush people in Australia was a harried one-hour stop in Sydney rushing from steamer to steamer on the docks. "Did you know, sir, that they believe a kangaroo can turn into a rock?"

Moor barked a small laugh. "Oh, my, my. If you think that is exciting, the people of Benin City will keep you occupied for years."

"Years?" Rip McCulloch jumped in his chair. He was a hand-some man, with tendrils of white-blond hair clinging to his shirt collar, and a dimple in his chin. After ten years as Elle's partner, it was still a pleasure for her to gaze upon him. He fanned his face with his Stetson hat. "We don't have years, do we, Elle?"

Elle laughed charmingly. "Rip is in a big hurry to take his photographs. He gets very edgy when he cannot be around native peoples."

Ralph Moor turned suddenly sober. "Well, surely you've heard of the saying . . . 'The Bight of Benin! The Bight of Benin! One comes out where three goes in.' "

Elle and Rip looked at each other knowingly, chortling with camaraderie, as if they had just been singing that very song. Elle ventured to say, "Well, then. We had better be three people in our party, hadn't we?"

The Consul General was too stodgy to understand Elle was joking. "Yes, and I have just the man for you. Mateus Barbosa. He speaks the corrupt Portuguese dialect spoken by the older inhabitants of Benin City."

Becoming sober herself, Elle said, "That is a good idea, sir. Where can I find this fellow?"

"He lives in Sapele. I'll write you a note of introduction. Just be sure to not look . . . agape at him or his surroundings. He can be very touchy. He lives aboard the old hulk *Hindustan,* and I daresay he's most sensitive about it. And be certain not to drink any palm wine when you're near him." He was already scrib-bling a note for Elle. She looked on eagerly, but could not read the spiky, upside-down handwriting. "While you're in Sapele, look in on another man for me, would you, my dear? This chap has been known to trade with the Benin people, which is some-thing the rest of us cannot say." He handed the note to a waiting servant for the man to seal, then looked at Elle with a sudden flashing of his dark eyes. "The place is a fortress, my dear. They refuse to trade with us and have cut themselves off from all contact. Many valuable trade products are lying in storage in this dusky king's territories due to the fetish rule of that unfortunate land."

"Oh, they won't refuse to deal with me, sir. I have methods for cajoling and coercing men into . . . dealing."

Rip nodded. "Yes, Elle . . . er, my wife has the power of persuasion, as they say."

"Well, then. Perhaps you can cajole Brendan Donivan into opening up the trade routes. We need the hinterlands trade, the palm oil, the ivory." An idealistic sheen came to Moor's eyes when he said, "Palm oil is the life blood of the Delta, flowing down the main artery, the River Niger!" When he got no reaction from the Yankees, he added gravely, "You'll find Mr. Donivan along the Ethiope River, in the house on stilts. He's an American also, so you should have a lot to discuss."

Elle was sweltering inside her hunting costume. She swore to hang her corset from the branch of the next tree she saw. And the boater hat was the height of absurdity. "I am not one for trade or politics, being strictly an anthropologist, but if you say Mr. Donivan has knowledge of Benin City, then I shall look in on him."

Moor accepted the note from the servant. He seemed about to proffer it to Elle, but he had something more to say. "If you can convince Mr. Donivan to speak with the king of Benin City on our behalf, the whole of Britannia would honor you. As you know, it helps everyone when the needs of three continents are met. Just think! Your country may have never fought the War of Independence, if such was the case."

"Yes . . . " Elle said vaguely.

"Yes . . . " agreed Rip.

Moor inhaled and exhaled. "Well, then! Good cheer to you." He held the note out as a tribute, and stood. "Now, be certain to hire the best canoe boys. These rivers are most treacherous." Moor turned his angry eyes onto Rip's innocent form. Rip stood, adjusting his corduroy vest. "Doesn't your husband have to attend to the bags outside? I cannot guarantee they will still be there. These natives are most—"

"Yes, sir!"

It made Elle jump when Rip saluted, his body all coiled like a rattlesnake. She wished he wouldn't do that. She followed Rip out of the room, a drip of moisture rolling down into her cleavage. The hunting costume with its tight belt of shotgun cartridges was smothering her, and she longed to be out of doors.

In front of the stone Government House, Rip guarded their baggage with his Colt in one hand, taking assiduous swigs from a flask with the other. Elle rattled him by the arm. "No palm wine!"

Rip exhaled happily. "I tell you . . . I'm still tickled to death whenever someone calls me your husband."

Elle relaxed at the sight of Rip's twinkling eyes, his dimples cuter than a baby's. One had to relax around Rip; his charming and guileless ways had extracted them from many a fix. "Well. Just make sure you keep up that front 'til we get out of this . . . joint."

Although the red-roofed citadel of the Government House had a nicely mowed viridian lawn, it was merely an oasis in the quagmire of mud, piss, and banana peels that comprised the rest of Old Calabar. Below, the Calabar River was exotic enough in a teeming mercantile sort of way, with its barges and giant canoes loaded up with puncheons of palm oil. This part of the coast was one colossal mangrove swamp, intersected by a network of creeks. The loud morass was sensational even to Elle, who after all was jaded, having been around the world and to every port that mattered.

"Anyway. We're not near that Matardus joker so I don't need to watch my palm wine."

"Yes; I wonder what's up with that?" Elle was looking for her umbrella in the cart full of trunks, knapsacks, and photographic equipment boxes.

"More'n likely he's some lowdown varmint." Without even

glancing at the cart, Rip reached in and withdrew Elle's umbrella. He was such a gentleman he even opened it before handing it to her. "Why else would Moor have given you a sealed letter of introduction? The letter probably tells him to ambush us at the first turn of the river."

"Oh, Rip." Elle looked to the cart boy, remembered she didn't know the local language, a frightening pidgin English, so just waved her arm to indicate he should start pulling the cart down the hill. "The note probably says something he's embarrassed for us to hear, like 'make sure you tighten my mother's truss.'"

They walked down Consular Hill through the magical air that caressed Elle's forearms. She had heard this part of the Niger Coast was the whiteman's graveyard and emitted noxiously mortal fumes by night, but so far it seemed like a happily tropical idyll.

"I'd like to tighten his mother's truss. That fellow is a traitorous villain if ever I saw one."

"Rip, don't be so skeptical about everyone."

"And don't you smell this air? It's got a decomposing aroma."

"It's the jungle."

They were always followed by a trail of innocently smiling children, like what America would be like without poverty. All right, it was an ignorant outlook. But it made Elle feel good, as though they weren't anywhere near the "City of Blood" yet. She wanted to see Benin City. But in another regard, she didn't.

— ✦ —

The leopard jumped him! Its powerful paws were around his neck, and it was sinking its incisors into the back of his head! He threw the beast off and roared to his feet. He could feel the silky bulk of his dog pressing against his thigh as she reared up in a fury of monstrous barking.

Where did the leopard go? Why was there no blood spilling

down his neck? Why was Ode laughing down at him from his perch in the karite tree?

"Iwi!" the boy squealed at the top of his lungs. "You look so funny!"

Brendan now pointed his rifle at the squirming form of the boy in the tree. "Where did the leopard go?" he yelled in Edo. He saw the bait monkey still tethered to the stake, and when he slid his hand beneath his helmet of leaves, he felt no blood. A creepy feeling came over him as though he had just fallen like a thousand of brick from the karite tree, and the leopard had never even been there. The dog's bark now seemed curiously full of humor.

Ode's trilling laughter gave forth. Leaping on the tree trunk, Brendan shook it so mercilessly the small boy, hugging his bow and quiver of poison arrows to his chest, crashed harmlessly to the duff of the jungle floor. Still laughing, Brendan noted.

"Get up. Let's go home."

It was too much to hope that the little critter would disremember what had just transpired. The boy held his stomach as though his guts would fall out from laughing as Brendan jerked him along the murky path. Ode trailed the monkey on the tether, the monkey shrieking at being almost laid out flat. Could anything be more mortifying?

"You looked so funny! You went to sleep and fell off the—"

"That's right!" Brendan shouted sternly. "And that's exactly what I was trying to demonstrate to you, Ode. This is the *wrong* thing to do when you're leopard hunting. You must make sure to take every precaution not to go to sleep—"

The boy was merciless. "But Iwi, you really were asleep! Your eyes closed, and then you started sliding off the branch—"

"I was only pretending, boy! This is part of your apprenticeship. You are much too young to join *iroghae* anyway, so I thought I'd give you a few more lessons that other leopard hunters don't get. It keeps you busy when you aren't helping

Ikponmwosa in the farm. Or perhaps you would rather be harvesting yams?"

That finally calmed the urchin. "No, sir. I'd rather be hunting with *you*." He beat the air with his quiver.

The way Ode puffed up when he said "you" made Brendan relax a little, confident the boy wouldn't tattle about the incident. After all, Brendan was Ighiwiyisi, "the hunter who shall not get lost in a foreign land." The Oba himself had given him a gift of the boy Abievbode, in return for two ferocious live leopards. Brendan wore a string of leopard teeth around his neck, and he was allowed to carry a leopard skin shield. If Ode ever doubted him, Brendan didn't think he could bear it.

After they had walked through the jungle for six hours and into daybreak, Brendan started speaking aloud in English. He knew this made Ode quizzical, but Ode's eyes had started to slide shut a long time ago. The lad stumbled ahead like a zombie, sleepwalking through the entire racket. "That leopard would've run all over me like fire in dry grass. I'm a poor worm of the first degree. This young one isn't going to respect me if I keep full of devilment."

For it had taken Brendan six hours of hard walking to admit to himself the reason he'd fallen from the karite tree. He wasn't asleep, quite. It was more like a hazy waking dream where someone dropped a gauze curtain over his head. He saw a woman, a white woman of sun-browned finery with a proud stately throat, flashing dark eyes, and loads of auburn hair shining like velvet pouring over her shoulders. The strange thing about the vision, the thing that made Brendan realize it wasn't a real memory, was that the white woman stood next to a chair of European design, yet carved with imagery from Edo. There was the Oba with his mudfish legs next to a leopard that had decapitated a critter of some kind. The most anomalous carving was a whiteman in a boat holding an oar. In the other hand he grasped a chain attached to a barrel, and behind him was a cannon. Brendan had never seen such a chair in Edo, only the carved square stools the Oba and *uzama* had. He knew then it was witchery that brought the vision to him, perhaps from the crossroads that morning, where the white-tailed ant thrush had called its harsh prophetic cry.

Brendan imagined a dead person was playing a trick on him. If a woman died childless with no one to bury her properly, she was stuck in this world as a ghost. Understandably, ghosts were irked with the living. A fellow from the *Igbesanmwan*—the ivory carvers' guild where men made glorious altar tusks, hand clappers, and ceremonial swords—had died recently, and if his children hadn't buried him with his feet pointing toward Ughoton, he couldn't take the canoe to *erinmwin*. He could be kicking up a fuss, not being able to travel to the world across the sea, heaven.

"But why would the ivory carving fellow be sassing me?" Brendan wondered aloud. "Why am I tortured by a vision of a white woman? There's no white woman here."

They were now emerging from the inviolate jungle cover and into the blinding chartreuse glare of yam farms. There were sacrificial yam heaps topped with cutlasses and hoes next to calabashes of palm wine. Along the road were *idiogbo*, three sticks planted upright in the ground to represent the ancestors who first farmed along the path. Brendan paused at a mound of red earth beneath a tree where there was a terra cotta pot of water. He withdrew a few cowrie shells from a pouch at his waist, paid for the water, and drank a coconut shell full before handing it to Ode. Ode was waking now, as he wanted to be sure everyone saw him returning from his important leopard hunting training.

Brendan was gratified to see that people stopped their work and stared respectfully. He felt silly as always in the bushy helmet, but he knew that even strangers would recognize him as the *Oyinbo* leopard hunter of the Oba's. He enjoyed the eclectic hodgepodge of his attire, his hunting vest of forest green duck, the brass leopard face hip ornament, and his black American river boots that just reached his kneecaps. He left his long chestnut hair free-flowing, but for hunting he applied palm oil and clamped it down with coral decorations, as a pigtail down the middle of his back. Altogether Brendan felt quite feral in his getup.

"There's a few white women in Sapele. Mary Wells, the missionary, but she's got moustaches to rival Captain Gainey's. Bradley Forshaw's wife, Caroline, but she resembles a manatee. I don't think either one of them was the one in the vision. That Victoria visiting Gainey was a peach, sure enough." His penis instantly stiffened at the thought of Victoria, her white skin unmarred by the sun, her delicate earlobes like seashells. He had spent many a pleasurable moment masturbating and thinking of Victoria, hating Captain Gainey all the more. Beneath his robust cheer, Gainey was ripe for the devil with his empire-building.

However, Victoria's hair was the color of strawberries, not lustrous auburn like the woman in the vision. Brendan's guilt at thinking of *Oyinbo* women overtook him, and at the next "silent market" he paid more cowries for plantains, some to eat and some to leave as tribute to his *ikegobo*, his shrine to his Hand. He was surprised to have been so aroused by the vision of the woman, when he thought he had put such superficial things behind him.

Onaiwu, a friendly fellow of the *ighele* grade, jumped in the middle of the path with one arm stiff in the air. Ode kept on toward the city gate, trailing the monkey on the leash.

Brendan and Onaiwu confronted each other near a shrine, a mound of raised rusty earth embedded with sticks upon which shreds of white cloth were tied. There were so many shrines in that land it was hard to understand them all, but Brendan knew this was a shrine to Osanobua, creator of everything in the universe. Brendan's Da would be turning over in his grave if he knew Brendan even listened to notions such as that.

Brendan made the three circles with his right hand. "*Kóyo. Vbèè óye hé?*" Hello. How are things?

Onaiwu was so clearly agitated he didn't even give the standard response. "*Oyinbo* are coming to the city!" On his forehead a vein bulged in perfect symmetry with his vertical cicatrices. Onaiwu had a retinue behind him of other *ighele* men who protected the city and acted as policemen. "A runner told me they left Ughoton this morning."

Brendan nodded. "So they won't arrive here by tonight. How many of them? Are they English?"

"Only two, all we know is there are *Oyinbo*. The runner said Mateus was with them."

"Well, ain't it precious?" Brendan exploded in English, striking the muddy ground with his pike. Mateus Barbosa was a swinish cane rat of a man who made a good way for himself playing each tribe against the other. He mainly acted as broker between Africans and whitemen in matters of palm oil, stirring up trouble wherever he went. Because he'd been born in the Oil Rivers— his ancestors were the Portuguese adventurers who stayed in Edo and intermarried—and because he spoke the secret language still understood by the top *uzama* and *eghaevbo*, he was free to come and go in Edo.

Brendan sputtered angrily, and had to turn aside and glare at the earthen city walls, seventy-five feet above the bottom of the moat from which they had been dug. He turned back to Onaiwu and his men. "*Oyinbo!* And just what makes them think they can come here, when we haven't allowed any others?"

"We think they must be very impudent, or else very stupid."

"If they have Mateus with them, they're not stupid. He'd enjoy scaring them with frightening stories of what they think are evil doings in Edo."

Onaiwu stuck out his lower lip. "So, they are arrogant."

Brendan exhaled. "Aren't they all? And don't worry. I have tricks that I know will work very well on *Oyinbo*."

The irate aura surrounding the group of men lightened as they turned as a unit and headed for the city gates, although some of the more bellicose ones continued to huff angrily through their nostrils.

Onaiwu enquired, "Will you tell me about your trick?"

Brendan knew he shouldn't be so averse to other whitemen, but he was. He had lived intermittently in Edo for three years now after jumping ship during a particularly boring sojourn on the Forcados River, and he preferred it to *Akpo r'Oyinbo*, the whiteman's world. That was one reason he should pay tribute at his *ikegobo* for thinking erotically about *Oyinbo* women—if he scorned the industrial crap of civilization, he should scorn the women as well. "Yes, I'll need your help tomorrow."

Ugiagbe, a bold *ighele* man, stuck his oar in. "We can help you now! If we intercept them on the Ughoton road, we can scare them with the deity to whom we sacrifice blood."

"No!" bellowed another. "We can kill them!"

Brendan glared at the men over his shoulder. "Do you want the entire Liverpool Army"—for that was the only town in England they knew—"coming to kill everyone in Edo? No, my plan is better."

"Ighiwiyisi knows what he is doing," Onaiwu chastised Ugiagbe.

When they arrived at the northern gate, Brendan was close to his house. He knew Ode had gone home—although given to Brendan as a slave, Brendan chose to have another family care for him. Ode was too young to hear the plans of *ighele* men, so he was right to have continued on without Brendan.

Brendan was in a jovial mood. What a day! He had gone from mortification to anger, and now fairly chortled with glee at the thought of those arrogant *Oyinbo* having the gall to come to Edo. He entered the courtyard of his house, laughing aloud at the new *kora* that sat atop a stool. "Hey! Ikponmwosa!" he shouted as he ducked under the lintel of his front door and into the relative cool of the red clay house. "All hands on deck!"

He wandered from room to room, sticking his head into the various chambers of the honeycomb house. "Ikponmwosa?" He passed through a freshly glazed and spacious atrium. At either end were altars inlaid with cowries, and alcoves filled with carved ivories, porcelain platters, and fine mats. He paused in one room to divest himself of the leafy hat and armament, and in another room to deposit his plantains, placing several chunks that he cut with his Bowie knife atop the brass *ikegobo* on its mud altar. His particular *ikegobo* was a monument to lofty pretension, adorned as it was with figures of warriors brandishing swords, spears, shields and ceremonial doings—and, of course, a figure killing a leopard. Only the Oba and *uzama* had *ikegobo* as elaborate as Brendan's, but they had allowed him to have it made. Folding his arms in front of his bare chest, he smiled with pride at the altar.

"What're those cops doing in the courtyard?"

Brendan jumped, and was embarrassed he had jumped. "They say smoke follows pretty folks."

"You know I don't like them. Can you get rid of them?"

Brendan snorted. "Well, you're a sight."

Evin's face looked even more lupine when he squinched it up like that, his smoke-colored lens spectacles perched atop his nose. His well-trimmed moustache and little monkish beard made up for the hair that wasn't on his head. "Maybe if you'd stop worshipping at your own shrine, you could clean and gut one of those hundreds of animals you just killed."

Brendan laughed, but moved back into the hallway to cover up his shame at not having killed even one animal. "You know I didn't bag anything, because Ode already told you."

Evin always followed him. Brendan knew he was back there, with his fancy-woven *eruhan* kilt, his bare feet, his head wrapped in a length of red silk. "We cancelled our lesson, I have to go back to the fields. But I can stay to give you another lesson."

"Are there still weevils in the corn? Ain't that poison you ordered from the States come yet?"

"Well, as usual it took the direct route through the South Pole on its way to bonny Old Calabar." Evin paused in the front doorway behind Brendan, pointing at the courtyard. "Look at those guys. What's up?"

Brendan waved at the *ighele* men, who scattered like a passel of parrots. "Come back tomorrow morning at sunrise," he told them. Evin couldn't speak but the most base of the Edo language, just enough to order things in the market. Brendan was proud of his own facility with languages. "I reckon my graphophone records got hung up in Casablanca, too. I'm waiting on that *Il Trovatore*."

"I'm waiting on those coon songs myself. Bill Newcomb over in Albertville's sending me Hogan's new sheet music. 'All Coons Look Alike to Me.' "

Brendan smirked. "That's a mighty ironic title to be teaching these Edo folks." For Evin had been amusing himself of late, whenever in Edo, by giving classes to men of the *iroghae* age grade and even some elders of *edion*. With his Washburn lyre guitar, banjo, mouth harp, and accordion, Evin had distilled an agreeable mix of music with Edo brass bells, ivory horns, rattles made from calabashes adorned with cowries, and the most boda-cious assortment of stringed instruments known to man.

"Well, I just won't sing the words," Evin agreed. "We can jazz it with hand clappers and *koras*. They'll never know the difference. Are you going to tell me what those cops were doing out here?"

Exhaling mightily, Brendan took a small leap off the front mud stoop and struck for his favorite umbrella tree. "Some beefeaters are headed this way." Was Evin's mouth open to let in flies again? From an alcove in the mud wall that enclosed his home and courtyard, Brendan withdrew his tobacco box, hoping beyond hope that there were some cigarette papers in there. Smoking pipes and chewing tobacco was all right for other folks, but Brendan enjoyed a good cigarette now and then.

He heard Evin sputtering as he followed him into the courtyard. "Beefeaters are coming here? Are the cops going to kill them?"

Praise be, there were cigarette papers in his wooden box. "Keep your shirt on, Ev. I'm going to make sure no harm comes to them." Brendan took a stool. He gestured vaguely at Evin, who still stood like a scarecrow in the middle of the yard. "Pull up a stool, or sit on the ground."

Evin sat. "Do you know what they want?"

"The usual, I reckon. They want to ratify the treaty that Gallwey tricked the Oba into making in ninety-two. But of course they're going to make out like it's a mighty grave thing, stopping the bloodshed."

Evin nodded earnestly. "Flint over at the Royal Niger Company's been having it up and down with old Moor, a-hollering about who's got the right to the Edo trade."

Brendan enjoyed it when Evin became so heated he allowed his Alabama patois to slip into his speech. "Yup, between those two and the Lagos Colony making a big fuss over a city that ain't theirs for the taking, mayhap all hands'll scupper one another and leave us alone. You can bet Moor's behind sending these beefeaters over this way tomorrow."

Evin barely moved his mouth when he spoke. "Moor's on leave in London."

There was a hush, as though all the air had been sucked out of the firmament above them. All the birds were still, and it seemed as though even the trees ceased dropping leaves for one part of a second.

Then the clamor resumed, the clanging of metal against anvils from the brass casters' guild yonder, children squealing gleefully in their rock-scissors-paper game. Brendan's mouth was shaped like an O, so he flattened it into a knowing grimace. "Well, then. Let the frolics begin." Moor had earlier been an inspector with the Royal Irish Constabulary, "standing at the back of the Irish landlords, bayonet in hand," stifling rebellion. Just for that reason, Brendan and Evin loathed him.

Evin picked up his *kora* and set it on his knee. Brendan could tell by Evin's avuncular disapproval what he was about to say. "I'm keeping a close eye on your frolics, Captain Donivan. No sense in stirring up a lot of trouble. We don't need to give them the excuse they're looking for to come rampaging in here with all the big guns."

Brendan happily rubbed his own bare chest with his hand. He smiled the delighted smile Evin termed "saurian" as he leaned back against the warm mud wall. "Don't be afeard."

His words didn't seem to soothe Evin any, as he snorted even more fiercely and set to picking his *kora* stridently.

2

Ugbini, halfway between Ughoton and Edo

"Oh, Lordy. I sure wasn't expecting a sight like this so early in the morn," said Rip.

Elle was certain she could feel the vaporous fumes of the jungle flowing like ichor through her veins. They stood shoulder to shoulder in a fetish house their local guide George had insisted they visit. It had probably once been a fine house, but the roof had caved in, and as a result the daily rains cast a moldy pall over everything. The molten heads they stared at had once been burnished brass; they now oozed rivulets of slime.

"I think they're beautiful," Elle opined with tilted head.

Rip put a protective arm around her. "I haven't seen anything this creepy since those coal-walking fellows in India."

"No, these are really gorgeous, Rip. You're just not looking at them the right way. And those fire-walking fellows weren't creepy, either. They were mystics and couldn't feel the coals."

"No, don't you see how those eyes have no pupils in them? And what's that stiff cast around that fellow's neck? Did someone strangle him?"

Elle shook him with annoyance. "But look at how exquisitely detailed it is! That's surely a *necklace* and not a cast, Rip, and look at the detailed work in that hat thingamajig. There are birds and dinky . . . delicate . . . faces of—"

"I'm telling you, Elle, it looks like a death mask, like it was cast right around the poor old dead lady, and I, for one, am getting out of here."

Elle spoke sternly. "Rip. Stop being so discombobulated. Don't you see? It's obvious the Portuguese made these heads. Or they trained some of the natives in their casting techniques. Surely you don't think it's possible for the natives to create such detailed and aesthetic works of art."

"Works of art?" Rip fairly spat in her face with indignation. "Don't you see what this is, Elle? These people are head-hunters! Cannibals! These heads are calling to their heathen gods to bring more victims to them, luring more addlepated dumbheads like us into their lair so they can—"

"These weren't made by no Portagees!"

It was a bark like a dog, but a man resembling a monkey stepped out of the shadows of the fetish house. Elle and Rip now clutched at each other's shirtfronts as they slowly backed away from the simian man.

"Do you think those wine-soaked blockheads could make something of this majestic grandeur?" he growled, holding his arms out from his sides as though his hands grasped cow dung. In the dim smoky light, his coarse black hair stuck out at odd angles like a woven wicker mat, and the whites of his eyes bulged like intestines. "No! Any fool can tell from the Queen Mother's hairstyle that it was Egyptians who taught the Edo about brass casting."

"Egyptians?" Both Elle and Rip scoffed.

"Egyptians!" roared Mateus. He waved a brutal arm as though scything wheat, and crabbed in a bow-legged stance over to the altar, where he indicated one of the heads. "You see this conical headpiece? It's identical to the hairstyle of the Pharaohs!"

Rip snarled at the fierce man. "Sure, if the Egyptians were accustomed to wearing roosters on their heads." He stomped out of the hut.

Elle wandered to the bust of the Queen Mother. She was perched on a shelf above fetish idols such as wooden water pots studded with metal, and three battered elephant tusks that had been carved as intricately as those in China. The Queen's eyes were inlaid with iron irises and were heavily outlined and bug-eyed. She wore a high cylindrical bead collar that reached her beautiful cupid lips. "Who is to say the people of Benin City didn't create this on their own? I have seen other situations where cultures have been separated by thousands of miles with no trade between, creating similar and advanced art."

Mateus seemed born with that cynical, disparaging sneer, as though his lip had gotten snagged on a tooth. "*E' incerto*. I would sooner believe that than say Portuguese cur had a hand in this."

Shaping her arm into a crescent, Elle steered Mateus toward the hut's door. She spoke in a seductively singsong tone. "Mateus . . . How much truth is there to all this buzz about human sacrifice?"

Mateus shrank exaggeratedly from her, cringing back with claw-like hands held to his chest. As though she had been about to touch his filthy skin!

"Reason I ask is, as an anthropologist these sorts of things interest me. I have no stake in the political doings of the various British factions; I could care less if they all kill each other. The English are dogs," she ventured, to see his reaction, "but I am most eager to know more about this human sacrifice I have heard rumored."

Mateus lifted his lips as though they slid around a large piece of liver. "The more British come . . . the more they kill."

Rip was shouting, "Mateus! The hammock boys refuse to budge! They say we haven't washed their mouths. What in Sam Hill does that mean?"

Elle and Mateus emerged from the hut into the dripping illumination of the jungle path. The head dragoman and guide George, an impudent fellow in an absurd woman's dressing gown of scalloped cornflower satin and a dusting cap that was set saucily askew, was beating the laughing men about the shoulders with a quirt in a half-hearted effort to get them to move. However, with adequate rum distributed to the men, blankets and waterproofs were lashed to rough poles with *tie-tie*, hammocks were raised, and the party resumed its way in a desultory manner. Elle insisted on walking, even in the most ridiculous of terrain, as she was a proponent of various healthy water-cures and outdoor activities, and felt that being carried in a hammock would be too embarrassing.

They had been told the road from Ughoton was a fine boulevard suitable for a four-wheeled carriage, but it rapidly became evident someone had been drinking too much *tombo*, for it was merely a cart-road through the coarse sandy ground. In places the jungle was so dense and teeming there were tunnels burrowed in the plant life through which they had to duck and slap fronds from their faces. Elle now traveled almost as bereft of clothing as Rip in his finer moments, her lingerie consisting of drawers, a linen chemise, and one deliciously lavender silk petticoat under her vertically striped skirt. She kept the straw boater, as she could stuff her long hair under it even when the pins slid out of its coils, and she was glad for the beaver congress shoes she could slide on and off, although they had grown an indelible film of mold she couldn't scrape off with a knife.

Mateus insisted on flanking the rear, his worn revolver banging at his hip to encourage the carriers to keep the pace. The partners bent down to enter another jungle tunnel.

"This has to beat all for our most *loco* idea yet, Mrs. Bowie," Rip drawled in his good-natured way. He spun to face her, holding a mass of lianas out of her way.

Rip had been a cowboy of some sort in Texas, and he had maintained the commendable physique Elle imagined all cowboys had, the easy, sloping muscles wrapped around long bones, the shimmering skin richly fawn from the sun. She often liked to appreciate Rip in a remote way, when there was nothing better to do. "Oh, I think the lunatic asylum was the most daring thing."

"Ah, well, you're probably right on that one," Rip said casually over his shoulder. "But seeing as how I wasn't able to accompany you, I can't have much of an opinion. Still, I've got a feeling the lunatics here will make those women in New York look like missionary wives."

Why was he taking off his corduroy vest? Maybe his vest was moldy. Ah, well, it would amuse her to watch the lovely inclination of his wide shoulders, and—Why was he taking off his shirt? He stuffed the shirt into the belt loop of his denims, and Elle became a little groggy watching the flickering sunlight as shadows slithered across his bare back. "They really incarcerated me there, you know," she called weakly. "It wasn't just a stunt on my part. It was more like really being incarcerated." In her idle moments it was pleasant to gaze upon Rip's nicely shaped buttocks, the haunches that moved so splendidly, like a stalking beast.

As a suffragist, Elle felt no shame in her feelings. She allowed herself the fullest luxury of fantasy, especially when it was not acted upon, or spoken aloud. Often, when her mind strayed in such a manner, she did wonder what was to become of her, or what was to become of Rip! Why had he thrown away a ranch full of cows, steer, or whatever they had in Texas, to join up with her, to traipse the world on such dubious missions? He could have had a wife and children by now. He was obviously perfectly capable. One could tell that easily from the wonderfully graceful plane of the small of his back, the sudden whiteness of his naked rear as the denim slid down over them, and—*oh!*

She nearly had the breath knocked out of her when she bumped into Rip's backside. He was bent over in that limber way of his, taking off his cowboy boots and sliding the pants down over his feet. "Oh, Rip! Must you?"

"Hell, why not, Elle? This place is made for this." Squatting before her now, he was tying up all his clothes like a beggar's bundle. He made sure to step back into his cowboy boots before turning to Elle in his splendor, arms spread wide, inviting her to encourage his stupid boldness. "I just thought I'd make these here natives feel a bit more at home."

Shoving him, Elle bade him to continue on. Some carriers were jogging back from the front of the line, probably to ask Mateus for more *tombo*. "Fine! I think it's *you* who has the need to feel at home, if you ask me. You and your nakedness!"

Her irritation didn't faze Rip one smidgen. If anything, it inflated him even more, as he sauntered ahead in his absurd boots and Stetson, and of course the ever-present Colt in his hip holster. "Nudity is a great relief and freedom, as well you should know, Mrs. Bowie, being a stumper for the freedoms of various down-trodden groups. Besides, we've already passed loads of cool clear creeks, and I just might get a hankering for a swim. Then I'll be clean while you're just melting away under all that material."

He had a point. Being a woman, Elle always had to find her own creek, preferably at dusk when mosquitoes were at their worst, try to hang a piece of fabric to cover her pool, and . . . That was it! That was why it annoyed her when Rip threw off all of his clothes! There was more *mystery* to a partially clad man. Somehow it was not nearly as erotic when he was in buff, revealing all. Now, shirtless with a vest, that was different—the top couple of buttons to his denims undone, sitting around a fire, the shadows playing havoc with the exquisite line of silky hair that ran from his navel—

"*Hey, camarada!* Mr. Bowie! I see you're getting into the spirit of things. You'll fit right in over there." Mateus had suddenly appeared behind them, abandoning his post at the rear, all politeness now. "You know, in the courts of Edo—that's Great Benin City to you—the Oba doesn't allow anyone to wear clothes. Yes, that's right. They have to *earn* the privilege. Until then every man, woman, and child must go stark naked."

Rip was happy as a pig in clover. "See what I said, Elle? When in Rome, do as the Romans do."

Elle frowned. "Well, that's all very fine and well, Mr. . . . Mateus. But do let us keep walking. I am not looking forward to spending another night in a leaking hut sleeping in the mud."

"It's like this . . ." Mateus said. "The bridge is out ahead. We need to take a detour. Right over here, you see this antelope trail in the bush? This will take us around the uncrossable creek, and—"

"Ah, hell!" Rip cried jovially. "I can cross any of these danged creeks. Then I'll get my bath in, too. 'Course, I used to have a horse, but no mind. These little peewee creeks don't scare me."

"But what about crocodiles, Rip?" Elle clung to his shoulder as she staggered behind him. "Remember in the canoe, we did see quite a number of them."

Rip paused to withdraw his Colt, and brandished it while looking coyly over his shoulder at Elle, one eye screwed up as though aiming.

Sometimes she thought it was a shame that he seemed to be oblivious to his own charm, but then again, perhaps it was a good thing. "All right, all right. You're going to shoot the crocodiles that leap viciously at you from all angles. How am I to cross the creek? On your back?"

"Well, that's not a bad idea. You can carry my bundle of clothes on your head like these here natives do, and I'll just hoist you up—"

Elle coughed. "What's that smell?"

Rip paused, too. His voice was suddenly cautious, and he spoke slowly. "I'd venture to guess it's some kind of dead . . . "

" . . . thing." Already Elle had her kerchief at her mouth and nose.

They slowed as they stepped over the dead body, as everyone ahead of them had done with nary a concern. Rip took Elle's arm and assisted her to walk around the dead person, and cradled her head into his warm armpit. But she forced herself to see it had been a man, now bloated, discolored, and partially eaten, sprawled in the path with little concern as to whom he inconvenienced.

He wasn't annoying many, as everyone behind them stepped over the body as well, including Mateus. Elle tossed a look back at Mateus as he crabbed from side to side trying to catch up.

"I'm real sorry about that, missus! I tried to get you to take the other path—"

"It's quite all right, Mateus!" Elle cried through her kerchief. "As an anthropologist, as an . . . a . . . "

Rip spoke over the top of Elle's head. "Are you all right, sweet pea? I don't like you having to look at that sort of thing."

Trying to smile, Elle allowed her face to rest against Rip's silken skin. "I'm going to have to get used to it. That *is* our goal, isn't it?"

"Yes . . . " Rip said, but he forged ahead of her once again. He had probably seen many bloated corpses in his path, back in Texas. He ordered back the carriers who were hauling his equipment, and he made several photographs of the corpse, everyone standing around chuckling to each other as though he were a potatohead tourist making photographs of a squirrel.

They continued through the rank fetor of the forest, passing village gates of poles that were draped with cloth and fringes of palm leaf. They passed clearings, rest huts, marketplaces, and crossroads where coconut shells and clay pots full of cool water were placed for the relief of travelers. Every new vista gave Elle indications of Juju, fetish worship: knotted cloths on branches, altars with kola nut offerings, a heap of chalk sticks, or earthenware images. The villagers on the path wore kilts of vibrantly patterned indigo, red, yellow, and green, the architectonic totems bringing to Elle's mind the symbols of Indians from Arizona Territory. She saw that the wealthier men cocooned themselves from the waist down with all manner of calicos and fine muslin 'til they resembled dinner bells, so perhaps George's dressing gown costume was his attempt at dressing to the nines.

In the vigorous foliage by the path appeared the figure of a fine youth with arms extended and wrists fastened to a scaffold framework erected behind him. He had been crucified, seated on a wooden stool with a white calico cloth draping the lower limbs. He had been garroted by a rope of *tie-tie* bound tight around the neck to a stake behind. The sacrifice was so fresh that, though flies were present, turkey buzzards hadn't found the eyes. No emotion whatever, save holding the nose, was shown by crowds of Edo who passed by.

"Where do they get these unfortunate victims?" Elle asked Mateus. "What is the criteria for selecting one man over the other?"

"They're all slaves, or criminals," Mateus volunteered readily enough, but then he waxed mysterious again, casting her a dark sideways look. "Just possibly they are increasing their sacrifices, having heard of the approach of *Oyinbo*."

It turned Elle's stomach to water to think their arrival had been the cause of such celebratory proceedings.

The jungle thinned and they emerged into a clearing of palm trees. Soon, they were skirting what looked to have been a city wall, but it was broken in places, and being encroached upon by vegetation. A man emerged from a whitewashed guardhouse and demanded they stop.

There was an intense negotiation with the guard, a conversation that apparently ranged from serious palaver, to humorous anecdotes, to surly confrontation. Mateus approached the two *Oyinbo* and said, "We have to stop here. Custom demands it."

Rip ejected a stream of tobacco juice onto the red ground and said between thin lips, "What else were you jawing about?"

This question pleased Mateus inordinately. His face became distinctly chipmunkish as though it would burst with nuts. "The Edo stand on ceremony. You'll get used to it."

There was a long silence. Rip finally said with narrowed

eyes, "All right, let's get on with it."

The three *Oyinbo* and the dragoman George were ushered past black pools of water made solid by aquatic plants. At the door to the dwelling, they were commanded by a slave who spoke a little English to "do wash feet," and herded to a little shed. Rip was reluctant to rid himself of his beloved cowboy boots. As a concession to formality, he had tied his shirt by the sleeves around his waist as a sort of kilt, leaving one naked hip. Elle's saturated stockings and shoes with their panels of elastic were a misery to put back on after the rinsing in the shallow brass Neptune. Mateus, who smartly wore only wide rubber sandals, was tickled to death, and beamed his simian grimace about the room.

They entered the mud house that was the abode of the Captain of War, a General Ologboshere. After passing through a courtyard and into a reception room, they were told to sit on a mat tucked inside an alcove. Elle sat between the two other *Oyinbo*, the steward George having been relegated to a subservient corner by the whipping quirts of a few attendants. It was apparent George's scalloped dressing gown did not stand him in good stead in this town, although the attendants, with their intricately beaded coral blouses, were not set to emblazon the pages of a Paris magazine.

The general appeared in an upper doorway, supported by two attendants who propped him up like a puppet. Elle and Rip shared knowing looks that the general was pickled; it wasn't until later they learned that upstanding members of this society were always supported in such a manner. And indeed Ologboshere was a hale and virile man of maybe thirty years, fine in form as well as feature. A stripe of white chalk adorned his forehead from brow to tip of nose, and over this was traced a narrow line of fresh blood. It seemed to Elle that he fixed her with his dolorous, long-lashed eyes, and something daring and bold stirred in her abdomen at the sight of his glistening lips. She was successful in putting this down to her too-delicate female nature, the same frailty that often had her riled in the middle of the night sleeping near Rip.

The attendants lifted Ologboshere by his arms, weighted down as they were with dozens of coral and brass bracelets. His head was shaven in contrast to the helpers who styled their hair combed toward the ceiling like roosters. Ologboshere did have a pigtail in back that appeared to be fastened with small birds' feathers and cats' claws. His hairless chest was bare and gleamed like oil spilled on a jungle pool, so well put-together and pleasing to the aesthetic eye Elle imagined she heard Rip snuffling in competition. Unfortunately, the general was of the same sartorial bent as his helpers, and below the waist he was swathed with what looked to be a petticoat embroidered with large daisies.

Elle could feel Rip just raring to let loose some remarks.

Ologboshere sat upon a stool and tapped the ground with a ceremonial stick to rally his attendants and eject some undesirables. Kola nuts were brought on a tray, and the *Oyinbo* were compelled to peel them and eat them with glasses of *tombo* while the general inquired about the war in Liverpool. Rip, who had taken off his Stetson for the occasion, replied that the war was going about as well as expected.

"I think he's friendly because I'm naked," Rip solemnly told Elle.

When he asked their business in Benin City, Elle explained she wished to study the culture. This story seemed to go over all right, for the general then launched into a round of demands for not only rum and cloth, but that they stay for dinner.

Rip smiled obsequiously. "Well, you see, sir, it's like this." He looked to Mateus for translation, and none was forthcoming. "We're in a bit of a hurry to see the Oba and get set up in a hut of our own. My wife here is tired from traveling, and—"

Ologboshere said something furiously, and Mateus translated with glee. "He says you absolutely need to have dinner before seeing the Oba. The Oba demands it. It's a custom."

Elle dared to interject, "Thank him very much, but—"

That was when the conversation took a definite turn for the worse.

"He says you must eat some beef."

Rip raised his eyebrows. "I haven't seen any cows over here."

"You must have boiled yams."

"We really are in a hurry to—"

"Then you will have palm oil chop. You must also eat some chicken."

"That sounds like a mighty hefty dinner there, Mateus. All we really want is to see the Oba and—"

"It's the Oba who demands it. He will be very unhappy if you do not eat a large meal before seeing him." Mateus interpreted some more of the general's commands. "You must eat melons. You must eat corn."

Elle interrupted. "Why can't we just have a large meal with the Oba? He has to eat too, so we could all eat together."

Mateus's normally fanatic grimace spread even wider across his imp face. Elle imagined she had struck upon a good idea. Mateus turned to Ologboshere and interpreted grandly, with much sweeping of the arms.

Ologboshere frowned something fierce. His lovely eyelashes now curtained the flashing eyes of a cracked axe murderer. It seemed to Elle that the attendants' jaws went slack, and they stepped aside to give the general more elbowroom.

Elle whispered to Mateus from the corner of her mouth. "What did I say wrong?"

Mateus shrugged. "Maybe the Oba is busy tonight."

Ologboshere raised his stick, pointed it right at Elle, and his shout boomed throughout the mud chambers. Several strong-arm men took long strides toward the *Oyinbo*, growling and shaking their leaf-shaped perforated brass swords that beforehand had seemed like flimsy children's weapons.

Elle rattled Mateus by the arm before the men reached her.

"What's wrong? What's wrong?"

They grabbed Rip first, dragging him to his feet and divesting him of his gun holster. Someone swiftly shackled his wrists behind his back with *tie-tie*. "Mateus! What is this, a necktie party? This better be part of the ceremonial welcome!"

Still, Mateus smiled that odd grimace that Elle now knew could mean anything. "I don't think so, Mr. Bowie."

"Well, *ask* the general what's wrong then, for Christ sake!" Elle said frantically, as the footmen were now tying her hands behind her back. She felt oddly calm, however, as she usually did in extreme predicaments. She had a fatalistic outlook that certain things were preordained, and she had no control over them.

Ologboshere was on his feet now, supported unnecessarily by the henchmen, pointing his stick and bellowing. "*Uku akpolokpolo!*"

"Oh!" cried Mateus in a stage whisper. "I think I understand! Though it doesn't make much sense . . . "

Rip yelled, "Spit it out, for God's sake!"

Mateus had a new, earnest expression when he explained to the prisoners, "He says nobody can say that the Oba eats. He doesn't eat. He's immortal, *Ikeja Orisa*, second in command to the gods."

"Well, she takes it back!" Rip sputtered, but the henchmen were already yanking him out of the chamber. "Explain it, goddamn it! She didn't mean the Oba would eat with us, just that we could eat in another room or something."

"To save time!" Ellie shouted, but Ologboshere was so preoccupied with his ranting Mateus couldn't get a word in, and she was bounced from the room as well.

"Don't worry!" Mateus called. "I'll fix it!"

The henchmen rudely jogged them toward the city. In the dank shade to the side of the path there were many moldy skulls scattered about like rocks. Elle was ashamed of herself for thinking Ologboshere a fine-looking man.

"I suppose this is one way to get to see the Oba," she sighed.

"They can't kill us!" sputtered Rip. "We're white people!"

They were commanding quite a crowd now, especially as Rip's shirt had fallen in the tussle and one of the soldiers had appropriated it for his own adornment. Their knapsacks, bundles, and hats were back in the general's quarters, so Rip was shoved along in a purely natural state save for his cowboy boots.

Rip continued to rave. "We're not even from Liverpool! Let's sing 'Battle Hymn of the Republic.' "

"It is *really* too bad that nice Mr. Donivan was out of town in Sapele."

"Why did we ever come to this jerkwater? This kind of thing doesn't happen in New York."

"Where did Mateus say Mr. Donivan was? Off hunting?"

"He said he was going to hookers in Old Calabar. So what good does he do us now? Let's think up a plan of escape. Think, Elle, think."

"Rip, this entire thing is perfect for our project. I doubt they're going to kill us. Don't you want to expose these murderers? You said yourself they're all *loco*."

"Hell, yes, Elle. I'll do anything it takes to put an end to this crackpot regime and get out of here. But we can't do much when we're tied up."

They were on a wide plain of yam farms and palm trees, with every farmer and bystander gaping at them as they were so ignominiously paraded. Filthy turkey buzzards clamoring in places indicated where other sacrificial victims lay, right alongside yam mounds or a herd of grazing long-horned cattle. Elle didn't have the heart to point out the cows to Rip.

Edo

Evin Jordan was yelling. His squinchy lupine face with its scraggly moustache and beard was worked up into actual anger, a sight not often seen in the normally placid man. "This is the limit, Brendan! I've seen you do some dumb ox things in your time, but this really takes the cake! I'm leaving; no one's going to associate me with this flatheaded gag." But he didn't leave the room. He seemed to prefer standing there with his filthy bare feet and Dr. Reihl's Sanitary Wool Shirt.

Brendan didn't care. He was having a high old time sitting on his stool in his front room, savoring every word from the loathsome Mateus's mouth. Mateus was such a vibrant storyteller Brendan could actually picture in his mind the events unfolding. "Quit wailing twixt me and our guest, Jordan."

"Oh, guest, is it now? Since when is this lowdown louse a guest in our house?"

Mateus didn't lose his permanent gleeful grin, but he sat up straight and said happily, "If it pleases you, *Senhor,* the name is Mateus."

"You're bringing a heap of sin upon us, Brendan!"

Evin was starting to annoy Brendan. Why couldn't he just let him have his fun? "Is that so? And where's the load of alleged sin coming from having it up and down with a couple of beefeaters? They all hate us, Jordan. First thing we turn round they're going to be coming here in armies, colonizing, building *Idjere ro Oyinbo*, cricket grounds, polo fields, all kinds of new-fangled humbug — after wiping out every last African, of course." Evin didn't know that *Idjere ro Oyinbo* meant wide, paved white-man's roads, because he couldn't speak Edo much, but that never stopped Brendan from showing off his knowledge of the lingo. It usually made Evin primp up his own speech with phrases that displayed his university learning.

"I'll tell you how it's going to go awry, Donivan. When Moor hears of English people being imprisoned and tortured, he's going to send a whole battalion of troops over here to restore 'law and order.' It's the perfect *casus belli* he's been waiting for."

"But you see it's all a joke, buddy."

"I doubt they'll see the finer aspects of that after having a feather pierced through their tongue. Isn't that one of your beloved people's favorite tortures?"

"The fact of the business is, we're just letting them sit in the jail overnight, Jordan. From the way you talk, we're making them pick tiny seeds out of hot oil, or take the sasswood ordeal."

Mateus craned his head around Evin's arse. "If I may suggest, it might be advantageous for you to spring them from the *prisao* a little sooner than that."

Brendan folded his arms across his bare chest and glared balefully at Mateus. "Mayhap you're right; might make them a little more kindly disposed toward our trick." Standing, he waved an arm at Mateus. "Come on, then. We're going to be the big dogs of the tanyard walking in and freeing the beefeaters."

Mateus protested, "No, *senhor*! No, thank you. If you don't mind, I prefer to keep distance between myself and this joke. They still haven't paid me for my services."

"Keep your shirt on. I'm going to make Ologboshere take the rap for everything."

Evin nodded. "And what if he doesn't?"

Brendan shrugged, devil-may-care. "He will. He's always raring to provoke the British. He's not a general for nothing."

"*Fortuna boa*," intoned Mateus, staring at his empty glass.

For this occasion, Brendan got ragged out in his very best rig. Being used mostly for hunting, his river boots were looking a little dog-eared, so Brendan selected his good palaver-with-Oba calf opera boots. He still wore the *eruhan* kilt, much cooler in the searingly poisonous tropical weather, and he went shirtless as always, but he donned his best double-breasted silk vest to which he attached some of the many medals and pins he had acquired over the years. For instance, his mother of pearl monogrammed cufflinks were from his riverboat captain days, but as he never wore a shirt he thought them striking on a pocket flap of the vest. His emerald tie-pin dated from that era as well, as were his gold hoop ear-rings, so small they were almost cuffs, although in his captain days he had worn only one. He had been told that wearing two denoted a queen in drag, but now he thought it made him look more like a pirate, a mode that hearkened back to his merchant mariner days.

He waited for Evin to come scoff at him as he regarded his entire getup. Dissatisfied with the amount of brass and ivory bracelets that clinked on his forearms, he added a turquoise bracelet he had obtained on the American prairie. He tried several hats before selecting his buckskin sombrero with a braided hat band from which hung a few agate beads, ivory tokens, and leopard claws. He took his Schofield revolver, and with his Bowie knife in his opera boot, he altogether made enough noise to wake the dead when he walked. Which was his intention.

Evin didn't come to scoff, so Brendan left the house.

"Why aren't you wearing your beaver top hat?"

Evin was lurking in the courtyard just inside the front gate, casually leaning against the mud wall, though a few of his music students sat under the umbrella tree waiting for him.

Brendan shook his head with disgust. "Have a break, why not." Mustering a haughty expression, he sauntered out the gate.

Brendan's house was in the quarter of the *Eghaebho n'Ore,* town chiefs, commoners who by their enterprise and the Oba's favor had risen to positions of power. They controlled many fiefs, and the Oba relied on them for tribute, labor, and troops. Onaiwu and some other *ighele* men were also town chiefs, and as Brendan passed their houses they all joined to follow him, as though they had nothing better to do. They all had wide smiles on their faces, and they slapped him on the shoulder with jocosity.

Onaiwu beamed at Brendan. "Ighiwiyisi. This is a very clever trick for you to be playing against your enemies from Liverpool."

"I agree." Brendan blew his own trumpet. "Do you think it will scare them sufficiently?"

"Oh, yes. They will go back to Old Calabar and tell the Consul that nobody ever dare come to Edo again."

"They will tell them to send soldiers, and we are prepared and eager to fight!" shouted Ugiagbe. He was an annoyingly belli-cose fellow who conscripted troops for the Oba, and his mind seemed to go in one bent only.

"Keep your shirt on," Brendan told Ugiagbe sternly. He had taught everyone what that meant in Edo. They all thought it a good bit of monkey business. "We all know the Liverpool men would win in a war, so calm down."

Brendan couldn't be sure, but it sounded like Ugiagbe muttered something that translated as, "No *Oyinbo* is telling me what to do."

Brendan took only Onaiwu with him into the large walled compound near the Oba's market. Brendan had spent some time in this jail himself during the first days of his residency in Edo, before the Oba had decided to pardon him thanks to the gift of a live leopard. It had not been that easy to spring Evin, for not only hadn't he caught a leopard, he had stomped upon an altar of ant-hills in the belief it was devil idolatry. Evin still probably didn't believe the ant-hill altar helped barren women give birth. Evin got very funny about devil idolatry. Brendan could not make him understand the Edo didn't care for the devil any more than he did.

Ologboshere was out training soldiers in the countryside, but the guard gleefully gave Brendan and Onaiwu passage. The guard seemed fit to bust with pride at his strange garment, what looked like a woman's vertically striped shirtwaist. He drew attention to this puffy finery, not nearly large enough to button up, by smoothing the front with his fingers, and dallying with the buttons.

"Very nice shirt," Onaiwu grudgingly told the guard.

The guard brightened. "Yes! The *Oyinbo* gave it to me!"

Brendan snorted. "Strange days are afoot, when *Oyinbo* take to wearing women's clothing," he muttered to himself in English as they entered another chamber full of uncanny alcoves with skulls, like a wax museum of horrors.

Outside the beefeaters' prison chamber, Brendan told Onaiwu, "You should stay out here. We don't know what will happen, and I don't want them accusing you of anything." Onaiwu nodded silently, and leaned into the mud wall as though it were camouflage.

There were not many doors that locked or even closed in Edo, but the metal workers had fabricated large iron grids for gates and hinges that were hammered into the hewn doorjambs with square iron nails. As the guard handed Brendan a candle and opened the rude lock with his key, Brendan poked his head around the corner, but could see nothing.

He tried to think of what beefeaters usually said to each other. "Good day!" he called happily, not bothering to disguise his accent. He was gratified to hear the rustling of fabric and limbs from within the cell. "I say. It's a jolly good thing I happened along just now. I've heard some white chaps were being held prisoner, and I said well, now, that's not a very jolly good thing, indeed, so I headed on over here, and—"

He now saw the *Oyinbo,* huddled back to back in the corner, trying to get to their feet by inching along each other's spines like two caterpillars, and manacled in irons to a bracket in the wall.

Brendan held the candle high above his head, and saw it was a hale blond man who shouted, "Who are *you*?"

Brendan paused. The blond man looked well nigh about to bite his head off. He would have been frightening with his powerful frame, had it not been for his utter nudeness save for a pair of cowboy boots. That was funny. He'd never seen a Britisher who would stoop to wearing Yank footgear such as that —unless it was all he had. He shouted imperiously, "I do not think it to be fitting for you to be questioning me. More to the point, sir . . . who are *you*?"

The pair had succeeded in almost standing straight, huffing and grinding their hips like vaudeville performers. The blond roared malevolently, "I'm Rip Bowie, photographer for the New York Anthropology Society, and if you let them kill us there's going to be an entire country in the shit!"

Brendan stopped breathing. "Americans?"

Rip spoke to his partner. "L! Say something! He might believe *you*."

The guy strapped to Rip's back emitted a loud sound of disgust. His hair was much longer than Rip's, and he tossed his head so that it nearly slammed against the mud wall, and shouted, "We're *both* Americans! Can you please get us out of this hellhole?"

A woman.

Brendan's eyes immediately dropped to her lovely clavicle that, divested of the striped shirtwaist, displayed a cleavage that was heaven to behold. Her ripe uplifted breasts rose and fell above the framework of some sort of lace and ribbon, Brendan didn't later remember what.

A woman.

He backed into the hallway and bade the guard lock the gate immediately. The guard did so with such trepidation and shaking of hands that the two of them and Onaiwu were soon running down the darkened hallway, though nobody was much sure why.

~ ~ ~

"*You* sure made a hit." Rip sighed.

"Like a hippo makes a splash."

Elle and Rip were already resuming their former positions, on their rear ends on the dirt floor. Elle rubbed the back of her skull against Rip's. "Do you think it scared him that you're from Texas?"

"Texas? More than likely he got scared 'cause you're a woman."

Even in these dire straits, Elle smiled to herself. Rip had not understood her joke. "Why would that scare anyone?"

Rip chuckled, and his voice turned velvety, which it was wont to do when he was tired. "Now Elle . . . in a country with only *one white woman* . . . now . . . why would you imagine that might scare a guy?"

They both smiled for a few moments, then Elle said, "He's American."

"Yep."

"Did you catch what he looked like?"

"Not in the glare from all those medals he had encrusting the front of his vest. He had an awesome tooth necklace."

Elle sighed deeply. The man had just looked like a silhouette, but a man with a nice rugged shape, as though he lived by his hands, the virile life where a man actually meant what he said; his voice, so lilting and kind, as though he really was going to help them before she scared him off by being a woman. "I miss my family." She shouldn't have said that. Rip had no family to miss. It was rude of her.

But Rip answered, "You're *my* family."

That was sweet of him. Elle snuggled her shoulder blades against him. It was so hot in their cell she had already saturated the top layer of her petticoat.

Men were much better as friends than as husbands or lovers, she thought.

The *ikegobo* represented Brendan's worship of his Hand. The Hand was his success in human society and the world. It symbolized his vigor, enterprise, and industry in hunting, as well as personal responsibility and self-reliance. The Edo said, "If your father does something for you, he makes you ashamed by telling everyone how much you owe him. If your mother does something for you, she makes you ashamed. But if your Hand does something for you, it doesn't shame you." So Brendan prayed at his altar now, in his own peculiar farrago of Catholic, Protestant, and Edo prayers.

He asked for guidance on how to proceed, having played a trick on some fellow Americans. What were Americans doing there? The New York Anthropology Society, the blond fellow had shouted. Well, that didn't bode too terribly awful: they wouldn't try to grab a part of his trade, and they wouldn't tell everyone they were bound for hell, like missionaries.

If the truth were known, it was the sight of that half-naked woman, L the man called her, that had rattled him—in a much more elemental way than Victoria with her almond-shaped green eyes, her pristine long neck, her small bosom as white as a dolphin. No, this woman seemed unleashed, bold. He had seen that in the brief flaring of her eyes as she leaned back against that brutish lout, her shapely bosom jutting out, so that Brendan no longer looked at her eyes. And with her thickly cascading dark hair, all loose and wild like that, she stirred something terrifying in Brendan.

He didn't want to be stirred. He had everything exactly the

way he liked it. He had his very profitable business, his waterside trade, his upcountry trade, the hunting he loved so, his partner Evin, and his proper life in Sapele. But the wild American woman pricked at his very skin, made him wonder, made him want to know everything about her, so he could find something to dislike and go back to his comfortable ways.

It would probably not be that difficult to find such a thing, with her penchant for getting tied up nearly naked to crazy naked Texan men.

"It is in your hands. *Ise*." *Amen*. That was what Brendan said at the end of a prayer. It meant the same thing in Edo as in English.

With Onaiwu, who had been waiting in the front room, Brendan walked swiftly back to the jail. The guard told them the prisoners had been taken away right after Brendan had left.

Before they could jog the few blocks to the Oba's palace compound, Brendan heard people laughing and discussing the event as they too raced toward the palace.

"I do not like the looks of this, Onaiwu," said Brendan.

"I agree most fully."

Ologboshere sat on a stool brought out for the occasion. The two victims were already kneeling on the wooden pedestals they would use to hoist them up the sacrificial *Iroko* tree, and the usual skulls and bones were strewn about as though the residue of a particularly rowdy celebration.

Brendan strode right over to Ologboshere and demanded, "We can stop the joke now! This is too much."

Ologboshere smiled with one side of his mouth. "But you wanted to scare them. They are not scared yet. Look, the man has gone to sleep."

Brendan didn't need to look to know Rip Bowie had fainted, but he didn't know the word in Edo. "He is not sleeping, Ologboshere. He has . . . " He didn't know the term for "keeled over" either.

Onaiwu assisted. "He has collapsed from fright."

Brendan nodded. "Yes. And there has been a big mistake. These people aren't from Liverpool. They are from America, Boston, the same place I am from. They are countrymen." The Edo thought all Americans were from Boston, as that was where all the merchant ships hailed from.

"They have had the impudence to enter Edo without an invitation. The last time an *Oyinbo* came here, we were tricked into a mistaken treaty that there is no way we can uphold without losing power. The man shows respect by not wearing any clothes, but Ighiwiyisi, we need to make sure these people go back and tell everyone we are such blood-thirsty crazy men never to attempt to come here again."

"Yes, but if you crucify them, how are they going to tell anyone?"

"*Hey!*" It was a lusty, smoky shout, from the female L who had disturbed Brendan so much. He saw her more fully now as she kneeled on the platform with her hands bound with *tie-tie* in her lap. Her upper arms crushed her bosom prominently into view, but Brendan was able to look at her face now, all round shapes, glistening lips as though stained with berries, and handfuls of shiny auburn hair that tumbled about her shoulders. She was much more darkened by the sun than other *Oyinbo* women Brendan had known, but then, if she was with the New York Anthropology Society, that would explain it.

"You American! Why are you doing this to us? What is wrong with you, you good-for-nothing toad?"

Brendan paused; that was some talk coming from an anthropologist. Weren't they supposed to be gentle, and concerned about native peoples? "Miss, there's been a mistake," he started to shout, but two of Ologboshere's *emada* attendants jumped between him and L, and Ologboshere was commanding George, that sallow wretch in the blue dressing gown, "Interpret for me."

The *emada* stood stiffly between Brendan and L, but he could still hear George telling L, "The leopard hunter says you are to die, but the good warrior Ologboshere says you are to go free and . . . " George looked back at Ologboshere, who reminded him,

"Go tell everyone in Old Calabar what devils live in Edo."

Tearing the *emada* brutally aside, Brendan shouted at L, "These are all lies, Miss L! This lousy varmint has been telling you a pack of lies!" But he was grasped by the upper arms and enveloped in an entire crowd of *emada* who, with their combined hands upon his limbs, entombed him like a mummy so he could not move.

He could sure enough hear Miss L shouting, though. "Oh, I'll tell everyone what devils live in Edo, all right! But it isn't the Africans; no, they're perfectly civil! It's the cracked Americans who *think* they're Africans and walk around with necklaces made of teeth and leopard skin loincloths carrying spears and poison arrows who are the devils!" It appeared she had vented herself to the maximum then, for her voice changed from a she-devil to a soft loving mother when Brendan heard her soothe Rip. "Honey, you'll be fine, they're letting us go . . . Let's just walk this way, follow this man and we'll cut out of here . . . "

And her rough, sweet voice faded into the throng of laughing celebrants, everyone set to have a high old time at the elaborate joke that had just been perpetrated. The *emada* keeping a bear's grip on Brendan loosened up, and when Brendan turned to glare viciously at Ologboshere, the stool was empty, and that worm George was gone as well. Even Onaiwu seemed to be laughing at Brendan.

"It seems the joke has come back in your face, Iwi."

He didn't care much about Miss L, although he was certain he'd think about her when masturbating, but that was only because she did have a shapely bosom. When Brendan spied a fellow clad in a vertically-striped skirt that dragged in the mud, he spun the fellow around, and he had never shucked a woman's clothes as fast as he figured out all the buttons and clasps to that skirt. It was all a whirl and a blur, but he remembered shaking the skirt in his fist at the fellow and yelling in English, "Mayhap you'll think twice next time, parading about in drag!"

CHAPTER

4

Sapele

"You wear that in the road, you're going to get mud all over those feathers!"

"I'll pick up the train when I walk," Elle said calmly, running her hands over the burgundy satin gown with lace and feather trimming. "It'll make an impression." It was her best gown by far, and she was glad she had brought it. The neck came off the shoulders and was trimmed with black ostrich feathers, and a black lace mantle passed over both shoulders and swooped down the back, gathered at the tailbone with a rhinestone brooch that allowed the remaining lace folds to sweep free nearly to the floor. Garlands of cultured pearls cinched the waist and draped from the fur-trimmed shoulders. Elle stroked the dress. She hadn't allowed any native Urhobo near it, as the last washing she had given them they had zealously beaten threadbare on rocks.

Rip leaned against the doorjamb, his thumbs hooked under his suspenders. He had remained shirtless, but thankfully now the planes of his lovely sun-browned pectorals did not distract Elle. She had completed her toilette, her hair wound around padding rats and pinned in elaborate style. She stepped into her dress. "Honey, would you please start cleaning up? Vince said half past five."

"Yes, and as it starts getting pitch black here exactly at six, I need to clean that lamp that was busted last night. I think it got clogged with mosquitoes. I bought all the mosquito netting in stock from that *Hindustan* fellow Forshaw, but I swear there were holes you could throw a pig through; all night long I was slapping—"

"Rip! Can you fasten me?"

Rip stepped over and buttoned the pearls at the small of Elle's back with a precision born of a decade dressing her, but he continued to vex her with his uncooperative talk. "So it's Vince now. Isn't it proper to refer to him as District Commissioner Gainey?"

"He told me to call him Vince."

Rip was being unnecessarily rough cinching in her bosom from behind. "Even with that hoity-toity lime-juicer girlfriend always swooning on his arm?"

"Oh, Rip, I don't care about his girlfriend. It's not like I want him to court me; don't be disgusting. You know I live to work, and work to live. Working keeps me out of the sort of trouble that courting brings."

And lately her thoughts had been straying in directions that were not of a toilsome vocation. She could be in the market shopping for maize or groundnuts, and suddenly remember the particularly luscious sight of Rip's armpit as he stood on his toes to hammer a brace for a wall shelf. Or Ologboshere, who had really turned out to be a kind man after all, how intelligent his forehead, how erotically strong his hands. So it was even with Gainey; she had briefly mused on the rigidity of his august bearing before she told herself to stop, it was just those delicate female vapors again, and probably had a medical cause. Being childless might have something to do with it. If that were the case, she would use the same vigor to focus on her work, and let the hearty life of sport and activity render her too tired for such frivolity. "Energy rightly applied can accomplish anything," she always reminded herself.

"You know it behooves us to be amicable with Vince. He's just full of information, and he gave us the best house in Sapele."

Rip turned Elle by the shoulders to face him, fluffing the ostrich feathers at her bosom. The dimples in his face deepened. "I'd venture to say, aside from the house of that Donivan fellow no one ever sees, compared to most of the mud and wattle shacks that comprise this fine burg, our six-room wooden mansion is just fine. It's definitely the best of the ten empty houses that are currently vacant because *somebody died*."

Elle brightened. "And the roof barely leaks. Now, please, honey . . . "

"I'm dressing." Rip loped off to his own bed room.

Elle was glad they finally had separate bed rooms. Married couples, after all, oftentimes had separate bed rooms. She had a proper bedstead and, thanks to the wife of a merchantman dead from country fever, a dressing table with only one crack in the mirror, and a pewter basin and ewer for washing. When it rained, the sound on the corrugated iron roof reminded Elle of New York summer storms, and she felt cozy and secure. She had been having daily lessons, along with a missionary's wife, Mary Wells, in the Edo language, and she took copious notes on all she saw around her, much as an anthropologist would. From their house in the Riverside Quarter, she could see the Ethiope River, dramatic and drenched, where sometimes it rained so hard the river ran backward, and malignant exhalations rose to enshroud the long canoes, the steamers, and launches full of palm oil puncheons.

She was just slipping her aigrette of green glass baguettes into her hair when there came a sudden clamor from the back of the house, as though animals the size of sheep had fallen from the roof. Rushing out into the hallway that bisected the house, she saw Rip's tall silhouette against the back screen door slamming a shorter fellow into the wall.

"Stop it!" she shouted. "What's all this?"

"What's all *this* is a no-count worm who's going out the back door he slid under."

"Wait, no, Rip! Let him go!"

"What?" Rip had Mateus by the collar; in fact, the shifty man seemed to dangle in the air with his toes brushing the ground. "I don't get you, Elle."

"I invited him over."

"What?" Rip exploded, and threw the small man against the wall without even glancing at him. Rip put his hands on his hips. "And just what might be the meaning of *that?*"

"I told you, sir," Mateus gasped. "The missus told me to pay her a visit."

Elle moved a hand near Mateus's arm as if to assist him, but didn't dare touch him. "Yes, you see? Come, let's go into the sitting room like civilized people."

In the sitting room, Elle lit the lamp that wasn't broken and took a chair. She bade the men to sit as well, but in their mutual distrust they both stood shuffling their feet, hands deeply embedded in their pants pockets. "It is true I initially thought Mateus was guilty of complicity in that cruel hoax that was perpetrated on us," Elle began loftily, hoping the mightiness of her words would at least numb Rip into submission. "But I soon realized it was all a misunderstanding."

"Misunderstanding?" Rip exploded. He punched Mateus in the shoulder. "It was completely obvious that whatever that Moor bastard wrote in the note we asininely gave Mateus, he followed it to the letter, down to *pretending* he didn't know that talking about the Oba's dinner would get us in the shit!"

Elle spread her hands out and faced the palms toward the floor. "I at first thought the same thing, Rip. Remember? We were saying to each other it was completely obvious that whatever that Moor bastard wrote in the note we asininely gave Mateus—"

"But you soon realized you were wrong," Mateus bellowed, as if to hurry them along.

Elle and Rip stared blankly, merely blinking. There was another silence of a few seconds. Mateus sliced his arm through the air impatiently. "You soon realized the whole thing was the doing of that *Oyinbo* you saw in Great Benin, and I couldn't agree more. Now, whoever that *Oyinbo* might be, I don't know, but he sounds like one of those palm oil ruffians who eke their way into these parts like termites into a termite hill."

Elle blinked. "But he had a native skirt on, and native . . . teeth around his neck."

Mateus spoke to the floor. "Well, then, he could be one of those *Oyinbo* who come to these parts and start dressing like natives, and acting like natives, and—"

"This is ridiculous!" Rip shouted. He took a couple steps toward Mateus with upraised hands, but stopped when Mateus shrank back. "That's completely *loco*! How many whitemen could there be like that around here? Well, I'm not sure, it could be the guy third from the left with the gorilla bone stuck through his nose."

"The point is." Elle stood. It was time for her brandy and gum guiacum. She had prepared for a moment such as this, guests present in her sitting room, by having the concoction already mixed in a decanter on the sideboard. "Mateus is a highly useful person to know in the Oil Rivers, wouldn't you agree? He has a free lunch over in Edo, and he has agreed to tell us all of the goings-on in that town. And besides, false executions are good enough for Dostoevski, so I don't mind. Right, Mateus?"

Mateus held out his hand in the shape of a glass, but Elle did not offer him anything. "Right, missus. It altered his whole life forever after. He was never the same."

Rip frowned. "Dostoev—? Now, look here—"

"And what news have you brought me today, Mateus?"

Mateus stood proudly. "I have heard through the grapevine that Dogho will be at Gainey's tonight. He's an Itsekiri chief, a most loyal supporter of the Protectorate. The British have appointed him Political Agent, and he's a very good fellow to play up to. He's got a frilly white gig upon which he flies the Union Jack. Now, signing treaties is the main activity of British colonial agents in the Oil Rivers. They have been showering corruption on Dogho, and in return it is said he leases them Urhobo lands in the hinterlands. Dogho would like to see Great Benin humbled and eliminated as a trading competitor. A very slippery fellow."

"Sounds like you're describing yourself." Rip was implacable.

Elle sipped her brandy. "Hadn't you better be dressing?"

Rip hesitated a few moments and stood there glowering, just to show Mateus he was not bossed around by his wife. "If this guy is going, you can count me out."

Beaming widely, Mateus said proudly, "Oh, no, sir. They wouldn't have a hulk rat like myself at such an upper drawer gathering. No, indeed not. Gainey likes to use me for his secret spy work for Sir Rawson and to help him train his Hausa company, for, as you know, my ancestors were elite Portuguese soldiers in Great Benin, and I have knowledge of—"

"All right, shut your trap! I'm leaving, but you better be gone when I get back!"

~ ✦ ~

The more time he spent in Edo, the stranger Brendan felt when he came back to Sapele. Sapele was the last civilized outpost in the Oil Rivers hinterlands, with a gathering of European houses in the Riverside Quarter, where the houses of Gainey, the District Commissioner, and Dr. Elliott, the Medical Officer, were built at the waterside. In the Farmland Quarter was the Prison Yard, and the barracks for the Niger Coast Protectorate Force. Sapele was the first market where Urhobo dared venture from upriver. Past there up the Ethiope, each bank was dotted occasionally with oil markets, a few houses on the riverside being a depot where Itsekiri middlemen lived and bought oil as it was brought from inland by Urhobo men.

Brendan had established new trading posts in Urhobo country, beaches with warehouses for palm oil and trade goods. The Oba had *eghen* at the waterside markets, and they often stopped all trade leaving Edoland if they weren't happy with the terms. Brendan's men were so accustomed to the embargoes they kept their palm oil in gourds with narrow necks that could be sealed until the markets reopened.

A ship named *Hindustan,* bought at Bristol, was sailed to the mouth of the Benin River, so called because it was thought you could reach Benin City on it. There it was dismasted, fitted up as a hulk, and towed to Sapele anchorage. A roof, first of thatch, later of corrugated iron, was built over her decks. In Brendan's first years in Sapele, the hulk provided good accommodations for several Europeans, a customs office, a Treasury, and barracks.

Brendan had offices there, where he'd trained men to make oil puncheons, and collect the oil as canoes brought it in. Steamers drawing fourteen feet of water could run up to Sapele from the Delta. When a ship arrived in Bonny or Old Calabar, she had merely to discharge the new supply of trade goods and take in the oil which Brendan had accumulated, then away home after only a few days in port instead of several months, as in the old days. The old-fashioned firms kept ships anchored in the noxious rivers for six or eight months loading and stowing palm oil; Brendan had sent home by steamer palm oil bought at the same time as the oil still on board the vessels at anchor in the Delta. He received returns twice or thrice over before the cumbersome ships brought their cargo to market.

To the ships' crews this change was for the good, but for the Agents living in the hulks, it was another matter. Condemned to a three-year stretch in "the graveyard of Europeans" by the cold-blooded firms that had sent them, the mortality rate was shocking. So Brendan and Evin built a house in the Riverside

Quarter above the river, a two-story house with the living story above to keep out the mud and varmints. They left their brethren swinging in the tides in their great mart of commerce, poisoning their blood with the malaria manufactured in the bilge-water. For every one of them who thrived in Sapele, there were many young traders who went under, defeated by disease and the harsh and lonely life, their skin jaundiced from years of ingesting quinine. Brendan was fortunate to have leased his fine, healthy acreage directly from an Urhobo chief, for he often thought of poor Cyril Punch (who really was from Liverpool) being in possession of "The Queensbury Estate of Sapele," a certain property consisting of 840 feet of water frontage situated between the grave of a dead Itsekiri and an indentation caused by an overflow of surface drainage.

"Now, I don't want to see you mooning over that Victoria of Gainey's," said Evin. "You know he's brought her out here to prove to everyone how harmless and jim-dandy the climate is, and if she hooks up with you, that theory is gone up the spout."

Brendan said, "You'll be glad to know I killed that Coast Smell by giving some Edo soap to Miriam." Miriam was their maid who had been converted by missionaries. To demonstrate, Brendan lifted one arm and breathed deeply of his armpit, satisfied he didn't smell the mixture of moldy dirty water, cockroaches, and something they variously defined as urine or something worse.

"Stop that!" Evin jostled Brendan as they were nearing the Vice Consulate's front stairs. Anyone who happened to be looking through the windows could have seen Brendan with his snout buried under his own wing.

Brendan didn't care. "Just 'cause you haven't mooned over anyone in years, let me have some fun. I can't see the harm in putting on a few airs at a frolic such as this."

"And speak regular English!"

Evin elbowed Brendan again, and Brendan elbowed him back.

They were both going up the stairs now, and with their competitive natures neither would allow the other to advance first, with the result that they arrived at the front door shoving each other aside in their race to be the first to greet Captain Gainey. However, it was only Gainey's majordomo who answered the door, and the way the fellow laughed at them like they were a donkey show must have mortified Evin properly, for he relented, and let Brendan step in first, not without muttering, "You're a sight!"

Brendan knew he was not a sight, not in the way Evin meant, for he had on his fancy Irish linen suit and had "toned down the native junk" to the point where its only evidence was the brass leopard hip ornament, and he still wore his hair in a pigtail fastened with coral decorations. Evin was more of a sight in his white duck pants and his cholera belt, a flannel cummerbund he imagined warded off the chill that led to cholera and dysentery.

Brendan handed the majordomo his coat and proceeded to the sitting room in shirtsleeves that were proper in the casual expatriate gatherings of the tropics. He gave Chief Dogho, already drunk as a fiddler's bitch, his most malevolent uppity look before moving past the missionaries Charles and Mary Wells in order to greet Victoria. The gibbering Itsekiri chief in his cardinal velvet cape and silk top hat waylaid Evin, and Brendan could hear the buffoon saying, "Mister Evin! Now we can finish our discussion on the palm oil trade in Edo."

"Chief Dogho, I don't think we ever had started a conversation along those lines . . . "

"My dear Victoria," Brendan babbled, overjoyed Gainey was not to be seen.

"My dear Captain Donivan," Victoria gushed, with such fervor to equal his, Brendan was taken aback. She grasped his hands and pulled him into a chair next to hers. "I am glad to see you again so soon; I was told you had been sucked up into the belly of some horrifying cannibal kingdom."

"Please, my dear, call me Brendan." He was aware he was suddenly following Evin's instructions to speak properly, but he didn't much care, holding onto the gentle white hands of such a creature. "No, I merely spend time in a more . . . primal civilization. There are no cannibals in Benin City." He certainly didn't want Victoria thinking he was barbaric. He had to let go of her hands and halfway stand in order to take an object from his pants pocket. He pressed it into her hands; her palms barely closed around it. "You asked me to bring you something lovely from the hinterlands."

Her shimmering blue eyes dilated as she looked down at her hands, but he saw her face fall a few dozen shades of emotion when she looked at the object. It was obvious she thought the ivory armlet much less than what she had expected. "What is this?"

Brendan's voice was void of cheer. "An ivory bracelet." He shrugged. He had thought it the finest he had ever seen, the Oba carved with mudfish legs, his hands raised to the sky, depicting his connection with the great god Olokun, ruler of the sea. The armlet Brendan had thought precious now looked like the naïve primitive carving of savages.

"Oh," said Victoria. "Now, aren't these cannibal peoples also the peoples with the gold? I have seen gold weights melted into attractive shapes and figures."

Victoria meant the Ashanti, who were from the Gold Coast, and not anywhere near the Oil Rivers. Brendan supposed he had some of those gold weights hanging around in one of his factories somewhere. "No, but I can get you—"

"Did you say *gold*, Miss Armbruster?"

Victoria stood at the sound of the American's voice, some-where over Brendan's shoulder. "Yes, Mrs. Bowie! Have you not heard there are kingdoms of gold around here?"

"Well, I certainly have heard about the Ashanti kingdom, where the revered golden stool is not allowed to touch the ground."

Brendan also stood, and turned. He didn't hear the rest of the

American's sentence, as all else after that was a blur of sight and sound, as though he had been imprisoned in one of those glass terrariums.

Indeed, the woman from the Edo jail resembled a resplendent angel all bedecked with foamy clouds that veiled the outer edges of her form, as Brendan's vision went all strange and fuzzy. All that was in sharp focus was her limpid face, the round brown eyes as though brimming with tears, the wet lips the color of berries, the rich auburn hair that fell in waves and ringlets, peppered with jewels that glowed with foggy light. And there, before his eyes swam blindly with phosphenes as though he had stopped breathing, were her proudly full and bursting breasts, encased in a bodice of delicacy and feathers he had never seen the likes of.

She was staring directly at him as he gaped like a dumb ox. She smiled devilishly, as though she knew what he looked like without clothes, the rest of her form fading away into luxuriant shadows of burgundy that coruscated like underwater plant life. Brendan knew then all else had become trivial, as though just by looking at the woman he was a changed man.

And then he swooned. He stumbled a little, and had to prop himself up by the back of the chair. He must have blacked out for a few seconds, for the vision of the American woman was gone, replaced by Victoria's bland visage as she said,

"He said he had a painful back . . . ."

He remembered to breathe. "Now, what were you saying about gold . . . ?" he tried to inquire politely. But before he could start feeling too normal again, the American woman L was gasping.

"This bracelet is absolutely astonishing! It's very delicate, so intricate. Why is this man sitting on top of a fish?"

"Oh, that is just some rather . . . folksy bracelet Captain Donivan gave me."

It felt unreal when Brendan spoke. Everyone else in the room faded out, like townspeople on the fringes of a dream. "That's the king, the Oba, he had mudfish for legs." Luckily he had rehearsed this speech to use on Victoria. "The mudfish has symbolic significance among the Edo people as it can live on land and sea, as is the Oba invested with divine powers from the spiritual world above and the secular world below."

L had been taking tiny steps even closer toward him, her face enraptured with his words, until she was standing almost on his toes. He continued, "I believe that Oba Ohen was paralyzed after he'd reigned for twenty years, and he built up this myth that he had mudfish for legs to explain why he always sat covered with a blanket in public. He would have been killed if found out."

"I see." L looked directly at Brendan as she caressed the armlet she had taken from Victoria. Brendan felt his jaw go slack at the manner in which she rubbed her thumb across the little mudfish Oba. His penis came to life before his head did, swelling and engorging uncomfortably against his thigh. "But is it not heresy to imply that the Oba did *not* have mudfish for legs? You must be very careful what you imply about the Oba, because as everyone knows, he is *Ovbi'Ekenekene ma deyo*, the son of beauty that never fades."

How had she learned that? Brendan doubted that the New York Anthropology Society had much knowledge of Edo. Nobody did. "Yes," he agreed, completely enervated and drained, as though the vital woman had sucked him dry of all vigor. "That's very astute of you, Mrs. Bowie. But it is also true that anyone who tricks someone into making a statement about the Oba, say, that he had palm oil chop for dinner, must make amends to his *ikegobo*, and sacrifice an entire goat."

L had a charming ability to arch one eyebrow. She continued coolly, "That might begin to be penance for such an odious trick. But there must be more, for such a heinous deed. Don't you agree, Mr. Donivan?"

This woman had devilment to match her charm. Brendan saw now that with her fine long arms, elegant wrist bones, and jawbone so sharp one could flay a buffalo with it, she was the epitome of a witch. If Brendan gave her some sasswood to drink, would she puke it up? Or prove her guilt by dying? "That would depend, ma'am, on how truly vindictive and heartless the alleged victim was."

L did not like that one bit. Her eyes narrowed, and she gave the armlet back to an apathetic Victoria.

"You two speak as though you were acquainted." Victoria smiled uncertainly.

Brendan came to himself swiftly enough to say, "You could say we had a punitive enjoyment of each other's company."

Before anyone could question this, Captain Gainey came in from the veranda with that rambunctious Texan, Rip Bowie. Rip was fully clad today in a corduroy vest, and he was taking off a tremendous ten-gallon hat when he laid eyes on Brendan.

"Well, bless my soul," Rip cried. "If it ain't the hangman, judge, and jury himself in the flesh. Clean out of bodies to crucify on trees, pal?"

Brendan stepped forward to say something that might smooth things over, but to his utter wonderment, the witch in burgundy came between them and said in a voice that seemed to put a spell over Rip, "Honey, I'd like you to meet Mr. Donivan, the trader Consul General Moor referred us to, remember?" She turned gallantly to Brendan and smiled. "We've just been discussing the judicial system in Edo."

While Rip was busy looking confused, Gainey was oblivious enough to barrel on ahead as though continuing a conversation he and Brendan had just broken off an hour ago. "Brendan, my boy! I take it you've brought me good news from your . . . vacation estate, shall we say?"

Evin said, in a sudden jovial mood himself, probably not wishing to palaver about the vacation estate, "Captain, may I crank your talking machine? I have some new cylinders from the U.S. I've heard them myself on our own machine, but I thought your guests might enjoy listening."

Gainey sprang to the talking machine as though Evin had just suggested a Roman orgy. "I'm always up for more coon shouters, Evin, but our other American guests have brought some very interesting records of their own. I've promised to play one called—what did you refer to it as, my dear?"

For some reason, Brendan was electrified with fear to hear Gainey call L "my dear." It implied some sort of intimacy that, for no apparent reason, Brendan hoped did not exist. He gulped the entirety of the drink that he held.

"A new musical style called rag!" cried L brightly as she went to the graphophone, watching with shining eyes as Gainey took the wax cylinder from its oblong container. "A friend of mine made this cylinder of a fellow he knew in New Orleans."

"And he sent it to Elle!" shouted Gainey.

Sadie Elliott, the sickly and moribund doctor's wife, said excitedly, "She's promised to show us the New Orleans dance step that accompanies it."

"Yes, who will you demonstrate with?" Mary Wells asked.

For such a normally reserved and shy fellow, Evin bounced up and said happily, "Brendan here has been known to cut a rug!"

"Avast!" Brendan cried in astonishment, but before he could stop the man from bloviating, Evin was shouting,

"Brendan has all this Irish blood, dancing and drinking, and all those sailor jigs running through his veins."

Gainey clapped Brendan on the back. "By God, my boy, he's right! Us Irishmen are known for that."

Brendan attempted a laugh. "Right about what? That all Irishmen are good dancers?"

But the witchy woman, who had now gone all soft-edged and shimmery again in the angel's guise, was blessing him with her brilliant smile. With her hands on his shoulders, she walked Brendan to the center of the room. "Yes, you're about the right height. Now, this is very easy, it's mostly a schottische, or a two-step."

Gainey was still obliviously shouting, "It's called the Slow

Drag! Right, Rip?"

Was Rip laughing at Brendan's predicament? "Yes, indeed, sir!"

The music came from the horn, tinkly and merry piano music. L put her powdery hand in Brendan's clammy one and began moving. It was true as Evin had said, Brendan had always moved well, had effortlessly mastered new dances—had always moved well with women. That was not what Brendan feared. It was being in proximity to the woman that put the fear of Olokun into him.

Indeed, L moved forward, dragging her left foot behind her; when she moved backward, she dragged her right foot. Brendan flowed with the ravishing woman, feeling the warmth of her hip under his hand as the fellow on the record sang something about a copper coming to his crap game, and no more would he buy his sweet thing pork chops. Brendan felt his eyes smiling at the woman. "L . . .Is that for Lucy? Or Lily?"

She frowned with happy consternation. "Lucy?"

"Your name. In the j—in Edo I heard your husband call you L."

She tossed her head deliciously. She swayed so firmly against his crotch Brendan knew she could detect his swollen penis when she rubbed her hip bone against his pants pocket. "Oh, L! It's Elle, E-L-L-E. Short for Eleanor."

Feeling more at ease now, even with the other women in the room following their every move as though they were a fireworks show, Brendan said suavely, "You accompany your husband in his work with the Anthropology Society? That's very brave of you."

"My husband accompanies *me*, Mr. Donivan!" Elle said haughtily with a splash of merriment in her eyes.

She was such a delight to behold, Brendan was already plotting ways to see her again, to talk to her alone. He had done worse things before than court a married woman. In the thousand ports of the world he'd sailed into, such things were commonplace.

And he was usually back aboard ship by the time the husband came after him. "What does such a ravishing woman do that needs to be photographed?" She was sashaying the front of her frilly lap against Brendan's crotch. What manner of woman was this, who came to Africa accompanied only by a naked photographer, who brought her own lewd records that sang about never hearing his sweetheart's lips going flip flop no more? This was a balled-up continent in every way!

She looked at him through lowered lashes, though he doubted she was coy in her heart. "I'm an anthropologist. I study clitoridectomy."

"But they don't do such things in Edo. Why would you go there to study that?"

She missed a step, and the toe of her shoe cracked Brendan right in the ankle. She looked so truly shocked and forlorn, Brendan thought to ease her by adding, "Well, they do sometimes clip off . . . a little of the . . . "

But he said it quietly, and he couldn't be sure she heard him.

Swiftly she regained herself, and with her face so close he could feel her breath infused with cloves and brandy against the side of his face, she said, "I have decided to forgive you for your tasteless stunt."

He cradled her hip in his hand. The cushion of her bosom was plastered against his shirtfront. They were glued together by sweat. Oh, how he wanted to kiss her! "I am glad. And I wanted to tell you I've never worn a leopard skin loincloth in my life. Perhaps a leopard skin scarf over one shoulder, but not a loincloth. Now we can meet again to discuss female circumcision."

The song was over, everyone was clapping, and Brendan knew he had to walk Elle over to Gainey or whoever was closest to the veranda door, to use her as a shield so that the entire room would not have the happy picture of his enormous erection poking out his pants pocket. But he wanted to hear her answer first, and he held her tight.

"Yes," she said. Her eyes looked sad, as though she was about to burst forth with tears. "We can discuss . . . "

It was Elliott, the River Doctor, who pried Elle from Brendan's clutches, insisting on learning the dance himself. Brendan had to shake off the other women who clamored for a dance, making out that he had to visit the head. Victoria in particular clung close, and Brendan dismissed her by saying, "Perhaps Mr. Bowie can demonstrate for you."

It was callous, but he was eager to leave the room, to breathe air, to rearrange his penis inside his pants. Evin was the last person he passed by on his way out, and of course he had to utter a cynical remark.

"You'd better prepare that goat for sacrifice, Ighiwiyisi."

Brendan gave Evin a look that burned him to perdition. "You're going to be dancing at the gratings." Which really had nothing to do with dancing at all. It was their seamen's saying for being flogged with a cat-o'-nine-tails.

~ ✦ ~

Elle was pleasantly surprised to see the handsome Irishmen through the screen door at Gainey's, even more pleased when Vince confided to her one of them was Brendan Donivan, the legendary Guinea trader, and his partner, Evin Jordan.

"They're quite colorful characters, really," Vince allowed. "Donivan in particular. Why, he was the one who thought of using the dane-gun cases for coffins."

"How inventive." Elle strained to view Brendan's features, washed by a curtain of setting sun, as he moved through the room, taking a chair next to that insipid Victoria. Not as tall as Rip or Vince, he had the nicely put-together form of a man accustomed to working with his hands and, as Vince had told her, hunting in the jungle.

Vince was waxing contemplative, leaning against the veranda railing, and analyzing his pipe. "Of course, sometimes the corpses were too long for the boxes, so the natives fixed that by cutting off their feet, and nailing top hats over their heads."

In particular, Brendan had the well-shaped bottom of a man who walked miles and miles every day. "And he's been away, in Old Calabar?"

"Old Calabar? No, why would he go there? He detests anything to do with civilization. Sapele is the apex of culture for men like Donivan."

So the hooker story was another fabrication of that highly inventive gnome Mateus. On a whim, Elle left the two men smoking on the veranda, and entered the sitting room. She stopped behind the man as he sat, talking with the beautiful yet annoyingly vapid Victoria, for something suddenly struck her. *She felt as if she knew him.* How was that possible? It was the curve of his thumb as he handed the white object to Victoria, the lovely lilt of his smoky voice, richly dripping with a delicious patois she couldn't put her finger on. *She had seen him before.* It was as though finally running into a very old friend one hasn't seen in years, decades even.

He must have felt her standing there, for he rose and turned. Elle was absolutely awestruck by his beauty. The last rays of sun, filtering through the oil palms and umbrella trees, rendered his dark chestnut hair all fired up with streaks of vermilion and gold. He had the arched eyebrow of the cynic, the trenchant aquiline nose that had always intrigued her in men. And his sharp turquoise eyes had a sly, seductive look, or perhaps she was imagining it. She felt faint, but then it came to her . . . where . . . they had met.

Rage fueled her from then on. This little juvenile toad with his life-defiling games! For, while she had pretended to Rip that the last-minute gallows reprieve had been a literary experience, she had remained utterly determined to return to Edo and hunt down that Cro-Magnon in his asinine skirt and humiliate him, after taking all the wind out of his sails of course, as he had appeared to think he was second in line only to the Oba. She ceased to feel faint, and plied her feminine tactics on him.

While it was true she thought the ivory bracelet a thing of great beauty, she was happy when that nice harmless partner of Brendan's suggested they dance. She was torn with anger and fear, fear because with every dragging step she took, the more she had hoped to lead and dominate him, the opposite happened. Elle was accustomed to tormenting men in order to get her way—it was simple, really, and she had a decade of practice in her career—but his confidence and ease, the way he held her, above all the way he moved with assured sexuality, all conspired to melt the furor in her stomach. She was no fool! She was an utterly driven woman who lived to work! Anything that threatened to distract her from her industrious goal was instantly excised from her life.

And his voice, that lilting dripping dialect was doing unspeakably erotic things to her innards. His enormous erection that had her slithering around him, a drip of sweat rolling between her breasts. It pleased her to think she was torturing him, yet by the time she remembered to discuss clitoridectomy, she was the one who was the drooling imbecile, merely a puddle of something viscous on the floor.

Then she was nearly crying at the thought that she, being a worker automaton, could never dally with such a man as him. He was gone from the room, and the anger returned.

Elle's eyes were rimmed with tears, and she was short and irritable with Dr. Elliott, who was the worst dancer she had ever met, and Charles Wells who was even worse, with his big clown shoes and nose like an elephant. She spent half an hour looking out for Brendan, then an interminable dinner was served, during which she had to sit at the opposite side, and the opposite end, of the table from him.

Her palm oil chop was a pool of grease, and out of frustration she drank more claret than usual. She had to tolerate the kittenish glances that Victoria, seated next to Brendan, gave him when she kept glancing down at his lap. Nobody noticed that Elle only pushed her forkful of food around the plate. They were too intent on shoveling their own forks crammed with gelatinous junk into their mouths.

"Vince," Elle piped up in a clear tone, "What is the difference between George Goldie of the Royal Niger Company and you government fellows of the Niger Coast Protectorate? Doesn't that cause confusion as to administrative boundaries, especially when the borders are so nebulous and ill-documented?"

"Confusing, yes, indeed," said Vince, wiping a bucket of lard from his glossy black moustache with a cloth napkin. "The offices of the Royal Niger Company, the Governor of Lagos, officers of the Niger Coast Constabulary, and the government of our Company each in turn give orders to native rulers, that is true."

"Do you ever consult each other beforehand? It seems as though some tribes would wind up with conflicting orders."

Vince was not eager to answer. He audibly gulped his claret, as everyone at the table was deathly silent now to hear his answer. "Yes, those other outfits often exercise authority in our territories without prior consultation. The situation is deplorable, and I daresay unheard-of in the history of *any* government of *any* country not actually in the midst of a war."

"Don't get him started on Goldie," jollied Lieutenant Henry Lyon, the assistant commissioner.

Chief Dogho said something that approximated, "Goldie a bad man."

Vince shook his head. "People have developed deep feelings of disappointment and neglect by the British government. It's just a quagmire of bureaucratic battles for control."

"Anarchy." Rip nodded. "We were in the midst of anarchy and revolution once, down in Mexico, before we were bounced from the country."

Vince brightened. "Indeed? And why were you down in Mexico?"

Rip went on, warming to his subject. "Elle likes to study cultures and civilizations that are downtrodden, in poverty, where there's corruption. She likes to root it out, figure out the workings of it, and expose it."

"Expose?" Vince sneered icily.

Elle squeezed Rip's thigh under the table. "Not 'expose,' that's not the right word, is it, honey. I like to point out ways in which the civilization can be made better, more healthy for the people. Suffering to me is an intolerable condition that no modern society should allow."

"Yes," Rip continued, "that's why she pretended to be an insane Cuban woman to get into Blackwell's Island—that's a lunatic asylum—in New York. You should've seen the furor when she wrote about the beatings, ice cold baths, forced meals. We lived in the Lower East Side on Hester Street in the most despicable tenement for an entire summer so Elle could write about the filth, the fire escapes filled with bedding, people living ten to a room—she's fearless, I tell you!"

Victoria pressed a hand to her bosom. "Oh, my! That sounds so . . ."

"Dirty," laughed Vince.

"Well, they needed baths," Elle explained. "Water doesn't hurt anyone, and can hardly be classed among the pauperizing influences. I believe they will open a public bath there soon."

"Thanks to her report!" Rip continued, "And the best stunt by far was the 'round the world in seventy-two days—"

Elle squeezed Rip's thigh so hard she felt her fingers would break. "Oh, honey, they don't want to hear about *that*, that has nothing to do with the poor or downtrodden. Mary, will you pass me the claret, please?"

Vince seemed to relax then, and laughingly said, "Well, if you can think of any ideas for improving the lot of these downtrodden people, particularly in Benin City, please let me know. Though I doubt you've had to deal with much human sacrifice in your time."

Brendan spoke for the first time. He leaned one arm against his chair back so he faced Elle down the long table, and said slowly with narrowed eyes, "And you are here to study clitoridectomy?"

"Why, yes," said Elle smoothly. "You must agree, mustn't you, that cutting off a woman's organ of sexual pleasure is certainly a situation that could use improving."

The beastly man skeptically lifted his own glass to his mouth and said, "An improvement for who?"

That enraged Elle all the more. She had to seethe through a dessert of cow's cream as hard as stone before she could excuse herself for the bath room, but when she returned to the sitting room Evin was playing his coon songs on the graphophone which enraged her afresh. She took herself to the veranda to smoke a cigarette.

Exhaling a mouthful of smoke out over the quietly chirping jungle floor below, Elle muttered to herself, "Oh, why is everyone being so impossible?" She was going to round up Mateus tomorrow, and get a head start to Edo before that yokel from the sticks could make his way back there.

Through the screen door she could see Rip and Evin laughing animatedly as Evin brandished one of his wax cylinders, and Elle wished she could just walk out into the night and away from the noise of so-called civilization. Then it occurred to her she was thinking like Mr. Donivan, and this angered her even more. He was probably only the "legendary" Guinea trader because he was the only one who had happened to survive that long. She started back indoors to get more claret and was nearly knocked into the middle of next week when the screen door flew open.

And there he was, alone. His finely drawn features in the lantern light made her shiver in the depths of her belly, and she backed up into the veranda railing. He smiled and advanced on her frontally, moving so close Elle went into a sudden panic that he was about to gather her in his arms.

But he was only going for the ashtray on the railing behind her. She felt silly for imagining he would touch her again. He withdrew a cigarette from his case but did not light it; instead he looked her levelly in the eyes and said, "It's very admirable, your work on behalf of the poor and downtrodden. If I'm cynical, it's because I see so much hypocrisy. What is it you wish to know about female circumcision?"

Elle was taken aback by his candor. "Forgive me for assuming you're an expert in such matters."

Brendan smiled at her collarbone. "More of an expert than most. You can ask Gainey, if you prefer."

The chutzpah of this palm oil ruffian! "All right, then . . . Does it not affect a woman's ability to urinate?"

"Not at all. What's removed is the prepuce, a small piece of the sheath that extends from the clitoris, the same sheath as is removed in men."

"But I thought . . . "

"That is generally thought. There are some tribes that remove the external genitalia, and even stitch the remaining labia together, leaving just a small opening—"

Elle shrank away, quivering unpleasantly. "But not the Edo?"

"No, and the Itsekiri don't practice it at all."

"And how do you . . . " Elle inhaled and exhaled. "Why do they do it?"

He responded with such alacrity, it was thoroughly suspect. "They'll tell you that it gives the man more pleasure because without the friction, it extends the act of love." He watched her with a placid face devoid of all emotion.

"Oh!" Elle steamed, shaking her head rapidly as if to rid it of dire thoughts. In her anger she took another cigarette from her case. "Men! It always comes down to men, doesn't it? Men and their pleasure!"

Brendan smiled, shaking his head too. "It sure seems that way."

"And who's to say it's a *good thing* if the act of love is prolonged? Who cares about that, anyway?"

"The men, apparently." Brendan answered the rhetorical question.

Elle was dazed, staring dumbly at his beauty. She jumped idiotically when there was a flash in her face, and she saw he'd withdrawn his match safe to light her cigarette. What a nice gesture, Elle thought. In the degenerating modern world of manners, it was rare to find a man who lit your cigarette anymore. Puffing smoke from her nostrils, she said, "These are very good things to know; now I *am* extremely angry about this entire subject, this is *all* going in my report, thank you very much for your help in this matter."

Now he said softly, his words like feathers against her neck, for he remained standing close after lighting her cigarette, "No, thank *you*, ma'am."

Elle frowned. "Oh, please don't call me ma'am, I can't stand that! I'm not an old biddy—Thank me? For what?"

"For having the grit to be the first white woman to ask me such questions."

He looked darling then, with smiles in his eyes. His open shirt collar framed his sun-browned clavicle, a few wisps of silken chestnut hair tantalized her, and the moisture between her legs expanded. Her nostrils flared, and her entire skin suddenly felt flushed with heat. She tried to regain her control, but her next stupid line of questioning did not help. "And in your opinion . . . this cutting of the prepuce . . . to please the man . . . does it work?"

Still smiling, he shook his head. "No. I prefer a woman in her natural state."

The thought of this man uttering any combination of those words had Elle's innards fluttering. She was in such a state of suspended anticipation the ash end fell off her cigarette and she didn't move.

The man grabbed the ashtray in one fluid motion, held it underneath her hovering cigarette, and continued speaking in a conversational tone. "There is a certain peculiar practice over in Abomey, to the west of here. Sort of an opposite practice to our subject I haven't heard of anywhere else. There, it's considered desirable for professional older women to manipulate girls' labia daily 'til they resemble the teats of a she-goat." He set the ashtray down, leaned against the railing, crossed his feet, lit his own cigarette, and looked impishly at Elle. "*It is said* the men enjoy handling the long projections."

"Oh . . . *it is said*, is it? And I suppose *it is said* in Edo that one of the benefits of female circumcision is the women remain more faithful!"

"Yes, how did you know?" Still, he smiled. "And that if women have too many orgasms, it injures their health."

"What?" Elle blurted.

But instead of answering, the infuriating man took a long pull of his cigarette, self-satisfied and assured. He must know he was riling her out of her head!

"What is this about too many—"

"Oh, *Brendan!*"

Elle finally tore her gaze from Brendan to see Victoria swishing through the screen door in her pink silk gown, calling gaily, "Brendan, Evin says you absolutely *must* join us, he says you have an absolutely angelic tenor, he says you have the voice of an angel. Did you know that, Mrs. Bowie?" She wrapped her hands around Brendan's arm and leaned into him.

Brendan tried to hold up both his hands in protest. "It's not true. Evin just loves to get me in trouble, haven't you noticed that, Victoria?"

Victoria held fast to his arm. "But I received the sheet music for 'Just Tell Them You Saw Me,' and you say you love my piano playing."

"That's very true, my dear, but as for singing—"

"But you absolutely must!"

Certain she wasn't wanted, and as she had no desire to sing sappy songs, Elle lifted her skirts a few inches and soared grandly back into the sitting room. Rip and Evin were still playing the funsters over by the graphophone. They were even swaying in unison, singing along as Mary Wells plodded out a tune on the pianoforte that resembled "Yellow Rose of Texas."

Shaking his arm, Elle whispered loudly in Rip's ear, "We have to go. I've forgotten to bring my medicine."

Rip relented to her lie, but parted reluctantly with much hale-fellow-well-met handshaking, and slapping of Evin's back. Elle was very nearly out the front door without having to see Brendan again, but Victoria was dragging him back in from the veranda and proclaiming to the room at large, "We are all invited over to Brendan's to see his naughty painting!"

Rip paused in mid-slap and asked Evin, "Naughty painting?"

Evin shook his head with disgust. "It's not naughty, really. It's pre-Raphaelite, which a lot of people confuse with naughty. Do you think Brendan would be so risqué as to have a real naughty painting?"

Rip paused with consternation for a moment, caught the joke, and laughed heartily while Elle tugged at his arm. That was when she saw Brendan, leaning against the wall detached from the rest of the guests, staring directly at her with a low, assessing gaze.

They were finally promenading down the dark muddy street. Torrential rain came down with a dull roar, Rip with no choice but to get soaked as he held their only umbrella over Elle's head. He scampered around Elle like a child.

"Did you know those fellows were buffalo hunters in the early eighties? They followed the northern herd just as they were all starting to disappear."

"Well, isn't that charming!" Elle snapped. "He can add that to his list of high and mighty accomplishments."

"Yep, they were even with Teddy Roosevelt on the last hunt in eighty-three."

"No doubt they showed him where the last lame, weak, albino buffalo was cowering."

"Ah, honey! I thought you were over that Dostooski thing."

"I am! I'm on a new fresh crusade—against men who denigrate women."

"Wait, now . . . " Rip had to skip to keep up with her, as she was stomping furiously in the mud. "I don't like the sounds of this one bit. By any chance are you hating this fellow because of a *look* in his eyes? Or the way his thumb curves around a glass?"

"I hate him because he's exactly the sort of man I had to run from, and I'll be damned if I come to the middle of nowhere and run into that sort of bastard over here!"

Rip finally shut his trap, but he kept shaking his head and muttering, "Oh, no . . . "

She was relieved to have a bed room to herself! She drank her brandy and gum guiacum, dressed in her most feminine nightgown with posies embroidered around the hem, flung herself into the bed, and blew out the candle. She enjoyed the luxury of heatedly pleasuring herself, her clitoris already swollen from suffering through hours of female hysteria. Her crisis came swiftly, almost without touching herself, and the convulsions were so violent she thought she might be having a seizure. She cried out unintentionally, and bit down on a pillow, the spasms like electrical shocks washing through her torso.

Was this what that man meant, about women injuring themselves? She didn't care! She would take pleasuring herself any day over relying on a man, longing for him and being disappointed. Back at home, her good doctor had provided her this service, and without him she had become inventive, but the climaxes had been increasing in strength.

If she had a seizure and keeled over, it would at least sound good in the obituaries back home.

5

She wasn't supposed to be at his house.

Brendan wasn't allowed in Gainey's Vice Consulate when Gainey was out in the field. Nobody had ever outright said that, but the few times Brendan ever bothered going there, it always seemed like Lieutenant Lyon or a clerk or a soldier was popping up right at the threshold, barring his way with that sort of nearby talking that had one backing down the stairs. Brendan knew Gainey didn't trust him (Brendan returned the sentiment with fervor), and Gainey only maintained jovial civility in the hopes of gaining some negotiating elbowroom with the Oba. Gainey would be apoplectic if he saw his precious Victoria standing unaccompanied at Brendan's front door in such a light summer dress, with her frilly pink parasol and what looked like a picnic basket at her feet.

Damn Miriam for telling her he was home. He would have to talk to Evin about that. Miriam listened to Evin.

"Oh, I am glad you're at home."

Of course she knew he was in. He had only just returned ten minutes ago from having an Urhobo detained for adding mud and chopped plantain suckers to his palm oil puncheons to make them weigh more. Now he was shirtless, cleaning his shotgun, preparing to return to Edo. He'd been itching to get back there ever since he'd gone to seek out Elle to give her a gift, only to be told by some lounging bystanders that the "scientists" had gone downriver to Ughoton, in a canoe with ten pullaboys. He wanted to whip himself for that—he could easily see Elle's house from the front windows of his own, and indeed had pulled up a favorite wicker armchair to the window with the broadest view.

He reckoned he'd wasted too much time down at his offices on the *Hindustan* ordering the loading of his own canoe. Brendan's canoe was the biggest war canoe on the Rivers; it had belonged to Chief Nana before old Ralph Moor waged war on him a few years back. He always brought the *eghen* of Edo plenty of calicos and fine linen, rum, brandy, champagne, glass beads, crystal ear drops for the Oba's wives, gilt looking-glasses, cooking pots, all manner of clocks, and tobacco. On this journey, the jewel in the crown of which he was particularly proud, he had a new Edison talking machine to present the Oba.

Yes, Elle had slipped away when he wasn't looking.

"Hello, Victoria. What brings you a-nigh this way?" For Brendan relaxed when at home. He relaxed when he took off his shirt, he relaxed when he cleaned guns, and he relaxed his language. And lately it just didn't seem that he needed to primp for Victoria anymore.

Victoria picked up her basket and entered. "Oh, Brendan! Well, you know Vince said before he left, if I need company and get lonely, I'm to go see you directly. He said he trusts me with you, because there aren't any scoundrels lying in wait to kill you."

Brendan doubted Gainey had said anything of the sort, but he had no choice but to let her in. He sent her to the veranda at the back of the house, as it fronted acres of palms and silk-cotton trees, and was enclosed with mosquito-netting. He put on a shirt in his bed room, but omitted shaving. He wanted to save that for

Edo, so he'd be newly shaven when he saw Elle.

On his way back out to the veranda, he ran up against Evin in the kitchen. "This doesn't bode well," Evin said darkly.

"I can't very well turn her out." Brendan shrugged. "She's got a picnic."

Evin scowled. "I'm just saying you beware."

On the back veranda, it did appear that Evin was prophetic, for the young woman had divested herself of her straw hat, had spread a cloth upon the floor, scattered pillows about, and was in the process of examining a champagne bottle.

"Allow me, my dear." Brendan sat cross-legged next to Victoria and, taking the champagne bottle, covered the cork with a linen napkin and twisted. It popped with a dull thud, and Victoria giggled with delight at the way it foamed over the lip of the bottle. Brendan poured it into the two goblets she had brought. "When is Gainey due back?"

Victoria pouted. "Oh, any day now. He has gone with Chief Dogho to sign more treaties with the Sobo."

"Urhobo," Brendan corrected her. He didn't understand why it was difficult for British to say "Urhobo." Nor why it was deemed easier to say "Gwato" instead of "Ughoton."

"Urhobo, Sobo . . . " Victoria giggled. "Jekri, Itsekiri, Ijo, Ijaw, it's all so confusing."

"Did he take the man-of-war?"

"Yes."

"Gun-boat diplomacy."

Victoria tilted her head. "I beg your pardon?"

"Gun-boat diplomacy. They bring the man-of-war in to scare everyone, to enforce their dubious treaties."

"But he's bringing them cases of gin as well! I know Vince is not a favorite of yours, but he really just does what Whitehall tells him to. It's not easy, you know, what with all these confusing tribes, treaties, tse-tse flies, and I don't think he's ever been the same kind man since they brought that head and body of that

Chief to him. Separately, you know. They said it was because the Chief had the nerve to decide some tribal matters without consulting the Consul first. And he's ever so shirty at being passed over for promotion again."

"Is he?" Brendan melted a little at this news.

"Why, yes. They're sending a younger man, a James Phillips, to Old Calabar to be Acting Consul while Moor's on leave, and Vince should have been chosen—after Gallwey, at least. As if this new man could possibly know a fraction of what Vince knows!"

"And who has he taken as dragoman? If he took Mateus, he's lost. That fellow has been known to disremember certain words and speak them all backward, all depending on who's paying him at the moment. Why, in one treaty last year on the Jamieson River, the chief thought he was signing for a free canoe full of umbrellas."

Victoria sipped and laughed at the same time, then held her hand to her face with a feminine choke. "Oh, my! No, not that strange little man, thank goodness. He went with Mr. and Mrs. Bowie up to Gwato several days ago."

"Traitor!" Brendan cried, without meaning to. Jumping to his feet, he spread his hands out in a conciliatory gesture. "I've got to go, my dear. You know I've been overseeing the packing of my canoe—"

"But wait!" Victoria, too, leaped to her feet, in doing so kicking open the picnic basket, betraying that there was only one tin of sardines in there aside from the champagne, glasses, and napkins. She rushed to Brendan, clinging to his suspenders. "But you can't go yet."

Victoria rocked off balance, and Brendan was compelled to put a hand on her shoulder to steady them both. She was so short her moist breath steamed against his sternum. "What's wrong?"

Her shining eyes searched his face. He could see she had rouged her lips, and the unmistakable wafting of gardenia caused his penis to instantly stiffen at attention, like a dog that had seen raw meat. She was delicate with tiny bones, and he was afraid of hurting her. "There is something I need to tell you, something you want to know. It's something I overheard."

"Something important," he prodded.

She nodded rapidly, reminding him of a doll with eyes that opened and closed. "Yes, oh, yes!" Her hands climbed his suspenders, and she stood on tiptoes, as though she had to tell him this urgent thing face to face. "But I feel so muddled . . . All that champagne . . . "

Brendan tried. He tried as much as a man could. "Is it something to do with Gainey? Mayhap if you took a sit over here, cleared your head . . . "

Victoria's eyes were half-closed. She wasn't sewn up, that was for certain, not after only one glass of champagne. "I think you're very handsome, and exciting, and I often dream that if you'd just carry me off, I wouldn't do a thing to stop you. Oh, Brendan!"

He surrendered then and kissed her, chastely at first as was proper for an upstanding English girl, so as not to muss anything on her. He remembered how much he had craved her, how he had imagined kissing her while getting himself off, and the reality of her felt much smaller in his arms. Within the space of a few seconds she had flung her hands around his shoulders and was pulling him down so that he nearly lost his balance. He lifted her by the hips, turning so he could set her on a wooden windowsill. She frantically licked his mouth and uttered small whimpers. Brendan had reached down and lifted her skirts to her knee, when there was an enormous clattering inside the house, as though someone stamped in iron boots.

Brendan stood up straight as a deer, but Victoria didn't seem to hear the rumpus. As she could only reach his chest with her face now, she began a hurried undoing of his shirt buttons.

"*Capitão!*" a man inside the house yelled.

That stopped Victoria. She didn't know that Brendan was also sometimes known as Captain, from his position on the merchant ships he'd worked on for years. "Vince!" she whispered.

The back door banged open then. A veritable Tasmanian devil of a man burst forth, bandy legs spread wide apart, hands outstretched in the shape of talons. His black straw hair stuck out every which way.

"*Capitão*, I've just come from Edo!" Mateus proclaimed.

"Edo, yes!" Brendan detached himself from Victoria suddenly; she fell forward off the windowsill and stumbled. "What's the news?"

Mateus erupted into a knowing smile, all sense of urgency gone from his demeanor. "Ah, perhaps we should discuss this at a later time, eh, *Capitão*?"

"No, goddamn it, give me the news now."

"All right." Mateus reported solemnly, "The Bowies are under the tutelage of Ologboshere."

That was the worst news ever. Brendan knew Ologboshere as a compatriot and warrior; he knew Ologboshere's proclivities for women. "Is there any way for you to, ah, create a few—"

"Wrinkles? Already done, *Capitão*."

"All right, I'll meet you down at the *Hindustan* and get the details."

Mateus leered at Victoria. His teeth pointed at odd angles like the oars of a war canoe. "Yes, get the details *later*." Dropping his leer to Brendan's crotch, he added, "You best start thinking about base ball, *Capitão*."

"Base ball!" In a flash Brendan had the gnome in an iron choke from behind, his knee in the back of Mateus's knee, just so he knew he could drop him at any moment if he took the notion to. He hissed in Mateus's ear, "Stick to business and we'll both prosper, *camarada*."

Brendan shoved Mateus toward the back door. Mateus looked

as if he would hide his head underneath his arm as he took his leave, walking sideways like a crab so that it was a wonder he ever got anywhere.

Brendan exhaled mightily and turned back to Victoria. She looked out through the mosquito netting at a kingfisher on a branch. He stroked her under the chin. "Darling." That might help, calling her darling.

She turned to him with moist eyes, her lips all aquiver. "Darling!" she echoed, gathering his hands inside her tiny ones.

"I must go; what is it you needed to tell me?"

"Oh! Yes! I heard Vince and Lieutenant Lyon talking two nights ago. They were discussing a dispatch Ralph Moor had sent to Whitehall before he took his leave."

Mayhap it would help if he continued stroking her paper-white throat. "Yes?"

"It said that every year the King of Benin exacts murderous tributes from all the towns under his jurisdiction, that he makes human sacrifices for *juju* purposes, and he's the last big hindrance to trade."

Was that all? Brendan's mind started wandering to an image of Ologboshere having Rip Bowie seized so that he could get his pillaging hands on that wondrous angel Elle. "Yes?"

"Moor went on to tell Salisbury that 'at the first opportunity steps should be taken for opening up the country, if necessary by force'!"

"Oh, God." Brendan backed away, rubbing his face with his palm. "That's good you told me that, Victoria. Thank you very much."

Nobody said anything for several long moments. Brendan swallowed the remaining champagne, staring at the same spot the kingfisher had been in before, but now there was nothing.

~ ✍ ~

The city of Edo was a marvel of primitive technology. Laid out on a spiral plan, all roads emanated from the Oba's palace. It was divided by tracts of bush and wide avenues into a number of distinct settlements, each bearing its own name. The streets were clean and not even muddy when it rained, as gangs of women were charged with almost constantly sweeping them. Some of the roads seemed to Elle to be two miles long.

The houses of tough ochre-red clay had thick walls, and roofs thatched with palm fronds. Most houses being very wide had great atriums within, supported by strong hewn planks of timber twelve feet tall, and in these atriums there were benches to sit on under the overhanging eaves, and open impluviums in the center to allow in air and rain, which washed away down clay drains. These atriums were finished with a red glazy paint, and this was where Elle met Iden, a young Edo maiden.

Ologboshere had made the introductions, after Elle had thanked him fawningly for saving her life. She knew he hadn't, but it worked to her advantage, for he said he knew just the girl to assist Elle in her studies. Iden was a slave, but lived in what Elle took to mean a sort of extended family, loosely-structured groups that lived in adjoining compounds. Elle thought this an ideal arrangement, with an old man as head and the families of his several sons all working in close contact. What problems would vanish if Americans adopted this method!

This was how Elle came to feel a warm attachment and affection for *Edo ne ebvo ahirre*, "Edo the city of love," as she discovered it was known to *Ivbiedo*, the citizens.

Iden must have been a slave of some standing, for she was at all times heavily laden with brass collars and chains of gold and ivory, and on her legs she had shackles of copper. She wore a handsome girdle of blue stones that, as far as Elle could figure, was a sort of coral from the sea. Iden was a stunning girl of maybe twenty years—ten or twelve years younger than Elle. Her hair, a bit shaved off the hairline, was gathered at the occiput into a huntress's knot, then divided into four large bunches, the knots defined by beads of brass and coral. She oiled her hair with palm oil so that it lost its natural black and turned almost chartreuse.

At first Elle had Mateus translating, and the three of them spent several days walking about the city. Iden told how wives and slaves were continually at market, tilling the ground in the farms, looking after housekeeping and children, and cooking every meal. Men worked in the trade guilds, but women weren't allowed to join, and had to weave the everyday cloth in their own homes. Yet all the women seemed jolly and vibrant, happy with their lot, and Elle placed them as equals with the women of New York's Lower East Side in industriousness and strength.

She learned that the Edo word for "wife" could also mean "my boy," or "my servant." When men greeted one another on the street they said, "Are your people well?" The greeting implied that a man owned his family.

But when it came time to inquire into womanly matters, Mateus visibly cringed and backed off, so stridently in fact that Iden and her friends laughed at him. Elle was only able to get Mateus to translate that she wished to know "about all female bodies."

That was when Mateus vanished, and was not seen again for some time. Iden seemed to understand, and took Elle back to her compound, where she disrobed and laid herself bare. Elle discovered Iden's nipples were dyed a dark dull blue she knew as indigo. She had patterns of cicatrices of horizontal stripes on her belly. And Iden willingly spread her thighs and showed Elle the circumcision, but Elle wasn't certain what she was looking at. It occurred to her she had never looked at herself in a mirror, so she wouldn't know the difference. She then divested herself of her shirtwaist, skirt, petticoat, camisole, and drawers, Iden laughing melodiously at every article of clothing Elle dropped to the mat, but too shy to pick anything up.

The women laughed, and Iden petted Elle's face with the back of her hand. Iden had two bright blue tattoos on either hip not unlike the leaf-shaped swords of Ologboshere's henchmen, with several dots and lines radiating from them. But of course Elle spoke only the most basic Edo and couldn't understand Iden's explanation of what they symbolized.

At length Elle proffered some items of her clothing to the younger woman, and she dressed Iden in her camisole and drawers. She knew Iden wanted to invite in some of the other women. By gestures Elle indicated this was all right, and a few girls who had evidently been waiting in the wings burst into the atrium to squeal and jump around Iden. Elle in turn donned the sarong Iden had dropped to the mat, but didn't leave her breasts bare as was the style, and instead yanked it up under her armpits. One girl made movements that told Elle she wanted to dress her hair with palm oil and coral.

Barely anyone noticed when an older *iye* woman frantically rushed in, raising the roof with her yells. Apparently she did this often, because none of the girls paid much attention, that is until a whiteman clad in river boots, shirtless save for a leather vest, stormed into the room and sent them scattering. He seemed to inhabit the entire room, leaving no space for anyone else; indeed, he mildly shoved aside the frenzied *iye*, as her screaming was doing nobody any good.

Elle wanted to die. Covering her clothed breasts with her hands, she shrank back to the wall until she hit a clay bench, sinking onto it with legs of sand. She saw Iden squeal happily and race over to Brendan, fling her arms about his neck, and ecstatically kiss his face. Brendan seemed not to notice Elle, as a few remaining girls jumped around the couple as well. Elle was grateful, for she barely remembered how to stand, her hands and legs were shaking with terror, and she looked for the closest door.

Brendan held the girl at arm's length, shaking her slightly, chattering in Edo. Elle heard him say *Oyinbo* at least once, so he was probably asking where she got the clothes.

By crawling with her back to the wall, Elle managed to slink behind Brendan before Iden decided to point out her newfound friend who had given her such pretty baubles. Brendan's expression, when he turned and saw Elle, was indescribable. It could have been horror, or humor. He uttered something that sounded like, "Land's sake." It was hard to be certain.

Elle was able to stammer, "Mr. Donivan?" before turning and skipping out the door.

6

Once again she was without clothes in Benin City.

She dashed down the wide avenue at first, but she eventually slowed to a jog. A few of the girls from Iden's house followed her to help, soon giving up when Elle indicated she wanted to be alone.

She entered the guest house Ologboshere had loaned to her and Rip. She was all the way into one of the interior rooms when her chest caved in with sobs. She leaned back against the cool mud wall and wailed without tears, a completely dry convulsing of the chest that left her empty, searching for some comfort. She stared at a dark wall, her jaw slack, and said quietly, "Bastard."

After many more deep breaths, she dressed in one of her remaining outfits, really a tennis costume with vertical stripes and high dog collar. She moved into the front room and sat down to write.

She was only writing for thirty seconds when Rip came barreling into the house, his shirt open at the collar as though he'd just come from breaking horses. Indeed, he ran so fast he had to hold his Stetson atop his head with one hand.

"Elle! Someone just told me—"

"Is everything everyone's business in this town?" Elle snapped. Angrily throwing her pen down, she stood and sashayed past Rip to the fresh air of the front door.

"Well, *no*, honey, that wasn't what I meant at all! What I meant was—"

She spun around in a flash. "What you *meant* was that I just had an extremely embarrassing scene wherein that Brendan Donivan bastard just swept in from one of his oily rivers and embraced his *girlfriend* and made me look like a complete sucker and gump! I know that's what you mean; I can see word travels fast in this burg!"

Rip approached her with open arms. "Honey, honey, honey …"

"Oh, stop it with that 'honey'!" Elle shrieked. He had just been out in the yam fields, Elle could tell; he was imbued with that wheat smell that was vaguely attractive. It was certainly much better than the soot and fumes of New York they both used to be saturated with.

Rip held her from behind, his chin lightly resting upon her shoulder. "Honey, what did you expect? Men are out here on their own, with no white women to comfort them. And you yourself said he's just like every other man, right?"

"Well, of course! And that's why I'm *here*, and I thought I left all of them *back there*!"

Turning her around to face him, Rip held his hands out in a feeble approximation of comforting. "Listen here, sweetheart. I know you have good reasons to think all men should just hit the road. I know it disappointed you to find out this guy who was supposed to be helpful turns out to be a rat. But look at it this way. He's here in the middle of nowhere. If it were me, I'd be taking myself a fine wench too."

Elle sniffed, glad to have something new to think on. "Why don't you?"

"Why don't I what?'

"Ever take another woman? I know, I know, we're always

traveling together, how can you get to know anyone in a port, I know all that. And you know I don't mean the temporary women you always find. I mean . . . back home. Why don't you find a woman? Look at you, God knows you're so handsome women stop and stare when we walk down the street. No, don't go." Rip wasn't going anywhere, but he glanced sheepishly at the floor, his hands sunk deep in the pockets of his denims. "I mean it, Rip! I feel like I'm ruining your life sometimes. Like you're bound to me by contract—"

"Which I am!"

"Which you are, but that doesn't preclude your finding a wife! The New York world doesn't say people can't marry and have children. You agree with me that all men are worthless, shifty liars, but *you're* not. You're sweet, helpful, dependable . . . Why don't you find a wife?"

"Well, you know, honey . . . Maybe I just can't see leaving you alone like that."

"Oh, Rip. I can always find another photographer."

"Not one who was apprenticed to Matthew Brady!"

She knew he would bring that up. Brady was in his waning years of fame and living on the wrong side of the other half when a young Rip had tracked him down. Still, it was impressive. Elle raised her face to his and kissed him sweetly smack on one of his dimples. "You're my closest friend. I love you, you know, you lunkhead."

"I know," Rip said, almost with disappointment.

~ ⚓ ~

Brendan at once knew who was the culprit at the bottom of things. It had probably been Mateus's idea to introduce Elle to Iden, but since it was so poorly unsatisfying to whale into such a mud-crawling varmint as Mateus, Brendan went directly to Ologboshere. As he stomped the half-mile or so from Iden's to

Ologboshere's abode, he muttered aloud to himself in English, as he was wont to do when riled.

"Now that woman thinks I keep company with such as Iden! Well, I reckon I do, but that's nobody's business but my own. The fact of the business is, she was given to me by the Oba, and . . . Well, why not? A man's got to find some small comfort in jungles such as this. But now the whole town of Sapele's going to know my business. Damn! What do I care what that high society *wife* of a photographer thinks of me, anyway? Sure, she's pretty . . . more than pretty . . . but if she's such a prude she'd frown on a man for doing what he can in a jungle, well then . . . "

He found Ologboshere in one of his atriums hugging up a couple of his wives, one of whom was the Oba's daughter. Brendan refused to take a seat, eat his kola nuts, or drink his *tombo*. Brendan said as politely as could be (for Edo was nothing if not a polite lingo), "I think there is more here than the eye can see, Ologboshere. I think you purposefully sent the *Oyinbo* woman over to Iden just so you could sit back and laugh."

Ologboshere drew himself up straight, no small feat, seeing as how he was still sitting on a mat on the ground, and looking at Brendan's crotch. "And what would I be laughing about?"

"Oh, I know you. You'd be laughing at the *Oyinbo* going back to Sapele and telling everyone that Ighiwiyisi sleeps with an *Ovbiedo*."

Ologboshere got to his feet by using a carved wooden stick to prop himself up. Brendan knew him as invincible as an elephant, so mayhap he was just accustomed to being held up by others. He boomed his disapproval. "And what would be so bad about that, Ighiwiyisi? Is it perhaps because you are ashamed of Iden, and don't want *Oyinbo* to know of her?"

Brendan had suspected for a long time that what Ologboshere said was the truth. He was, after all, from Alabama. A yellowhammer from Alabama could reconcile in his mind the needs of a man and think it was imperative, and a big sight better than

the random *Ivbiedo* he had dallied with before, when you never
knew the outcome, or indeed what they'd be saying in the morning.
He did feel avuncular affection for Iden, but even with his fluency
in Edo there was not much they could talk about, nor did Brendan
ever expect there would be. "That is not the topic I came to discuss,
Ologboshere. There are hundreds of other women you could
have sent the *Oyinbo* to, and you chose Iden. I think this was
deliberate devilment. I just want you to know I will be keeping
my eye on you."

With no formality, Brendan turned on his heel and marched out.

That was the apex of rudeness in Edo, and Ologboshere shouted
after him. "The Oba has been good to you, Iwi! He has allowed
you to trade within the city walls."

Instantly cognizant of the threat, Brendan once again turned
on his heel and stormed back to where the tall, prideful man was
sneering at him. "To prove to you I am not on the *Oyinbo* side, I
will tell you that Consul Ralph Moor of Old Calabar has written
to the Queen in Liverpool that he intends to take this city by
force. And I will *not* be among his soldiers."

He turned again, this time intending to make it out of the
house, while Ologboshere shouted after him, "When, Ighiwiyisi?
What have you heard? Tell me everything you heard!"

Since he really hadn't heard much more than that, Brendan
chose to change it into a grand exit, stalking out of the house with
his head high in his whiteman's clothes, pants tucked into his
boots. Fingering his leopard hip ornament, he thought how he
couldn't wait to get back into his Edo attire. The *eruhan* kilt was
much more soothing and cool than the impractical wool pants,
and he could effectively go shirtless, his favorite mode of vest-
ment. And he did fancy his jewelry.

Mayhap he'd head directly back to his house, or down to the
creek off the Ikpoba River where he liked to bathe. Two days in
his canoe and he felt as funky as a dog. Speaking of dogs, where
was Pequod? Ode looked after Pequod, and they usually came

running down to the canoe landing, somehow knowing ahead of time when Brendan was due in, but this time they hadn't.

He stopped abruptly, surprised to find himself in front of the guest house. Mayhap it was a sign from Osanobua. Inhaling deeply, Brendan squared his shoulders and entered the courtyard.

Nobody greeted him, as they would in other houses. There were no family members hanging around the yard, and since it was starting to rain again, Brendan ducked inside the front door just in time to catch an eyeful of Mr. Bowie voraciously kissing his beautiful wife. Well! If that wasn't a sight! Brendan felt a pang of envy that the Texan was over six feet tall, unlike Brendan who in a similar position would probably just look directly into that tall woman's eyes.

If that wasn't enough, that jackass then murmured, "I love you too, Elle."

They proceeded to stare sappily into each other's eyes until Brendan cleared his throat and said, "Excuse me?"

The two happily oblivious faces that turned to him changed rapidly, the husband into a mask of rage, the woman into something similar. It was a toss-up as to which one would vent on him first.

"What do you want?" Rip shouted.

"If it's all right, I'd like to speak to Mrs. Bowie."

Rip looked down at the woman. "It's up to you, Elle." Then he strangely added, "This is your job."

The woman was ravishing in a vertically striped costume that covered almost every square inch of her fine form. She must be sweltering in that getup, and indeed lovely tendrils of damp hair were glued to her forehead and sun-browned neck. She shrugged. "Certainly. Fine. Do come in."

Which was strange, since he was already in.

"I'll just get some film," Rip snarled, "and head on over to town." He left by way of an interior hallway, while the woman turned her back and flipped over some papers she'd apparently been writing on that lay on a wooden table. Brendan found the sight of the thick curlicues of auburn hair at the back of her neck incredibly stimulating.

"Brandy?" Elle enquired politely, holding aloft a decanter.

"Yes. Listen here, Mrs. Bowie . . ."

"Call me Elle."

"Elle." How it pleased him to be able to say that name aloud! "I must apologize for a few things."

She looked up from the table brightly, her warm brown eyes brimming with fun and amusement. "Only a few?"

Brendan accepted the glass from her. He wet his lips with the liquid. "I realize it's . . . highly unconventional, some of the things I do. I just hope you take into consideration the strife of living in these parts, and that the discomforts are sometimes over-whelming."

She stood boldly not more than a few inches away. He got a whiff of her jessamine scent, and something else that was indefin-able that he knew was an inner, secret female smell. "Mr. Doni—Brendan." She smiled. "If I were to get up a tree about every tiny thing that appeared to be unconventional, I truly would be nowhere. Now, how did I expect you came by all that knowledge of female circumcision, if not by firsthand study? So, please don't apologize. Your dirty linen is none of my concern."

Should he be relieved? Her reference to dirty wash seemed to indicate something sordid. He now heartily swallowed the fiery brandy. "For some completely divine reason that appears unknowable to me, Elle, it matters to me very much your opinion of me." It occurred to him he was breathing liquor into her face, but she only continued smiling maternally.

"I am glad . . ." she whispered, searching his face with jollity, as though he were a sideshow spectacle. "I did enjoy dancing with you the other night. I've only been away from home for a short time, but already I miss the companionship of other *Oyinbo*. Since Rip seems to have taken a shine to your partner, maybe we can pass an evening. Do you have a talking machine up here?"

The idea of spending more time with Elle so overpowered Brendan, he moved even closer to her until he was very nearly standing on the toes of her shoes. "Yes, we have one."

"Oh, wonderful!" she cried like a young girl. "And please do dress in your normal Edo attire. I find it very wild and savage."

He would dress in palm fronds and walk backward if Elle found it wild and savage. "Anything," he whispered.

"May we eat the animals that are sacrificed? I haven't tasted a nice smelly goat for a long time."

"I've only been back in Edo a few minutes, but the first thing I'll do is kill that goat." Brendan still whispered. "You can eat it from my fingers."

Elle laughed beautifully. "That's not necessary. Although I'm sure you can be of continuing assistance regarding some of the more . . . " Her eyes seemed to go distant then, as though she gazed right through him at the wall beyond.

Brendan finished her sentence. "Anthropological things."

She said nothing, merely glimmered her eyes at him, and once more it looked as though she was about to cry. What layers of hidden feeling and mystery there were in that woman! All at once he needed to touch her, so he lifted his hand to her chin and took her delicate jawbone in his hand. His index finger ran underneath her chin, as smooth as cream. She didn't stop him, or try to pull away; no, she inclined her head erotically, as if daring him to kiss her.

"Ighiwiyisi!"

The dog reached him before Ode did. Leaping and growling like a rowdy bear, the dog jumped on Brendan's arse from behind. Luckily Brendan had heard them coming and had braced himself for such an event. All at once he wasn't touching the woman anymore, he was dancing with a dog, one paw in each hand, and a boy was attached to his right leg, hugging him mightily.

"Avast!" He rubbed both dog and boy on their heads. Elle

was laughing, leaning with one hand against the table as if she'd fall over without the support.

"Iden told me you were here. Obadesagbon told me he saw you come into this house. I wanted to bring Pequod, so you knew I took good care of her. We went hunting." He pronounced the dog's name *Pika*.

"That's good, Ode, but I'm in the middle of an important palaver—"

"This dog!" cried Elle. She came forward, sinking her hands into Pequod's mane while the dog happily slobbered on her wrists. "It looks just like one of those Newfound-land dogs, except brown."

"Yes, it's strange. I found her taking a French leave from an American steamer, and I decided she would be my hunting dog."

"And the boy? Is he yours also?"

Brendan shoved the dog down so that she stood on all four paws. He moved closer to Elle again. It was suddenly unbearable being even slightly apart from her. "He is my slave," he said soberly. "When I first came here, I gave the Oba some live leopards. To repay me, he gave me two slaves, Ode here, and Iden."

"Oh. Then Iden . . . "

"Is my slave. To do with what I wish." How he wanted to kiss those luscious lips! "Instead of taking her as a wife and living with her, I gave her to a family so she'd have relatives around her. She can still marry an *Ovbiedo*."

"Oh," breathed Elle, as if what Brendan said changed her mind altogether, whatever mind that may have been.

Ode was dragging the brown dog by the scruff of the neck. "Come, *Pika*! I will see you later, Iwi. I have a music lesson with Evin now."

"*Òkhíen òwie*." Brendan merely nodded, but Elle waved jubilantly at the boy.

"*Ób'ávàn!*" she called.

Brendan laughed, and had the nerve to run the back of his hand against her cheek. "You just told him good afternoon."

Elle's face went all liquid again, as if she teetered between laughing and crying. "Ah, well. I am still learning." She even inclined her head toward his hand, as if to rub it like a cat.

"I have to tell you," Brendan started. He dared to lift his thumb to lightly touch her lower lip.

"Elle! There's some kind of strange old sacrificial ceremony going on over by the—Oh." Rip stopped cold in the doorway, as if seeing a disemboweled critter in front of his very eyes.

Slowly Brendan lowered his hand from Elle's face, turning suavely to Rip and saying, "I was just telling your wife that there's some concern about the safety of being in Edo these days. I have it on good authority the British are planning an attack on this city, probably not before Ralph Moor returns from leave, as he is the main instigator of the plot."

"Ah!" cried Rip.

"Oh," Elle breathed calmly, as though the news were old.

Brendan stepped away from the woman and shook Rip's hand robustly.

"But Brendan—" Was Elle standing in the doorway as if she wanted to say something more?

"OK," Rip called as Brendan stalked out into the rain. "We'll see you . . . soon . . . "

Suddenly Brendan could not get far enough away from Elle. He needed to think, to ponder. Spending ten minutes with Elle was enough to fill one's thoughts for an entire week. What did that poet say, the poet Evin had urged him to read . . . ?

Women, nurse those fierce invalids home from hot countries

CHAPTER 7

Edo

Elle was very confused about how Brendan made her feel. His proximity—when apologizing for having a mistress! how silly—had all at once evaporated whatever steel will she had formed against him. The boldness with which he touched her face should have felt impertinent, but it shook up some deep atavistic longing in her. She became distracted with thoughts of Brendan fucking that lovely maiden, detailed picturesque imaginings that riled her anger once more, and she was glad if a day went by without laying eyes on him.

Still, how very handsome he was, with that long lustrous chestnut hair to rival her own, his hoop pirate ear-rings, that brass leopard nestled at his hip, atop the pants pocket where his thick turbid erection had so provoked her.

When her washrag started taking off enough soot from her face to paint a horse, she went down to the swimming hole Evin had told Rip of, on a creek off the Ikpoba River. She had not considered a bathing suit to be an essential item of attire in Africa, and she merely stripped down to her chemise and drawers before plunging into the cool pond. She figured she was washing her clothes at the same time, so she took into the water a cake of the Edo soap made of palm oil, banana leaves, and wood ashes. The Edo soap was much better than that awful carbolic soap sold by the Royal Niger Company. How marvelous it felt, skimming the filth from her skin. She lifted her chemise to scrub her breasts, and dropped her drawers in the shallows to thoroughly soap between her legs.

After she washed her hair, dipping her head into water lilies on the surface of the water, she waded back to the bank to pin her hair up with clips. She wanted to swim and frolic as Rip was doing one pool over. It sounded like he was swinging from the lianas that were draped from the ebony and mahogany trees, as she could hear prodigious splashes as though from on high into very deep pools, accompanied by yells of joy. Elle gathered everything in her arms—she should learn to make a bundle for her head like the women here did—and clambered barefoot over the giant tree roots. She would feel safer swimming with Rip and his Colts should a gargantuan crocodile leap out—

She shrieked and dropped everything save her Derringer, which she had a safe grip on under the bundle.

"Avast, woman!" cried Brendan, holding his hands out at arm's length.

"Oh, you *bastard!*" Elle whispered fiercely. Her heart began its staccato pounding a second too late to inform her to fire. Brendan had been on an intersecting path leading down to the creek, and they had nearly taken a header together.

He allowed a smile now that she had lowered the pistol. "You've got a right smart quick draw on that piece. That's a good talent to have."

Elle's eyes dilated as her fear drained. Now, instead of a ravenous leopard she saw the *Oyinbo* man, clad in his woven Edo *eruhan*, leather vest, and not much else save for his eclectic mélange of bracelets and his incisor necklace. His enviable silken hair was loose about his shoulders, giving him the look of an angel sent down from heaven. "Well! How did you move so quietly? All these plants, I think I would have heard you."

"I'm sorry. I'm accustomed to moving quietly."

As he didn't offer any further explanation, Elle made as if to move past him, but he held out a hand to stop her.

"Excuse me," Elle said, trying not to look below the man's chin. He did indeed have a glorious mat of satiny hair covering his chest, creeping upward over his clavicle, and a darker stripe of the soft pelt between his pectorals that disappeared beneath the vest buttons. "Rip and I are bathing." They heard another of Rip's rebel yells as he cannonaded himself into the water.

"Thought you might want a taste of this," Brendan said with uplifted eyebrow. He hoisted an unlabelled bottle that had been corked.

Elle remained placid. She was, after all, in her wet lingerie rendered nearly transparent, so she squatted to retrieve her clothing where she had dropped it. Brendan squatted as well in one fluid motion, balancing perfectly on the balls of his bare feet. He was still smiling, damn him! "What is it?"

"Brandy. I had a shipment a few months ago, and I've managed to save some." He handed her the light blue stockings she had worn under her mannishly tailored outing gown, and she snatched them from him. What if they had been drawers! "You have such an…inspirational jessamine scent."

How dare he! Maybe his crude and low attempts at chivalry made women around here clamor, but Elle was from New York City. Further, she didn't even clamor when she was in New York City. "Brandy."

"Yes, you were drinking brandy at your house."

They both stood together, Brendan keeping his eyes level with Elle's. "Well, yes, I do drink brandy from time to time. But my brandy is medicinal."

Brendan frowned, a sweet expression that made his turquoise eyes flash. "Medicine for what?"

"How impertinent," breathed Elle.

"Reason I ask, there's a passel of *Ewaise,* medicine men, here in town who can help you with whatever ails you."

Elle felt herself finally smiling too. "If they are so wonderful, why is your back problematic?"

She knew she had flummoxed him then, for his frown took on a look of concern for himself. "Back?"

"Yes, Miss Armbruster seemed to have a detailed knowledge of the state of your back." She allowed Brendan to lightly take her wrist and lead her to a large root of the silk-cotton tree that had several indentations for seats, as though worn down by many derrieres.

"Miss Armbruster takes familiar liberties that I don't encourage," Brendan said mildly.

"Oh, don't you, now." Elle had nothing to sit on, and didn't fancy getting green moss on the back of her light blue drawers, so she shook out her outing skirt. "Seems to me from having talked with you and danced with you that you can be very . . . *seductive* in your encouragement."

"Is that so?" Brendan asked evenly.

"Why, yes. You have a very slick way that a poor girl like Victoria, who is starved for attention, would be affected by." The last thing she wanted to do was to step into her skirt in front of Brendan, so she sat on the tree root.

"No, wait." Brendan took some glass tumblers from a knapsack, which he then flattened and smoothed over the tree root. He then allowed her to sit on his knapsack, using her skirt as a lap blanket. "Slick, eh? The cat is out of the bag. I'd let you sit on my *eruhan* but that'd mean I'd have to take it off, and that might make me appear even slicker."

He had two tumblers with him, but then again no blanket to sit on. It was mysterious. "How long were you there?"

"Where?"

"In the bushes. Before we collided. Did you see me . . . swimming?"

The lascivious grin this notion brought to Brendan's mouth made Elle sick and dizzy with shame and lust. She had to steady herself with her hand on the tree root.

Brendan handed her a few goodly fingers of brandy in the tumbler. "I'm not one to spy on ravishingly bewitching women when they soap their bodies."

But it sounded like exactly the sort of thing he *would* do. "You didn't answer my question," she tried to say, but it came out a whisper, as when raising her eyes from her glass she took notice of a conspicuous bulge under the cloth at Brendan's right hip. She thought *if he has nothing under that* eruhan, *he is as impressively hung as these Edo men.* She was fairly slithering down off the tree root at this thought.

He smiled wickedly. "You look ravishing when you swim."

Elle's mouth formed an O. "Sir, I am a married woman," she said weakly.

Brendan closed his eyes briefly in obeisance. "I apologize. You are a ravishing *married* woman when you swim."

Elle had to shut her eyes too. The gall! She wanted to scream, and at least stand and stalk off in a huff. But his impertinence weakened her, and she had not been this aroused by a man's bawdy talk in years, perhaps decades. She felt like a bitter old spinster growing cobwebs in the moldy recesses of her body. She lived to work, she must work more now, ah perfect, she could ask Brendan something anthropological—

"How long have you and Rip been married?"

What? Brendan was refilling her brandy glass. "Married? Oh, ah, ten years. Yes, that is right. Ten years."

"And you're very happy with him?"

"Of course! You ask such questions!" *If that is his flaccid penis under the kilt and nothing else, fucking him would be like riding a bull. He would kill me. Especially after so many years . . .*

"I just ask that because . . . While Rip is certainly an

admirably robust fellow, he doesn't seem to match your intellectual heights."

"Intellectual? Well, Rip can certainly hold a candle to me in the brains department, if that's what you mean. Just because he's from Texas one shouldn't assume he just likes branding bulls and burning cow chips."

"No, I meant you seem much more educated."

He really got to her, the way he inclined his head, his face serene and sincere. What would it be like, kissing such a rough-hewn trader who had probably humped thousands of women by the time he had turned thirty?

Elle, despite her weakness of limb, continued to drink the brandy copiously. "Hardly. I didn't have the opportunity to attend university; I'm a self-educated woman. I had to start working, writing articles before I'd even left my mother's house at fifteen. I had to give my mother money."

"Ah, so you're not educated then. I thought since you'd mentioned Dostoevski . . . "

"Dostoevski! How . . . ?"

"Mateus said you mentioned him."

"Why, that lowdown sewer rat!"

Brendan waved Mateus's existence away with the hand that held the tumbler. "It's what you can expect from him. Then how do you know of this writer?"

Elle shrugged. "I've taken it upon myself to read all manner of literature. Dostoevski especially had such feelings for and knowledge of the poverty-stricken masses, which is the element of society I hope to elevate. Have you read him?"

"No," Brendan said vaguely. "I'm just starting to 'read book.' Evin told me I should be impressed by your knowledge. He's the educated one, he graduated from university in Tuscaloosa."

" 'Read book'? What do you like to read? Aside from palm oil manuals, or how to shoot leopards."

"Capture leopards," Brendan corrected her. He sat proudly

when he told her, "I am currently reading a book of poetry. Evin says I'm to call it a 'slim volume of poetry.' Nothing can beat it; I read it every chance I get."

Elle was truly impressed. She had not expected such fripperies from him. "And who is it?"

"Oh, I lifted it off a Frog in Lagos."

"No, I don't mean who did you steal it from." Elle had to laugh, that he would freely admit his thievery.

"It was either that or get involved in some long-winded yarn in Frog lingo. Oh, the poet? I can't tell you that. Just mayhap I'm writing some poetry of my own, and I wouldn't want you to think I was taking after this fellow. Evin says I'm to find my own personal mode of speech. He's already set some of my poems to music."

Elle found herself hopping forward on the tree root toward Brendan as she warmed to the idea of him writing poetry. "But you *must* recite something!"

"Something I wrote? Not a chance."

"Then recite me something from the French poet. Please! You have such a beautiful, syrupy voice. To hear you recite verse would send a woman into paroxysms of . . . " She inhaled and exhaled sharply. " . . . education. So please, please, enlighten me. It is a long time since I heard anything to do with literature, especially while sitting . . . in the jungle."

For the first time since she'd known him, Brendan looked shy. He was always cocky and brash. Now he looked at his own knees and kicked his feet that dangled in the air. "I don't think I can remember."

"Of course you can! Here, just recite into my ear." Elle shuffled herself even closer until they were sitting side by side, their thighs lightly brushing. "I'll close my eyes, and you can just quietly recite into my ear. That way, I can imagine what you're saying." To demonstrate, Elle held her head high and closed her eyes.

"You're going to get more'n you bargained for," Brendan said in a new, low voice.

She had no idea what he meant. "Recite!" she commanded.

And he began in his lovely lilting drawl to whisper,

Sweeter than the flesh of sour apples to children,
the green water penetrated my pinewood hull
and washed me clean of the bluish wine-stains and the
splashes of vomit,
carrying away both rudder and anchor.

"Vomit." Elle giggled, but did not open her eyes.

Where, suddenly dyeing the blueness, deliriums and slow
rhythms
under the gleams of the daylight,
stronger than alcohol, vaster than music
It is boiling, bitter, red; it is love!

How hot his breath was. It caused gooseflesh to rise on the side of her neck. Her fist was balled on the tree root to prop herself up as he sat almost on top of her hand with his powerful thigh nestled against her. Her nipples were so erect she felt he could see right through the measly material of her chemise.

Glaciers, suns of silver, waves of pearl, skies of red-hot
coals!
Hideous wrecks at the bottom of brown gulfs
where serpents, devoured by vermin,
fall from the twisted trees with black perfume!

There was a dull thud that must have been his glass falling to the jungle floor. She felt from the heat his body radiated that he lifted his right arm and lightly slid his burning fingertips across her breastbone. They were callused as she already knew, but her skin felt particularly pliant beneath his roughness. He dipped his fingers with feathery touch beneath her chemise strap, as he continued to seduce her with his words drenched in lilting sexual patois.

Sometimes, a martyr weary of poles and latitudes

The sea rocked me softly in the sighing air,
And brought me shadow-flowers with yellow stems—
I remained like a woman, kneeling . . .

He bit lightly into her earlobe, his tongue snaking around it, his moan barely discernible. Elle emitted a small sigh, her lower jaw drooping. She fought against the overwhelming craving to vault herself into his lap, to rotate her pelvis against that stupendous erection, to hump him with such ferocity they crashed to the duff below. When he slid his fingers into her armpit and gripped her pectoral she felt him swing his foot around so he straddled the tree root. Her hip was firmly glued in his crotch now, and she whimpered when he moved his mouth with slow slurping kisses down the side of her throat.

"Brendan," she whispered, whether to say yes or no, she didn't know.

"Elle, you're an amazingly delicious piece of ripe fruit," Brendan panted steam against her throat. "It's a mighty solemn occasion to hold such a precious bit of ripe beauty like you."

The fingers of his left hand started a painfully pleasurable spidery route across her bare shoulders, her vertebrae so sensitive she cried out, a small, strangled animal sound.

"It's all right, Elle . . . Elle, it's all right, don't be afeard," he whispered as he moved his right hand down, over the chemise just barely brushing the point of her enflamed nipple, supporting her breast in his hand as his mouth moved with new intent.

"Elle! Dear Mrs. Bowie, where are ya, honey?"

Rip was shockingly close by, his voice so loud it was as though he shouted through a speaking trumpet. Elle jumped, but Brendan seemed content to lick a slimy snail's trail across her breastbone. His sweet sensitive mouth had her sliding off the tree root, she was dripping so between her legs. She had to push his head away from her breast as she scooted back on the tree root, and even then the vile man merely grinned up at her, the tip of his tongue erotically touched to his upper lip. Rip's face popped out of the greenery almost behind his very shoulder.

What if Rip *had* been her husband! And that was what Brendan believed! Even as hot and excited as he had just stirred her, Elle compelled herself to loathe him even more. She felt fonder than ever of Rip when he swaggered over, his sluggishly flaccid cock swinging freely in the humid air. He was as sun-browned as Brendan, and probably over a larger percentage of his body! And he was so tall he hovered over them like some Sun God, his Stetson casting a shadow on Brendan's obliviously upturned face.

"Well, *buenos dias*. Going for a swim?"

Elle got to her feet too, holding the skirt in front of her lap as though Brendan hadn't already seen her in her drawers. She wound her free hand around Rip's admirable bicep. "Sweetheart, Mr. Donivan was just telling me more details about clitoridectomy."

Brendan still sat, casually picking up his fallen glass and refilling it. He was probably hesitant to stand, as his prodigious pole of beef might knock the couple into the creek, and make her husband irate as well. He was even searching his vest pockets, as nonchalant as to want a cigarette! "Say, Mr. Bowie, what was it you were saying at dinner about the around the world in seventy-two days thing?"

Rip crinkled his dimples. "Oh, that. Well, as the missus here said, it had nothing to do with helping the poor, really."

Elle inserted, "I was soliciting some funds, in order that I could *later* help the poor."

"By doing what?"

Elle hated herself for feeling crestfallen because when Brendan finally did stand, his kilt was smooth around his hips. "By going around the world in seventy-two days." She would raise the roof later at Rip for even mentioning that in the first place at Gainey's dinner. It did not sound even vaguely anthropological to pull off a stunt like that.

Rip explained, "She had a bet with someone."

"Yes, a very well-known captain of industry in New York. He said it couldn't be done. Especially not by a woman." Oh, how she wished she weren't standing in her lingerie, bare for all the world to see! And this odious man who thought nothing of mashing a married woman, he just stood there, disinterestedly scratching his stomach as though to draw attention to his hip ornament, or the fact that he did not have an erection.

"But then you accompanied your wife as well, right, Rip? Then it wasn't all her glory, nor was it all her effort; it was shared equally by both of you."

Elle and Rip turned into statues. Nobody had ever asked that exact question. Rip was the photographer. Elle was the girl journalist. It was such a bigger feat for the female half of the team that nobody had ever patted Rip on the back. "I suppose," she said coolly. She narrowed her eyes at Brendan. "Rip was there *the entire time*, yes. By my side. He shared equally in the glory, yes."

Brendan actually had found a cigarette in his vest pocket. He lit it, and with the cigarette still in his mouth, he squinted at the couple. "Except for the time in Cairo, right?"

Why was Brendan doing this? Elle shook Rip's arm to indicate her displeasure, and said, "Well, it appears I am about done with my female circumcision research, Mr. Donivan. I doubt very much if I will be needing your know-how."

"Oh," said Brendan, with as much emotion as a hansom cab driver ejecting her at her destination. "I expect I won't see you anymore."

"No, I will be here, I am just moving onto the next phase of the research. I shall study men next, and their *anthropological* rituals and surgeries."

Brendan cocked an eyebrow. "Is that wise, Mrs. Bowie? You'll need supervision. You don't know a thing about the men of Edo."

"Well, I expect to find out!" Elle cried brightly, pointing to

Rip to fetch her clothing from the ground. "Ologboshere is going to be my teacher."

She was heartened to see a flicker of concern in Brendan's eyes. "Mrs. Bowie, I wouldn't trust Ologboshere. He's a touchy sort of player. Not the sort a demure married woman such as you should be messing about with."

"I'm not worried. Good evening, sir."

Elle put on her clothes once they had almost regained the main path back to the city. Rip, of course, didn't have to put his clothes on at all.

"Now honey," whined Rip, "what's going on with that shifty fellow?" He buttoned her shirtwaist as she fumbled with her skirt.

"I find him very odious!"

Why was Rip always that appallingly relaxed? "It's obvious you've rather taken a shine to him."

"Oh, obvious, is it?"

"Well, it's obvious to anyone that *he's* taken a shine to *you*." He straightened her collar as though dressing a little girl. "Leastways, that's the picture I got from his bull's balls hanging out of his skirt, and the huffing and puffing you were doing practically into each other's mouths."

Elle could not believe Rip had just said that. She slapped his hands away from her shirtfront. "We were not! You know how I am, Rip! How could you think such a thing?"

Abruptly Rip stopped smiling charmingly. He regarded her with tilted head. "Maybe because it's true. You seem to have found yourself a new convert. I, of all people, can tell these things when you can't . . . Colleen."

What was Rip saying? Had everyone suddenly gone completely insane? "Would you *shut up*? What's gotten into you?" Elle turned and started furiously down the path.

Rip followed. She knew he was back there, looking ridiculously naked as always. Why couldn't he at least put on some drawers? "What I'm saying is, how do we expect to write a paper on how dangerous and murderous this place is, *when you keep liking it too much*? How treacherous is that going to sound to the New York world when you write 'I swam in beautiful jungle creeks, paddled around in canoes with smiling natives, and went practically buff'?"

Elle had never wanted Rip to know her original reason for coming to the Guinea Coast. It had nothing to do with being sensational or saving a civilization from despotic, rank savagery. It was simpler, really. Six months ago she had had a dream that she was in an African village. As she awoke, she heard in her mind a word: *Benin*. When she went downtown to the New York World Building, she ran to the research department, and with the help of the geographer, found a map. With nauseous foreboding, she saw the city there. She had not figured out the other part of the dream yet, a vision of a blue pictograph that resembled a large cat.

"I *don't* like it! The smell of death is everywhere! You never know when you're going to fall over a half-eaten dead person! How can anyone like that?"

"You like your women friends. You like that war-mongering devil Ologboshere. And you like your white traders! I'm telling you, we better start stumbling across a few more burning flaming corpses, or this piece is going to run on the Ladies' Page."

Avast! Elle almost cried, until she realized it was a word of Brendan's. She twirled around, allowing Rip to run into her. She pressed a forefinger into his sternum and hissed, "I'll tell you what's so likable about that disgustingly perverted white trader, Rip, and I don't want to hear one more word about it. He is *so low* he makes goo-goo eyes at a woman he thinks is married, while trying to romance the fiancée of a high muckety-muck in Sapele who could possibly ruin things for all of us, all the while running a circus with a harem in the jungle! How many other women does he need to satisfy his stallion lust? Now, you know my views on rutting and romancing, so stop shooting off your mouth!"

She stormed back to the city in silence, Rip trailing behind. The only thing Elle thought she heard Rip mumble was, "I just want you to be happy. I think you're making another mistake."

As if he were such an expert on sex or love!

He was the big dog of the tanyard.

Brendan and his retinue marched to the palace down the northern road, past the Queen Mother's Palace, past all the wards where guild members hammered, melted, and carved: the road where they were likely to garner the most attention. So as not to make it appear he'd had too much assistance trapping the leopard, Brendan took up the prominent front position at the litter where the hanging head of the poisoned leopard might possibly come to life and bite him in the arse. Brass workers dropped their tongs and clay to come watch, bringing clouds of wood smoke from the wax-melting furnaces. Metal workers ran out carrying half-finished spears, hoes, and fans for aerating the fires. Gangs of women rushed from the Oba's market with baskets on their heads, brandishing whole catfish, parrots in wooden cages, and cane rats.

And of course, Brendan's procession had to pass by the guest house where Elle resided. Only Rip, however, came to the front gate to gawk and run back inside to grab his camera. In an increasingly foul mood, Brendan refused to answer Rip's questions as the lanky Texan (clad this time in denims and cowboy boots, praise be to Olokun) scuttled sideways next to him with his camera box in outthrust arms, pushing buttons and turning dials.

"How'd you catch that cat? How long did it take you to find it? Are you bringing it to the Oba? What was your hunting experience prior to the buffalo thing in the Plains? What do you hunt in Alabama, possums?"

Brendan remained placidly silent, as the other men of his retinue laughed and caroused and told stories that made themselves out to be the lions of the day. All Brendan wanted to do was shout at Rip, *Where's your beautiful ravishing wife, buddy? Why aren't you looking after her?*

The procession passed the house of Ologboshere, close enough to the Oba's Palace that Ologboshere could conveniently consult with the *Iyase* whenever he liked. As though Brendan's internal screaming had been heard clear down the road, Elle emerged from Ologboshere's gate skipping excitedly, looking a thoroughly changed woman from the one he recollected. Her skin was fairly glowing from the sun-drenching she'd evidently received, apparently from sitting in Ologboshere's atrium having her hair elaborately braided and stacked into architectonic shapes on her head with coral ornaments. She was sporting a particularly intricate cloth wrapped around her body, her shoulders tantalizingly bare. The fact of the business was, the only *Oyinbo* items she displayed were her black pointed beaver congress shoes and some gold and garnet ear drops he had seen her wear before.

Elle jumped up and down like a little girl at a parade, waving at Brendan, but stopped with a crestfallen look when she saw his impervious face.

Ologboshere sauntered out smiling then. He beamed proudly at the leopard lolling on the litter behind Brendan, then took Elle by the arm and guided her back inside the house. It would have been unseemly for Brendan to continue looking, so he forced himself to look at the Palace, its walls of ribbed mud and designs of spirits and lackadaisical critters, the five-story tower emblazoned with a massive snake running down its length, a brass Bird of Prophecy crowning its crest. Squeezing his eyes shut, Brendan thought of the *onwe vb'uki* symbol on his own hunting armband, a sun and moon. He chanted to himself, *What you throw at the moon cannot strike the moon. What you throw at the sun cannot strike the sun. Death cannot kill the sun in the sky.* Brendan thought his Hand would forgive him for reciting the offertory with a completely different aim in mind, that he might remain immune to the glances and words of the captivating Mrs. Bowie.

Inside the Palace gates, they were joined by *emada*, pages carrying swords and spears, as well as court musicians who created a racket with trumpets, drums, and rattles. Brendan did not expect to present the leopard directly to the Oba. The raucous column passed through many more gates to reach the head *uzama,* where Brendan was put upon his pins to relate his experience capturing the leopard. He gave them the particulars, how he had waited every night for three nights by the pit, how the leopard finally came to kill the goat he'd staked out there. How he shot it with his poison-tipped arrows after which Onaiwu came to help with his blowgun and poisoned darts. It was very important to get the right amount of poison before the leopard wearied itself thrashing about the pit for hours. A dead leopard was only second best to a live one. Brendan was then able to leap upon the cat and hog-tie its feet and muzzle while Onaiwu and a few others held it down. Now he had a fine leopard to give the Oba, *Ovbi'Ekenekene ma deyo*, the sun of beauty that never fades, though Brendan was never sure if the *uzama* would even tell the Oba, them being fond of keeping secrets from him, and taking it upon themselves to dispose of goods. Nevertheless, he had to blindfold the cat then, for the leopard was the Oba's animal counterpart, and as such, "Two Obas cannot see each other's faces."

The pomp and ceremony finally over, Brendan made a beeline back to his house. There was no one in front of Ologboshere's this time, even though Ode proudly led the sacrificial goat that had been the bait for the leopard, and Brendan led Ode. The greetings of *"Ighiwiyisi!" "Kóyo!"* and *" Vbèè óye hé?"* from all doorways and benches of the street did not improve Brendan's spirits, and the first thing he did inside the walls of his own compound was to cut the goat's throat with his Bowie knife. He didn't want to shoot it in the head, as he needed the skull intact to place in front of his Ogun shrine to ensure good hunting. He left Ode in the back yard to supervise the goat's demise, and he entered the dark corridor of his house.

Evin must have heard the goat's bleating, for he fairly slammed into Brendan, apparently just as eager to exit as Brendan was to enter. Brendan pushed on past Evin in his haste to access the brandy keg in the kitchen.

"Are we going to get to keep the goat this time?" Evin demanded, following Brendan like a dog. In his endless attempts to enshroud his vanishing hair, Evin had a red silk scarf tied over his head, the tail ends hanging down his back.

"No." Brendan banged a mug onto the wooden counter. He shifted the brandy keg from where it was wedged among calabashes of palm wine, gin, and whiskey.

"Ah, you're making good on your goat promise to the comely Mrs. Bowie."

"I've got mighty little of this world's goods, and I can't take it with me."

Evin frowned. "I thought you could. Leastways, as far as your Edo religion goes."

Refreshed with a few healthy gargles of brandy, Brendan asked Evin, "Do you? Think she's comely?"

"About as comely as they come, I'd say."

"Would you take her over Victoria?"

"Lickety split. Maybe it was that Dostoevski thing Mateus

told us of. Maybe it's that I always see her in her courtyard writing something. Or maybe 'cause I like to see her sucking you in."

"Sucking me in? What's that supposed to mean?"

"I mean she strings you along. It's the funniest sight ever. She's so smart, she's got you drooling at her feet like a dog. And she's the one woman you *can't* have."

Brendan narrowed his eyes at his partner. "You like that, don't you, seeing as how you only gets the ugly ones. Well, I'm telling you right now, I'm sending Ode over there with that goat, because I'm finished with her." He swallowed more brandy ferociously. "That's right, I'm not going anywhere near her. She's a married woman and that's that. I'm not going to dip my wick into that stewpot."

One would have thought Brendan had just informed Evin he was running for Oba the way Evin's jaw dropped to his chest. "Jesus H. Christ! Well, don't that take the rag off the bush."

"It's not like I haven't refrained before, you sassy old rascal."

"This is the first I've seen!" Evin gaped. Since it was usually so difficult to get much reaction from the poker-faced Evin, Brendan allowed him to carry on. "You've got a lifelong legend as a fancy man, Donivan; you're telling me you're putting a stop to it now? Let's see, it was back in Marengo County when you were courting that judge's wife."

"That was in Lee County, which is why I never consummated it. She was a big old heifer!" Everyone knew things were better in Marengo County, the county Brendan was from, and that only heifer women came from Lee, the county Evin was from.

"Nah, she was from Marengo, which is why that old judge caught you diddling her in the pigsty!" Evin was having such a good time roasting Brendan, he even filled a mug with brandy, though normally he was a tub-thumper of the Anti-Saloon League.

"It was in Lee, in a hay barn."

"Ha!" Evin pointed at Brendan with his mug. "I thought you

didn't consummate it."

Brendan fell silent, sipping his brandy. "Mayhap we're thinking of the district attorney's wife."

"In Marengo," added Evin.

They both nodded, silent.

"Well." Brendan pushed himself off the wooden counter he'd been leaning on, and struck for the back yard. "I'll tell you one thing. I was having the darnedest time finding something to dislike about that woman."

Evin followed. "Your usual method when dumping a woman."

"Olokun knows, she laid in the shade all the other women. Smart as a whip, a right stunner." Brendan hefted the goat Ode was guarding onto his earthen game-dressing shelf. "Real forward-thinking, not afraid of the truth. She well nigh shamed *me* for her straightforward talk, if you can picture such a thing." With his Bowie knife, he sliced open the goat from belly to breastbone.

"She's a peach, all right. Not like Victoria. Victoria's a doll, but she's got a face like a sea-boat." Meaning she didn't have much expression.

Brendan waved the bloody knife as though he were a professor making a point. "It's like comparing mangoes to bananas. And aye, when I happened to gaze upon her bathing." He started pulling out the slimy eels of intestine, Ode helping just to get his hands bloody.

Evin jabbed his brandy mug. "Wait. Happened to see her bathing? I can see you just happening onto a scene like that."

Holding his hands full of entrails in the air like a man surrendering, Brendan pleaded, "I didn't know she was there. I think you told her husband about the bathing place in the creek off the Ikpoba."

"Oh, aye, I did," Evin admitted.

"And oh, what a sight. It struck me clean to the heart. I fixed myself and watched her swim, lathering up her body like she was setting to pleasure herself, if I didn't know any better—"

"Avast!" Evin slammed his mug onto the earthen shelf. "It's enough I have to imagine it without you making me see it in more detail."

Brendan didn't mind seeing it in more detail now, because his new vow gave him the strength to hold out against such vivid imaginings. "But then I remembered . . . *she's married!* Not only that, but I think that naked pumpkinhead husband of hers is a tricky jackass. And he might be a few inches taller than me, but I've got a whaling bigger cock."

Evin near about died when Brendan said that. He laughed so hard (though he knew it was true) that Brendan had time to yank out the goat's lungs and had started sawing the breastbone with his bone saw before Evin regained his composure enough for Brendan to add, "There's something fishy about that around the world thing. Didn't some of that strike you as smoke?"

"Most certainly." Evin still giggled, already three sheets to the wind, not being accustomed to booze. "It probably really happened, but as to *why* . . . "

Brendan shrugged carelessly. "Nevertheless notwithstanding. I don't care none, because I'm finished with that woman. I wrote a new poem while I was setting waiting for that leopard to make his appearance. It's in my knapsack if you want to set it to that new music. Can you take over cleaning this goat?"

"Sure."

"I've got to get to the creek before I need bush lights to see. I'm as funky as a—"

"Week-old Edo body crucified on the *Iroko* tree," Evin finished his sentence.

Brendan paused. "Yep." He handed Evin the bone saw. "Well, I'll get that new poem for you, and strike out for—"

"*Capitão, O Capitão!*"

Brendan and Evin stared at each other.

"He's in the house," Evin warned.

"Out here!" Brendan yelled.

Mateus emerged in the yard, grinning so vehemently it seemed he aimed to break his jaw. He evidently wanted the *Oyinbo* to admire his new coiffure, a strangely opposite style from the men of Edo, who often shaved it on top and left a fringe around the ears. No, Mateus had taken a razor and shaved everything save a brushy strip down the middle of his head, leaving it its original length so it stood out stiffly like a rooster's comb.

"*Capitão!*" the clown said again. It was an affront to Evin, who had only been the First Mate.

"What's the news, Mateus?" Brendan asked instantly, not wanting to hear a long-winded yarn about coiffures. "Anything about the new fellow in Calabar?"

"*Certamente.* He's a Captain James Phillips. He took a degree in law from Trinity, and was in the Gold Coast Colony as Sheriff and Overseer of Prisons. He's only met up with Moor once, in London before he came over here, so we don't know to what extent he's a follower of Moor's policies. He arrived in Old Calabar several days ago and has already—"

Brendan interrupted. "Mateus. Remember at my house in Sapele when you said you had fixed some things regarding Mrs. Bowie and Ologboshere?"

"*Certamente.*"

"I thought you didn't care . . . " Evin called in a singsong voice from over where he was excising the goat's heart.

"Hush up. What did you do, exactly? You said you'd keep them apart, and it doesn't seem to have worked."

Drawing himself up proudly, Mateus sauntered about the courtyard, a hand to his chest. Above the usual odors emanating from his person, a mixture of sweat, moss, and crocodiles, Brendan detected a whiff of gin. If Mateus was oiled, it was a bad omen, for bad things happened when Mateus drank liquor. "I merely used the old *cabeça*, *Capitão*. I told Ologboshere that

Mrs. Bowie wasn't really a missus, that they just said that because it made it safer for them to travel together, so he didn't need to worry about Rip killing him if he felt like smooching with the young—"

"What?" Brendan took two long strides forward and grabbed the peewee vermin by the front of his obnoxious woven Portuguese vest that was probably drenched in a decade worth of palm oil. Lifting him to his face until Mateus stood on tiptoes, Brendan yelled, "Why the hell would you say something like that, you flatheaded dodo?"

Evin stood next to Brendan, waving the bone saw. "How is that supposed to keep them apart?"

Mateus's fingers scrabbled at Brendan's fist, trying to pry it open. "I'll tell you my logic, sirs, if you let me go!"

Reluctantly, Brendan unhanded the louse, not without tossing him back against a mud wall. Straightening his befouled garment, Mateus explained. "I figured the best way to get that fine woman to run screaming from the general, was for him to insult her so grossly with his smooching and feeling—*besides!*" he cried afresh, as Brendan was starting for him once more. "I am of the opinion that those two are not really as one, are not really married in the legal or true sense of the word!"

Mateus had found a way to pacify Brendan and Evin, for they both went rigid and silent at this revelation, allowing Mateus more room and relaxation to expound on this subject. "I am of the opinion that they merely maintain this seeming state of affairs because it gives them the ease to travel freely and without question, but I think the true story is they are merely working partners."

Brendan squeezed his eyes shut, then opened them. "And what . . . gives you . . . this idea?"

"They sleep in separate rooms, *Capitão!*"

"Lots of married people do."

"They don't wear rings!"

"Mayhap they're afraid of the rings getting stuck on . . . the spokes of . . . "

"They don't have that flowery way of talking that married people have."

"Mayhap they're bored, being married for ten years. Oh, this is tomfool stupid!" Brendan finally exploded, throwing up his arms. He made as if to go, but returned to poke Mateus in the chest. "You're going right to Ologboshere and setting him straight."

"If Mrs. Bowie hasn't already," Evin pointed out.

"Then you're going to Rip and telling him that Ologboshere is manhandling his wife and if he doesn't get over there this very second she's in danger of losing her . . . her maidenhood. Anything, anything to get that lazy jackass to move. Tell him to put his camera down and go save his wife!"

Brendan began to storm back inside, pivoted on his boot heel, and pointed at Evin. "Keep the head."

She didn't want to return to Iden, she really didn't. Though she could care less about the Alabama ruffian, it still irked her in the pit of her stomach. Disgust, that was probably it. Not that Iden was Negro—in New York, reformist suffragists such as herself didn't concern themselves with such things. It was disgust to imagine him licking her, holding her body above his, or kissing which appeared to be anathema to *Ivbiedo*. Iden couldn't be more than twenty years of age, at least ten years younger than Elle, and thinking of it made her uneasy, perhaps unsure of herself.

She went to Ologboshere, where she might get more information on human sacrifice, while her interest in circumcision and other tribal rituals had sincerely deepened. Ologboshere was always very merry when he saw her, when he wasn't out training in a way-camp at Obadan about twenty miles north, with sixty European cannons, from what she could gather from their happy mixture of sign language and rudimentary Edo. He had some of his wives, some thin and many tending toward the desirably corpulent, remake her coiffure until it resembled theirs, and Rip made many photographic portraits of her that would make for good accompaniment to her articles.

Elle grew to feel genuinely fond of Ologboshere, his magisterial presence, his willingness to cheerfully tell her almost anything she wanted to know. He drew pictographs in chalk and ochre in the dirt of the courtyard. In this manner she discovered that Brendan had traded them the cannons and firearms for palm oil. Elle wasn't sure how she felt about this, but she knew she wasn't about to inform Gainey. She knew Brendan and Gainey were competitors, as Brendan seemed to compete with almost everyone, including Ologboshere.

One day he called her into his inner chambers decorated with leopardskins and large hands on the wall painted in blood and lime. He didn't often sit on his stool in her presence anymore, and he squatted down on a leopardskin in order to hand her the most precious object, a brass fellow he explained was a dwarf playing a flute. It was quite old, he told her, from the reign of Oba Eviwua, three hundred years ago. He looked at her with such moist, inviting eyes then. Maybe it was her womb hysteria coming to torment her again, perhaps assisted by the ever-larger amounts of brandy to dull her pain. But she threw her arms around his neck and kissed him.

Why did it seem that throughout her entire life she had always been with the one she *didn't* want? She kissed him to feel the sensuality, the sleekness of his dusky shoulders, what it would feel like if she were Iden, about to couple with a dangerous warrior. But it was more akin to another one of her societal investigations, and she soon broke the embrace, stood, bowed politely, and left.

As she entered her own courtyard, Rip was there, and he leaped up from a chair in his enthusiasm to greet her. "Elle!"

She frowned. It seemed Rip had been living more and more like a native lately. He still wore his Stetson and denims, but now he went barefoot. "Rip, your feet. You're going to step on a scorpion."

Was he drinking too much *tombo*? His eyes swam with glistening happiness. "Our *Oyinbo* friends have sent over a goat! I've got Ogiso to cook it, she's making a stew."

"It's only payment for making us think we were going to be killed. I was hoping he wouldn't actually give us a goat."

Rip happily rubbed his lean belly. "Well, I'm hungry enough to eat a goat."

"No. We have to go to their house now, to thank them."

They walked to Brendan's house. Elle thought about Brendan parading through town manfully with his leopard slung behind him, how heartless he was, how cold inside.

They could hear the unbridled singing before they even entered Brendan's courtyard. It had started to rain, the ceaseless roaring rain that saturated everything and tended to put one into a blue funk, if one was alone. It gave the American singing the effect of an oasis of beatitude in the clutches of the insidious jungle.

As Elle drew closer, she could plainly hear Brendan's fine tenor soaring and rising over Evin's earthier tones. Above the unsteady weavings of two guitars, Brendan sang angelically, entreating someone to stay. A banjo tickled the melody, and Elle wondered who the third musician was.

"Come on," Rip encouraged her at the door.

"No, wait 'til they're done."

"Ah, they're just howling at the moon. Come on."

Their house was one of the grandest in Edo, on the scale of Ologboshere's with its many chambers. The courtyard at the front was a marvel of tropical botany, with plants hanging from the wooden eaves, blood-red blooms showering from tall bushes that hugged the mud walls, and terra cotta pots scattered at artistic intervals, spilling forth their exotic vegetation. There were pathways of kiln-fired tiles through the undergrowth, some leading to little pools, some with wooden benches.

To stall for time, Elle stooped to pick up a fallen banana palm leaf. They were handy as hats during the monsoon, she had learned.

That was when the banjo stopped, and Brendan stopped singing.

"There's someone here," he said.

"Who cares?" roared Mateus.

But in a portion of a second, Brendan's silhouette was standing at the open front door. He brandished his Schofield on his shoulder, in fine form wearing only his holster, *eruhan*, vest, and river boots. "Who's there? Aye, Mr. Bowie!"

Why did he mention only Rip by name? Irritated already, Elle came forward reluctantly. She knew her lower lip protruded petulantly, but she didn't try to correct it. Rip was slapping the son of a bitch on the bare shoulder with familiar jocosity, even greeting Mateus who stood by with a new Red Indian tonsure.

Elle tried to smile and nod at Evin as Brendan ushered them into the front room. She cringed back into a bas-relief brass plate of Edo warriors marching with their *eben* swords and shields. The room, in fact, was peopled with brass objects as gorgeous as the one Ologboshere had given her, masks of striated terra cotta, carved ivory tusks, and intricately woven mats. There were a few *Oyinbo* items; several rocking chairs were gathered around a low Oriental table. In an alcove in the wall, a flow blue china platter supported a human skull. It did not quite warm Elle's heart.

With the guitar slung around his neck, Evin rose and offered Elle his chair.

"No, we've just come to thank you for the goat. Our cook has already made some lovely stew."

Evin gestured at an empty chair. "Please. I have to go check on our own dinner."

"Don't let the fire go out," Brendan told Evin before Evin disappeared down a hallway.

"We interrupted your dinner," Elle proclaimed, for the first time able to look Brendan in the face.

He slowly licked his lower lip, as though he would like nothing more than to gobble her up. He probably hadn't seen her new Edo garb, as he hadn't even glanced at her that morning when he had paraded with the leopard.

"Not at all," Brendan said distantly, lost in his inner thoughts. "Please join us." He took one of the three chairs and motioned for Rip to take the third, leaving Mateus to sit cross-legged on the floor.

"Yep," said Rip in that expansive happy tone that annoyed Elle. "See here, Mateus? I've brought my wife with me. You don't need to worry about me not looking after her. Can you imagine," he cried, turning to Brendan with merriment, "this here fellow came barreling in my door this afternoon, his eyes all bugged out, shouting that I had to look out after my wife or Ologboshere would get his paws on her." He laughed boldly, but nobody else in the room shared his glee.

"What?" In horror, Elle shrank farther back into the rocking chair.

"I can imagine," Brendan said evenly. "Mateus is prone to strange outbursts."

"Yep! He's drinking gin out of this flask, and carrying on like Elle is his sister or something! 'Rip, if you don't get over there pronto, you're going to lose your wife to that monster!' Say, buddy, ain't you supposed to be on the water cart?" Rip carried on obliviously. "Well, I just needed to tell this guy that my wife does what she wants. Yes sir! Have I ever been able to stop you, Elle? No, she'd yell blue murder if I tried to stop her from doing what she wants." He turned to Brendan again, all chummy, as though in their mutual shirtlessness they were somehow related. "She's a mighty headstrong woman, if you haven't noticed yet."

The effect of Rip's speech on Brendan was nothing short of electrifying. His face rapidly melted from its mask of marble, and he lowered his gaze as if to finally take in Elle's neck and bare shoulders. His look was warm, making shivers rush from her tailbone to her jawbone. "I've noticed. I think it's an admirable trait."

Elle uttered, "Now, how strange of you, Mateus. What on

earth prompted you to say that?"

"Here, please have some brandy!" Brendan cried, leaping to his feet. He went to a sideboard that held decanters of expensive cut glass, and he babbled as he set the glass tumblers right. "You drink brandy, don't you, Mrs. Bowie?"

"You know," Mateus boomed, also getting to his feet and swaggering to the sideboard with sudden inflated puffiness. "I don't just get these ideas out of nowhere. There is often a factual basis for the things I say, believe it or not." He grabbed one of the tumblers, placing it first in line as Brendan poured. Mateus intoned loudly, "These are not the ravings of a *louco* maniac, Mrs. Bowie."

Brendan elbowed the midget so brutally he actually had to take a faltering step, but Mateus once again banged his tumbler in front of Brendan's decanter. Rip was taking great pleasure in the vaudeville act, slapping his knee and *hoo-wee*ing. Mateus punched his tumbler at Brendan, and Brendan drew back with the decanter as if to brain Mateus with it.

"Yes, indeed, Mrs. Bowie," Mateus continued to shout theatrically. "There are some who are of the opinion that you and Mr. Bowie are not even married, can you imagine that?"

Elle insinuated herself physically between the two men locking horns, backing Mateus rudely away from the sideboard. She gently eased the decanter from Brendan's rigid grip. "That's all right, Mateus," she said serenely, looking Brendan directly in the eyes. "Strange theories have abounded about me my entire life." And she smiled what she hoped was a dazzling smile, pouring her own tumbler without even looking down at it. In a low, sultry voice, she whispered to Brendan, "You and Evin sing very well together. Victoria was right, you have an angelic voice. Why are you ashamed to sing?"

It seemed the cat had Brendan's tongue then. Elle soaked her lips in the brandy and looked coyly up at Brendan as he struggled to speak. He gazed at her with blank eyes, stunned. She stood so close to the man she could have put a palm on his silken chest hair.

"My Da," he finally said, "loved to sing opera."

"Bren, do you want to eat in the dining room or the front room?" Evin shouted from the hallway.

"Whoa, partner!" Rip cried. "Let me help with them bowls."

"Let's eat at the dining table," Evin continued yelling. The rain was now clamoring, hitting pools and puddles about the downspouts outside. "Can you bring one of those lamps in here?"

"Opera?" Elle spoke in a stage whisper, though no one was paying attention to them anyway. "How wonderful . . . and how odd. My mother used to sing opera, too. Do you have any opera recordings?"

"Yes, I just got the Anvil Chorus from *Il Travotore*. Did your mother sing with an orchestra?"

Elle smiled. "Only in her head. She would sing around the house. Then she went into an asylum and . . . didn't sing very much anymore." She couldn't believe she had just told Brendan that. It was the brandy that had loosened her tongue.

Evin continued bellowing from the next room. "Mateus! Can you bring some matches in here?"

"Ah," Brendan said, as if he already knew. "I'm sorry about that."

"Don't be sorry. She needed to be there. We were happy to put her there."

Rip was shouting, "Evin, partner, are we supposed to eat this with our fingers, or is there some cutlery?"

"Ah," said Brendan. "Then I'm not sorry. Can I ask you, then—"

"We should help with the dinner."

Brendan reached out as if to touch her bare shoulder, but stopped short. "Is it true then? Are you and Rip really married?"

Now she knew what it meant when your blood ran cold in your veins. Why did Brendan even question it? If anything, people had suspected they *were* married when in the States, because they were always together, and got on well. Yet they had never shared a passionate kiss, not even when in danger, or when the possibility of death might have made them act rashly. They were just as sister and brother. "No, we're not really married."

It was his sweet pleading expression that got to her. She noticed a few freckles scattered on his sun-browned cheekbone, and she was incapable of lying anymore to him. Just by standing there, he usurped the virility of every man in the Oil Rivers, emasculating them utterly.

"Not . . . " he whispered.

The other men were busily clattering pots and dishes in the next room, shouting instructions to each other. She whispered too. "No, we never were. We're partners, that's all. We just find it safer to say we're married when we travel. People in other countries understand it more readily than a working woman who is assigned a male photographer."

Brendan shook his head slightly with a smile of disbelief. "But you were kissing him."

Elle frowned. "Oh, I was consoling him or some such thing. We *are* quite close, you know. We've been together for ten years and have been around the world together. Now, don't tell anyone, please. Except of course *your* partner, Evin. Don't tell Vince; it would be just my luck to have him making goo-goo eyes at me. It behooves me to act like Mrs. Grundy around him."

Brendan had a look as though gazing upon a chocolate éclair. His dilated eyes went all soft, and Elle could see his rapid heartbeat in the pit of his throat. "I'm not breathing a word."

"Bren!" shouted Evin from the depths of the house somewhere. "Are we supposed to eat this squash right out of the gourd?"

Brendan shouted back without taking his eyes from Elle, "Yes, the gourd is the bowl. Sprinkle cinnamon on them and some of that brown sugar."

"What wine do you want to go with it?"

"Use that California claret." With the "t" still in his mouth, Brendan breached the few inches separating him from Elle in one fluid motion and kissed her. Shocked at his brash spirit, and washed away with lust, Elle felt all the blood drain from her head as she slid down his body, clutching at his bare shoulders with her fingertips. He kissed her tenderly at first, slowly sucking on her lower lip, his hand planted firmly at the small of her back, the other hand cradling her cranium as though it was a crystal globe. She felt him snort hotly against the side of her face, and he seemed to quicken then, assiduously licking the backside of her front teeth, sliding his talented hand over her tailbone to gather her to him.

She clung to him with an ardor so intense it scared her. It felt natural to be kissing him lasciviously, to squeeze his bare biceps in her palms, to press her pelvic bone against the sluggishly alert breadth of his erection. It was the same knowledge of him when she'd seen him at Gainey's, as though he were a long-departed lover she had finally smoked out after decades of worldwide searching. Elle Bowie, the last woman to be a strumpet, taking such loose and pervasive pleasure in pinching his hoop ear-ring between her fingers, sucking on the tip of his tongue, in slithering her bare breastbone over his sleek chest hair.

"I can't ever figure out how to use this fucking corkscrew."

"Don't look at me. I'm a gin drinker."

"Here, let a New Yorker show you. Damn! How do you use this fucking thing?"

With her entire backside in both his hands now, Brendan backed Elle up against the sideboard. A brandy tumbler thudded to the earthen floor. Now his fingertips tickled her bare shoulders, as he had by the bathing pool, as they licked each other's mouths. He was so strong, so forceful! She could not sit atop the sideboard in her narrow and closely wrapped sarong, so he bent his knees and leaned into her, swaying his hips upward so that if not for the thin barriers of cotton betwixt them, she would have been shamelessly compromised. He didn't seem to care. And she cared even less, to her completely delighted shock. She was working one of the coral ornaments out of his lustrous hair when a goonish male voice shouted into the room. "Bren, nobody can figure out how to use this fucking corkscrew—Oh. Say, Rip, maybe we can push the cork into the bottle."

"Nah, forget it; let's not ruin the good wine. Where's Brendan?"

Elle came to her senses when that voice blared into her ear. Detaching herself from Brendan with a slurping sound, she squirmed from his clutches, panting so heavily little phosphenes swam before her eyes. Brendan leaned against the wall with one hand up high by a brass plaque, his other hand adjusting his penis inside his *eruhan*, and she had to smile, though Rip was barging into the room now, bellowing,

"Hey! Chop's getting cold! You wouldn't believe what they whip—Oh." He looked blankly at Brendan over by one wall fondling his prick, and his business partner all in flushed disarray. Before the shocked anger could spread over his face, Elle strode forward, setting her features into a stolid pattern that approximated boredom.

"Yes; I'm famished. What has Evin cooked up?"

The table was astonishingly long, as though the ruffians were accustomed to entertaining large groups. Since the Irishmen chose to sit as far apart as possible at opposite ends of the table so as not to taint their masculinity, this left such wide expanses of tabletop between each person they had to slide bowls and gourds to each other with the gusto of base ball players. Elle tried not to look at Brendan overly much more than chance would dictate, but she admired the way he opened the wine bottle with the complex contraption, then went around the table pouring it into artistically etched goblets.

Rip asked, "Now, we just eat out of this gourd, like the red men?"

Elle answered for Evin. "Yes, like it's Thanksgiving."

Rip smiled his sexy lopsided grin. "Thanksgiving in Africa. Wonder what that'll be like."

Elle babbled on happily, "Or Christmas. I suppose we shall be gone by then."

"Oh, don't go." That was Evin, surprisingly. "Christmas is the best time of year in Sapele. Remember that year we put candles on the custard apple tree?"

Smiling warmly, Brendan said, "Do you mean the year we started the fire on the custard apple tree?" The lit candles in the center of the table cast an intimate, softening light over his excruciatingly well-arranged face. Elle adored in particular the tip of his pointed nose. All she could think was *I have kissed him* . . .

Evin pointed at Elle. "Everyone gets very gay in Sapele at Christmastime. Even old Gainey gets sentimental. One year he invited us to come around and sing carols."

"He plays piano about as well as he plays golf," Brendan noted.

Rip looked agape, his mouth stuffed with the chicken concoction. "*Golf?*"

"We mowed out a nine-hole golf course once upon a time," Brendan said. Briefly he looked at Elle, slaying her with the delightful merriment in his eyes. "The hard part was keeping it clipped so the balls rolled somewhat straight. Some fellows always came around with cutlasses, but things grow so fast over here, and nobody likes a straight line in Africa."

Rip guffawed like a donkey. "That'd be a sight to see! Say, this *is* chicken . . . isn't it?"

Elle added, "Not some other thing that swims in the lagoons?"

Brendan nodded. "It's chicken, right enough. We got a passel of them over at some other folks' yards, so we just take what we want."

"Though we eat the things that swim in lagoons too." Evin smiled.

"*Crocodilo*," Mateus burbled into his squash gourd.

Glad she could turn to Evin now, Elle asked, "And what are these little seed things in here?"

"Peppers," Brendan answered.

"And this okra-looking thing?" Elle continued to ask Evin, but Evin pointed at Brendan.

"He's the chef. He wrings their necks, he cleans them, he cooks them."

Brendan said, "He just grows the stuff I cook with."

Elle had to look at Brendan once more, and admire him all over again so strongly her heart actually felt pained. God knew she didn't need to like or admire any man, especially one as entrenched in such an out-of-the-way place, one who wore kilts and leopard teeth, and who would surely turn out to be as heartless and cruel as the rest of them. But she let herself relax for the moment, due to brandy and now wine, and she thought perhaps she was strong enough in heart and will to have a wanton, gratifying affair with the delicious man, and walk away as unconcerned as men always did. Such a rapaciously delightful possibility made Elle as giddy as in her early twenties, when she had last embarked on a tryst with a man who had the frightful ability to stare right into her inner core, and make her feel special, adored, even loved.

Love! What a frightful word! How had that cuss word entered her brain? The only love Elle knew was the affectionate protective love she felt for Rip, for her family in New York. Oh, how she missed them! Pulitzer had promised to send them checks while she was abroad, so Milos and Sal would not have to resort to questionable practices to remain afloat. They were very resourceful, but came up with some puddingheaded schemes that were adorable, and sometimes dangerous.

When they had quite polished off every scrap of food, and the men were smoking and enjoying a second bottle of wine, Elle felt compelled to clear the table. Brendan said nothing, indeed had not paid undue attention to her during dinner, as though regretting his impetuous kiss. As she hauled the fine china out back to the cooking area, certain she had a wet area on the behind of her sarong, she was beginning to feel amiss, that she'd been fooled, and would not get a chance to practice her rusty seduction techniques on this world-weary "palm oil lamb." Perhaps he was embarrassed that Evin had seen them kissing, for she was no lovely quail, she was a seasoned woman of thirty years and then some.

She was prepared to march back to the dining room, coldly thank them for the meal, and march out with Rip, when Brendan came sweeping grandly into the kitchen with a few goblets and pieces of cutlery in his hands. He tossed everything into the brass neptune that stood for a sink, and grabbed her by one arm as she attempted to leave.

"Elle," he breathed urgently, his sharp eyes casting about her face.

"Brendan," she said uncertainly.

"What is it, what is it about you," he muttered, brushing her face with the back of his hand. His eyes searched her face, neck, shoulders, as though he couldn't make up his mind which part to take a bite from first.

"What do you mean?"

"When I saw you I felt a strange feeling . . . that I had seen you before. Where, I can't remember. Do you know what I mean?"

"Yes, oh, yes! Do you mean when something small happens, it can be the way someone's hair is combed, or a trivial statement someone makes? And you have the strongest most overwhelming feeling you've seen that exact thing before?"

"Right, only . . . this isn't trivial. It's some strong *uxumu*, some potent medicine, Elle, and you're it. What is it, what is it about you? Where have I seen you before?"

"Isn't it usually a dream one had a long time ago? That's the feeling I always get, that maybe I dreamt it months or years beforehand." She was happy he had sought her out, had followed her back to this dank and mildewed room, yet she wanted to push him away, he was that completely unknown and frightening to her. And she was convinced that no matter what she did, he would wind up stamping all over her, running roughshod. After all, was there emotion in the jungle? Living in this undrained swamp months on end, slowly withdrawing more and more into oneself, with gruesome perversions of Christian symbology, corpses dripping ooze under the pestilential dew, how could one bother having finer emotions?

"Yes, yes, a dream, that must be it." As if to rub out the frustrating inability to remember, Brendan gave his head a little shake, then slowly inclined it so she could prepare for the wretchedly exquisite feel of his mouth kissing her forehead, the bridge of her nose, the tip, slowly sighing into her mouth. Her mouth actually watered with aching to taste him again. He smelled feral, of Edo soap, ferns, and civet. She allowed her hands to brush across his fantastically well-developed chest, and she was not ashamed that she uttered a little surprised cry of arousal as she sucked his upper lip into her mouth.

"Bren, Mateus is at the brandy." Evin spoke in stentorian tones, but he kept his face discreetly behind the mud wall.

"I'm coming," Brendan breathed, hardly audible to Evin in the hallway.

"He started hammering away at Rip about a certain subject again," Evin said politely.

Brendan exhaled with resignation against Elle's mouth. "I'm sorry," he whispered to her.

And it was the most captivating thing, to be sorry for something someone else was doing!

Before Brendan could detach himself from her, Elle heard snarling oaths, and the banging of bodies against dull mud walls. The couple turned with mild interest to the hallway, where Evin ducked into the kitchen and took cover behind a wooden charcoal

refrigerator. All Elle could make out was Mateus growling something that sounded like, "*Você é tolos!* Why can't you admit to
the world what anyone with eyes can see, Mr. Bowie—if that is
indeed your real name? Who knows who you really are?"

There was more thudding as Rip presumably threw Mateus
against the wall. Mateus's fingers appeared around the doorjamb,
scrabbling in the packed mud. Rip shouted, "Are you *loco*?
Nobody wants to hear your cretinous ideas!"

Several times, Mateus tried to make a break for the kitchen.
First Rip's arm was around his throat, holding him back. Then
Rip tore Mateus's fingers from the wall and cinched both his
wrists together in the small of his back, so Mateus appeared as a
marionette with legs akimbo as he tried to run in one spot.

Elle called out gaily, "I want to hear his cretinous ideas, Rip."

"Yes, let's see his act," agreed Brendan.

At that, Mateus was manumitted, and stumbled forward into
the room. Drawing himself up, Mateus intoned, "It is no secret
that Mr. Bowie—*if* that is indeed his real name—and I don't get
on, and I feel no hesitation in announcing that I don't believe his
real true name is Rip Bowie. Do you know why I think this?
Because Captain Gainey, being an educated sort of man, has
shown me in his world atlas that there is a town named Bowie in
Texas. Yes, indeed, *certamente*!"

Brendan and Evin shared mute expressions and gestures that
said *That's it? This is the cretinous idea?*

Elle laughed, glad of an excuse to weakly lean against
Brendan's shoulder, aroused by the pressure of his bare arm
against her breast. "Mateus, has it occurred to you that maybe
Rip has relatives in Texas who founded that town?"

Mateus looked uncertain for one fraction of a second. Then
he gathered his wits and roared, "*And* invented the Bowie knife?"

Rip slapped himself in the forehead. "Oh, for God's sake!
Who said anything about inventing—"

Evin ventured out from behind the safety of the wooden box.

"You know why I doubt that story? Because Gainey wouldn't let him into his house in a pig's eye, much less show him his atlas."

"Hey, what's this?" Quick as a flash, and in a very brilliant move to change the subject, Rip had plucked what looked like an envelope from Mateus's back pocket. "It's got big letters that say 'Brendan Donivan,' but it appears the envelope has already been opened; the seal is broken."

Mateus swooped his claw-like limb to tear the envelope from Rip's paw, but Rip was faster, and in a flash he'd met Brendan in the center of the room to hand over the envelope. Mateus glowered something fierce at everyone in general. "One of the Kroomen got his hands on it and opened it. You can see how it's wrinkled and smudged, that's from us fighting over it."

Brendan sneered. "The same Krooman you fight with over every private dispatch you're entrusted with? Or is this a new Krooman?"

Evin inserted, "Maybe it's the same Krooman who showed him Gainey's atlas."

"Who gave this to you?" Brendan demanded.

"It was relayed to Gainey in Sapele, I just picked it up when I was there a few days ago. Gainey asked me to give it to you. I'd forgotten all about it." Mateus made sure everyone was watching him before he announced, "It's from James Phillips, the new Deputy Consul General in Old Calabar!"

As Brendan was now avidly reading the dispatch, Elle gave Mateus a reassuring smile over Brendan's shoulder. To be polite, everyone should have engaged in small talk unrelated to the dispatch. Perhaps it was the strange atmosphere of the tropical swamp, but everyone instead rudely remained with eyes fixed on Brendan as he read.

Rip swatted Mateus on the shoulder. "And what does it say?"

"Just that he's invited to a meeting with Phillips in Sapele," Mateus retorted. "Nothing to get excited about. Nobody died."

"A meeting?" queried Brendan, handing the message to Evin,

who was crowding Elle in his haste to read it. She was crushed between the two male bodies, and had not been in a more pleasurable position in many years. "Who else will be there?"

Mateus swaggered about the room. "I heard there will be all the merchants of the Oil Rivers, Harry Powis of Miller Brothers, Coxon and Gordon of the African Association, Swainson of Pinnock's, Cyril Punch, Chief Dogho, Ralph Locke . . ."

"Yes," Brendan told Evin. "They've petitioned the government for aid to enable them to keep their factories open."

Mateus chuckled gleefully. "You fellows are the only ones whose factories aren't suffering, so why would you care? The only reason Phillips wants you is to see if you can't get the Oba to open trade."

"Well, I'm not going 'til *Isiokuo* has finished," said Brendan.

"What is *Isiokuo*?" Elle asked.

Brendan spoke to her as though she were the only person in the room, in loving tones. "The festival to honor the god of iron and war."

"Brendan parades around in his leopard outfit," Evin clarified.

Elle smiled with amusement. "Oh, the loincloth?"

A slow smile spread over Brendan's face. "I've got something for you . . . your anthropology research." And he vanished into another darkened hallway.

Rip had ears like an owl. "Festival? Will there be human sacrifices?"

"*Certamente!*" Mateus chortled.

They moved back into the front room as Evin explained. "If you hang out by the *Iroko* tree in front of the palace, you'll soon see the events you're looking for. However, I hope you make it clear in your report that the motive of human sacrifice isn't blood lust. It's a deep-seated belief in appeasing the gods. The dead will bring messages to the gods, and most of them are quite eager to be dispatched. There's authority for that in the Old Testament."

"Well, appeasing or not," Rip said, "it's downright wrong.

We know that the gods don't give a hoot how many poor slobs you decapitate."

Evin said, "I have to agree with you, Rip. I'm not raving over the finer aspects of it myself. And the more the British press them, the more people they sacrifice."

Mateus freely poured some booze into a tumbler. "See?" He pointed proudly at Elle. "I wasn't lying about the sacrifices."

Brendan's sudden voice at the other side of the room made everyone jump. "In judging the African, don't forget that Englishmen hanged men for sheep-stealing and exhibited their heads on Temple Bar. Before that they were drawn and quartered." He stepped forward to hand Elle a folded garment—her striped skirt from the experience in the jail. She laughed, and started to shake it out, but Brendan closed his hand around hers and stilled it, and she felt there was a cylindrical object wrapped in the skirt.

"Later," Brendan told her.

"We'll see you tomorrow, then."

"Parading," Brendan agreed.

They took their leave. Elle wasn't eager to hear Rip's interpretation of the night's events, but he regaled her nonetheless. "Well, well. And just exactly why did our leopard hunter friend have to stuff his cock back inside his skirt? And I have to say, you've never looked lovelier than you did with all your hair and clothes messed up like that."

Elle snorted hotly. "He wasn't stuffing it back *in*, Rip. He was just . . . arranging it a little."

"*Hoo-wee*! And I am sure you gave him your famous celibacy brush-off."

"Oh, keep your pants on. Nothing's going to happen. He's just a small-time merchant in the middle of a godforsaken jungle, and after tomorrow I'll never see him again."

Rip corrected her. "He's a moneybags merchant, Elle, the richest in the Oil Rivers."

Elle hadn't known that. Not that it made a difference. "Then why does he live in such shacks?" she sniffed.

At the guest house, Elle waited until she was safely in her own bed room before unfolding the skirt. She gasped with delight when out rolled an ivory vessel about a foot tall. A sophisticated carving topped with what appeared to be an *Oyinbo* mother cradling a child and *Oyinbo* men holding hands encircled the lid; the base depicted coats of arms, scenes of hunters, and men with swords and fancy costumes. It was such a delicate piece of work Elle felt unshed tears burning behind her eyes. It was a far better piece than the armlet Victoria hadn't appreciated, she thought triumphantly.

She placed it on her dressing table and positioned her standing mirror so she could see it front and back.

"Brendan," she whispered.

10

Several times Brendan rode his bicycle past Elle's guest house in the hopes of seeing her coming or leaving. He wanted to find out what she thought of the saltcellar; he hoped she wasn't as apathetic as Victoria had been. He saw Rip, who claimed Elle was at market, but nobody in their right mind would be at market when the Oba was set to parade in his finery through the city.

Brendan took his place in the column with Evin, who was a warrior on account of he could shoot almost as well as Brendan. Evin had taken seventy-two buffalo with seventy-two cartridges from a Wyoming buffalo stand once. One would kill the leader cow, and while the rest of the herd milled in obtuse bafflement, one would pick them off. Hardly an admirable trade and not sporting at all, which was why Evin abhorred it, and agreed to become a mariner. The indiscriminate slaughter angered and nauseated Brendan, and he vowed thenceforth to kill only for human comestibles.

There was no standing army in Edo, but young men were expected to learn the art of warfare. Each war-chief had his own army of relatives, slaves, and followers. The palace associations also had soldiers, and men came from outlying villages when needed to fight, for honor and status.

Evin had become an Edo warrior simply because he knew he had to if he lived there, although he spent more time in the fields with his crops and plants, trying to graft strange hybrids. Well, Evin was a strange man. He kept trying to get Africans to believe that they must let fields lie fallow for a season or plant something different, but Africans did not grasp the idea of wasting land like that. Brendan had offered Evin Iden on occasion, but eventually gave up when Evin kept insisting Brendan was bound for hell by having an African mistress.

They marched in their decorative *eruhan* made of fibers spun to the texture of fine silk, both men armed with pikes and cutlasses, armor rendered obsolete by their possession of rifles and holstered sidearms. And of course Evin had to point out that Brendan's leopard skin shield was almost as bad as a leopard skin loincloth.

The Oba was grand in his mantle of coral beads, coral collar, and coral bead crown, the entire rig of which probably weighed a hundred pounds. He thanked Ighiwiyisi for his most recent gift of a leopard, but Brendan had to march a dozen rows behind him, in back of Ologboshere, and he wanted to stick the warrior general in the buttocks with his pikestaff. Brendan was chagrined to not see Elle among the spectators, though there was old Rip again vigorously punching the air and waving his ten-gallon hat like he was at a roundup.

Elle wasn't at the *Iroko* tree either, where a prisoner Brendan knew as Thompson Oyibodudu momentarily distracted his attention.

"Isn't that the fellow who dresses in whiteman's clothes?" Evin asked him.

"Sure enough." Brendan nodded grimly. Oyibodudu traded directly with *Oyinbo* and had adopted their customs.

"He will not go quietly," Onaiwu said.

Oyibodudu's eyes bugged out as though about to explode before the executioner even wrapped the garrote around his neck.

Though hobbled, and with hands cinched behind his back, Oyibodudu lurched to his feet and shouted in booming, foreboding tones, "The whitemen that are greater than you and I are coming soon to fight and conquer you!" Henchmen leaped to subdue him, to wrestle him back to the properly submissive execution stance. "Kill me quickly!" was the last thing Oyibodudu yelled before he was muffled. The jovial crowd shrieked in both horror and humor, many of them reflexively turning to laugh at Brendan and Evin.

It was of the utmost effort to remain placid through all of it.

"He doesn't mean you," Onaiwu assured them needlessly.

However, Evin was a bit perturbed. "What did he say? Why's everyone staring at us, laughing?"

Brendan explained, but that didn't soothe Evin's nerves any. His squinchy wolf's face was all atwitter with excitement. "I'm swallowing the anchor, buddy." His fingers were wrapped stonily around the grip of his cutlass. "Can I take a few carriers back to Sapele? If you're not coming, I'll just take enough men to carry the recent batch of rubber. Can I take the war canoe from Ughoton?"

"Bear up!" cried Brendan. He didn't even look at the weaver finally collapsing in the death dance, he had seen it so many times. Men scrambled forward to raise him on the *Iroko* tree. "Let's go see the *amufi*, that's always your favorite part of *Isiokuo*."

"Oh, those treetop acrobats?" Evin was unwinding a bit, now that passersby leaving the execution were grinning effusively, slapping Evin on the shoulder, and generally letting him know they didn't consider him one of the *Oyinbo* coming to knock seven bells out of them. Evin was just a nervous fellow.

"Right, the acrobats who swing from the ropes. But first, the sun is over the foreyard; me and Onaiwu are going to repair to the men's *tombo* hut and . . . "

The rest of Brendan's sentence disappeared completely from his brain. On the other side of several curtains of milling people racing to and fro, shoving and greeting each other gleefully, Brendan saw Elle as though through powerful binoculars. She stood quite alone, not in synchronicity with anything around her, but refulgent with her inner smile, amused and detached. Her hair was still stacked in the *Ivbiedo* manner, but she had attired herself in a flattering *Oyinbo* rig, the shirtwaist with the leg-o'-mutton sleeves, the striped skirt Brendan had returned, her little heeled shoes.

"All right, you can go get sewn up," Evin was saying with disgust. "I'm going back home. I'll meet you at the mahogany grove. What's wrong? What're you looking at?"

Brendan shoved men aside blindly without bothering to see who they were. He even stepped on a few people's feet in his haste to reach Elle before she was sucked into a hypothetical vortex. She didn't see him; she merely glanced around with moist assessing eyes, her hands in front of her lap. She might have been searching for Rip, who was as always nowhere near her.

"Brendan. By the mahoganies, right?"

"Ighiwiyisi!" A fellow Brendan vaguely recalled was a hunter greeted him, attempting to joke about the oaths Oyibodudu had uttered on the gallows, but Brendan shoved that guy aside too.

If Elle was gone . . .

"Elle," Brendan breathed with vast relief. With his body smack up against hers, and the crowd pushing them ever closer together, he took her in his arms.

"Bren—"

They kissed for several long minutes. This was a bad thing in Edo, where nobody kissed much even behind four walls. But Brendan was swept away by lust. He wound his fingertips up into the silky myriad of braids at the base of her skull, he squeezed her so tightly around the waist he felt he might hear her bones crunching, but he didn't let up. The woman, for her part, slithered her fingers through his hair, sucking on his mouth with omnivorous fervor. Her other hand clutched at the small of his back, massaging his bare skin under the vest, pressing him to her.

A floating butterfly alighted on their faces, tickled them with its miniscule feet, and flew off again.

Elle was the one who pulled away, gasping for breath. "Brendan, I'm leaving."

"Come," Brendan grunted, grasping her by the hand. Scooping up the shield he had dropped, he pulled her down a narrower avenue, away from the flowing creek of humans. He clanked like a mobile armory when he marched, while the woman gracefully skipped to keep up with his pace.

"I'm glad I found you. I wanted to tell you I'm leaving Edo today."

"I know." Ah, there was the house of a fellow warrior. Brendan yanked Elle through the gate in the mud wall and pressed her into a confusion of cassia and hibiscus that tumbled over the wall. She sank back into the greenery languidly, as though Brendan was just laying her abed to rest. The damp blooms of the hibiscus matched precisely with the coral beads in her richly adorned hair.

His shield, cutlass, and pikestaff thudded to the earth at their feet. "I know your work here is done," he panted, unbuckling his holster. "You've seen enough killing and sexual deviance."

Elle laughed with merriment. She was probably completely amused by the idea that he looked set to fuck her. "No, my work isn't done." With her thumb she traced patterns on his face, down the side of his nose, along his upper lip. "I haven't seen nearly enough sexual deviance."

"Will you wait in Sapele for me?" Bending at the knees, Brendan leaned into the woman, crushing her back into the vines and blooms, lewdly rubbing his aching penis against her satiny lap. He knew then he wouldn't last long, and he set to unknotting the men's tie she wore around her neck.

She spoke against his mouth, as though she didn't dare kiss him. He felt a tremor in her voice now. "Yes, I intend to do more

. . . studying . . . in Sapele . . ."

His face slid down her neck, and he heard a moan that must have been his against the pit of her throat. "Elle, I'm sorry I'm . . . " He took a slurping bite from the delicate skin there.

"Don't apologize for being so forward, Brendan. I don't mind. There's something about you that's bewitching and desirable. I think it's a dream I once had . . . "

"No, I'm apologizing . . . " Were her fingers assisting him in undoing her tie? All at once her glorious chest was bared to him. His mouth slithered down her slick skin as his thighs clamped down on one of her hips. It was Elle who at last rent the front of her chemise, and a couple of buttons went flying, allowing a ripe breast to bounce free. She squirmed and whimpered as he shamelessly humped her fully clothed like some unforgivable satyr. He felt the crest of her hipbone against the head of his penis as he rubbed its entire length against her, licking tiny squiggling patterns down the uplifted slope of her breast, white in the verdant copse of plant life. " . . . for being too quick to . . . " He sucked her aroused nipple between his incisors.

She cried out. Whether in pain or pleasure Brendan didn't know, for all sense in his head had shut down. He climaxed with a massive ferocity against the woman's hip, straddling her like a donkey, unashamed. Grunting and snorting against her buoyant breast, he strangled the poor woman between his strong thighs. He didn't give a damn, he felt on the verge of tears, as though he'd just run twenty miles through the jungle, a kind of religious gratification washing over him.

It took several moments before he realized she too was panting, so shallow and rapid he feared she might faint. She cradled his head to her breast, but she whined with muttered words, and it occurred to Brendan she might want release too. Not one to shy away from more submissive pleasures when it concerned women, Brendan straightened up, lightly fondling her heavy bared breast in his palm, and he spoke gently while licking her earlobe. "I'm sorry I'm so quick with you—I've been imagining you in my bed since I first saw you, and it's difficult to keep a lid on it." He dropped his hand to her lap, and began gathering her skirt in his fist, lifting it above her calves, knees.

"I've imagined you in my bed dozens of times. All night, all day . . . I think it's incredibly erotic that you're so . . . quick with me."

There, a hot expanse of bare thigh in his burning palm. With his thumb he rubbed the trickle of wetness that slid down her inner thigh.

"Oh, Christ, Brendan!" she cried all at once. Grasping his head between her palms, she kissed him brazenly on the mouth, turning to him so that her bare breast was smashed against his chest, and a few more drips of honey rolled over his slithering fingers. He must've gone crazy then with the silken ichor between his fingertips, for he groped his hand to the slit in her drawers. Dipping his fingers down over the velveteen mound of her pubic bone, he swiftly played a glissando with his middle finger over the hard swelling of her clitoris.

The woman bucked, swaying her hips in circles like some wobbly sort of toy. He licked a tear from her cheekbone as he set to caressing her elongated clitoris, his penis at half-mast coming back up for air against her belly.

"I hate to break up such a heated coupling, but the boss has sent me for you."

What?

"I've heard it's bad for your health to stop in mid-rut, but I don't have any choice. He said to come *rápido*, the carriers are threatening to mutiny."

Brendan was the first to come to the surface. He removed his dripping fingers from Elle's honeypot and straightened his back. Her eyes rolled up in her skull, her head banged back against the mud wall. She looked utterly edible and delightful in such a state.

Without looking over his shoulder, Brendan snarled, "One of

these days you and I are going to have some serious words, Mateus." His voice changed sensibility when he whispered to the woman, "Elle. You have to go." He covered her bare breast with the ripped chemise.

"What?" Elle opened her eyes. "What are you talking ab— *Oh!*" Leaping, she clutched the fabric at her bosom and stared at Mateus over Brendan's shoulder. *"What the hell?"*

"It's all right, *amebo*." It felt good to call her that. He helped her tie the length of satin about her throat again. "You have to go now. Your party is waiting."

"Mateus! Not a word about anything to Mr. Bowie!"

"Not a word to Mr. Bowie," Mateus said unctuously.

"Oh, Lord," Elle sighed, going all to pieces again in Brendan's hands. "I'm sorry . . ."

Brendan frowned. "Sorry for what?" Now that she was properly attired, Brendan couldn't help but kiss her again, in front of Mateus and whatever carrier minions he had standing behind him gasping with glee. "Listen, Elle," he said against her mouth. "You wait for me in Sapele. Don't you dare go. I have to meet with Phillips—"

"I know."

"—and I need you to be there when I'm finished. Stay."

"I'll stay. I'll chase you down the monsoon winds if you don't come back."

Then Mateus had the crust to grab the woman by the hand, and she was stumbling off next to him. Brendan didn't need to punch that low-down rat in the back of his square head. He already knew what Mateus looked like with his coconut all knocked chockablock. He looked stupid, like some damnfool effigy about to be strung over a tree.

Elle looked back, her men's tie knotted incorrectly, fluttering over her shoulder.

Brendan knew he had never laid eyes on a more glorious female.

11

The war canoe was delayed by half a day arriving in Sapele from Ughoton due to the death of a pullaboy from what seemed to be dysentery, but was of course really due to "witchcraft," according to the Itsekiri who accused a Krooman of causing the death. Brendan tried to get them to wait until they reached Sapele to build a coffin, but the Itsekiri got into some rum and soon were demanding the Krooman endure the poison ordeal with *esere* beans.

Brendan had been in the midst of such accusations dozens of times before, and he was all for overdosing the poor accused with esere bean so that he vomited, thereby showing his innocence. But Evin, still edgy from the gallows pronouncements of the weaver, shot the accuser in the foot to shut him up. Brendan was determined to row only with Kroomen from here on in.

They didn't reach Sapele until after two o'clock, and Brendan had to rush about checking on his house, raising his warehouse-men to ensure the goods were stored, and arrange for transport of remaining goods.

He had walked by Elle's house several times and seen no activity. How he longed to bang on the door! But that would look strange at the door of a supposedly married woman.

Brendan went to the post office on the *Hindustan* to send a cablegram to New York. On his way out of the office, he bumped into John Swainson, an agent with Pinnock's who had a factory next to his in Warri.

"Did you get hung up somewhere?" Swainson queried, much to Brendan's consternation. "You missed a decisive meeting."

"Missed?" Brendan recalled the dispatch, written in Phillips' handwriting, and he knew it definitely said three o'clock. "What time was it convened, then?"

Swainson frowned in delighted superiority. He had those waxed moustaches Brendan couldn't abide. "Why, noon of course."

"I see. And what was so decisive about it?"

"Well, it appears Phillips is quite in the saddle, as you Americans say. Already, he has informed all the Oil Rivers Chiefs not to comply with your Oba's demand for additional tribute for partially opening the hinterlands markets. We raised quite a cry against the king's restrictions on rubber, gum copal, gum Arabic, incense gums, and the newest ban on woods."

"Yes, I've heard of this move on his part. It sounds like Phillips has fallen out of the saddle, John."

"Well, my boy, Phillips said pacific measures were useless. And now the Oba's demanded twenty thousand corrugated iron sheets before he even allows a trickle of palm oil into the delta. Phillips has instructed all Itsekiri not to deliver the iron, or any tributes at all."

Brendan knew of that too. The Oba wanted the sheets for palace roofs. Brendan had brought a few hundred sheets, and the Oba delighted in the dandy manner they resisted deterioration, and the way the rain sounded sluicing off the roof. "So what's the plan of the Niger Coast Protectorate, then?"

"Phillips said he had a clear picture of the situation now. As for his plans for your Benin City, you had best run see him yourself. Odd thing, telling you three o'clock."

After the subdued majesty of the jungle, the baking metals and shiny facades of buildings hurt Brendan's eyes. He felt like a Cro-Magnon walking up the front steps of the Vice-Consulate, even in his *Oyinbo* attire, with only his Schofield at his hip. He found Gainey in his office chatting up Phillips, a gangly serious fellow with a hairline so severely in retrograde Evin would be proud to stand next to him. He seemed so young his face was still peppered with ruptured follicles.

"Brendan!" cried Gainey, standing. Phillips didn't stand. "We were just discussing your king. The Itsekiri middlemen are extremely irate about the extra tributes he's demanding, cash and ivory and so forth."

Brendan shook Gainey's hand—why not?—and accepted a gin and quinine drink from a servant. "Well, the Oba was awful irritated with that whole mess about Moor overthrowing Chief Nana."

"He's made enemies," intoned Phillips with disgust. "Please sit. I've sent for you, as you're the man, they tell me, who can convince the Oba it's only to his benefit to open up trade routes with us."

Brendan sat. "You sent for me at three o'clock. The meeting was at noon."

Phillips smiled at his own devilry. Meanwhile, Gainey was backing across the room, as though he would make an unobtrusive break for the door. "I've heard you've a hard head, Mr. Donivan. The Bini people are your friends, and you've no wish to hear your fellow traders speak badly of them."

"I wish to hear the truth about what your plans are."

Phillips inhaled and exhaled. "Donivan, the whole of the English merchants represented on the river have asked us to help enable them to keep their factories open. The revenues of this Protectorate are suffering due to the stubbornness and backward ways of the Oba."

"I can understand your frustration at seeing your palm oil trade dwindling. Everyone can understand when income is suffering. However, to force a king to trade when he clearly doesn't *wish* to . . . How would it be if I went to the Midlands and started shooting miners for not selling me coal? It's the Oba's prerogative to sell to whom he wishes."

Phillips' eyes narrowed. "And he *wishes* to sell to *you*."

Brendan nodded. "Indeed." He crossed an ankle over his knee and shrugged. "The Oba likes me."

"Yes, you shoot his leopards." Phillips said this as though stating that Brendan was a fratricidal sodomite. "And you sell only to American firms."

"No, I just made a contract with John Holt and Company. I've no patriotic fervor when it comes to business. Which brings to mind . . . It seems to me that this is an issue of commerce, not government. You're using this palm oil matter for empire-building purposes."

Phillips coughed out something that approximated a laugh. "Oh, hardly, my dear boy!" It was funny, him calling Brendan that, when Phillips was obviously the more youthful. "Who do you think we could get to settle in the hinterlands? Who would be suicidal enough to try to prosper in such a deadly environment?"

Brendan looked levelly at the jackass. "Yet you're considering deposing the Oba."

Phillips swung his empty gin glass between his fingertips, leaned forward, and said confidentially, "My dear boy. There is every reason to believe the Bini people would be glad to get rid of their king. He's a liability, a throwback to an earlier, primitive, tribal way of dealing. You've seen for yourself the hundreds of human sacrifices. Now surely, even Americans don't stand behind that sort of behavior."

"The sacrifice is a very holy belief in appeasing their gods. When they see us impinging upon foreign countries in the name of our God, quite possibly they think the same thing of us." Brendan paused meaningfully. "And the only sacrifices are criminals and unauthorized traders found in his domains."

Phillips sighed, and stood for the first time. "I see. You are quite content with your monopoly in Benin City; I didn't think you would happily help open up trade routes."

Brendan stood too. "When do you intend on sending men to get rid of the Oba?"

"I've no such intentions."

"You said pacific measures were useless."

Phillips was mixing himself another drink that involved mainly gin. "Well, of course, first I want to meet with this king. I don't expect him to come to me, so I shall have to go to him. You could assist me with that, couldn't you?"

Brendan nodded. "Certainly, yes. I have to warn you, though, he doesn't take kindly to foreigners cutting into his domain."

Phillips sniffed. "Any attack on us would be suicidal. But Moor's assured me of their cowardly nature, so my mind is at ease."

Brendan did not bother setting Phillips straight. "I mean it might take awhile for you to get an audience. Hell, I didn't even get an audience last week when I brought him a live leopard."

Phillips stopped just shy of swallowing his gin glass whole. "Live?"

"Yes. They're royal symbols of his sovereignty, and he likes to parade with them." Phillips continued to gape, so Brendan added, "On chains, of course."

Phillips sniffed. "Indeed." He gulped his gin.

Brendan said by way of departing, "One thing, Phillips. If I help you get a meeting with the Oba, would you be so kind as to tell me beforehand your plans to attack the city? I have friends there, and I don't want them injured."

Phillips' mouth was a thin line. "Oh, you can be assured in the extreme unlikelihood of something of that nature, no whites would come to harm."

Brendan nodded briskly. "That's good, because it's an extreme unlikelihood there are any whites in Benin City to begin with."

He took his leave then, striking for the *Hindustan's* saloon. On the quarterdeck he found Beazley, Swainson, Gordon, Powis and several other cohorts. He drank for many long hours with them in the malarial exhalations of the river.

~ ⚓ ~

" 'Help, I am drowning,' " said Rip.

They had steamed in the launch *Daisy* to Ughoton along with everyone else. They were following the nebulous trail far behind the party now, as Rip had insisted on looking for chewing tobacco in the town. Why there would be tobacco at Ughoton and not in Sapele Elle had no idea, but he claimed he'd found some, and they were at last on their way to Belzoni's grave.

" 'Get up, you lazy scamps,' " Rip read from a guidebook. "Does this give you any indication of the sort of land we're in?"

"That book is called 'Phrases in Common Use in Dahomey,'" Elle mentioned. Above in the canopy of hardwoods, hordes of gray parrots squawked, complemented by a band of frogs singing in the undergrowth below. "Dahomey is farther west."

Rip wasn't listening to her. How could he walk while reading? " 'Why has this man not been buried?' Oh, here's the answer to that. 'It is fetish that has killed him, and he must lie here exposed with nothing on him 'til only the bones remain.' "

Mateus brayed like an ass with merriment. "That could be useful over here." He liked to hack needlessly at the jungle with his cutlass; it gave him something to do.

"Now, Elle," Rip said in a renewed tone of exasperation, "why exactly are we still here? Why can't we go back to New York so you can publish your report?"

Elle did not look over her shoulder at Rip. "Report's not

done. Mateus, what was that thing in the river that looked like a hippopotamus but wasn't? It had a tail, not two hind legs."

"That is a sea cow, a relative of the elephant."

"Elephant? How—"

"*Elle* . . . What do you need to finish the report? I've sent loads of film boxes back to New York, and I'd like to live to develop them."

"I want to find out what is going to happen," Elle replied lightly. "It seems to me there is a Mexican standoff between the Oba and the British. Brendan can give me some idea of that when he returns from Edo. If there's trouble, it'll make things sound more dangerous. You know, 'Civilization Encroaches on Jungle,' that sort of thing."

" 'British Imperialists Save Africa from Cannibals,' " Mateus added.

Rip muttered something, and Elle did not want to ask him to repeat himself. She knew it was something bound to irritate her.

The women of the party, Mary Wells, Sadie Elliott, and Caroline Forshaw, were spreading out the picnic blankets near the drooping boughs of Belzoni's tree of poison apples. Victoria should have been assisting them, but she had not left the side of the newcomer, the intensely exotic Brazza. He had arrived yesterday from Libreville, stopping over on his way to Algiers. Commissioner of the French Congo, Brazza was an Italian, and his beloved adopted France had thrown him overboard, recalled him due to greedy machinations over red rubber. Brazza and Gainey were now warm chums, as they currently hated the two-faced French, so when Phillips left Sapele, Gainey arranged for this expedition to the grave of Giovanni Battista Belzoni, which naturally Brazza would be interested in, both men being Italian explorers. Belzoni had been a traveling circus giant who had discovered the Pyramids in Egypt, and had died near Ughoton in 1823 when setting off to discover the source of the Niger.

Elle hadn't been able to speak to Brazza yet, as Victoria had monopolized the *Comte*, as she was fond of calling him, with her knowledge of the flowery French language. Elle's head was stuffed enough with the Edo language as it was, and too crammed with thoughts of a palm oil ruffian to appreciate Brazza's towering, olive-skinned elegance with more than the detached admiration of the museum visitor.

However, when Elle emerged into the little clearing, Brazza's face lit up, and he waved at her party. "It is the Bowies!"

"There's that crazed Frog," muttered Rip.

"He is not crazed," Elle whispered loudly. "He's merely in hot water for being a 'negrophile' and making a mess of that French expedition."

"For which all of Liverpool is eternally grateful," Mateus sneered with glee.

As Brazza was now waving his arm in an arc to herd them in, Elle marched on over. Victoria pouted under her parasol.

"I would like more news from America about the automobile," Brazza declared. "You know, the Belgians are having a 'rubber rush' in Leopold's Congo Free State, and now the French think my French Congo has rubber. It is the craze for bicycle tires, but next I think it will be the craze for automobile tires."

Rip poked his trigger finger at Brazza. "You're probably right there. I was just reading earlier this year, some fellow built a horseless carriage that ran on gasoline."

Elle nodded. "I read that too. Henry Ford. His quadricycle went twenty miles in an hour, and it ran on bicycle tires. Why did you not desire to stay in the Congo, and exploit all the rubber?"

Brazza rubbed his own face wearily, rolling his eyes. "It is the politics between France and my mortal enemy, King Leopold of the Belgians."

"Really? Will you explain more to me? But please, come over here." Elle motioned toward the blankets the women sat upon, where they arranged dishes, glasses, and comestibles. "I've been so very thirsty, and we forgot to bring a water skin."

"Of course." Brazza did not ask Victoria if he could bring her a drink, he merely followed Elle to where Mateus was already squatting at the edge of a checked blanket, eviscerating an orange with a simian voracity. Mary and Caroline must have liked Mateus, as the three were chattering happily, and paid no attention to Elle and Brazza when they took a seat next to a champagne bottle.

Brazza opened the bottle with an elegant flourish and poured it while explaining, "King Leopold decided he owned all vacant land in Congo Free State."

"Vacant? How is that defined?" Elle frowned.

"He meant every square centimeter not being sat upon by an African. So all the ivory and rubber they used to freely trade and be paid for, they now have to run and harvest to give as levy to Leopold's agents. Failing to deliver the levy results in whipping, imprisonment, or death."

"That's impossible! How can such a monster get away with that?"

"Every Sunday they must bring a certain quantity of rubber as tribute to the commissaire's headquarters. They grab it with force. The soldiers run the people into the bush. If they will not go they are shot down, their left hands cut off as *trophees* for the commissaire. Most of time, they shoot poor helpless women and innocent children. The hands are put in rows before the commissaire, who counts them to make sure soldiers have not wasted *balles*."

"*What*? For God's sake, why has no one stopped him?"

"Because it is making him richer than anyone dreamed. He has persuaded France to replace me, to introduce their system of *pillage* to my Congo colony. I run on principle of trade; they wish to run on robbery! I am too nice to Africans. I have one motto: Hard on self, never to others!"

"Oh, I can see that you're too gentle and kind of a man," Elle said dreamily, so absorbed by Brazza's wicked tale she had stopped monitoring Rip and Victoria, who had taken their seats on another blanket. "Such an idealist you are! To think you can run a country without corruption or torture. Silly you!"

She didn't know if Brazza understood the sarcasm, but he laughed beautifully anyway. "I am explorer, not *administrateur*." He shrugged. He took off his solar topee and shook out his gloriously glossy hair.

Elle then felt a quickening of attraction toward Brazza that accelerated her heart, that hysterical weakness taking control of her blood and womb. Was the only solution the bearing of a squalling nipper that would render her unable to work, and die in the poverty of the Lower East Side? "Now, this is very interesting, *Comte*." She laughed to use Victoria's snobbish appellation like that. "I am just comparing this atrocity to the situation I've been studying—Benin City, have you heard of it?"

"Yes, yes, I am wishing to visit there, but Captain Gainey has told me it is impossible."

"Well, *Comte* . . . I have seen these human executions with my very eyes, and where I at first was prepared to be thoroughly horrified, mortified to my very core, I have now come to believe that it is the very opposite of barbaric. Do we not publicly hang men in our own countries? Most of the victims in Benin are criminals, or enemies of the state. They believe that the dead spirits are taking messages to their gods, appeasing the gods, and we are here to put an end to this? Is it that much worse than chopping hands off innocent children, or even the hands of men who may not be that innocent? That is torture; it is worse than slavery! Has Captain Gainey heard of your friend Leopold's colony?"

Brazza smiled with understanding. "Ah. Yes. And he has said—"

"I have said this is the exact example of the difference between the styles of the British, French, and Belgians!" Gainey suddenly appeared, towering over the couple before he creakily hunkered down into Indian position next to them. "The French and Belgians come in to exploit, not govern. They set up no public works, no education, no incentives for natives to better themselves. When they pull out, as they inevitably do, the raped countries have been stripped of their vegetation and citizens. They come only to extract what they can, then they move on."

Elle closed her eyes with patience. "And your style is to govern—"

"With benevolence!" Gainey pointed to the heavens with jingoistic fervor.

Laughing, Brazza laced his fingers between his knees. "Benevolence is not the Belgian way."

"Yes; it's bloody horrific, the things you tell me in the Congo. Oh, and I'm sorry to intrude on your palaver, my dear Elle, but—" and here Gainey adopted a sneaky playful tone of voice— "Victoria's palaver looked more intimate than yours."

Elle tilted to one side to look over Brazza's shoulder. Victoria was laughing appealingly, giving Rip the same coy glances at his crotch area she had bestowed upon Brendan during that dinner— that dinner that seemed a hundred months ago now! And Rip, dimples permanently engraved in his cheeks, leaned back casually on his hands with that open-collared abandon Elle had always admired. Victoria held a hibiscus flower in her hand, and she gestured at Rip with it as she spoke—in fact, she did all the speaking.

Brazza looked, and gave Elle a sympathetic shocked look. "Is your husband very close with Miss Victoria?" In his kindness, he refilled her champagne glass.

Elle turned to Gainey with a gracious smile. "You tell me, Vince. Is your fiancée very close with my husband?"

Gainey shook his head rapidly. "Oh, my, no, she is not my fiancée! My dear Elle, do not labor under that delusion. She is merely a friend of the family who wanted a little adventure." He chuckled. "Just tell me if she is getting too adventurous with your husband."

"No . . .My husband can do what he wishes. We have a very . . . *relaxed* sort of marriage." Elle turned to Brazza. "That is the American way."

"Ah." Brazza smiled knowingly, but knowing of what, Elle had no idea.

"Very good. Then I hope you shall join us in a round of croquet?"

"Croquet?"

Gainey pointed to where some servants had been chopping away grass with cutlasses.

"*Croquet*," smiled Brazza.

With the guenons that resembled Mateus leaping in the jungle cover above them, Elle learned to play croquet. Brazza and Gainey were both eager teachers, but Gainey preferred to grasp his mallet in both hands and swing it from between his legs, a position not tenable for a woman in a skirt, so she preferred Brazza's method similar to golfing. Elle went all shivery and clammy when Brazza posted his gangling form behind her, encircling her with his arms to demonstrate the correct stance. Still she was clear-headed enough to know that the hysteria was much more diluted than when she was anywhere in the general location of Brendan. In fact, she thought so often of the Guinea trader that, while Brazza was taking his expert (and therefore long) turn at the mallet, Elle became emboldened enough to quietly ask Gainey, "Did Mr. Donivan make it to the meeting with Phillips?"

Gainey didn't take his eyes off Brazza. "Yes, he did," was all he said.

That was how Elle came to be standing in a compromising position, with the exotic Count Pierre de Brazza snuggling her to his long warm physique, instructing her how to knock one of his balls off the lawn, when Brendan made his appearance in the clearing. It was a most unfortunate position to be in; she could not very well shake Brazza off her back, and he was now muttering some unsporting things into her ear.

Evin was with Brendan, and his brown Newfound-land dog that romped like a gigantic puppy in the grass, tossing some kola nuts in the air. Brendan was a vision that stopped Elle's blood in her veins, his seraphic face with the intelligent dazzling eyes that could bewitch one from a mile away.

"Ma chere Elle, vous m'avez tout enchante."

"I'm sorry I don't speak French." Elle wiggled to show her displeasure with Brazza's closeness, but that probably encouraged him more. Gainey and the Assistant District Commissioner Lyon were now greeting Brendan and Evin by the pathway, shaking hands formally, leading them to the picnic basket that probably had the most booze.

"Vous etes delicieux," Brazza insisted in her ear.

"Excuse me?" Elle turned to face Brazza. "Why don't we eat? It took us five hours to steam up here; it shall be midnight when we get back."

She sat with the Count, eating mangoes that he scored with a very sharp knife, inverting the skin to easily bite off the little squares of tangy fruit, but the tough threads stuck between her teeth, and she had to laugh. She was trying to hear what the men said in their palaver one blanket away, where they all smoked pipes or cigars, as though camouflaging themselves as a cooking fire. She heard phrases such as "fetish veto," "steps taken," and "Itsekiri . . . most loyal tribe." Oh, why were women always excluded from the most interesting conversations?

At last Mary Wells clapped her hands and proclaimed, "Now, everyone must partake of these treats Captain Donivan has brought from America. Doctor Elliott, Sadie, gather around." She held aloft a tin that she now opened. "Brendan? These are called what again?"

Brendan stood. "These biscuits are called Newtons, they've got a fig filling."

Mary took one, and passed the tin to Gainey. "And to

accompany it, we have this most interesting soda drink." She held aloft a bottle, and Brendan lifted a chain that jangled about his belt and snapped the top off the bottle with an opener.

"Coca-cola," he said, "made from kola nuts." He took a few sips, and Elle was gratified that he handed the bottle to her with a smile.

"Kola nuts?" she asked him. "From here?"

"From here and up the Guinea Coast."

Lyon exclaimed, "We've known about this drink for years here in the Rivers. We've often held a kola nut in our mouth and drank tonic over it to get the essence. A very bracing drink!"

There was a general commotion of handing around the biscuits and sodas, and Elle heard Victoria sneer, "Are you sure they aren't poisoned?" Elle turned, and saw Victoria and Rip share a laugh.

Brad Forshaw said, "I've seen this before, Brendan. Doesn't it come from your Atlanta?"

"Right." Brendan was snapping tops off bottles for everyone. "Remember Jacob's Pharmacy in Atlanta, Evin?"

Caroline Forshaw sighed with a mouth full of Coca-cola. She swallowed. "The trading life is so endlessly fascinating."

Elle surprised even herself by piping up. "Oh, I've always thought that! The 'old coaster' traders are so very tough, yet kind. They don't try to alter native culture to a white one, they just want to understand it."

"Here, here," intoned Brad Forshaw, hoisting his Coca-cola.

Gainey did the same. "I'll agree with you, they are rather tough old birds. Have to be, to last more than six months here."

However, Victoria didn't seem interested in the traders' encomium. Rather loudly, her high-pitched voice queried, "And how is it you have come to know this many 'old coaster' traders, Mrs. Bowie?"

Elle's eyes narrowed. "I've met many: Fell, Brownridge,

Gordon, Beazley, Powis, and of course Brad, Brendan, and Evin here. They seem to know the African well in order to keep the peace, and they seem quite fond of them, as all whitemen who get to know Africans must do." Her recited list met with nods and silent approval from everyone, except Victoria, who continued to berate.

"Yes, but they also, by nature of their profession, must also be not a little duplicitous, not a little full of cunning and deception."

"Hey, now!" protested Brad Forshaw.

But it was Brendan who stepped forward and interrogated Victoria. "You sound as though you have someone in mind," he said levelly, with a menace that sent an excited thrill up Elle's back.

Mateus's chortling was the only sound in the clearing.

Victoria looked daggers at Brendan, but oddly it was Rip who smoothed over the moment by saying, "She means that because you have to deal with the masters of deception, the Africans, you have to alter your methods to meet theirs. Tricks like pouring boiling lead into the bottom of elephant tusks, taking out the staves in puncheons, things like that." He leaned back casually with one hand planted on the blanket, comfortably close to Victoria's behind. Elle had thought Victoria could take Rip's mind off leaving, so she should have been happy for this abrupt coupling, but it made her uneasy.

Slowly Brendan withdrew a cigarette from a case in an inner waistcoat pocket, but he did not take his assessing eyes off the frivolous Victoria. "I am sure that's what Miss Armbruster meant."

Elle stood. She said soothingly to Brendan, "I think it's admirable how the traders look after Africans when they're sick or in trouble. It seems as though you traders call upon God and ask why you're condemned to such a godforsaken hellhole, but God sends you home and you hanker to get back to the Coast."

"Here, here," Brad exclaimed, dimly.

Brendan smiled so beatifically it seemed as though tears glazed his eyes. He said nothing for such a long time, just gazed at her as though they were alone, his dilated irises regarding her with abandoned warmth, that the people around them became fidgety, and turned to remarking upon the warm kola drink and suchlike. Elle felt perfectly comfortable beholding the savagely civilized man; she felt no need to say a word either.

At length Brendan said quietly, "You *do* know."

"I'd like to think so."

But Brazza was on his feet now, shaking hands with Brendan. "I know who you are. You are the man who can get me behind the walls of Benin City. This most beautiful woman has told me you helped her get in."

Elle had to burst out laughing. "Yes, he did do that."

Brendan was laughing too. "I nearly had her kept inside there on a more permanent basis."

Brazza of course was puzzled, but he was probably accustomed to that with the English, for he suavely put a hand on Elle's waist. Immediately Elle saw Brendan's eyes shrink to pinpoints of black. "Ah, then *Monsieur* Donivan, it would be an easy thing to get a disgraced Frenchman into the city."

"Easy? Mayhap. Full of glory and crowns, I daresay you'd think you went to perdition, Count." And then Brendan did something that so shocked Elle, she well nigh thought she had fallen in love with the man for a moment. "*Ce peuple est inspiré par la fièvre et le cancer. Les infirmes et les vieillards sont tellements respectables qu'ils demandent à être boullis. Le plus malin serait de quitter ce continent. Oui, la folie rôde pour pourvoir d'otages ces misérables.*"

A look of complete enlightenment came over Brazza's face then. He spread his arms wide and babbled some more in French, causing Brendan to say, "I'm sorry, that's the only French I know."

"What did you tell him?" Elle asked.

"I think I told him the smartest thing would be to leave this continent where madness lurks and gives hostages to these miserable people."

Brazza asked excitedly, "How you know only a piece like that?"

"Your Frog poet." Elle beamed.

Brazza cried, "You must have good faculty with French to learn such words! Come, as favor for bringing me Benin City, I teach you French."

Brendan shook his head, smiling. "It's not the smartest thing to do, Count. I can't put you in danger."

"But you can put the beautiful Madame Bowie at danger?"

Brendan looked shyly at Elle. "No, I don't want the beautiful Elle ever to return to Edo. In fact, I have to go there now. I have some messages for the Oba from Phillips."

Elle was shocked at how chagrined she was to hear Brendan wouldn't be going back to Sapele. How could she be that thoroughly disappointed about a man to whom she had only a carnal attraction? For she had decided that's what it was. It was his animal look, his sulfurous aura of danger, and her virulent female weakness.

She was equally elated when Brendan said to her, "Will you walk with us down the path a ways?"

"Yes." And Brazza might as well not even have existed anymore.

Brendan gave one low piercing whistle for Pequod, and gave merely a look at Evin, who was over chatting up Rip and Victoria. They would have passed by the party without incident, except that a grey parrot got it into its head that Victoria's pink parasol made a good backhouse, for just as Victoria was letting loose a peal of charming laughter in Rip's direction, the bird splashed her parasol. Her shriek was piercing, like metal against metal.

"Oh! A filthy bird!"

Rip jumped back like any cowboy would, reaching for his

Colt, but Brendan was calmer, and quicker with his handkerchief. When Victoria saw Brendan make a swipe at her parasol, she too jumped back, against Rip's drawn Colt as it were, and spat, "Perhaps I am *too fat*, and shouldn't allow you to touch my parasol!"

Almost everyone nearby was stunned wordless. Brendan had an endearingly quizzical look on his face, drawing back with his handkerchief like a flag of surrender fluttering in the air.

Rip put his gun back in the holster. "Now, honey, I don't think he meant anything, he's just trying to help."

"Let's go," suggested Evin, but Brendan had already turned away, taking Elle by the forearm.

Elle didn't care who watched her walk into the jungle with the Irishmen. Let them think she was loose! She would never see them again after a month or so.

Evin walked ahead with the dog. They were under cover of the tree canopy for not thirty seconds before Brendan tugged her to the side of the footpath that was only a line of crushed ferns and grass, and under the spiky fronds of a screw pine. Still clad in his *Oyinbo* attire, he had divested himself of his silk tie, rolled up his shirtsleeves, and his chestnut hair was coming undone from the coral ornaments that held it back at his neck. His chest shone with sweat, and had not shaved in several days, but Elle felt grasped by such vaporous desire for him she fairly melted into the bristly tree trunk behind her back.

He did not touch her. "I couldn't find you in Sapele."

"Oh, we went downriver to Warrigi, Rip, Charles and Mary Wells, and I. We spent the night playing whist at Beazley's factory."

"If you're not Mrs. Bowie, then what is your real surname?"

"It *is* Bowie. It's Rip whose real last name is McCullough."

A slow smile expanded over Brendan's face. "McCullough? Another Mick?"

Elle furrowed her brow, then burst out into laughter. "Mick!

I like that. Yes, I suppose Irishmen made it to Texas at one point. They didn't always stop in Alabama."

It was only then that Brendan stepped up to her. He seemed hesitant, and shy in a way to which he was unaccustomed. "Ah, *Miss* Bowie . . . " He touched her forehead with the tips of his fingers, his thumbs smoothing away stray tendrils of dripping hair that had escaped her coiffure. Now no longer in the Edo style, she had unraveled all that styling, and pinned it back into fluffier curls. "Every man at that picnic wanted you."

Elle half-closed her eyes and sighed. "Yes, my whole life it's been that way." It was true, but it was always the men she didn't want. When she realized that sounded full of swagger, she amended it. "But no, I am glad, if by 'everyone' you mean you."

Brendan chuckled at her seeming immodesty. "Yes, that is what I meant."

"Then I am flattered."

She admired the way he always looked directly into her eyes when he spoke. So few men did that. "I don't want to see you anywhere near Edo now, do you hear?" he said softly.

"Why?"

"Because if there's trouble, I don't want you hurt. Now, I have to go back to Edo and—"

"Tell me about the trouble! You can trust me."

Brendan's thumb traced the outline of her upper lip. "I'll warn you ahead of time. And then I want you to leave . . . And go back to America."

A sickening trickle of cold metallic blood slithered through Elle's gut. He wanted her to leave! She tried to take a halting breath. "Why should I go back to America? If there's trouble I want to know about it, I want to write about it—"

His hands dropped from her face, and he took a step backward. "If there's trouble it's going to spread out like fire in dry grass, and everyone in the way is going to get stomped, that's why. Now listen here—"

Elle took a step forward. "No, *you* listen *here*, Mick. I don't know who you think I am, but I'm not a woman to shrink from danger. I've been around the world, I've been to Mexico, I've been in the booby hatch—"

"Can you shoot?"

"Shoot? Why, of course I can, I've my Derringer I carry all the time, and—"

Brendan scoffed, waving a hand at the jungle floor. "Derringer? A little pea-shooter like that won't scare away a dwarf." He pronounced it "skeer."

"Then what about your Victoria? Why don't you warn her off?"

"*My* Victoria? You seen for yourself how close we is. I done told you, she takes liberties with her familiarities."

"Then why was she acting like you'd called her fat?"

Brendan threw up his hands. "I ain't never called her fat in my life! Womenfolk gets things into their brains, and us men ain't fixed to figure out why that is."

They were having an argument. How had this happened? Elle took several deep breaths, and smeared the hair back from her forehead with her palm. She looked at the ground. "I think I might know where she got that idea." When she looked back at Brendan, he was standing with his hands helplessly at his sides. It was such an appealing stance, Elle was carried away with the warmth of affection that was brought on by carnal attraction. She was about to move to him, when there was a harsh bark in the foliage behind them.

"*Capitão!*"

Brendan's face collapsed with chagrin. "Oh, he's a caution! Sometimes I think that fellow was put on this earth to haunt me."

"He's like those cracker people who live in the hill country," Evin called from his covert post down the hill. "You can never get rid of them."

There was a crashing of vines, and the sliding of Mateus's sandaled feet in the mud. "Boss, I need to go to Edo. I have some palavers to attend to."

Elle wrapped her hands around Brendan's neck and pulled him to her against the spiky trunk of the pine. "Are you coming back?" she said against his mouth.

His mouth was suddenly hot and slick against hers. "I'm coming back for you."

It was she who kissed him then. She had found the daring somewhere in the memories of a love she had once felt. She remembered being bold with Joe, stopping him in random alleys when she could not prevent her hands from searching out his skin beneath all the layers of clothing. She sucked on the delightfully cynical bow of Brendan's upper lip, and she felt obscene when she grasped his hand and moved it down over her breastbone.

"Ahh . . . " Brendan sighed into her mouth. He rubbed his face against her neck. "I crave you something fierce, you lovely jungle flower."

And Elle felt better then, even when Mateus sloshed right down to their side and gasped, "The Count is asking for Mrs. Bowie! He says she promised to go bicycle riding with him."

Brendan breathed against Elle's neck, then detached himself and cried, "You're a sight to scare the witches, you hulk rat! Well, get on down there with Ev."

"If we don't get to Ugbini by sundown, we'll have to bunk out, as we don't have any country lamps to see."

"Right, right, get on with you!"

Brendan kissed Elle on the mouth, over and over. When he pulled away to leave, going down the hill with one hand raised to her, there was a painful rock in her throat, as though she'd swallowed a coconut. The sun was setting, cutting wide swaths of lemon-yellow light through the foliage where thousands of bugs tittered. He turned back to her, radiant chiaroscuro movements of orpiment and cadmium sun slithering over his form.

"I'm going to touch you, woman. And when I'm done, you're never going to want another."

Elle shivered, and delighted in the vision of him, holding up his arm, then reluctantly turning and bounding down the slippery hill. The wet crashing of Evin, Pequod, and Mateus, she embraced it all with her heart, knowing she could coast along for months or years on the sheer happiness of this moment. Just the knowledge that a man would care enough to come back for her was enough.

No man had ever done that; they had always just left.

Edo

" 'I will arise and go now, and go to Innisfree.' "

Evin nodded, serious. "Good. That's good."

Brendan read from the 'slim volume' in his hand. " 'And a small cabin build there, of clay and wattles made. Nine bean-rows will I have there, a hive for the honeybee, and live alone in the bee-loud glade.' "

"Excellent, Bren! You're doing well."

Brendan looked at Evin, poker-faced. "Ev. I just memorized some of this. I'm not actually reading it. Besides, what in hell is a 'bee-loud glade'?"

Evin stared across the courtyard, at the pond where curtains of climbing grasses and lycopodium sheltered the outer mud wall. "A glade where the bees are buzzing loudly."

Brendan looked down at the book. "It was probably one of those things that looked better written down." He dropped the book when Evin jumped like a bullet to his feet.

Pointing one stiff arm at the pond, Evin shrieked, *"Avast! A fucking snake!"*

Brendan stood and struck for the pond. "Where? In the pond?"

"On the fucking wall!"

"I just see lianas and creepers and climbing grass. Can you come closer and point it out?"

But Evin didn't budge from his scarecrow's position by the bench. He just kept saying, "On the fucking wall. Can't you see it? It's bigger than my leg!"

"What kind of snake? How big? Oh, I see it. It's a rhinoceros viper! Those make for good eating."

"They make for good killing too. Don't go near it! Those adders strike like lightning."

"Can you get my shotgun from the armory room?"

Evin wouldn't go near the snake, so Brendan had to back up and grab the shotgun from him. Luckily the snake was still in the same position on the wall. Brendan smashed its head with the gun butt, folded the snake up, and brought it back over to Evin.

"Why didn't you shoot it? How do you know it's dead?"

"Because its head is flatter than one of your botanical specimens, Ev." It was a beaut, with its velvety red-brown and yellow patterns. Brendan laid it on the bench. "I'm more wondering who had the audacity to put it in our garden."

Evin was cringing back into the trunk of a raffia palm. "Who's to say it didn't just slither over from the jungle?"

"Have you ever seen one in the city? These critters don't tolerate civilization."

"Maybe it's got someone's bush-soul inside of it."

Brendan looked at Evin and blinked. "For a fellow who thinks we're all ripe for the devil with heretical ways, you sure sound like you believe in it right sudden."

Evin hugged himself as if shivering. "Of course I don't. But what do they say happens if you kill someone's bush soul?"

"They fall sick or die. I'd better call in the *Ewaise* to make offerings to whoever I offended."

Evin exhaled mightily. "I reckon whoever drops dead next, we'll know who did it. I'm telling you though, there are a lot of those chiefs I don't trust. Ologboshere, to start."

"Ever since that devilment last year between the *Iyase* and the *Iwebo* association, there's a passel of young upstarts fighting amongst themselves." The Oba's own *Iwebo* men had assassinated the most senior palace chief, and before the Oba could root out the perpetrators, four had been killed or committed suicide. The *Iyase* had influenced the remaining murderer to surrender and seek reconciliation. "I suspect that *Iyase* of currying favor with the British for such a time as they take over, so he can be lion of the day."

"What did the Oba say when you said Captain Phillips wanted to pay him a visit?"

"Oh, for land's sake!" Blood from the dangling viper's head had dripped on the fallen "slim volume."

"Why didn't you shoot that thing? Seems it wouldn't have been half as messy, or potentially deadly."

Brendan scooped up the book and rubbed it against his thigh so the *eruhan* would clean it. "I'll allow I could've, if I wanted to bring a crowd of some as yet unknown persons racing over here to see what the commotion was."

"At least you'd know that whoever *didn't* come racing over was the evil bastard who put the snake in our garden. So what did the Oba say?"

"I'll just let them think the viper's still sliming around our house. Oh, I didn't get past the *Iyase*, he's a type of Secretary of State for the Oba what commands the military; he bosses around even Ologboshere." Brendan shrugged. "He seemed to take me serious, but you know how deceptive these chiefs can be. I told him that old Jim-bob didn't seem the patient type to cool his heels. He gave me the usual palaver, that *Ivbiedo* don't want to trade with the English."

Evin nodded. He had warmed up enough to stand just outside of striking distance of the dead viper's fangs. "Right, those notorious Liverpudlians. What's she doing here?"

She? Brendan saw where Evin's frowning gaze was directed,

at the end of a pathway of terra cotta tiles. Iden stood, a regal and immobile figure. She wore the parasol Brendan had given her rolled up laying flat atop her head, the handle sticking out over her forehead. This was the popular fashion, as was her style of wearing the pink silk tassled shawl neatly folded in a square balanced on her shoulder, rendering it practically useless. Her sober face belied the unintentionally satanic cast given by the two long pins of carved river ivory she had woven between her plaits, poking up over either ear.

"She's not allowed to come over here, is she?"

"No, she's not," Brendan breathed. It was not acceptable for a female slave to call at her owner's house; Brendan always went to her house. Or he could bring her to his house, supervise her, then take her home. He put the poetry book down atop the snake's head without looking, and strode down the path.

"Iden, *vbo ye he?*"

"*Oyo ese,*" she replied with lowered eyes.

"Why are you here?"

It took her many long seconds to answer. "I know I should not come."

"It's all right, now you are here. What is wrong?" To soothe her, he took her by the arm and led her to a bench, indicating it was all right for her to sit.

She sat formally, hands atop her knees, eyes cast at the ground. "I thought you might go away and I wouldn't see you again."

"I'm not going anywhere. What makes you think that?"

"The talk of the British coming. And then what Oyibodudu said at his . . . ceremony."

"Why, Iden . . . is there a *reason* I should maybe go away? What have you heard?"

She shook her head. "No, nothing. I was only . . . " She looked at him now, and he saw her dolorous eyes were swimming with tears. Taking a jump toward him on the bench, Iden laced her fingers around the back of his neck. "I was afraid you might get married!"

"Married?" Brendan tried to laugh it off.

"Are you marrying someone else?"

She was practically clambering into his lap, and Brendan tried to peel the clinging creepers of her hands off his person. "No, Iden, no, there's been no talk of marrying anyone. Who did you think I might be marrying?"

Now she was rubbing her lips all over his face, muttering, "You can't marry . . . I won't let you marry anyone else . . ."

Grasping her by both shoulders, Brendan held her at arm's length. "*Who did you think I was marrying, Iden?*" He was being harsh with her, but she was nigh about acting like a banshee.

She blubbered, "The . . . the *Oyinbo* woman . . . with the upright bosom."

"Land's sake!" Brendan cried in English. He tried to speak calmly. "Iden, I barely know that woman. Now where did you get these ideas? What made you think that?" A thought then appeared like a blaring sun in his mind. "If you tell me, I'll give you that green necklace." Iden had been admiring a malachite necklace Brendan had meant to give one of the Oba's wives.

Iden looked down again. "Someone said you were caressing her."

Brendan was speechless, partly at Iden's nerve to be upset over that, and partly at the nerve of the third party to be blathering such particulars. He clamped his jaw into its proper position, set Iden back onto the bench, and stood. "All right, that's enough. *Who said that, Iden?* Who is telling you these stories?"

"Mateus. He said you were—"

Brendan's arm shot out; he yanked Iden to her feet, jostling her mercilessly. "Don't you listen to that lying cane rat! He's a crazy, evil person, Iden, you should know that by now. Now, I need you to leave. No, wait. Let's go inside and get the green necklace."

On their way to his bed room, Iden pointed toward the back kitchen. "You must hide that brandy. Mateus is in town, and he might drink it."

"No, he drinks gin." It was a good idea, though, because in a pinch Mateus would drink paint. Brendan would bring it back to Sapele, as they had been smack and smooth out of brandy for weeks there.

When he finally got rid of Iden, Brendan scouted out Evin, who was reading in the courtyard. Evin had pulled a stool up a goodly distance from the dead viper, where he could keep an eye on it if it should suddenly get it into its mind to take a bite out of him.

Evin looked up mildly. "Slaves! Can't keep them in line these days."

"I'm telling you, Ev, things are all hugger-mugger on a sudden. I feel the need to be striking back for Sapele. Can you finish the deal with the *ekhen*?"

"I feel the need to strike back there, too. Just you and me?"

"I certainly ain't taking that traitorous gnome. Guess I'll need to skin that snake first."

"Let's just give it to Onaiwu."

So they folded the snake as many times as they could and jammed it into a burlap bag. They covered it with a length of dyed cloth, and made out they were taking Onaiwu a sack of sugar.

~ ⟶ ~

It was the middle of the afternoon, and she was doing such a thing. How awful was she? Surely there would be some punishment.

She had skipped up the muddy red avenue, away from Gainey's house where Brazza had worked her into such a lather she just wanted to scream. With his experienced, Parisian-Roman manner, he was constantly leaning the entire length of his lanky body into her, backing her against bookshelves, tables, mosquito curtains, his hands always fluttering just above her skin, and she knew with those long tapered fingers he could bring her to orgasm within a few short seconds, were she to give him the chance. She was fairly slithering from his grip, and nobody impinged upon their solitude overmuch, especially now that Rip and Victoria were always together on a couch or divan somewhere.

She could not cave to Brazza's delicious insistence. It made it easier to remember that the loutish ruffian Brendan would eventually come back to town, when everyone seemed to mention him in every conversation. Assistant DC Lyon called him a "muck snipe in a rookery," Chief Dogho said he was a "most brilliant traitor in the Oil Rivers," and Victoria variously termed him a "bounder" and, most memorably, an "arrogant walking, talking John Thomas." It excited Elle, the rancor one man was able to stir up among that many people.

She had excused herself, citing some vaguely appropriate female necessity back at her house. She locked the front door and strode to her bed room. There was no lock for that door, so it was expedient for Elle to merely fling her wracked body back against the door, her fingers tugging at the velvet tie about her throat. She had nearly succeeded when she abandoned it in order to fumble with her skirt buttons.

"Too many clothes . . ." she muttered. The striped skirt slid to the floor; her lavender underskirt seemed to stand on its own with its confectionary frills below the knee, and Elle merely let it drift down around her behind while she finished with the velvet tie at her neck. The pearly buttons slid around her fingers, and at last she was able to rend her shirtwaist asunder, allowing her engorged breasts to lift free from the tight chemise. She took a big lick out of her left palm and applied it to her right nipple, rubbing the entirety of her breast at first, then raking the tips of her nails across the nipple. Her more adept right hand entered the opening of her drawers, and she assiduously rubbed the enlarged plum of her clitoris, already enflamed with inner female juices.

She panted, in through the nose, out through the mouth. " . . . too many . . . injures health . . . I don't care!" She didn't care! She just floated, awash with hot surges of thirst, feeling the craving build in her hips, manipulating her bursting plum. "I don't . . . care . . . " Images of Brendan's devilish mouth, the impish tip of his nose, the helix of his ear popped into her mind. She knew that if just once, if Brendan got to his knees before her, nuzzled his head between her thighs, spread her like a torn orange, and lapped at the very core of her, she would combust in an inferno once and for all.

Before she could realize that this orgasm was stronger than all the others that had gone before it—for she wouldn't have believed it possible for it to get more intense—she was falling into a vortex, as though someone had opened a trap door beneath her feet. *He was right . . . too many injures the health*. The air in her lungs was sucked out into the atmosphere, and all she could see in the sudden dark were big red balls of light barreling straight for her head, but passing without pain.

And then, many minutes or hours later, pain. Her head pounded like someone was compressing it beneath an iron anvil. When it occurred to her she might open her eyes, she found she was staring at her bed room ceiling. She knew she had to stand, but was entangled in various garments. Her chemise strangled her like the canvas jackets with buckles they used in the nut house; her under-skirt was a crocodile trying to suck her into a creek. She finally stood by climbing up the side of the dressing table, and she leaned over it panting, choking on her own breath.

"He was right," she wheezed. It helped to hear her own voice. She hung over the porcelain neptune, her trembling arms prop-ping her up. "What the hell happened?"

But she had no time to ruminate, as large crashes of thunder were now rolling through the floorboards of her house, rattling the empty scent bottles on the glass shelf of her dressing table. Gasping loudly, Elle twirled to face her bed room door. It couldn't be thunder—it was in her house. Dipping down, she grabbed her voluminous skirts about her waist and was fumbling with rebuttoning everything when the river boots stopped at her bed room door.

"Elle?"

Elle, still swimming in the murky void of the brain attack she'd just suffered, was now gripped with a stab of fear. The fear cut through any sense of nicety, and she automatically answered him. "Yes!"

Brendan must have kicked the door in, for suddenly he was standing there, river boots shedding red mud planted apart on the floor, hands at his sides. He loomed larger than ever to Elle in her miserable state, in his Edo attire of *eruhan* and vest, clanking with armory as though he'd just come from his canoe. Remembering a modicum of manners, Elle attempted to peel off a curl of hair that was stuck to her forehead.

"I'm sorry, I wasn't feeling well, and I—"

"Land's sake!" Brendan leaped forward, dropping at least some of his ordnance clattering to the floor. He leaned over her so ardently she was backed against the dressing table, and she breathed his river essence, the water lettuce, ferns, and palm oil. With her eyes not four inches from his face, she could see the scattered freckles on his cheekbone that had moved her. so much. "What happened?" His thumb rubbed something oily into her forehead.

Her hot breath made steam against his face. "Happened? Nothing, I was at Vince's and—"

"Hush," he whispered, closing his own eyes as though in demonstration. "I was just disembarking, and I had the most urgent call in my head to see you—I was struck clean to the heart that you needed me. Now I come in, and you're bleeding." Reaching clear over her, Brendan grabbed a towel and dipped it into the neptune.

"I'm bleeding?" Elle pulled away to regard herself in the mirror on the wall. Sure enough, there was a goodly gash on her fore-head, and blood trickled down the side of her face and neck, all the way down to the strap of her chemise.

Turning her to face him, Brendan wiped the blood from her breastbone. He was overly gentle, as though cleaning a baby chick. "What's going on?"

Elle reasoned then the jig was up. Brendan hardly seemed the sort of man to be mortified by her confession. "Actually, I . . . fainted. I ran home because I, too, had a sudden need . . ." If she spoke faster, it might seem more casual, more an everyday occurrence. "A need to pleasure myself, so I did, but it's been getting stronger and stronger lately, sometimes so strong I believe I might fall into a sort of fit, if you will, and I thought about what you said about how too much pleasuring can lead to health injuries, and . . ."

She had lost Brendan's attention about when she said "a need to pleasure myself." He had cleaned the blood up to her jawbone, but now he seemed content to cradle her face in his hand with the damp bloody towel, his eyes stupefied as though he'd been hit with a handful of stars. He shook his head vaguely. "No, that's what the *Ivbiedo* men want the women to believe. That's all I was saying." Now the beginnings of an amused smile appeared at the corners of his mouth. "I don't think there's harm in it at all. If frigging your-self caused bodily injury, my judgment day has surely come."

"Oh!" cried Elle, aroused by his sultry admission. "Then what could it be?"

"What happened?"

"Well, I . . . fainted. At the moment, you know the moment . . ."

"When you came."

". . . when hysterical paroxysm overcame me . . . I must have fallen to the floor. I was standing against that door"—Elle pointed—" and suddenly I was on the ground there, with this pain in my head."

Brendan gently sponged her forehead, and blew on her with his cool breath to dry her. "You must've banged your head on the edge of the marble dressing table."

Elle shut her eyes tightly. "Oh! This is terrible! Why should I have to become afraid of something that is so good for the health? Doctors in New York, you pay them a visit, and it's all very discreet, they manipulate you and it eases the congestion in the pelvis, and . . . Now why should something that is so good for the digestion and the blood . . . "

She felt Brendan's mouth lightly brush the undamaged side of her forehead. His talented lips moved over her cheekbone, grazing her earlobe. "It isn't bad for you, my *amebo* . . . you are just what we call oversexed. It only seems to get worse and worse because you have no release, you don't do it enough."

"I do it plenty enough!" Elle pouted. But he had tossed down the towel and was weaving his fingertips into the damp hair at the base of her skull, sending a torrent of shivers down her back. "*Ah!*" she cried sharply as he exhaled hotly in her ear and arched his gloriously full-blown crotch into her lap. She had earlier succeeded in only buttoning up her underskirt, and she could now spread her legs apart as he lifted her halfway onto the dressing table, his fingers squiggling around her backside. The heat instantly built to a near crescendo in her hips when he rubbed the full length of his stupendous erection against her pubic bone.

His voice was a hot purr. "New York doctors . . . pleasure you?"

"Well, yes," Elle panted, unabashed. "If one says one is hysterical they will generally agree with one to get one's payment, and . . . "

"Manipulate your quim 'til you come?"

"Yes; to release the pent-up juice. It is particularly satisfying when one has . . . this particular doctor who is recommended . . . a young Jewish doctor who is very . . . well-hung, and would diagnose hysteria in only the beautiful young women, and . . . " She was going out of her mind with a raging womb hysteria that was threatening to suck the very thoughts from her head. " . . . and would put a lot of professional keenness into the treatment."

"Aye, a difficult job, vigorously frigging beautiful young

ladies." He uttered a deeply leonine growl against her neck. "No, you don't get it enough. Not nearly enough for your own special beauty, my darling." He pronounced it "darlin'." Bending at the knees, he took big slurping bites from the soft flesh of her throat. "A gorgeous jungle flower like you needs tending . . . often."

Elle had never felt anything as delicious as cradling his head to her breastbone. "But Brendan, if it hurts me . . . makes me faint—*oh!*" He had lapped up her nipple into his mouth, and the stinging electrical pleasure of it shot through her clear to her clitoris. "Oh God, Brendan, you mustn't—you're going to kill me." Yet she cradled his head to her bosom, cringing with joy at every nip of his teeth.

He expertly stripped her chemise from her shoulders while he nibbled on her breasts, his tongue like a giant warm slug of the devil. "No, no," he panted, "you need pleasure...*more* pleasure." His penis was slathered up like a tree limb between the petals of her labia. Her female juices soaked clear through her drawers; she could smell the distasteful fishy odor of herself, warmed up by the friction he created.

Before she knew it had happened, he had unbuttoned her petticoat and tossed it to their feet. The scorching of his long clothed penis against the flimsy covering of her lavender nainsook drawers scared her into bleating, "I'm going to faint if you keep on riling me, you awful . . . nasty ruffian!" Yet she still massaged his skull with her fingertips, and she knew she was smiling.

It worked; Brendan detached his mouth from her nipple with a sloppy sucking sound and straightened up his spine, devilishly rubbing his silken chest against her on his way back up, sliding over her painfully bursting breasts. He had that leonine grin when he faced her. "My *amebo,* Elle," he breathed on her mouth. "There ain't nothing better for your health, since you're so concerned about it, than a good fucking to straighten you out."

He kissed her then to shut her up, his mouth delectable and warm, but inside she was fuming. The epitome of oafish gall!

Pretending it was her *health* he was interested in, when his hands were all over her body! He was smoothing his hands over the small of her back, hooking one thumb into the waist of her drawers, tickling the sensitive skin below her navel to distract her from his untying of the silk ribbon. His tricky fingers slid the drawers over her behind, and he snaked his fingertips over the rise of her bottom, opening up the saturated lips of her labia with expertise, then flicking against the strained erection of her clitoris.

She cried out loudly against his mouth and bucked away, her spine arching in a sudden twist, her feet lifting off the floor as she balanced herself on the edge of the table by sitting on her hands. When she cried out again, Brendan pinned her to the table with his hips and played his insistent *glissando* with even more flourish and vim. "Oh, do stop! I'm going to burst into flames!"

He laughed with a deep groan against her chin. "Ah, my *amebo* . . . Good! We'll both go to perdition together." And he lowered his terrible punitive mouth to her upraised nipple.

Three or four little bites were enough to set off a wrenching orgasm that compressed every last bit of air from her lungs. With her thighs gripping his hips like a vise, her shoulders crashed to the table, sending bottles twirling and flying. Spasms rolled down to clutch insanely at every last sensation from the fingertips of both his hands as he leaned into her, panting brazenly, "Good . . . ah, Lord, that's good . . . keep coming . . . come all over my hands, Elle." He slid one long middle finger up inside her as she snorted and bucked like a roped animal.

That was it. There was no more reason. Ten regiments of the Niger Coast Protectorate Force could have marched in armed to the teeth, and they could not have prevented Elle from getting more. With her legs wrapped around his waist, Elle laced her fingers at the back of his neck and lifted herself to kiss him, a long whimpering sucking that had all her senses shutting down one by one, as she jumped with electrical jerks against his slowing fingers.

It was she who slid her hand down the exquisite plane of his belly, her thumb delighting in the silken line of hair that dipped down into the dry heat of his pelvic bone. Under the brass hip ornament, she felt the raised welts of four claw marks that must have been the leopard's. She discovered then that *Ivbiedo* wore a sort of breechcloth under the *eruhan*, and as her fumbling hand could not reason out the fancy knots, Brendan helped her. He unbuckled a belt that sent more weaponry crashing to the floor. She had the scorching width of his massive penis in her hand, and before she could take her pleasure in sliding along the length of it, with one sly arch he had shoved it inside her to the hilt.

Unaccustomed to such rapacious assault, Elle cried out in awe. She could feel her eyes rolling up into her head right before it banged against the mirror on the wall, then suddenly she was swiftly accommodating. She reveled in the feel of his slippery back muscles under her palms, and she slid them down over the rise of that astounding backside she had always admired. She found that with her long arms she could tickle the underside of his balls, all contracted and hard up against his body, as he humped her.

She smeared her face against his; she wanted to be covered in his taste and smell. "Give yourself to me," she panted. "Brendan, oh, dear heart, give it all to me. I'm wide open . . . wide open as the sky." She sucked on his penis with her inner muscles, wanting him as close to her as was humanly possible.

She felt him cave then, in that gloriously vulnerable minute pause of men on the verge of orgasm. He caught his breath, and all was silent. Then he flung his head back, the ends of his hair tickling her hands at the small of his back. He uttered one long strangled cry as he convulsed inside of her, letting his head fall forward, their bodies bowing together.

She was surprised he still had strength to lift her, to walk backward until he came up against a rocking chair, stepping ably over all the detritus of their frenzy, where they sank down together.

Elle curved her spine until she could place the tops of her feet on his knees, and they kissed sweetly, for many long moments. He cradled her cranium as though she were a dearly cherished lover. Elle heard the singing of a clockbird nearby.

"Clockbirds are like drummers who have to keep vigil while others are asleep," Brendan whispered against Elle's neck. Tenderly, lock by lock, he plucked her hair from her dripping skin and replaced it atop her tousled coiffure.

She raised her head erect to breathe in deeply of the evening air that floated in the mosquito-curtained window on a choir of frogs and smoke from cooking fires. "I didn't faint," she marveled.

"No." Brendan smiled against her throat. "Rip's the only one who faints."

It took Elle several moments to realize what he referred to, and then she had to laugh. "But I'm telling the truth, I did faint earlier today."

Brendan licked her Adam's apple. When he brushed the back of his hand against her nipple, she reflexively clamped down around his penis, causing him to gasp. "I tell you, my darling . . . you need a man handling you. It's just not the same vigorous outcome when you do it to yourself. I think you should rely on me in the future."

"Doctor Donivan," Elle whispered, rubbing her swinging breasts against his face. "What is *amebo*?"

"*Amebo* is what a man calls his favorite wife."

Though certain it was meant as a compliment, it irritated Elle for its indirect reference to Iden. "I'm never going to forgive you for reminding me how good fucking can be."

"You mean 'forget you.' "

"No, I mean *forgive* you."

Brendan quieted, as though he didn't know what to make of her statement. Then he rocked back in the chair, jamming his rigid penis farther inside her. "I'm glad to find you're not cut."

He smiled devilishly. When he rotated his thumb against her clitoris, Elle jumped with nerves, and had to dismount.

Shy suddenly, and acutely aware she had only a dangling shred of chemise hanging from her elbows, Elle turned her back to Brendan and stepped into her discarded drawers and underskirt. Brendan, his body, his mouth, was such a transport of heaven she had to remind herself sternly it was only a temporary predicament, an "oversexed" satiation of the physical, and it had no emotional merit.

"Thought you was going to snap off my finger, when you got off," Brendan observed, and it rankled her. Was that all she was good for, "man-palaver"?

Stepping through all the fallen scent and powder bottles, Elle lit a lamp on the dressing table and poured only herself a dainty snifter of brandy, adding a teaspoon of guiacum tincture from another jar. She was more than a little raw between the thighs, a situation that did not displease her.

Brendan exhaled loudly. "I had better go—people shouldn't see me at your house."

Elle turned. Naked save for the river boots, leather vest, and leopard hip ornament, Brendan was in an attitude that would have made normal men look absurdly ridiculous. But he looked even more delicious, if such a thing were possible, wrapping his loins in the breechcloth without embarrassment, sliding his hand down the front of his belly and jutting his hips to adjust his penis inside the cloth.

"If you mean Rip, he's only my photographer. I don't care who he sees at my house."

"But seeing as how you're supposed to be wed, mayhap we should meet at my house from now on."

Elle slung an exasperated arm. "Oh, wed, who cares? I am starting to tire of that whole charade. The only reason I even maintain it is to keep Gainey and Brazza off my back." Then it occurred to her, he might think she was trying to make him jealous, and she breezily changed the subject. "I'd like to see your house, to see that illicit painting everyone spoke of."

"Yes, come anytime." Cinching his *eruhan* around his waist, Brendan asked calmly, "What is that you put in your brandy?"

"Gum guiacum. Thank God they've given up on bleeding people. 'That scientific form of sudden death.' " Elle laughed frivolously.

Brendan stepped up to Elle, frowning. "What is that for?"

"Oh, Mrs. Bowie!"

"Ah," Elle breathed, as though she had been expecting this. She made haste to find her shirtwaist on the floor by the bed room door. Standing erect, she frowned at the garment, as it had some drops of blood on the sleeve.

In the meantime, Brendan's clanging of metal as he garbed himself or otherwise draped his armaments about his person was enough to keep the leopards awake. He took Elle's jawbone in his hand and whispered, "I'll jump out the window if you want me to."

Frowning, Elle shook her head viciously. "I won't have it!" she called, loudly. "What have I to be ashamed of?"

Rip's cowboy boots navigated to the bed room door. "Oh, Mrs. Bowie," he sang, sounding three sheets to the wind. "Have you forgotten? Tonight is our anniversary. We have a big night planned. Or have you forgotten?"

Elle and Brendan glared at each other, both probably for different reasons.

"I'll be right out," Elle shouted stiffly.

Rip's muffled voice chortled at the door. "I can't wait, girlie. Now if you put on that negligee rig, the pink gown that's kind of sheer, well then, I expect we'll be in for a high old time. You *did* remember to bring that negligee, didn't you, girlie?"

Elle stared into Brendan's eyes, thoroughly horrified. *"Girlie?"* she mouthed. Brendan looked equally perplexed, and none too overjoyed with the new turn of events. Having finished clothing himself, he unsheathed his Bowie knife, and hefted it as though for practice. Elle took three long strides to the door and swung it violently open.

Leaning against the doorjamb, Rip had one boot crossed before the other, his fingers in the pockets of his denims. He looked as though he should have a long piece of grass in his mouth, the lascivious way he was eyeballing Elle up and down. His happy expression didn't change one iota when he spied Brendan, who had followed Elle, shadowing her in a protective manner that pleased her very much.

"Rip, what are you talking about? I've never had any gown like that, much less one I'd wear on a so-called anniversary, and you—"

But Rip swept Elle into his arms, dipping her so low she later found balls of dust in her hair. "Ah, girlie, it excites me when you talk like that."

Elle clawed her fingers into Rip's bare shoulders. "What is wrong with you, Rip? What the hell is this 'girlie' garbage? Let me up!"

Rip stood her up in time for her to see the crazed cowboy amiably shaking Brendan's hand. Presumably Brendan had put his knife away, having discerned that Rip was merely unhinged, not murderous. "Ah, Mr. Donivan. Always nice to see you. It'd be nice to have dinner with you and all, but seeing as how this is our anniversary, and I know how the missus loves her romantic interludes—"

"That's all right, I understand," Brendan was saying serenely. "You're entirely right about her enjoying her romantic interludes. Mrs. Bowie?" And he had the panache to kiss her hand then! His lips lingered, and he drew her close, all but seducing her with his eyes all over again. When he looked up at her from under those lashes, and the leonine grin started at one edge of his mouth, Elle just about died.

I have just screwed him, she thought. *I have just screwed*

*this gorgeous, edible, and thoroughly fuckable man, and I feel
wonderful.*

"Tomorrow," Brendan told her, and although she could not
remember any talk about tomorrow, she found herself agreeing.

"Yes."

She followed him to the front door more because she enjoyed
watching him walk than out of any courtesy, the exquisite sway
of that backside, the brash clanking of the weapons, the dull thud
of the boots. And most of all, his savage bare chest under the
leather vest, when he turned to smile at her before jumping down
the front steps.

Elle watched him go, hugging herself, even humming tune-
lessly, until Rip popped up and goosed her. She shrieked, and
slapped his shoulder rather harshly.

" *'Girlie?' 'Girlie?'* "

"Ah, now, honey, you know why I put on a show like that! It's
for your own good! You should be thanking me for saving you
from that lowdown brute!"

Elle slapped him back inside the house so she could shut the
door. "Saving me? And whatever gave you the notion I *needed*
'saving'? Honestly! If I didn't know any better I'd say you were
drinking something a little stronger than *tombo*!"

Rip's eyes flashed. " 'Not need saving?' You had that two-
faced pervert in your bed room, Elle! And where'd you get that
big gash on your forehead? Listen, you want me to, I'll go down
there and plug him right now."

Elle was so steamed her teeth were clenched. "That 'pervert'
was in my bed room because he was *helping* me, Rip. I fell down
and gashed my head, and if it wasn't for him I might've laid there
bleeding to death."

Rip's head took on a saurian shape Elle had never noticed
before; she fairly expected a forked tongue to slither out from
between his lips. He hissed, "Helping, is that so? And how was

he helping you by tearing off all your clothes and giving you a bare-assed poke on top of the table? Now how exactly is that helping you stay away from men? Men the source of all evil in the world, men whose center of existence lies in their dicks, men the people you don't *need* anymore? Tell me how that louse helps you, because unless you've suddenly become possessed by the spirit of a dead hooker, I don't even recognize you, and I'm ashamed to say I'm your partner."

Elle was so apoplectic all she could do was storm to the chair where she grabbed her pocket book. She marched back to Rip and hissed, "I want a divorce."

She did not want to go to Mary Wells's house in the state she was in. She could not bear the ecclesiastical tranquility of that house, Mary always finding a proverb to liken everything to and saying that everything was the will of God. Nor could she tolerate Gainey's. Brazza and his letch for her would just be irritating, when she longed so for Brendan. Elle headed directly down to the river and the trading hulk *Hindustan*, where she could chat with the men and have a cocktail in the saloon.

If she would be accused of being like a hooker, then she may as well act like one!

13

Brendan didn't see Elle again for several days. He received a message from a runner about a mishap at his factory in Warri. The wife of one of his warehousemen had given birth to twins, an event the natives regarded with such horror and fear the infants were usually murdered and the mother run out of town. The belief was that the father of one child was an evil spirit, and that the mother had been guilty of great sin. As the infants were never seen by outsiders or allowed to live, no one could tell otherwise. Their backs were broken, they were smashed into a calabash and ejected—not by the doorway but by a hole that was knocked in the back wall. They were thrown into the jungle, where carrion birds and carnivores ate them.

But perhaps because of Brendan's stewardship, the warehouseman had been able to hold off the killing until Brendan arrived to sort it out. He had to leave Evin in Sapele to finish a deal with a supercargo from Boston, and paddle out to Warri with the strongest pullaboys he could muster. It was too late; the grandmother had smothered the twins, and the warehouseman and his wife had struck out for Duke Town where they could find asylum with other lepers and thieves.

"Who'd you leave in charge?" Evin asked. They were walking, or rather, Brendan was dragging Evin down the road from their house to Gainey's. Evin hated calling on people. In particular visits of an official nature disgusted him, which was why he was always left behind when something involving other people needed doing. "Not that albino storekeeper, I hope."

"No, he's too good at keeping the store, I can't spare him. I left Victor Ekeh, the fellow with the spectacles with no glass in them."

"Right, he likes to be called Johnson." Evin approved.

"That's the one. I'll tell you one of many things to be said for Edo: this kind of devilment doesn't happen there. There's no killing of twins. Fact, it's esteemed a good omen. What's that?"

From his knapsack Evin had pulled something that looked like a sweetmeat, a pastry rolled into a cylinder with cream squashing out the edges. "Maybe if we get to the next twins in time, we can send them to Edo. It's a sweetmeat."

Brendan stopped walking, and jerked on Evin's arm that held the confection. Evin's hand hit his mouth, leaving him with a cream beard, like Santa Claus. "Where'd you get that?"

Evin frowned in irritation. "Miriam made it." He wiped his mouth on his shirtsleeve roughly, making him look like he'd just shaved.

"Hm." Brendan continued walking. "Miriam sure seems to favor you. *I* never get any sweetmeats."

"Hm," said Evin. "There are words flying around town about you bedding the anthropologist, speaking of never getting any—"

"Hush up!" They were nearly to Gainey's now, and Brendan again grasped Evin's arm and pulled him behind the safety of a mud dwelling. "Now who's been saying what? 'Cause I know the only person who saw us was that cowboy."

Evin shrugged, disinterested. "Probably the cowboy who started it, then. All I know is, Victoria says to me where's Brendan, I says Warri, and she says oh good, maybe he's going back with the strumpets where he belongs, after trying to force himself on poor Mrs. Bowie."

Brendan, too, became unconcerned then. "Oh, she just said I *tried* to bed Mrs. Bowie."

"Why's she so sour on you, on a sudden?"

Brendan shrugged, and started around the side of the house again. "Mayhap 'cause I bedded Mrs. Bowie."

It was Evin's turn to grab Brendan by the arm. "Wait just one minute, you right bastard! Just what are you referring to?"

"Get your dirty paws off me." Brendan tugged the lower edges of his vest to straighten it, though Evin hadn't rumpled it. "I'm saying I bedded Mrs. Bowie. Only you know she ain't a missus, so I don't want to hear your high-falutin preaching."

"In case you've forgotten, the cowboy is supposed to be her husband."

Brendan jutted his lower jaw. "Right, and her fancy man husband's dallying round with Miss Armbruster, so I'd say we're just about even. And I'd appreciate having that poem if you're ever finished with your courtly calligraphy."

"Ho, ho!" Evin's eyes crinkled when he smiled that hard. "I see you're in a bad way for the anthropologist. I knew when you started talking about regal broad shoulders and foaming auburn hair setting atop a carved chair—"

"*Flowing* hair, you tomfool blockhead. And if I recalls correctly, you was saying she was a peach, and right smart too."

"I was saying she had awesome titties."

In a flash the Bowie knife was in Brendan's fist, the steel cold against Evin's throat. "Take that back." It wasn't often they fought like this, even though both knew they were just funning.

Evin giggled, his voice all high-pitched like a woman. "I ain't! It's the truth!"

After scowling and breathing in Evin's face for many moments, a laugh escaped from Brendan too. He resheathed the knife. "All right. I'll allow that's the truth."

All the same, Evin felt his throat. "I'm just saying. I know you're doing it for one reason only, same as any sane man would, but you might want to avoid getting that Missy Prissy all worked up. She could use her pull with Gainey to raise a heap of trouble."

Brendan scoffed. "As if my name ain't already mud around these parts." He started back into the road. "And for your edification, I'm not doing it 'for one reason only.' I'm doing it for a whole passel of reasons."

"Ah, that explains your poem . . . 'she is a woman, lithe and able . . . ' I've never seen you so riled by a woman."

"And I'd really take pleasure in seeing *you* riled by a woman. You're a caution, Ev! You need to forget about that witchy wife of yours, and leave her in Lee County along with all the mules with five legs, and the rats as big as horses." He shortly noticed Evin wasn't following him, so he turned.

"You oughtn't to have said that, Brendan."

Brendan walked back to his partner. "I take it back, Ev. I know you can't forget about them young ones, even if they wasn't yours. I'm just saying you need to have fun, you need to loosen up. You're a fine-looking fellow and don't need to be withering away in these rivers of corruption. Avast, what about Missy Prissy? She seems capable of relieving a hard-on."

"She set her sights on you. And now on that cowboy."

"Right, which proves she's on the town. You need to have some fun, buddy."

"Ah. You might want to hush up." Evin looked pointedly up at a spot beyond Brendan's head.

When Brendan turned, he saw Victoria on the top veranda of Gainey's, her hand on the banister, merely standing there staring directly at the two men. Brendan smiled and waved cheerily, presumably annoying Victoria, for she frowned even harder, and slammed inside the front door. Brendan didn't care much; he struck for Gainey's steps. "I think it's a good idea, Ev. You need to shake some of the dust from your bones."

"I don't need no uppity bore," Evin grumbled.

Up at Gainey's, Lieutenant Lyon insisted on being present for the meeting, though nobody had asked for him. He also insisted on plying them with the black tea that Brendan hated, perhaps to get them to leave sooner.

"The fact of the business is," Brendan said, hands tented between his knees as he leaned forward in the wicker chair, "I get the distinct feeling Phillips isn't a man of patience. He might give the Oba one chance, and one chance only, to agree to a palaver. I can't guarantee that I can get the Oba to agree to that. Hell, they wouldn't even let me in to see the Oba when I brought the message from Phillips."

Gainey was not his customary hearty self. He seemed introspective, downright chilly of emotion toward the Americans. "Yes, it could be that our perception of the power you hold has been greatly exaggerated."

Brendan and Evin looked sideways at each other.

"Perhaps simply because you are the only white man who can even verify that the king still exists. For all we know, since Gallwey visited Benin City in ninety-two he has passed on to that great devil beyond, and the city is in anarchy. Still, you are our best hope of avoiding a confrontation."

Brendan tried again. "Just possibly, Gainey"—for he always called him by his surname to irk him— "the Oba doesn't particularly want to *hear* my message. As an omnipotent sovereign, he doesn't need to back down. He can make all the white people go away by ordering more human sacrifices."

Gainey frowned. "Is that happening?"

"That is happening."

Now Gainey and Lyon looked sideways at each other. "It's horrifying," muttered Lyon.

Gainey cleared his throat. "Well! Then we shall have to put an end to this despotism once and for all, one way or the other, although I do not go along with the extremities of Captain Phillips. Punitive measures have a proper time and place, but in

Benin City the result would probably be to drive the natives into the bush and make them greater savages than ever."

In a very rare event, Brendan was surprised speechless. While he didn't entirely agree with the part about the savages in the bush, he was surprised that Gainey wasn't going along with the imperialistic zeal of Ralph Moor. When Brendan opened his mouth to speak, Evin beat him to it.

"Then we're in agreement, Captain, about what's best for the city. Fine nations were never built on the aggression of a foreign power. It's trade, to the mutual benefit of both parties, that's the order of the day."

Gainey and Lyon both visibly started in their chairs, to hear Evin speak. Putting his teacup down, Gainey stuttered, "Why . . . yes! I suppose that's it."

Evin continued on then. "Look at what's happening in the Congo Free State. *Disaster!* I don't know what fancy term you would use, but I call that wholesale massacre, pure and simple. Now wouldn't you be doing the same thing if you went in and slaughtered everyone, merely because they refused to trade? You should set an example by following the high moral ground, Captain. England *is* superior to France, after all."

Gainey even chortled a bit, to hear this long-winded soliloquy coming from the American "silent partner." "Why, yes. One can't reasonably hope to abolish in a short time customs that have been in practice for centuries."

Lyon spoke. "Right you are. We send soldiers in there, why, they'll simply keel right over after a week from the climate." But he was silenced by a baleful look from Gainey, who was clearly eager to end the palaver.

When Gainey stood, so did the other men.

"With respect to the climate," Brendan could not help saying, as Gainey hustled them to the hallway. "It has a very bad name, but whitemen don't give themselves half of a chance. How could a man in Devonshire keep his health if he lived in a crude cottage, never took exercise, and never changed his scenery, but sat around smoking, eating, and sleeping, with no other excitement than the monthly arrival of the mail steamer? That's how most of the whitemen live here."

"True, my boy. True and pitiable."

Brendan could see Victoria's sleeve and the side of her skirt in the parlor as she stood beside a bookcase with her back to the men. "And this is presuming he indulges in no excesses. The chances of his remaining sane in body and mind would be vastly diminished if he went to bed corned on bad booze every night, as most do here. An utter lack of change, exercise, and excitement kills him in a year or two."

"Well said!" cried Lyon, who after all was known to swim lustily in the Ethiope, and was always after the soldiers and traders to organize footraces and suchlike. "In the days of the Druids, the swamps of England were called 'the Roman's grave' as well."

Brendan knew Victoria was pretending not to listen. "And if Africa was cleared of mosquitoes, it would lose the title 'the graveyard of Europeans.' "

The majordomo held the door for them.

"Good day," said Gainey. "Keep me apprised on what the king's answer will be to Phillips."

Gainey and Lyon retreated back down the hall to the office. Victoria was now casting Brendan dark, sooty glances. Brendan gave Evin an informative expression and gesture, and went to accost her in the parlor.

"Victoria."

He was mistaken about the meaning of her glances, however, as she snapped shut the book she pretended to read, and shied away from him. "Miss Armbruster to you, sir!"

Brendan appealed to the ceiling above for assistance. "Victoria, what have I done to make you take such a sudden dislike to me?"

"Oh, that is very funny, sir. You think it is perfectly acceptable to slander someone when their back is turned, yet make a pretense to their face otherwise."

"What are you talking about, Victoria? I thought we were rather close acquaintants, and suddenly you act as though I killed your pet canary. Why would I slander you?"

Sidling over, Victoria steamed in a stage whisper, "Oh, I heard about how *fat* I am, yes, sir! And about how ridiculous you find me, how frivolous and inane!"

"I have never called you fat, Victoria, for the simple fact that you are not fat. Now could it be that a certain cowboy named Rip Bowie has been filling your head with these ideas?"

"If I had known how little you thought of me, I should *never* have allowed you to kiss me!"

In order to shout her whispered words more effectively, Victoria had edged over so closely she was fairly spitting onto Brendan's shirtfront. When Brendan lifted his hands to hover over her delicate shoulders, he saw her look soften. It was a disgrace to use his masculine wiles in this manner, but it served him. "Victoria, I am telling you that cowboy is a no-good louse, a worm of the first degree. He thinks—"

"Oh, yes? And what reason would he have to malign you? You're helping them with their anthropology project."

"He thinks I'm . . .Can't you see, he's trying to separate us because he has eyes for you? Surely you can see that. A woman like you must be accustomed to having many men vie for her. Besides, he's a lowdown operator, a married man flirting with you."

She melted enough to look from Brendan's boot to his holster. "I see that marital station did not stand in the way of your forcing yourself on Rip's wife."

Although he hadn't forced himself on Elle, Brendan said, "You got me there."

Victoria looked to the St. Christopher medal nestled in his clavicle. "They have an unusual union that is far . . . looser than most. You might be interested in knowing, the *Comte* de Brazza has determined to charm Mrs. Bowie. And knowing what a shallow money-mongering woman she is, who is going to look more attractive to her?"

Frowning, Brendan took a step back. "I don't appreciate these lies, Victoria. Elle isn't money-grubbing, and she possesses depth that a man could plumb for a lifetime."

She spun around and glared at Brendan. "Miss Armbruster to you!"

Brendan bowed deeply, as befitted Victoria's formal mood. He made as if to leave, then turned to Victoria as though with an afterthought. "Miss Armbruster, I don't want to hear of any more slanderous lies coming from your mouth, is that clear?"

Balling her hands into fists at her sides, Victoria squealed. "*Oh!* I can't believe I ever allowed you to touch me!"

Turning without backing out the requisite few steps, Brendan left Gainey's house. He found Evin a bit further down toward the river, leaning on a mud building and eating a guava. Together they marched toward the *Hindustan*, moored upstream from the deep-water anchorage.

"Dumped again?" Evin asked rhetorically.

"Why don't you wipe that shaving soap off your chin? Ev, I am staking my affidavit that Phillips is in Gainey's bad books, as he felt he should've been made Consul General instead of some time-server fresh off his daddy's commission. Mayhap he's not such a raving empire-builder after all. What he said about driving the natives into the bush . . . "

"I have to agree with you on that one. He sounded downright amenable toward a peaceful solution."

The *Hindustan* floated in the river like a behemoth ark. Small canoes ferried people back and forth from the beach in the twinkling of an eye for the price of a cigarette. The Irishmen boarded a canoe, not bothering to sit down. At the hulk's edge, they made great acrobatic leaps onto the wide ladder that served as a staircase. They scrambled up to the quarterdeck, jostling descending men carrying casks of oil, kegs of brandy, and all manner of livestock on their shoulders. Brendan didn't even pause when he plucked a banana from a bundle a fellow hoisted on his head.

Cool and sheltered as the deck was with the palm thatch matting, Brendan and Evin nevertheless slid about in the pools of oil, phlegm, banana peels, and piss that coated the floor. Curtains one could raise or lower at will comprised the arch of the taffrail, each curtained section being a stall where merchants conducted business, with hammocks festooned between columns, ratty old Madeira wickerwork chairs tossed in the glassy slickness, brass spittoons positioned at random as though the deck were a stage in a Wild West show. Above all was the deafening din of the bargaining voices that bounced off the iron sheeting, trading can openers for brass wire, tobacco for pigs, ivory for guns.

Brendan slogged his way to the companionway that led down to his offices, fellows clinging to his arms with good cheer, waving fish and gargantuan lizards in his face, expectorating kola nut juice onto his person. Brendan bore it all with stoicism, vigorously slapping the men back and winding up with a hand full of grease. It was the ins and outs of his profession.

"We opened a jar of that palm fruit that we put up last autumn," Evin told Brendan.

"Is that so? Was it any good?"

They passed the saloon now. With its solid mahogany doors, tables, and sideboards, it still retained shades of its former glory days, though the gilt moldings had faded to dull yellow, the velvet seats worn threadbare by palm-oiled posteriors. A group of *Oyinbo* were gathered colorfully around the largest and grandest table, the odious Mateus Barbosa among them. From the darkness of the corridor Brendan could see the dwarf's white teeth gnashing together.

"Ah, Bren, it was even better than when we put it into the jar, over a year ago." Evin waxed poetic. "Tender and sweet; the sugarcane didn't coagulate at all."

Brendan swung open the saloon door. "Is that so? Is there any at home? I'll try it. If it's good, those African Oil Nuts fellows said they'd buy a quantity."

"Avast, Bren, not in there! I don't want to look at that disgusting cane rat!"

Regardless, Evin followed Brendan to the *Oyinbo* table, where the Count de Brazza held court, clad today in a white linen suit that showed off his beautiful walnut brown skin. Brendan took solace that Brazza had made an unfortunate choice of head-gear, one of the solar topees that always gave the wearer the look of a boy playing jacks.

But Brazza's exotic splendor was outshined by Elle's stunning beauty. She had prettified her usually mannish attire, and was sporting a light yellow satin gown. The bodice was high-necked, of accordion-pleated silk so sheer one could see her lacey chemise, apparently also yellow, against the golden brown she had allowed the sun to color her skin, as she usually went about without a parasol. Today, however, there was a fluffy brocade parasol hooked to the back of her chair. Brendan felt a pit of smoldering jealousy in his stomach, wondering why she had spruced up for the accomplished explorer. She clearly had not expected Brendan by the way her mouth formed an O when she finally deigned to tear her eyes away from Brazza, who was reading aloud something from a newspaper.

" 'He keeps on practicing philanthropy, not colonization,' " Brazza read in his seductive mélange of accents.

"And what is so wrong with that?" cried Caroline Forshaw. "I don't see how the two have to be mutually exclusive."

"Gentlemen!" Brad Forshaw was the first one to get to his feet when he saw the Irishmen, grabbing vacant chairs from another table for them. "Please, take a seat. The Commissioner here is entertaining us with an article written about him in a Paris newspaper." Evin took a seat next to Caroline, and Brad indicated that Brendan should sit there as well, but Brendan rudely grabbed the chair and banged it down squarely between Brazza and Elle.

"*Tombo, tombo*," Brendan said irritably, waving away the white-jacketed attendant who had had his nap interrupted by their sudden intrusion. "Please go ahead, Count. I am sure this is most interesting."

"The French are so awful to him, Brendan," Elle said, giving him a chance to turn and look at her. "I'm surprised he doesn't go back to Italy and renounce them."

Brendan was stunned by how much he craved Elle; all he could think to say was "Yes . . . "

Elle had taken her lacy and flowery straw hat off, allowing everyone to gaze upon her glossy auburn curls, all held back in a pigtail to display the most delicate ear drops of lampwork yellow glass. He was a goddamn sappy gump to think a woman of such refinement could have it bad for a crass "River Gentleman" such as himself.

He continued looking directly at Elle while Brazza expounded behind him. " 'With regard to the natives, he behaves like a teacher who crams his pupils with sweets and asks them to learn Latin and Greek on their own.' "

"Oh, that's the height of absurdity!" said Caroline.

Elle couldn't seem to decide where to look—Brazza or Brendan. Her eyes went back and forth between the men, an insipid smile pasted to her lips. She was the most gorgeous woman Brendan had ever seen—and since she was an anthropologist, did that not mean she was accustomed to ragged ruffians in her travels? There was a casual demeanor about her, she was brave and bold, unafraid to ask sensitive questions or to delve where most women would be calling for the smelling salts, or at least blushing until the steam from their rain-soaked clothes went up in a cloud. Elle did not blush. She had been vocally unrestrained when he took her the other day. A surprising feat, considering her "husband" might have taken it into his head to come in to get a shave at any moment.

"The aim of colonization is the development of the material wealth of the colonized countries, and this aim will only very occasionally be achieved by"—Brazza stumbled on his next words, causing Elle to raise her eyebrows and lean toward him in a conciliatory fashion, the only result being that her knees touched Brendan's—*"precher la 'bonne parole.'"*

"Oh," said Caroline eagerly. "That is like 'talking nicely.'"

Brazza continued. "'Talking nicely to the natives, and above all respecting their habits and their customs, which are based on laziness, while ours are based on foresight.' *Bah!* Idiotic!"

"Land's sake!" Brendan surprised himself with his own utterance—particularly as he didn't know he'd been listening to Brazza. "Who's the potatohead who wrote that?"

"This is anonymous author," cried Brazza. "He doesn't even have bravery to sign his own name."

"All you have to do is look around this hulk to see what 'laziness' has brought to Africa." Brendan frowned.

"For better or worse." Brad laughed.

Brendan pointed at the table. "That 'laziness' notion is one that gets me smoking. It's usually a case of a problem with the African lingoes, which can be fairly convoluted. For instance, there's no distinction between living or dead things, or things you can see and invisible things. I once spent half an hour trying to get to the bottom of this crocodile that was chasing a fellow, only to find out it was in his dream."

"And I am constantly being called 'sir'!" said Elle. "Do you have that problem, Caroline?"

"Oh, yes, it is very amusing."

Elle continued, "I consider myself a ladylike woman, to a certain extent—"

"To *all* extent," Brazza bootlicked.

"—yet I am continuously being referred to as 'sir.' Why, the other day I was caught in a downpour with no umbrella or water-proof; I was downriver on a little expedition by where the falls and fish traps are, and I recalled the trader Brownridge had a factory around there, so I struck for his shelter only to find he wasn't home. His steward-boy said, 'Massa live for Mister Swanzee's house.' So I said, 'Go tell him I live for come from,' and 'I fit for want place,' naturally."

"Naturally," agreed Evin and Brad.

"I had nothing to write with, but I thought the steward-boy could remember this message to Mr. Swanzee's house. Well! I was wrong, because he returned with a note—here, I kept it for humor's sake." Elle withdrew a folded note from her pocket book and gave it to Brendan petulantly, with a child's pout. "Here. Read it aloud."

All the blood stopped moving in Brendan's veins. He had no time to reason anything out before his hand clutching the note shot over toward Brazza, and he found himself saying, "You have the honor, Count."

Brendan could breathe again when Brazza also declined the note laughingly, saying, "I have hard enough time with French," making the women giggle.

At last the learned Evin was in possession of the note, and he read, " 'Dear Old Man,' " causing the entire table to give forth in mirth. " 'You must be in a deuce of a mess after the tornado. Just help yourself to my dry things. The shirts are in the bottom drawer, the trousers are in the box under the bed, and then come over here to the sing-song. Yours, Ed.' "

Everyone continued laughing uproariously as Evin handed Elle back the note across the table, saying, "You do know that from now on you'll be known as 'Old Man.' "

Elle had laughed so hard she had to wipe drips of tears from her eyes with the back of her gloved hand. "Oh, my, yes. I don't think I shall ever live this down. When poor Ed finally saw me, he said it took several years' growth out of him."

"I'll bet my bottom dollar," Brendan agreed. He found the nerve to lift his hand to Elle's face and rub one remaining tear away with his thumb. It was a loving gesture that Elle did not seem to mind, for she gazed upon Brendan bleary-eyed with a relaxed joy.

The rest of the people at table seemed to go quiet over it until Brazza barged ahead. "Mr. Donivan, you are an experienced man in these waters . . . Can you give a reasonable explanation for the human sacrifices? For if you can find explanation that will make sense to the British, perhaps they will not look down on it."

Brendan was disappointed he had to lower his hand from Elle's face. "Well, mayhap not much of an explanation that would give all the facts in this connection, Count. It's a sort of form of fatalism. The sun that rises and sets, the moon that changes, the tides that come and go—they don't give a damn about the African. He looks to the gods that are always smiting people with unexpected catastrophes, drowning, heart attacks, malaria. It's obvious these spirits are ripe for the devil, so the African flatters them with sacrifices—and the more pain and loss it causes the African, the happier the spirits be."

Elle interrupted with a question that betrayed her anthropologist's leanings. "How do they explain it, then, when some of these sacrifices don't work? For that's bound to happen—as in the case with the encroachment of the *Oyinbo*."

Glad of a chance to face Elle again, Brendan wondered how long-winded he could make his yarn. "The power's been lured away by some more highfalutin gifts than his, of course."

"So . . . He has to keep sacrificing until his account has built up so high that it cancels out the rich fellow's?"

"Oh, the African knows his fetish might fail. Here's an instance for you. There was an admired and trusted fetish doctor in Edo. He himself fell sick, so he made *juju* against the sickness, but it had him in its clutches, and he became sicker. He made more *juju* of greater power, but again it was for naught. He knew he was dying, so with the little strength he had left he broke up and destroyed all the fetishes in which the spirits resided, threw them into the river and died like a man."

Elle looked tremendously moved by his story. Her lips trembled. Brendan just wanted to lean forward and lick her mouth, and he was irritated afresh by the presence of the others. "That is so . . . sad," she whispered.

"But what happened then, when people see what he did?" asked Brazza.

"Well, they all busted out hollering, of course. They burned his house and everything belonging to him, and wailed to the four corners of the earth not to forsake them, not to blame them for one miserable critter's mortal sin."

There was a brief silence, then Brazza observed, "I do not think the spirits have returned to favoring them."

At that, everyone continued in silence, weighted down by the profundity of this situation.

At length Mateus, who had heretofore been content to grind his teeth in exhilaration and drink gin, leaped to his feet brandishing some papers, proclaiming, "*Capitão*, the Cross River Transport has brought the mail!"

Brendan, too, jumped to his feet to snatch the papers from the oily man's paws, while Evin covered his face with his hand, shaking his head in pity. Brendan stuffed the papers in a hastily arranged cone shape into one of his back pants pockets. "And you couldn't just leave my mail in my office."

"Well, no, *Capitão*, for it's your cablegram from New York City in there, *certamente*. I thought it best to keep it in my possession."

"*Onwon min mfanifa.*" *He drinks palm wine like a fish.* Brendan glared at Mateus, afraid to say anything else for fear of the revelations that might spout forth from the shrimp's lungs. As Gainey was the Postal Agent, Brendan would speak to him, ask him not to hand out his mail to every Tom, Dick, and Harry. "I must check my office now. Count, Caroline, Brad." He nodded at each one in turn, leaving Elle for last. "Mrs. Bowie, you might want to come to my office and discuss that earlier matter . . .?"

Comprehension washing over her face, Elle stood and gathered her pocket book and parasol. "Yes, that palm oil . . . banana matter."

While it was completely preposterous that Brendan and Elle would be discussing anything like bananas, Brendan didn't care much what the others, least of all Brazza, thought. He took Elle's forearm and led her from the saloon and back to the mucous-washed corridor. It seemed that she walked purposely close to him, rubbing her pleated bosom against his bicep, and he was so dizzy with lust he couldn't formulate a proper sentence.

"Why does he call you Captain, Mick?" Her tone was playful, teasing.

"Oh, ah, I was a pilot on a sternwheeler in the seventies, on the Chattahoochee River. I had a house in Eufala, which of course we called Eufala Downs. We'd haul cotton, turpentine, tar, produce from Columbus down to Apalachicola on the Gulf. That's how I hooked up with all these Liverpool fellows, when we'd off-load everything to their ships."

"Oh, how romantic!" Elle gushed. "So you've been on rivers your whole life?"

"Not exactly. Evin there used to come ride with me when he'd get a break from his studies at university; that's when we decided to become buffalo runners. *Amebo*, pick up your skirts. These floors ain't fit to be mopped with satin."

"My, I guess I am so used to filth I hadn't really noticed. But buffalo running is not a classy endeavor, from what I had heard. Oh, I am sure you made money, but you contributed to the noble animal's extinction."

Brendan held a door for Elle that led to another corridor. "Exactly my feelings too. Those animals is deaf, blind, and couldn't smell a rotten hippo carcass if it was lying atop them.

And then you're wallowing in blood and guts all day. No, we soon tired of that, and joined up to become merchant seamen. We did that for many years, sailing round the world, educating ourselves at all the different ports."

Elle stopped walking then, she seemed to be so overwhelmed with information. She closed her eyes and shivered. "Such romance! You've had such an exciting life."

Brendan shrugged. "Don't reckon it could hold a candle to yours. You traveled round the world too."

When she opened her eyes again, Brendan was instantly sorry to have ruined her picture. "Yes. In seventy-two days. I was hardly able to find 'education' at any of the ports. No, I'm afraid I spend a lot of my time in an office writing up reports." She held up an idealistic forefinger and recited, " 'We will always fight for progress and reform, never tolerate injustice or corruption, always fight demagogues of all parties, always oppose privileged classes and public plunderers, never lack sympathy with the poor . . .' "

Brendan smiled. "What is that?"

"That's the motto of my boss. A very great philanthropist. And a man with the vision and foresight to hire a woman."

"Oh, aye." Brendan moved as close to Elle as he dared, and then some stevedores bumped him from behind with their armload of mahogany wood, shoving Brendan into the woman's front. She caught his elbow with her free hand, and he steadied her with his hands on her shoulders. They merely looked at each other for several long moments. Surrounded by the raucous jostling of the hulk men, Brendan thought he had never felt this right, this normal to be standing in the oily banana peels and groundnut shells with this jungle flower of a woman in a yellow satin gown.

"You're a ravishing jungle orchid," Brendan breathed.

Elle looked down at his sternum, smiling. "I am hopelessly attracted to you. You have some power, some way of mesmerizing me . . . I am desperately stricken."

A wave of joy swelled in Brendan's stomach then to hear such words. "Aye, then I shall practice my sorcery on you every day, so I never lose the power."

"Good." She looked him in the eyes then, and he thought she might kiss him there, in front of all the heedless men slogging about with their crates and pallets, but she pushed him away to continue walking.

"Where's Rip?"

"Oh, I don't know where that crazed cowpoke is."

Brendan held open his office door. "Are you angry with him for his stunt of the other day?"

"If you mean that girlie stuff, yes. And he's been acting . . . strange."

Brendan's office was a grand cabin with square portholes, the former vacation home of admirals, princes, and fair ladies. Now it was chockablock with stacks of papers, manifests, purchase orders, shipping logs, stacks held down by nautical instruments that threatened to topple on the heads of the lounging Africans should the hulk take a sudden wave. "Yes, I'm beginning to suspect your 'husband' of muddying the waters with his own plot to keep us apart." Brendan yanked the arms of a couple reclining men, jerking them toward the door, and they went with nary a whimper, accustomed to being booted. "If he's just your photographer, what does he care what you do?"

"Ah, well, it's like this . . . He's more like my brother. He feels he's protecting me from your damaging influence."

Brendan turned to face her, the arm of the remaining clerk in his fist. He shook the fellow for emphasis, as though he were a handkerchief. "What could possibly be that scary and destructive about *me*?"

There was a pause, then the woman erupted into melodious laughter. It was so funny in fact that she had to put her gloved hand to her mouth, and turn aside in mirth. It slowly came to Brendan that, especially brandishing an unarmed African, a Coast

Gentleman such as himself might possibly give a refined woman pause for thought. He tossed the African out the door, locked the bolt behind him, and faced Elle afresh with a soft tone. "*Amebo*...surely you do not share Rip's opinion that I might damage you in any way? I'd rather see myself hanging from the *Iroko* tree than to ever cause you harm."

Elle cringed. "Oh, don't say that! No, it's not physical damage Rip is thinking about. It's more just that . . . I haven't had a . . . sweetheart in a long time."

Brendan poured brandy into two small snifters. "Long? How long? I can't see a stunning beauty as you without a sweetheart."

Elle inhaled and exhaled slowly, as if it pained her to admit. "Four years. There was someone who . . . did not turn out to be who he said, and ever since I have sworn off men." She continued in a lighter tone as she accepted the brandy from Brendan. "It is just not meant to be, for me. I am just not good at that courting sort of thing. It is much better for me to be disciplined in my work. I get much more accomplished when there is not a man distracting and annoying me."

"Ah, darling. No, that's too much of a shame." Brendan attempted to hurriedly get the ceiling fan to work, as he could already see the sheen of moisture on Elle's throat. His office was an oven, at the best of times. "Working all night and day is a mighty solemn bore. You got double-crossed by some heartless bast—some thoughtless fellow. You can't carry that heartache inside forever, and doom yourself to a loveless life, with no chance at happiness."

"Work gives me happiness!" Elle proclaimed. He saw her make a face at the brandy snifter. "This brandy tastes watered down. And sort of . . . dirty."

Giving up on the fan, Brendan went to sip his own brandy, and before he knew what he was doing, he was spewing the small mouthful of shit over his paper-covered desk. "Olokun! What happened to this brandy?" He looked suspiciously at the glass decanter that was just like any other that had been filled from a brandy keg. "This is the brandy I brought back from . . . Wait."

"What's wrong?"

Pouring yet more into his own snifter, Brendan poured more for Elle too. "I know why this tastes like this. Drink."

"But you just spat it out! Why should we—"

He stepped so close to her their noses nearly touched. Gently, he urged her, "Drink. Trust me."

She did, not appearing to despise it as much as he had, for she was able to swallow. "Now tell me why."

"In Edo, a great love charm is made of water that someone has washed in. Mingled with the drink of the loved one, it is held to soften the hardest heart."

Now it was Elle's turn to spew, though she had nothing left in her mouth. "Oh, you right bastard! Are you telling me that *someone* put your bathwater into your brandy?"

Brendan could not help but laugh, though he tried to soothe Elle by undoing the gold buckle that held a ribbon about her waist. "Doesn't it taste that way? A mighty fortunate thing you were the first to drink it."

"Oh, you . . . Brendan!" she cried. She lightly pounded her fists against his shirtfront, but it was without malice, and she did not protest when he deposited her belt on the desktop and started slipping her lacy basque off her shoulders. "Does this mean I shall love you now? That's a mean, terrible trick. And who made the charm? Iden?"

"Iden. What is so awful about loving me?"

Elle sighed. Brendan's fingers were stuck on the high dog collar buttons, so she replied leisurely, "Oh, it is not you in particular. It is love in general. I despise that word! People who claim to love only act in ways that truly loving people do not. I have seen that word misused so many times it doesn't mean a thing. Much better to use true, strong words if one feels forcefully about a person."

Brendan was mortified into silence, for he knew that he already loved her, and now, knowing how she felt, how could he ever say it? The pearl buttons slithered between his fingers, and he drew away the accordion-pleated bodice while giving the side of her neck gentle sucking kisses. His penis was nearly rupturing the seams of his pants he was so full and stiff, but he did not want to appear to be a heartless bastard. "And what words would you use to describe how you feel for me?"

"Ah." Elle gave out a happy sigh as she gathered him in her arms, shimmying her torso against his chest as he raced to tear off his vest and shirt—he never wore a collar, merely a tie. "You? I think that I . . . *respect* you very much. Yes, that's it. And I *admire* you for how brave and bold you are. Don't you think those words are much more honorable, much more believable?"

A soaring gust of happiness washed through Brendan to hear her words. *She admired and respected him.* He tickled her mouth with his own. "I do so *love* that you admire and respect me."

She giggled and sighed some more, tasting his mouth tentatively. "And what words do you use for me?"

"I am . . . entranced by you, in awe of your beauty." Sliding his palm down her chemise, Brendan scooped her full breast into his hand, rubbing her erect nipple. "I'm so enraptured by you not an hour goes by that I don't think of you. I want to devour you, to protect you from all harm, to keep you safe."

"Oh," she sighed. "That's good."

"And I'm so jealous of that lout Brazza if I see him near you again I'm going to drop him in his tracks."

To prevent Elle from responding, Brendan eased her into a long, deep kiss that had her squirming like a fish on a hook. He dropped her petticoat to the floor, allowing her to retain her chemise, drawers, and stockings when he slid down her body to his knees, licking her womanly white belly, lightly biting at her navel, before dipping his mouth to the slit in her drawers, finding her swollen labia with his fingertips.

"*Aah!*" It was a high-pitched sharp sound he elicited from her, as though she had suddenly realized his intentions. "Oh God, Brendan. Oh God. You can't . . . No."

He licked her hard clitoris with the flat of his tongue, his palms gathering the globes of her ass and pressing her to his face. She panted shallow, rapid breaths that might have been the cause of her fainting the other day, if she did that while pleasuring herself alone. Squirming and whimpering, uttering little sounds of struggle that only enflamed Brendan all the more, she grabbed a handful of his hair and squeezed. The knifing pain only worked him up, and he sped his ministrations to her straining button, covering it with his mouth and lapping like a famished dog. She tasted sweet, like honey and cream.

When she commenced sighing like the harmattan wind through the masts, Brendan bore down, sliding one middle finger inside her tight quim, and lightly crushing her engorged button with his teeth. When he heard her catch her breath at the apex of orgasm, he lit into her anew with his tongue, and was rewarded with the crashing, rolling spasms that traveled down the length of her channel.

She stood like a demented heron on one leg, the other heel of her shoe hitched up in a drawer of his map chest. Brendan slowed his tongue as her strangled cries weakened, and just then an enormous explosion hit the cabin door. The door banged with a thunderous metal boom against the wall, Elle uttered a feminine shriek, and without thinking beforehand, Brendan twisted to face the door, his Schofield at the ready in his hand. He covered Elle with his torso, and she clung to him, cringing her head behind his shoulders, her long legs tangled up in his.

It was only a ferocious sphere of brown fur that spun about the cabin. Brendan replaced his gun in the holster, breathed again, and turned to the woman. "Pequod."

"Oh!" Elle laughed with lopsided exhaustion, flinging her arms weakly about his neck.

"She was just protecting me, I'm sorry." Brendan laughed before Elle sucked up his lower lip in her mouth, and they kissed sloppily, the woman wiping her moisture from his chin and neck with her forearm.

He was sure the Africans peering around the doorjamb had never seen anything like this. He gave them an eyeful, as he wasn't in an overmuch hurry to release the woman, but the dog insisted on saving him by jumping up and tugging at the back pocket of his pants, the only element of clothing he hadn't tossed to the floor.

"Ah, I'm sorry," he murmured against her mouth. "Mayhap I should shut the door again."

"If you wish," she panted.

He detached himself and went to the door, his enormous erection tenting his pants, and glared at the giggling faces that festooned the doorway.

"*Okhien owie*." *Until tomorrow morning.*

His chief shop steward was handing him a bundle wrapped in Edo cloth and *tie-tie*. Taking it, Brendan slammed and bolted the door once more. He returned to Elle, who leaned out a porthole, taking great gulps of the humid air.

Brendan caressed her bare shoulders. He could take her right now, from behind like this, but he felt it would seem heartless and crass. "I'm sorry about the dog."

Turning, Elle flung her arms around his neck and kissed him over and over, sweetly and gently, his nose, forehead, chin. "Oh, Brendan . . . how you make me feel . . . I'm overwhelmed. I feel I will never be the same person again."

"Is that good? I like the same person."

"It is my female weakness," she whispered. "*Ah* . . . What did that man give you?"

"I don't know. He said it was from Edo."

Elle's face went ashen. "Oh, no. More *juju* from Iden."

Brendan smiled against her mouth. "No. More'n likely it's

another pike. I asked the metal workers to make me a new one, and it wasn't done by the last time I left Edo."

"In such a small package?"

Still smiling languidly, to appease the woman Brendan went to his desk and cut open the *tie-tie* of the bundle with his Bowie knife.

"Maybe I should have a palaver with Iden," Elle was saying. "I can tell her that I am no threat to her, I can soothe her—"

"You'll do no such thing, darling. Why upset the poor girl with a passel of lies?"

"Lies? Oh, I see. You are saying that I *am* a threat to her? Oh my, what is that?"

Brendan did not want to believe what he was seeing. He leaped for the door, yanked it open, and shouted at the shop steward who was of course still standing there. The steward said only that it had come on a canoe from Edo along with the usual puncheons of oil. Slamming the door again, Brendan approached the thing on his desk, a thoughtful hand to his chin, stepping in wide arcs around it as though afraid it would become animate.

"Dear heart, what is wrong? It looks quite gruesome, but then much of Edo art can be seen that way. I have found that some of the scariest things are really quite friendly."

"It is Ofoe. The Messenger of Death."

"Ohhh . . . " Elle clung to his arm with her fingertips.

Brendan pointed at the brass plaque, a depiction of the usual Edo face with broad nose, the walleyes inlaid with iron irises. The head sprouted limbs, and had no torso, only more limbs. "The legs relentlessly pursue his victims to death. He is also called Aguanaihon, which in English means 'we plead, he does not listen.' "

"Who sent it to you?"

"I don't exactly know, but I better get to Edo and find out. This is not good."

"Well, what does it mean? Why would someone send you this?"

Brendan looked away from the horrific statue, looked to Elle. "He symbolizes the Oba's power of life and death over his people."

"Yes?"

"If the Oba sends this to someone, it is a warning that they will be put to death if they do not behave."

Elle desperately missed Brendan. It had been years since she had been subjected to this physical yearning that hurt her, made her unable to sleep or eat. It all came rushing back to her what she loathed about it—the trepidation, the jumpy blue funk. She was so dead-set certain something catastrophic would happen around every corner at every hour she could not relax, could not even finish the first chapter of *Moby Dick*, the only book anyone had been kind enough to leave behind inside her house.

After three nights of lying abed listening to the chorus of cicadas, the singing and drumming around fires over in the Farmland Quarter, Elle took a stroll down to the anchorage. It was the beginning of the dry season, the "rest and chop" season after the yam harvest, and the banks of the river were covered with mounds of white lilies. The air was alight with butterflies, their canary, crimson, and peacock wings dancing out a cyclorama that was much too happy for Elle's mood. She did pause under an oil palm to throw some rotten lemons at the monkeys in the fluffy branches, but didn't bother to catch them when the monkeys threw them back. She kept walking jauntily along the beach, stepping into a canoe to take her across to the

Hindustan.

For Elle was hoping to talk to the chief steward who had handed Brendan the idol, to see Evin, in her loneliness to speak to anyone who might have once known or even sat in the same room as Brendan.

Instead, she saw Rip and Mateus having a palaver over a cocktail in the saloon.

Swiftly, she surveyed the layout of the saloon to see if there was anywhere she could effectively eavesdrop. But the windows all let onto the river, so she settled for slipping inside the door as unobtrusively as possible.

"—doesn't bother him that she's really a reporter, and he starts liking her even *more*? What then?"

That was Rip. They were both hunched over one of the smallest tables, heads put together like gargoyles on a lintel.

Mateus rejoined, "Not a chance. If all his business in Edo is ruined, what money will he have to attract her?—what're you doing?"

"*Elle!*" Rip shouted cheerily after kicking Mateus under the table. Standing, he gestured to an empty chair. "Why don't you have a seat, join us in some gin. Well, he's having gin, I'm having whiskey of course."

Elle glared up and down the entire length of Rip's body. "Whose business will be ruined?"

The men laughed an octave too high to sound genuine.

It was Mateus who answered. "Oh, pretty much everybody on these rivers, if we keep having to rely on the Itsekiri middle-men for our palm oil."

Elle folded her arms before her chest. "And just what are you two monkeys up to? I never knew you to be such back-slapping buckos."

She refused to be eased into a chair, so Rip waved a relaxed arm instead. "Ah, you know, honey. There's not much to do in Sapele, so we like to hang out in the saloon."

"And you can't drink at home?"

"Hey, I've got a question to ask you." Rip forcibly guided Elle to the farthest window in the saloon. He leaned on the sill with casual aplomb, but his question was the last thing she expected. "If you took my French letters, I'd like you to replace them. I'm sure you can easily get some from Mr. Donivan, since he's a trader."

Elle was astonished into silence for a full half a minute. Her mouth was so agape that a fly actually flew into it. When she finally spoke, it was in a screamed whisper. "*French letters*?"

"Yes, you know, those tubes made out of rubber that a fellow puts on his dick when—"

Elle slapped Rip, hard, on the arm. "Rip, I *know* what French letters are! I'm just so completely shocked that you would think *I* would take them!" They stared blankly at each other. She was about to add, "Why on earth do you even have them?" before she realized how silly it sounded.

Rip seemed angry now. "Listen, Elle. You're the one always spouting about how contraception should be free for all women, how it puts the necessity for undesirable marriages back in the middle ages, how it takes the fear out of sex—"

"Yes, of course I say all those things, because it's all true! But that's all propaganda for the general population—not anything I would ever need to practice myself. I am hardly the rutting sort. Why would *I* steal your French letters?"

Rip's head took on that nasty egg shape again. "Maybe because you need them."

Elle narrowed her eyes. "Maybe *you* need them."

They were silent in their Mexican standoff. Many statements, all of them hateful, went through Elle's mind, but she bit her tongue.

At length Rip surprised her again by saying in a conciliatory tone, "Elle . . . I wasn't the one who told Mrs. Pulitzer about you."

Again, Elle dropped her jaw. "I didn't think you did, Rip. I know that Joe would never have chosen me over her, anyway. Does it matter who told her?" Her words were blasé, but the poisonous lump in her stomach was the same sick permeating bile she always felt when anyone had the nerve to mention Pulitzer, though it was finally getting a bit better. The past month she had succeeded in even making light comments regarding him, such as his creed she had flippantly recited to Brendan. She thought perhaps giving voice to it was a way of expunging it.

"OK. I just thought you might be thinking that, the way you've been acting. You know I'd never hurt you, Elle. You're the person closest to me on this cold cruel planet."

Elle smiled a little, genuinely. "I know." She turned to leave, but Rip's next sentence stopped her.

"That's why I want to prevent you from making the same mistake as you did with Pulitzer."

Elle turned back. "All right, Rip. Now exactly in what manner is Brendan the same as Joe? Does Brendan have a wife he will never divorce?"

"No." Rip's luminous aquamarine eyes glittered. "He's just the same unfeeling, good-for-nothing bastard that Pulitzer is . . . when it comes to women, least."

Elle rolled her eyes. "And just how do you know these things?"

"Wait. Just you wait. He doesn't know who you really are." Rip did seem awful serious. "When he finds out, you'll be seeing his true colors."

Elle shook her head. "You're so moony sometimes, Rip."

She didn't think more about it as she went around to Brendan's office, where she was told "Jordan live for Donivan house." Once the canoe touched land, she set off up the shoreline to the house she had been curious about since first knocking on the door looking for the "trader Donivan" who would help them enter Edo. She talked quietly to herself as she strolled purposefully along.

214 — KAREN MERCURY

"Perhaps I should have stolen—no, borrowed—Rip's condoms. After all, why have I not thought of pregnancy 'til now? Maybe because normally there is no need to think of it. Perhaps I should, if only to avoid the possibility of becoming . . . oh, don't even think of it! The horror! Now why on earth did Rip bring condoms to Africa? Oh, what a silly question! I should be glad for him."

Brendan's house was the grandest in Sapele, unless you counted Gainey's, but that was a combination of vice-consulate as well. The front veranda, protected on all sides by sheets of mosquito netting, was a verdant explosion of plant life—palms, orchids, cassia, and hibiscus displaying their papery blooms, even some screw pines that had been stunted to stay within the confines of the awning. There were terra cotta pots Elle could see were made in Edo, wicker tables, and a wicker chair with a cushion. Elle smiled to see *Leaves of Grass* setting there.

Elle took a peek through the screened door into the sitting room. Surprisingly populated with dark American furniture, there was even a china cabinet with pheasants and guinea fowl on the dishes, and above all a magnificent turkey platter, recalling to Elle the turkey platter displaying the skull at Brendan's house in Edo. A guitar sat on a leather armchair, and on another, a banjo.

These sights encouraged Elle's heart. She called out politely, "Evin."

It took quite awhile for a woman to come from a side hallway. Perhaps as much as the same age as Elle, she was beautiful in that smooth refulgent African way, unadorned save for some surprisingly expensive and rare quartz point dangle ear drops. She was fussing shyly with her clothes, probably just awakened from a nap, and stepped back soundlessly to admit Elle.

"Mister Evin he come room."

"All right, that's fine. *Vbe oro ni rue?*"

"Miriam," the woman answered quietly. "You want gin?"

"No, thank you—but if you have some brandy I'll take that." Elle continued speaking while the woman moved to the adjoining dining room to a sideboard. She didn't much care if Miriam understood her; she felt like talking. "I had some magic love potion brandy the other day, and it was quite good, it tasted of bathwater, have you ever tried that? It's to make you fall in love with whoever's bathwater is in the brandy."

"Love potion," Miriam agreed shyly, handing Elle her brandy.

A happy boy of about four years ran through the dining room, babbling away, just as Evin made his appearance in the sitting room.

"Elle," Evin said with surprise, as Miriam went off to chase the boy.

"Evin, *ob'owie,* I am so happy to see you."

Evin, too, looked a little dizzy-eyed, fingering the buttons of his shirt nervously, and a thought suddenly struck Elle, that he and Miriam were lovers. It was probably a wrong thought, as Evin had always seemed disdainful of the concept of combining Africans and sex.

"I'm glad you're still in town," said Evin brightly. "Come, taste our palm fruit."

Elle followed Evin through the dining room and the kitchen illuminated by skylights, looking all the while for the "lewd painting" and seeing nothing more scintillating than an Albert Bierstadt color lithograph of the Sierra Madres.

The back veranda was a greenhouse of tropical lushness, and it was difficult to tell where the jungle stopped and the decking began. "You're very good with plants," Elle said in wonderment. "I can't grow a thing. People have on occasion given me ferns and suchlike, but I always wind up killing them. Not very maternal, I suppose."

Evin merely smiled. On a tall wicker table topped by a piece of glass, there were a few jars, a relish tray, and some tiny condiment forks. "It's easy in the jungle. You pretty much leave everything alone and it grows itself. Of course I have to water everything that's under the awning." Evin took the jar that was already opened and speared a few of the red fruits, placing them on the relish tray. "Here, try one. Brendan and I canned these exactly a year ago."

"And you're very good with crops as well. Rip was telling me you experiment in Edo with all sorts of grafting and new plants that you have sent over from America and other countries."

Evin shrugged. "It's not always successful. I just nursed a whole crop of rhubarb that went belly up. I seem to be having great success, though, with European mistletoe, and my kiwis are doing great. What do you think?"

"Oh, it's delicious! Do you have any jars to spare? We're sometimes short on edible foodstuffs around our house. What was it you studied in university?"

"Horticulture."

"And you became a . . . merchant mariner?"

"Brendan Donivan. What else can I say? That guy is so persuasive, it's impossible to not believe him."

His statement gave Elle pause for thought. "Yes, he can be quite a charmer."

Perhaps Evin realized his remark was thoughtless, for he quickly said, "Brendan is really very fond of you, and I daresay I approve. Living in the hinterlands of the Oil Rivers can be downright hot and pointless at times, and you seem to have given him a stable foundation. He seems happier. We're such close partners, God knows if one of us ever got married, the other one would go live in a dog house in the backyard."

Elle was happier now, as well. "I'm very fond of him too, though I can't say I have much of a stable foundation myself. Traveling about, going on different assignments . . . "

"Yes, what was that around the world thing all about?"

Elle sipped more brandy and said haltingly, "Well, it was more of a publicity thing. You see, I work for a newspaper . . . the New York *World*. One day we were in a restaurant, my editor, some reporters, and I, and we were discussing Jules Verne, you know his *Around The World in Eighty Days*. Well, I said I could do it in less than that, and everyone thought what a grand idea for a woman, and—"

There was a sharp squeal at the back door, and something flew through the air and collided with Elle's thigh, a warm wet blob.

"Oh!" she cried automatically, as Miriam scolded and dragged the small boy back indoors. Evin shouted something at the lad too, and strode over to see what was the matter.

"What did he do?"

"Oh, it's nothing . . . It appears he just threw some water at me. It doesn't smell," said Elle.

Evin wouldn't touch her with the piece of towel he proffered, so Elle took it and bent at the knees to blot her skirt.

"I'm sorry about that. He doesn't normally act like a prankster, I don't know what got into him."

"And whose child is he?"

"Miriam's. His father was killed in Edo, so we took her here where she'd feel safer."

"Oh, how terrible." As she blotted her skirt, Elle saw a bit of rag by her foot, and she picked it up. It only took a few fractions of a second for her to realize, by its rubbery smell and the thickness of it, that the boy had made a water-filled balloon of a condom. "Was he killed as a sacrifice?" She dropped the rubber rag.

"Yes."

When Elle straightened up, she saw Evin's faraway, gloomy face, and she wanted to cheer him up. "Miriam is a lovely girl, and the boy is just adorable."

The glaze faded from his eyes, and Evin's face assumed its normal chipper countenance. "Yes! And that reminds me." Stepping to another wicker end table, Evin leaned over and scooped up some papers that were lying there, next to some other scraps of paper, pens, and books. He offered the pages to Elle like a child at a birthday party. "Brendan wants you to have these."

Evin continued babbling as Elle took the pages, so suffused with awe she probably only heard half of what he said.

"He wrote this for you, and just forgot to give it to you. He's an amazing poet, really. What I mean is, read that! *'Hands of bronze and twist of fate will find me in these shards of bones'* . . . It's amazing, really."

Elle was stunned. She stared at the curvilinear handwriting as though the words contained her death sentence, afraid to read any of them in sequence, like lights strung out on a wire. " *'An ever-licking turkey plate, she is not mine, I am my own'* —"

"Yes!" Evin encouraged her. "The part where *'for in my hut of mud-red leaves, the dwarf decries, it's all for naught!'* " of course he's referring to Mateus, so don't let that out of your sight. He's incredible! I've never heard such lucid, flowing jewels."

Elle realized her hands trembled. " *'A peasant fable, I bought one where I'm the sole surviving son.'* " She had to lower the paper in order to ask Evin, "And how does he relate these lines to you?"

Even uttered a small sound that approximated "Mm?" He laughed, and went back to the palm fruit table. "Relate?"

Elle followed him, saying gently, "Evin, I know Brendan can't read or write very well. And I saw this, your handwriting, on some contracts in the *Hindustan* office. Fact, I saw your handwriting all over everything."

Evin closed his eyes. At length he said tentatively, "Brendan can write perfectly well, it's just that he has bad penmanship. He says his handwriting—"

"Evin," Elle said gently. "I don't see anything wrong with not being able to read or write. Land's sake, I've met thousands of people like that living in New York City! There's nothing shameful in it at all, so you needn't be protective. Fact, I find it somewhat adorable, if the truth is known."

"If he ever knew I admitted to you—"

"Evin! It's all right. Some of the illiter—people who cannot

read that I've met have been the most mellifluous speakers—
they're writers in their heads!"

Evin warmed to the subject. "Well, yes! He can remember
line for line every poem he's ever written, and there are hundreds,
and he can recite them to me."

That explained his ability to recite the Frog poet into her ear .
. . Elle was filled with such happiness it seemed to fill her outer
limits of endurance, and she was uncertain she could sustain any
more. The pages in her hands felt as though they glowed with the
warmth of gold. She looked Evin in the eyes. "I shall treasure
this poem, and read it over and over." She walked up as close to
Evin as she dared, hugging the precious pages to her chest,
knowing her shining eyes were giving him his most passionate
glimpse of a white woman in years. "No man has ever written me
a poem before."

Evin raised an eyebrow. "Mm. That's odd. Brendan has
never written a woman a poem before."

～ ➻ ～

Mateus Barbosa squeaked something fierce in a woman's
falsetto when Brendan choked him held high up against the wall
of the boathouse. Brendan was as strong as a Dick horse when
riled, and Mateus's little sandaled feet were kicking like those of
a man at a necktie party, clearing the ground by about three feet
like they were.

"I swear, it wasn't me!" Mateus sang.

Brendan growled, "Is that so? Mayhap it was that time we
went to the picnic at that Italian's grave, and you came running all
over me like fire in dry grass saying you had some palavers in
Edo." Mateus was sweating on him, spraying it from his face,
and dripping it down Brendan's wrist. It was very unpleasant.

"I had palavers! It's not what you think! I had—let me go!"

Brendan choked the hulk rat's filthy neck even harder. "I

know you're hot for Miss Elle. Well, let me tell you, you lowdown cur from the bottomless pit. You won't get a chance to say boo to Miss Elle when you're bound for hell down in the creek swamp swimming with the crocodiles."

Mateus's increasingly limp fingers scrabbled at Brendan's strong wrist. "I . . . I had palaver . . . *help* . . ."

When Mateus's eyes started rolling back in his skull, Brendan shook him some more like a sleepy child he was trying to awaken. He took note of the cobalt hue of the cur's face, and that was behind his decision to toss the fellow to the ground where he flopped like a beached mudfish, gasping and grabbing his own throat. Brendan straddled him, one booted foot planted firmly astride each of Mateus's ears, waiting impatiently for him to catch his breath. "Who was your palaver with?"

Mateus's lips looked like two pieces of goat's liver moving together. ". . . With Iden . . ."

Brendan bellowed, "All right! I've had just about enough of your sacrilegious yammering!" He reached down to grab a fistful of Mateus's vest and yank him around some more, but he realized he wouldn't glean any useful information that way, so he merely picked him up with one fist and set him back against the side of the boathouse. Mateus cringed, and tried to make himself two-dimensional against the wooden wall. Brendan tried a new approach.

"You're lying about Iden," he hissed, jamming his knee into Mateus's testicular region and pinning him back against the wall again, gripping two wrists in one large hand. "Now, if you didn't tell General Ologboshere that I was in cahoots with the British, who did, *Senhor* Barbosa?"

"Ow! Stop! I don't know for certain, sir, but I have my feelings. And my feelings are always right."

"Do tell." It was extremely odious being this close to the unwashed swine. Brendan wondered if next time he could accomplish his goal by prodding the gnome with a very long mangrove pole.

"I do believe it was Mr. Bowie who told Ologboshere about your alleged involve—Ow! Let me go!"

Brendan tossed Mateus onto the ground again just for good measure, even though he was already rubbing his hands with a scientist's glee to have stumbled upon such a universal truth. "Rip Bowie, aye . . . "

"Why would I do such a thing? You pay my wages . . . "

Brendan had instantly discerned it was Ologboshere who had sent him the Ofoe idol. The only other high muckety-muck who would have the knowledge of such a nefarious god would be the Oba himself, and the Oba had no reason to hate Brendan. Brendan plied the Oba with leopards. Ologboshere had reasons down to the ground.

He barely heard Mateus hacking and sniffling behind him. "If you don't mind, sir, I just came down to the anchorage to tell you Mrs. Bowie has given me a task to carry out. Namely, to keep an eye out for you, and at the first sign of you to go running and tell her. Now, I can't very well go carrying this important news to her if I've got the essence of life choked out of me, can I? So if you don't mind, I'll just be getting on my way now, and—"

"Avast!" Brendan shot out one stiff arm that had the little shrimp jumping nearly clear out of his sandals and into the river. It was just the mention of Elle that had Brendan edgy. "Yes, please, Mateus, do go run and tell her I'm back, and have her meet me at my house." He looked down at his own grimy palms. "But can you wait several minutes?" He took some coins from his pants pocket and handed them politely to the shaky smaller man. "I'd like to wash. Can you find me some wine?"

"Wine, *Senhor?* I can find port."

"All right, port then." They started walking up the slight incline to the market stalls and fish cleaning stations that lined the beach. "I actually like port, Mateus. Why don't you?"

"Ah, you see, it was the drink of my ancestors. They were all a crazy bunch."

"But port's the same thing as wine. Anyway, what does a dwarf like you know? You only drink gin, when you shouldn't."

"Stop calling me a dwarf! I'm not a dwarf; they are much smaller. Besides, dwarves are sacred to the Oba. He always has those two dancing behind him in parades."

"Dwarves haunt lonely places and seize passersby. That pretty much sums up your existence."

"I beg to differ, *Senhor*. Dwarves help people find out their true path in life. Port is OK for you?"

"Port. And is there any jessamine around these parts?"

～ ✎ ～

Elle happily marched the short way along the busy road to reach Brendan's. Breathless with anticipation and the knowledge that although she was wearing her dull striped tennis dress and the straw boater, underneath she was clad in her most feminine lacey lavender drawers and frilly violet petticoat. And she had donned her only mauve corset, as she knew men to be rather partial to them. She carried a flask of her own medicinal brandy, as she didn't want to be tricked with any of Brendan's bathwater again. Love potion, indeed, what loads of pure smoke. She was walking proof of that.

Sometimes she forgot what he looked like. There were great gaping holes in her memory trying to construct a full mental image of him. She was unprepared for the stunning beauty of him when he opened his door for her. His hair was down, rather than tied back into a pigtail as was his wont, wet as though he'd just washed it, and he had a shy demeanor when glancing at her, self-conscious, unaware of his own magnificence.

He did not kiss her, and the former jittery creeps began sinking their tentacles into her stomach. What was wrong? "Mick." She smiled. "I'm sorry to be busting in this unceremoniously, without an invitation. I was just eager to see you."

Now he smiled, that lopsided crooked grin that got to her, that latched onto the very core of her and told her she was doomed. "Miss Eleanor, you can bust in to my house any time the mood strikes you."

She was doomed, done for. "Well? What did you find out in Edo?"

"Come." He took her forearm and led her through the dining room to the kitchen, a large room comprising skylights and windows that let out onto the arboretum Evin had created out of the veranda. The filtered sun lit up the whole room without the use of lamps, suffusing it with a cheery glow that made Elle instantly happy. Brendan had the fanciest, largest Home Sunshine range she'd ever seen, with a high elaborate shelf in back.

"This is incredible," Elle marveled. "There's room for six pots to cook on this stovetop. What are you making?"

"Roast saddle of antelope." With his shirtsleeves rolled up, Brendan was sharpening a variety of knives that were laid out on a huge wooden chopping block planted squarely in the middle of the room.

"Oh, are you expecting company?"

Looking up at her with that devilish glint in his eye, Brendan replied, "Yes. You."

Elle was so shocked, a hot flush rose in her chest. "Oh, my. No man has ever cooked for me before! I can't allow that."

The blades flashed in Brendan's hands, and he didn't miss a beat. "It's a privilege for me, Miss Elle. There's no one to cook for here. Gainey and Victoria's idea of good cooking is a base ball park sausage, ancient mutton boiled 'til it's white, and beans boiled 'til they're mush. I, however, learned the great cuisine of the Chattahoochee River. Evin wouldn't be alive today if it weren't for me because he'd be subsisting on slugs and bark."

Elle laughed. "No, dear heart, you absolutely must let me

help. What can I do? I'm afraid I'm of the same gastronomical learning as Evin."

"You can chop that mint." Brendan handed her one of the freshly sharpened knives, then went to a counter and came back with a wine bottle. If he kept grinning with that seductive look, Elle was going to chop off one of her fingers. Uncorking the bottle, he said, "Sorry it's only port. Port for the chefs."

"Oh, I adore port. Now you must tell me . . . what happened in Edo? What did you find out?"

"Oh, it was Ologboshere, sure enough, I could tell by the cut of his jib. And he flat out admitted it, of course, being such an all-fired arrogant ass." He handed Elle her port glass, and cleared his throat. "Excuse me. I had forgotten you are fond of him."

Elle shook her head, frowning. "No, don't apologize. You know him much more thoroughly than I. Why would Ologboshere wish you dead? What can I chop now?"

Brendan slammed some garlic cloves down before her on the butcher block. "Smash them with the side of the cleaver first, it makes them easier to peel. Oh, he seemed to have gotten an idea into his head that I was in cahoots with the British, that I was the factotum for Captain Phillips, and that it was really my wish that the Oba open trade, and I would stand to gain by being set up as head merchant between Edo and the British."

"No! You wouldn't! Why, you *love* Edo!"

Brendan nodded grimly. "My feelings exactly. And that's what I told him. I said I'd stake my affidavit on it that someone had been filling his head with these ideas. He wouldn't tell me who, but I done finally put my finger on it. It were your erstwhile husband, Rip McCullough."

Elle put down the cleaver. "Rip? But he doesn't even speak the tiniest of Edo! How could he tell Olog—"

Brendan rested his knife too. "Miss Elle. Can you not see that man is hot for you? Why do you think he's followed you around the world all these years? Never taken a mate? Elle, he hates me, am I not correct?"

Elle finally shut her lower jaw, as she knew she looked despicable gaping like that. "Well, I have to say no, Brendan. No. I mean, if that were the case, you'd think he would have tried to kiss me before now! No, you are dead wrong. He has never tried to kiss me." As if to change the subject, she returned to chopping the garlic.

Brendan shrugged. "But you will admit about Rip hating me."

"Well, yes. But he only so-called hates you for the reasons I stated before. He's protecting me in his own way."

Brendan threw all the fat trimmings into a bucket. He hauled another bucket full of water to the chopping block. "Darling." He reached into the bucket to withdraw a beautifully fresh oyster. Elle's eyes widened and she went to his side to look into the bucket, which was chockablock with the living shellfish. Brendan, however, had other thoughts on his mind. "Darling . . . Just what was it this bastard did to you?" he asked gently.

Elle looked down at the ground. "Oh, it was more like a succession of bastards. It's just that I've never been the number one priority in any man's life, and I kept fighting against that. I wanted to be the number one important thing in a man's life, I thought it was natural to expect that. It was a fruitless fight. There was a man to whom opium was the most important thing. Then a man who worshipped his daughter above all. Then a man to whom his wife was the most valued thing."

She shrugged. "Then I finally stopped fighting for it. I decided to give up all men, that through celibacy I could concentrate more fully on my career." Shrugging again, she picked up the cleaver. She hadn't meant to tell Brendan anything of other men. "Now I know. I'm just not the type of woman a man wants to marry and be faithful to. I don't know what it is about me, but I am not the stuff of which wives are made, in the minds of men. I am always a mistress, whether it is to a man's daughter, morphine, or wife.

How did you come by oysters?"

"No," Brendan nearly shouted. Easing the cleaver from her hand, he took her by the shoulders. "*Amebo*, no. You just met up with a passel of jackasses. Don't you want a normal life, husband, children? Don't give up on it."

"No!" she cried, surprising even herself with the force of her outburst. "No children! Never. I would not risk it."

Gathering her to him, he held her firmly. "Risk? Would it be hurtful or dangerous for you to bear a child?"

Elle didn't want to talk about this, either. Why was he forcing her to discuss painful things? "Well, you see . . . My mother was confined to a lunatic asylum with a fundamental mental derangement. There is some worry that it might be handed down, hereditary. Although, as you can see, I am completely normal in every respect." She laughed and tried to make light of it, but Brendan continued to hold her tight.

"Why, yes, that's true of course. You're the most normal, lovely, enchanting woman I've ever known. Who wouldn't be completely enthralled with you? I don't understand these bastards . . . And I don't agree you should give up having children, darling. There is no proof lunacy is hereditary. People say the same of boozers and rummies, that their children will turn out the same, and I've not seen it."

"Yes? And what do *Ivbiedo* say?"

Brendan seemed to stop breathing. His eyes flitted sharply about her face before he said, "No man from a hoity-toity family would marry a woman from a family with a known history of insanity."

Elle touched his hot throat. How she wanted to kiss him! "There is more than just that. I have no wish to inflict . . . I'm afraid I might be as bad a mother as my mother was. She was terrible, Brendan. We raised ourselves after the age of seven, we had to steal food. We slept in carriages and barns. I told myself I would never repeat this, that I would work to fight for the honorable cause of the poverty-stricken, that I would always be well-off so as not to want, that I would never turn the other cheek to a person in need. And to do this, I have to be free of encumbrances, of men who make demands. Does this make sense?"

Brendan shook his head. "It's one of those ideas that looks good written down, but doesn't work in real life."

"But it does! It works splendidly. Rip is perfect, because he's not my sweetheart or husband, so he doesn't ask questions like 'where were you last night.' You see, it's perfect. Fact, he revels in and laughs at my adventures!"

"No. Because what happens if you're so dead set in your boring, staid existence that a man who could bring zest and thrills to you walks right by, and you don't even recognize him?"

"Oh, land's sake, Brendan!" Elle realized with a chill she had used Brendan's favorite saying. "That's the whole point. What if I don't *want* the zest and thrills because I don't consider them as such? Therefore for such a man to walk by without recognition would be a blessing indeed, for it would spare me the agony of finding out that he prefers his wife to me, or his backgammon to me, or his goat to me, don't you see?"

Brendan looked at her as though he would find the secret to a buried treasure map. "No. You'll be lonely."

"I have family."

"No. A sister isn't the same thing, Elle . . . No. It's too much of a shame for a gorgeous jungle flower like you to remain chaste, to turn into an old maid. Don't you like our sex?"

His abrupt inquiry startled her. "Of course I like our . . . 'man-palaver,' of course I do." She ran her fingertip down the bridge of his exquisitely sculpted nose. She brushed her lips against his; she could feel him panting, sweating like a horse at the bit. "Really, you are the most adept and talented lover of them all. That's why I'm drawn to you."

"Aye, is that why?" He licked her lips salaciously, sending electric shivers down her spine, and without thinking she opened and clamped her thighs around the side of his hip. They breathed into each other's mouths as his fingers hovered around the edge of her collar. "Fucking . . ."

"Yes . . ."

"Being fucked right smart, reamed deep by a stud such as myself?"

She ground her pelvis into Brendan's hip as he spoke lewdly into her mouth like that. "Oh yes, Brendan. You are the best. I cannot keep my hands from you." She slid her palm inside his opened shirt collar, sighing at the feel of the silken chest hair. She craved to slide her hand down the plane of his belly to grasp that prodigious cock by the root, but was afraid he'd think her too bold, too hungry, too crazed by female hysteria. "I'm addicted to you like an opiate, it is that painful being separated from you."

"Because I can satisfy you?" he whispered obscenely. He bent slightly at the knees, humping up and into her against the solid wooden chopping block, taking a great bite out of the side of her throat while tearing her tie from her throat, popping the buttons at her dog collar, laying her entire chest bare to the air. "Because you need my Irish meat inside you?"

"Yes, dear heart . . . yes!" Brendan buried his face in her cleavage, brutishly snarling, licking the entire length of his tongue into the cleft. "You drive me crazy, my dear one." How lush, the silkiness of his still-damp hair against her breast, how erotic, his long thick penis humping her thigh as he mounted her like a satyr, brutish and bald of desire. It was such power to hold a man in thrall like this, to make him hot and delicious as aroused men are. "My mouth waters to taste you, I dream of your body all day and night."

"Like this?" He divested her of her skirt, the petticoat swiftly following to pond up at her feet.

"Oh . . . here? Where are Evin and Miriam?"

Brendan swept the chopping block free of all knives, but when he grasped her by the shoulders and turned her to face the block, she could see he'd left the food she'd chopped. A raw hunk of meat was setting there.

He took her brutally, dog fashion against the block of wood.

His long thick penis seared her from stern to stem. She suffered, because she had not been used in the past four years. In one aspect, it was divine to stand there on her little heeled beaver shoes with back arched, and to be ravished by such a fine specimen of man. His curving over her back, having his way with her, all of his lust and desires and fears concentrated in his crotch, it was almost too painful to bear. Elle clawed at the wooden block, her bare breasts smashing the mint into the wood, making mincemeat of the garlic. *Is this what his cooking is like?* she wondered vaguely. And *does he do this with other women in his kitchen? For he seems capable.*

However, his moment of crisis had her melting, warming around him. His quickening, the enlarging of his penis inside of her, the vulnerability when he gasped out, *"Olokun!"* Bowing her back toward him, she knitted her fingers at the back of his neck behind her, her belly tight and strained, engulfing the entire length of his maleness. He cradled her, lowering her back to the wooden surface. He gathered a handful of her hair in his fist and lifted her face to kiss her, and both had the fixings of their dinner smeared to their chests.

Elle felt a surprising tear squeeze from her right eye. *It must be the garlic*, she bitterly told herself. She felt closer to Brendan in that moment than she ever had to Rip or her own brother, and the intimacy terrified her.

Brendan yanked her back to stand erect, disengaged his penis from her, and casually stuffed it back inside his pants. After rinsing his hands in the sink, he went around the chopping block to refill the port glasses. Elle was relieved not to feel compelled to engage in personal talk. She rearranged her clothing as though it were an everyday event, a man taking her in his kitchen, and she felt much more mature and in control of her emotions.

"You never told me what was so medicinal about your brandy," Brendan said, almost darkly, as he handed her the glass.

"Oh, didn't I? Well, I have, it's nothing really, just a touch of rheumatism. It really only affects me when it's cold and damp, which is why this climate is refreshing for a change."

His startled eyes stopped their roving, and alighted on her. "Rheumatism? Ah, that's no good, darling." He then set his jaw, and picked up the knives he'd swept onto the floor. "I suppose brandy'd help for pretty near anything."

"I mix it with gum guiacum—that's the medicinal part, not just the brandy, mind you," Elle giggled. "Should you think me affected with alcoholism."

Brendan continued to pat herbs onto his antelope, seemingly uninterested in her tale. Elle meanwhile entertained herself by shaping the chopped herbs back into their discrete little piles. "Evin gave me your poem. I was so impressed, I must have read it twenty times."

Now Brendan bent to a low cupboard and was clattering around with what sounded like an arsenal of medieval armor. He said nothing until he withdrew a large cast iron pot, brought it over, and banged it onto the chopping block. "Yes, I'm sure it was impressive calligraphy."

Elle frowned slightly. What had she said or done wrong? Maybe she was a failure as a lover; he was disappointed in her, that was it. She gushed even more effusively, "You have the ability to paint such a picture with words! I was able to mentally imagine almost everything—though what did you mean about the 'bang and the clatter'?"

"Just poetic license."

"Oh," Elle said, crestfallen. Why was he belittling his own poetry?

The evening continued like that. Elle was increasingly aware she had done something wrong, and she squirmed all night attempting to find out what it was. All she could conclude was she was an unsatisfactory lover, and how could she improve that? She would be damned if she'd ask Rip for advice. And there was no other man in the country who would know as much about it as Brendan! The few women, of course, would probably advise her she had allowed Brendan to take too many liberties, and should practice reading the Bible with him instead.

She knew she had committed some irrevocable blunder in his eyes, and she should do as Rip said, gather her papers and go back to New York. She was a failure as a woman! She had always known that. Wasn't she just telling Brendan that very thing?

She should stick with her work. Work never let one down, or made one cringe with shame.

15

"All right, enough beef, iron, and wine." Brendan set aside the brown bottle of thick slime. He dumped the contents of his tumbler out the porthole, and returned to his chair "I don't care how depraved my blood is, I'm not touching this stuff. You can tell that fellow that."

That was one of the many good things about Evin. He sheltered Brendan from the few eager supercargoes who made it that far into the hinterlands. All Brendan had to do, with Evin as middleman, was to sample a small bit of the wares, a procedure that oftentimes had both men holding their stomachs with the grippe.

"What's next? That better not be Pasteur's Microbe Killer again."

They leaned back in their wooden chairs, feet up on different stacks of papers on different desks. Brendan still hadn't succeeded in getting the ceiling fan to work, and flies crawled around their necks and hands.

Evin frowned, brandishing the tall bottle and reading the label. "I think that Pasteur's killed more than just the microbes. This here is Peruvian Wine of Coca."

Brendan nodded, clenching a cigarette between his teeth as he proffered an empty tumbler to Evin. "Peru, eh? Pour it, for land's sake. What's it supposed to do?"

After pouring Brendan a goodly two fingers of the stuff, Evin read from the explanatory leaflet. "It sustains and refreshes both the body and the brain. They urgently recommend its use for consumption, nervous debility, biliousness—"

"Oh, good," declared Brendan, and downed the entire glass.

"—malarial complaints, loss of forces and weakness caused by its excesses—"

"*Ah!*" Brendan exhaled mightily, so astringent was the brew, but pleasing and invigorating. He looked blankly at Evin. " 'Loss of forces?' "

Evin squinched up his face. "Ah, you know, those advertisement writers."

"I really like this! Try it, Ev!"

Evin poured himself some as well. "Is your body refreshed?"

At the mention of "body," Brendan remembered to be bitter and hard, and he said, "No, thank Olokun. Only my brain."

He knew Evin was looking at him quizzically, as well he should. Brendan had had a weed on ever since his antelope dinner with Elle. It hurt him that she wanted a man who didn't ask questions, who didn't want zest and thrills. She wanted to sail through her life as a man'o'war, getting fucked by the longest dick in town, and then continuing on her journey around the world. Sure, she seemed witty and gay, and full of a poetry that was richer and more meaningful than any other woman's. That was just part of her hard New York façade.

She had admitted she was only drawn to him because he was a talented lover, leaving him bitter and angry. He ducked from her the next few days, spending most of his time on his war canoe, doing some mud-fishing with Evin, and target practicing in a nearby clearing. He knew that if he ignored her long enough, she'd get bored without sex, and return to New York.

How fickle modern women were!

Evin snorted. He sounded skeptical. "That's too bad."

"And what's that supposed to mean, old partner?"

Now Evin frowned something fierce, gulping his glass and slamming it onto a stack of papers. "Nothing, of course! Jeez, I'm starting to think mayhap you ain't fit for the likes of Miss Elle! Yes, we had a good talk at the house. In my books she's a right fine woman; I had the best feelings about her, better than the last thirty women you brought over, and I don't want to see you get worse and worse, Bren!"

The men glared at each other.

At length Brendan snarled, "How'd you know it had to do with Miss Elle? I don't goes around—"

"Keep your shirt on," Evin snarled back. "Here are the shipping papers for this Peruvian wine. I take it you like it. Why don't we get some; it'll go over good with the Portuguese crowd." Reaching down with one sweeping arm, Evin snatched several papers from the floor. He didn't look at them, just shoved them at Brendan. Brendan in turn snatched them so vigorously that a few pages tore right in two.

"Now look what you done!" Brendan cried. He took the pages to a porthole, sticking a fresh cigarette in his mouth, trying to match up the edges of each page. "God-damned Peruvian coca wine, turns men into a cyclone hurricane . . . *Avast!*"

But the last was said in a hushed tone, and Evin didn't hear, just poured himself some more wine.

It was the cablegram from New York City. Brendan had completely forgotten about it after rolling it up in the saloon and shoving it into his back pocket. It must've somehow fallen out when he was . . . Well, he didn't want to think about it.

With renewed steel to his limbs, knowing he could angrily face whatever the cablegram said, Brendan held the two pieces of paper together. He realized his hands were shaking.

As far as he'd gone in his reading, he could make out some of the cable:

OCTOBER 25 1896 NEW YORK

DONIVAN

INFORMATION ELLE BOWIE STOP IS SO CALLED xxxxx REPORTER FOR NEW YORK WORLD xxxxxxx PUBLICATION OWNED BY JOSEPH PULITZER A DAGO OR JEW STOP AROUND WORLD WAS TO GAIN xxxxxxxx FOR PAPER STOP ELLE BOWIE REAL NAME COLLEEN VOLJACEK ANOTHER JEW NO DOUBT STOP HOWEVER ELLE FAMOUS IN NEW YORK MUCH BELOVED STOP DO YOU WANT MORE VIRGINIA TOBACCO YOUR SERVANT BOB GRIMES

Brendan felt as though his brain was bleeding. It sent a cold ichor running through his head, as if a huge ball of ice had been flung at him, and the pieces were running down his shoulders. He was stunned for several long moments during which Evin kicked papers around on the floor, muttered to himself, and tried to fix the ceiling fan.

Then it struck Brendan: *the treachery*. She was a reporter, someone who pulled off flamboyant tricks to gain attention, sort of an advertisement-writer for a newspaper, and this Joseph Pulitzer was probably the man she'd mentioned, her "mentor."

She was only here to write an exposé of the Oba, the human sacrifice, to gain attention for her boyfriend's newspaper.

Brendan's brain fairly seeped onto the pages he held in his rattling fingers. And what of this name . . . Colleen Voljacek? Her *name* wasn't even real.

The jig was up. If he ever let her come a-nigh to him again, he would shoot her.

" . . . and I think if you'd just manfully lay to waste all these highfalutin feelings you've been throwing around, you could just admit to yourself—What?"

Evin stopped bloviating when Brendan socked him in the ribs with the cablegram. Brendan even went as far as to grab Evin's shirtfront in his fist. "*Read this.*"

To give Evin enough time to read, Brendan found the bottle of Peruvian wine and poured himself a few more healthy fingers. He steamed such fire through his nostrils, he had to go to a porthole and lean out of it, as though that would do any good with the humid effluvium of mankind rising from the river below. *She was a traitor.*

When he finally turned furiously back to Evin, Evin looked somewhat ashen. His face had fallen like a corn cake, and he kept whispering, "Land's sake . . . land's sake . . ."

Brendan blew a lungful of cigarette smoke onto Evin's head. "Well? Well?" Impatiently, he tore the papers from Evin's fingers simply in order to have something to shake around. "Does *this* help in your highfalutin eulogy and tribute to the divine Miss Elle? She's a *reporter*, Ev, does that explain what her aim is here in Edo? She's out to *expose* the blood-letting human sacrifice, to rile up the public outcry, to give the Army an excuse to march on in and slaughter everyone! If anyone is in cahoots with the British, it's her!"

"But . . . but . . . " Evin looked like a doll, with black buttons for eyes. "But she's *American*! What does she care about a British colony?"

Brendan rattled half of one page in front of Evin's face. "What does this say? She's a *what* reporter?"

"Stunt reporter. That means someone who does things to get attention, to gain publicity for the newspaper. Such as, remember her talking about going into that asylum? Except I'd call it more of *investigative* journalism; that's how it's done. A writer pretends to be someone they're not in order to gain entrance—"

"Exactly! So it weren't no high-minded spiritual thing of helping the downtrodden and poor and suchlike—no! She made that up, just like her name—what's that name?"

"Colleen Voljacek. Sounds Polish, not dago as our illustrious friend Bob notes. She probably changed it for her job, a pen name, people do that all the time. Bob's a fine one to talk, anyway, with a last name like Grimes."

"Never mind that! What I'm saying is, we have to double-cross her back again." Unable to tolerate this betrayal any longer, Brendan roared and waved his clawlike hands at the heavens above. "Oh *why*, *why* did I not let Ologboshere make her dance on air from the *Iroko* tree? That's it! I'll go back to Edo, tell Ologboshere everything, and—"

Evin was on his feet now, holding out calming sacerdotal hands. "Keep your shirt on, Bren. First things is first. I think you should go to Elle and tell her what you know. Mayhap there's a decent explanation for this. Mayhap our upstanding pal Grimes got some of this information wrong. This Joseph Pulitzer—"

"That's the boss she mentioned. Probably a lowdown, no-good—"

"—is hardly a cheesy operator, Bren. He owned the *St. Louis Post-Dispatch*, if I recall rightly, before apparently going on to buy this New York *World*."

"—toad who is one of the men responsible for turning Elle into such a conniving, craven excuse for a girl!" Brendan helped himself to more of the deleterious coca wine as he continued to rant. "Not that that excuses her, because it doesn't! Oh, she got more than she bargained for if she calculated I'd just let her run over me like fire in dry grass. I'm striking out for her house, you had better bet, Ev. But I'm just going to tell her that I know her for the lowdown witch she is, and—"

"No!" Evin's shout was so unexpected, Brendan buttoned up on the instant. "No, you're not, Donivan. You're in such a state you're liable to get in a tussle with that cowpoke photographer, and he looks like he could be lethal if he put his mind to it. No, a much better plan is for me to talk to her. I'm reasonable, I can state things clearly."

Brendan put his face right up to his partner's, and he spoke "reasonably and clearly." "Was you the one holding that woman in your arms like she was the treasure at the bottom of the sea? Was you the one on your knees with your face in her muff, slathering at the trough like a starved bull? Was you the one so besotted and blinded by desire you entertained the notion you was in *love* with her?" Brendan shook his head. "I think not, buddy. Now. You just let me handle this my own way."

But he didn't. He went to bush, hunting alone for several days to stew and seethe, to wonder how he could have been so stupid as to imagine he loved Elle. He caught guinea fowl, turkey, boar, and a nice duiker, and busied himself cleaning and dressing the game at his hunting hut. He paid tribesmen to bear the critters back to Evin in Sapele, but he himself stayed out in the jungle. He wrote poetry that seemed to be spurred on by his anger, surprising himself with the memory of many words Evin had shown him.

Above all, he wanted to be beholden to no one.

~ ~ ~

At first she was patient, and waited for him to come around, to show at her door with his sparkly eyes, his brass leopard hip ornament. Out one of her front windows, she saw him come and go from his house, surrounded by sycophants and assistants, never once glancing her way, going to the anchorage. And then he must have left town, for she saw him no more. Then she saw tribesmen bringing game birds and animals to the house, and she knew he was hunting.

She could have easily gone to chat up Evin, as she still saw him around his house. But she didn't, for her pride prevented it. It was one thing to be that rudely dumped after having given her body so freely after so many years. It was quite another thing for her to slither over and try to obtain information from his partner. She could not, would not do that.

Still, she could not leave. The rheumatism decided to take a turn for the worse. It had not been true what she'd told Brendan about the warm climate alleviating the pain. She had never found a correlation between weather and pain, and she drank more medicine than usual. As a result she was in a state of sluggish torpor much of the time. Then, Rip was having such a gay time with Victoria, he no longer asked when they would return home. She saw the happy yet somehow evil glint in his eye whenever Brendan's name came up, or his absence noted, and he started inviting Elle along on his social outings.

So Elle went, becoming necessarily more intimate with Brazza, but squirming from his clutches when she felt he might move with impunity.

One evening after she had begun packing her things in preparation for departing back to Old Calabar, Elle lay on the sofa, enervated. A copy of Tolstoy's *Master and Man* loaned her by Caroline Forshaw sat open across her breast, and her fingertips swept against the floor. There was a slight commotion at her door, but she paid it no mind, accustomed to the natives' dramatic upheavals. Her eyelids barely fluttered.

And then there was the once-beloved stomping of river boots into her living room. Elle hardly dared to hope, and she forced her eyes open.

There he stood in the flattering yellow glow of the oil lamp. Fresh from hunting, he wore his Edo costume, his hair smeared back into a pigtail, the earthy mossy smell of the jungle emanating from him. His face was unreadable, and he lowered himself onto an ottoman.

"I didn't mean to wake you," he said quietly.

"I'm not sleeping." Elle struggled to her elbows, clearing her eyes as she curled up like a cat on the sofa. Although wearing her striped tennis skirt, she had dispensed with the shirtwaist and had been lounging in her camisole. She didn't care. She had an instinctual feeling the outcome of this meeting would not be to her liking anyway. Still, she made a feeble attempt by managing a smile. "I'm glad you came by."

He had no expression. "I know who you are . . . Colleen."

She felt sick. Her bowels turned to water, and her heart sped so fast it rattled her chest. She took deep breaths to clear the phosphenes from her eyes, but it didn't work. "Yes, Colleen Voljacek was my birth name. I thought Elle Bowie a much better *nom de plume*. Why does that bother you?"

Narrowing his eyes, he shook his head. "It's not just the name . . . Colleen. It's the entirety of who you are. You're a stunt reporter for the New York *World*, not an anthropologist. My only conclusion is that you're here to expose the bloodletting of the Oba, to help the British, to give them an excuse to invade Edo."

Oh dear God. Her voice was weak and faint when she said, "Brendan, no. I admit I'm not an anthropologist with any Society, I admit I work for the New York *World,* which by the way *is* a newspaper dedicated to 'expose all fraud and sham, fight all public evils and abuses, and to battle for the people with earnest sincerity.' Joseph Pulitzer hired me to fight the good cause."

Brendan snorted. "Your *boyfriend*," he seethed. "A damned good way to get a job . . . Colleen."

Oh, how she wished he would stop calling her that! It was as though he thought Colleen a lowdown traitorous snake, and could never call her Elle again because Elle was the virtuous, upstanding crusader he had imagined her to be. Now it was Elle's turn to frown, and snort hotly. "The boyfriend part had nothing to do with the job part, Brendan, and came much later, I'll have you know. I was hired based on a study I did of divorced women, and through that I was able to change some of the unfair marriage and divorce laws. I've investigated unsafe child labor in factories, unsafe housing and inadequate plumbing facilities and—"

"And just how did your around-the-world stunt fit into this philanthropic picture?"

Huffing and puffing, Elle flounced to her feet. Brendan sprang to meet her, muscles coiled up and bunched. She hissed, "It was strictly a stunt, as you said, Brendan. I told the paper I could best Phileas Foggs's record of eighty days, and I did. If you're looking for signs that I am a shameless manipulator, well then you will find those signs. A woman doesn't become a successful reporter without being ten times better than the next man. I was told I couldn't be a reporter, that I couldn't go here or there, and I shouldn't go here or there. So I did! I had to go ten times farther than any man merely in order to keep abreast of them. And you come here accusing me of being tough and callous, well then, I suppose that's something that happened to me along the way, and I can't change that."

Brendan didn't immediately answer. Elle panted, out of breath from her uncustomary outburst. She felt a twinge of hope that he might melt from his apparently murderous position, but that hope evaporated when he said, "If there's anyone who's a traitor it's you—maybe that idol was meant for you."

Elle was stunned speechless. Hadn't he heard a word of what she just said? Suddenly she hated him! Rip was right after all; wasn't that always the unfortunate case? Tears welled in her eyes when she finally uttered, "If you think I would really do that, then you *are* a heartless bastard." She snorted acrid air through her nostrils, oozing malignancy at him. He looked to soften a little bit, but Elle continued to speak. "I first came to this coast because of a *dream* I had once, Brendan—yes, a dream! The kind where you fall asleep at night and have a vision! But I had to come up with an idea for my editor, so I proposed the human sacrifice angle that Burton had written of. I needed an excuse, for why would he pay for me to follow a stupid *dream*? So yes, at first it was a 'stunt' as you call it. But the more I knew of Edo, the more I knew I couldn't write an exposé that was so one-sided. If I were doing that, I could have seen the corpses and left, but I stayed to find out more, the beauty, the traditions, the beliefs behind the sacrifices. And in that way I do consider myself an anthropologist. If you think for one minute I've been pandering to the British, then you need to hone your trader's and hunter's intuition and tracking skills, Brendan."

Brendan blinked at her, all rage apparently dissipated. He spoke tentatively, quietly, poised like an animal about to pounce. "A . . . dream?" He frowned.

He attacked her, then cared about her *dream*? What kind of man was this, anyway? Elle couldn't let him see her cry, so she started to the sideboard for more brandy. With her back to him, she said, "Yes, a dream! A dream of a jungle with a walled city, with red mud houses, and a twenty-foot long brass serpent atop the king's house, if you must know. So I researched, and found Burton's description in *Fraser's Magazine*, and—oh! What do you care?" Pouring her brandy from the decanter, she spoke to the wall. "I knew then that if one would become great, there are two necessary things. To know yourself, and to not let the world know you."

His voice was suddenly reverent, though to Elle's foggy mind that was probably an illusion. "A serpent? And what else?"

Elle sniffed, and turned mechanically. Why did he have to look that devilishly handsome, even when accusing her of rotten things? "And brass heads of the Oba, and a drawing of a leopard— Oh, what does this matter, Brendan? You've already set your heart against me. I think you should leave now."

Brendan nodded. Wordlessly, he walked backward, never taking his eyes from her face. Why he should be so transfixed Elle had no clue, nor did she care anymore. Yet another man to whom she wasn't the most important. What was more important to him was Edo.

Pausing at the door, he seemed to want to say something. He lifted his hand, but dropped it, and was gone.

Elle did burst into tears then. She flung herself onto the sofa face-first, and sobbed into the pillow like a toddler. Oh, that devil was so lucky Rip wasn't at home!

CHAPTER
16

The hot dry harmattan winds started blowing from the north, from Sokoto and Kano, caking the soil and bringing clouds of impalpable dust. This relief from the humidity was usually a call to celebrate *Oyinbo* rituals such as Thanksgiving that brought on a month of festive soirees, white citizens happy they had survived another year.

This year, however, Evin was quiet and distant, obviously disapproving of the harsh way Brendan had dealt with Elle. He stuck to the *Hindustan* and his arboretum where he was ensconced crossing his lilies-of-the-Nile, orchids, and cannas. Miriam assisted him constantly; in fact she must have learned to be a plant expert herself, and was virtually worthless as a maid. It sent Brendan into an even deeper funk to see his dirty clothes still lying where he had thrown them, and he tried to stay out of his own house. Then he was constantly running into Elle on Brazza's arm, Elle and Brazza in the market, Elle and Brazza in the saloon, Elle and Brazza taking a fishing party upriver in the launch.

She was still the most beautiful woman he had ever seen. He forgave himself for having thought himself in love with her, for her beauty was overwhelming; clearly every other man in town was in agreement with that. That dashing Count with his elegant aquiline nose, long tapered fingers, and seductive accents was probably vastly more suited to the sophisticated Elle than a corn-fed hick such as himself, who after all couldn't even read that well.

One day he had been unable to avoid them; they had called for his taxi canoe to stop as they ran up the beach in their attempts to reach the *Hindustan*. Brazza and several other men laid their hands all over Elle, draped in a stunning new crimson velvet frock Brendan had never seen before, in their efforts to help her into the canoe. Her eyes met Brendan's, he didn't lower his, and he did tip his panama hat to her. But it was Brazza who did all the babbling.

"Mister Donivan. You see this most amazing woman?"

Brendan blinked to indicate he did indeed see her.

"She has brains, she has smarts as well as beauty of the highest degree. I tell her if she comes to Algiers with me, there are news-papers of international reputation, she can write about war and famine and corruption, but no!" Elle sat looking forward with compressed lips. "She say she rather stay and write of gruesome human sacrifice." Brazza bowed low to the stolid Elle with a face of unabashed devotion. "*Mademoiselle* Elle." Did Brazza know Elle was unmarried? A sudden claw of apprehension grabbed Brendan by the throat. "Algiers is much more cosmopolitan for a beauty such as you."

"Perhaps *Mademoiselle* Elle finds things of a more fascinating nature here in the Oil Rivers," Brendan stated. He hadn't thought before the words left his mouth, and he had no idea of the meaning behind them, but the effect they had on Elle was frightening. It was as though all the sun drained from her browned face, her eyes went circular, and she swiveled her head toward Brendan like a figure in a wax museum.

"Yes, there are endlessly diverting things to be seen here," she intoned without emotion. "Exotic plants, skulls on platters, tattoos of leopards, absolute poetry in everything."

"You see?" Brazza expounded. "She is the most interesting woman!"

The canoe had reached the hulk now, and although Elle continued to bore holes in Brendan with her scary deranged eyes, a dozen men's hands hustled her up the ladder, and Brendan was left to bob unsteadily in the canoe, wondering to himself: *tattoos of leopards* . . .

Shortly after the canoe incident, Brendan finally received word from the Oba about Phillips's request for palaver: the Oba would be celebrating *Igue*, the annual tribute to the ritual of Head worship, and he asked Phillips to delay his visit until after the ceremonies. Brendan knew the Oba had postponed his reply until he was able to accurately say he had begun celebrating *Igue*, so the reply was expected. Brendan set about preparing to personally carry the message back to Old Calabar to Phillips, who had been hounding him for an answer, but was further perturbed by another interruption.

He was in his pantry, checking if anything should be thrown out before he left, when Miriam appeared in the doorway with bugged-out eyes.

"Daddy Massabren, whiteman, whiteman say he no can wait, whoa-whoa!"

"Berrah well, Miriam, I'll see the whiteman; does this look like weevils in this flour to you, or is it just pepper?"

But Miriam was too distraught to look at the weevils, so Brendan handed the canister to her as he exited the pantry, and was nearly smacked in the head by the full height of the imposing Rip McCullough, who had taken it upon himself to enter Brendan's house.

Rip poked Brendan in the chest with his forefinger. "Donivan, you've been griping me for quite awhile now, and I aim to have it out with you."

Brendan instantly matched his rival's voice in tone and volume. He grabbed the hammy forefinger and wrenched it away, shouting, "If that's your aim, it will please you to keep your hands off my person." He strode past the lout into his kitchen, knowing that by putting his back to the man he was showing complete unconcern about the cowpoke's punitive abilities.

"Listen here, you good-for-nothing rogue," Rip roared. "I'm here to tell you that Miss Elle is much too good for the likes of you, and I want you to put a stop to this brutality right here and now."

Brendan didn't turn to face Rip until he'd reached the far wall cupboard, where he folded his arms across his chest and laughed with disbelief. "I don't know what continent you've been on, partner, but you obviously haven't noticed, Elle and I called it a day awhile back."

"No," Rip shouted. "You may have viciously and ruthlessly given her the bounce, but the effects of your heartless carousing still linger on."

What? Brendan was stunned to the bone. Did he mean what he thought he—

Rip cut him to the quick. "Nah, praise be to Olokun I don't mean that. I mean that that good woman, intelligent, sensitive, creative, with a heart so good she doesn't deserve to have it splattered about by the likes of you, she's still pining and heartbroken, and I want you to put a stop to that."

The idea that Elle pined for him infused Brendan's soul with happiness. "How exactly do you know she pines for me?"

Rip swept Brendan's existence away with a swipe of his hand. "Wouldn't you just like to know? I can see it in her eyes, you bastard! She barely eats or talks, can't sleep, doesn't do nothing but pace all night and read pumpkinheaded Russian novels, she has no hankering for fresh out-of-doors exercises, because *you* dumped her and all for what? Because you found out she was a reporter?" Rip shook his head with exaggerated denial while Brendan's heart swelled painfully with happiness to hear of Elle's disability. "Hoo-boy, are you ever on the wrong tack."

He approached Brendan closer now, looking from side to side as though someone were eavesdropping, and he spoke with gentler, more confidential tones, pointing at but not touching Brendan's chest. "Buddy, that gal is *the* most respected journalist in all of New York City. She's had murder threats because she stepped on the wrong toes by being the only person who cared enough to squawk about deadly and unfair labor laws and living conditions. Why, she wrote a story that had them building a new public bath with fifty thousand customers paying a nickel apiece in the first year alone. She posed as an unmarried mother to expose the baby-buying trade. I say to you, buddy, that you're not even fit to shine her shoes. How *dare* you give her the boot just because she had the nerve to write about human sacrifices!"

Brendan splayed out his hands, palms toward the floor. "Rip, I had a fit of anger when I first heard things such as her real name is Colleen Voljacek, and that she meant to show the Oba for a bloodthirsty maniac. You have to admit that looks pretty low and shady to someone like me whose livelihood depends on commerce with Edo. That's all. I have never denied that she's a woman most deserving of the highest respect. Fact, I agree that I'm not good enough for her, she deserves someone more like Brazza."

This time Rip did poke Brendan in the chest, but Brendan didn't budge. "I'll tell you she deserves respect. Why, she met Jules Verne himself in France! Do you know what the city of New York did when she returned from going around the world in seventy-two days? They threw her a tickertape parade! Yes sir, buddy, right down Broadway! Banners welcoming home Elle Bowie, the Daredevil Female Journalist!" Now Rip's hands, and his rapturous eyes, described a scene of grandeur as he looked to the heavens with his memories. "They wrote songs about her, buddy, and had dolls in her likeness! Why, her face was in advertisements for soap and chewing gum. A racehorse was named after her!"

Brendan stammered, "I had no idea . . . "

"Why, of course you didn't, buddy, because you're just a dumb-headed stiff! And then she goes and chooses the Guinea Coast for her next assignment, when she could have been in Moscow for the coronation or covering the Battle of Adowa in Ethiopia!"

Brendan was appalled. He was shocked to find himself in agreement with Rip. "And just how do you propose that I help make Elle happier?"

"By being such a hell-fired bastard that you leave her no choice but to leave this place. Go and tell her to stop moping around, that you're done with her forever. Only don't tell her that Brazza is the better man, for I don't like anything about him, neither."

Brendan exhaled deeply, shaking his head. "That I can't do, Rip."

"What? And exactly why not, buddy?"

"Don't you think Elle can decide for herself whom she prefers?"

"But I thought you were eager to set her free, and—"

There was the clamoring of more boots, and from the hallway Evin appeared, brandishing Mateus with an eagle's grip on his shoulder. "I found this one lurking out front as usual, Bren, and I couldn't get rid of him."

Mateus flung his arms about like an acrobat to shake off Evin. "Will you let *go* of me?" Straightening his greasy vest, he swaggered into the kitchen waving a piece of paper in the air and proclaimed, "Mr. Bowie"—for he still felt compelled to maintain the farce that Rip and Elle were married—"I have the most upsetting news to impart to you. What we thought was Elle sleeping quietly in her bed was in reality a lump of clothing, and she has left this note."

"What?" Brendan and Rip yelled at the same time, both leaping to grab the note from Mateus.

There was a brief tussle, and it seemed then that Mateus gave

Brendan the advantage, as he leaned in toward Brendan and took the brunt of Rip's scratching on his back. Brendan leaped back the victor, praying to Olokun he would be able to read the note.

Rip, he read silently. *I have gone to Edo to set right what you have done wrong by Brendan. Please wait for me, but if you won't, please leave my papers and xxxxxx in the care of Mary Wells. Your xxxx servant, Elle. P.S. It was not I who stole your xxxxxxs.*

As Evin was now looking over Brendan's shoulder, Brendan pointed to the last word. "What did she not steal?"

Evin read aloud, "It was not I who stole your . . . " then he grabbed the note from Brendan. He read it intently while Brendan told him in a low voice, "I've got to go to Old Calabar to give that message to Phillips. Can you follow her to Edo and make sure no harm comes to her?"

Evin didn't look up from the note. "What?"

Impatiently, Brendan repeated, "Can you follow Elle to Edo and make sure she's all right?"

Rip had Mateus in a stranglehold on the floor and shouted, "Why'd you give that note to Donivan, you rotten dwarf!" Brendan tore the paper from Evin's steely grip and thrust it at Rip. Rip had to let Mateus go in order to wrest the paper from Brendan.

"Will you—"

"Follow her to Edo, of course I will. Of course I will, Bren."

Rip was reading aloud now. " 'Your obedient servant, Elle. P.S. It was not I who stole your condoms. Well, then. Who did?" He looked down at Mateus, who was sitting Indian fashion on the floor.

"Don't look at me, *camarada!* What use would I have for those things? Women are like a foreign nation to me."

Brendan pointed out, "You could use them to store things, flour and sugar and suchlike."

Evin added, "Or fill them with water and throw them at people."

Rip snarled, "You lousy toad!" and resumed throttling poor Mateus. Brendan and Evin headed for the hallway.

"Bren, I want you to patch things up with Elle. If I'm following her, I warn you, I'm going to build up your reputation so high you're going to have nowhere to fall but down."

"You would do that too, Ev. I never told you. The reason she came to this coast was a dream she had. Ev, she dreamed of the Oba's palace, of the brass serpent he's got on his roof. She dreamed of the gates, houses, and the heads that are *inside* the palace gates."

"Aye, that's a mighty profound thing."

"I know it. It scared me well nigh into fits, Ev. There's no denying she's got all kinds of power."

Standing before the front living room window, both men folded their arms in front of their chests and stared out. One could see Elle's house from here, the wooden one-storey structure raised on stilts above the mud, but plain with no garden, as it had always been a temporary house for visitors. The thought that Elle wasn't there, would not be returning, was a frightening one to Brendan.

"And you're going to patch things up with her," Evin told him.

Brendan shook his head. "She's not for the likes of me. What would a renowned gal from New York want in Sapele?"

It seemed that Evin frowned at him then. "Maybe plenty."

~ ✒ ~

When Elle reached Edo, she discovered that Ologboshere and Lieutenant Ugiagbe were away at their training camp in Obadan. She sent messages to Ologboshere through his minions and while she waited, first Evin and then Rip turned up in Edo.

Evin took her out to his farm and showed her where he was crossing blackberries from Himalaya with berries from California. He had Oriental plum trees, quinces, and walnuts. It was a strange dichotomy of pain and pleasure to walk with Evin, Brendan's partner, the man closer to him than anyone in the world, and be unable to talk about him. When she staggered a little crossing an irrigation ditch, Evin caught her elbow in his palms, and he kept his hands on her as they walked down the line of shady fruit trees. It was such a reassuring gesture for him to make that Elle took his arm and held it tight, and felt emboldened to say, "I have come to set things straight with Ologboshere. I know it was Rip who fouled Ologboshere's mind about Brendan, made him think Brendan was in cahoots with the British, and I want to clear that up."

Evin nodded at the trees in his quiet, shy way. "That's admirable of you, since it was none of your dirty doings to start with. I'm sure Brendan will let you know he appreciates it, when he gets here. You do know he had to go to Old Calabar to tell Captain Phillips—"

"Yes, that the Oba has the gall to insist on retaining sovereignty and trading independence."

"Yes. There will be trouble. I don't see Phillips fixing himself when he hears."

Elle sighed. "Serenity and peace breathe inexplicably from this place of 'savage chaos.'"

"Yes. Brendan says it's the *Akpo r'Oba*, the Oba's world, and *Akpo r'Oyinbo* is coming to oust it."

"No," she said, vague now. "It is too big of a shame."

Elle met with Ologboshere, using as a translator an *ekhen* who had helped her learn Edo in better times. She explained that she was very sorry that her husband had seen fit to lie about Brendan, but he was severely jealous of her friendship with Ighiwiyisi. There was nobody in cahoots with the British; all Americans from Boston thought the Liverpudlians the height of imperialistic chicanery.

"Tell him they are like big oafs—no? Big idiots—no? Big dumbheads? Oh, my."

Ologboshere waved away the chattering *ekhen*. In his formidable leopard skin soldier's outfit, he shook his staff so barbarically it was a toss-up as to whether he was radiating rage or friendship.

But at length the *ekhen* told Elle, "He say he understand. He say he want to keep you close to him."

"Yes, but does he *believe* me, that Brendan is completely innocent? That Brendan worships the Oba above all else, and would *never* bring harm to any *Ovbiedo*?"

More chattering, and the *ekhen* told Elle, "Yes. He say he want to keep you close to him. He say when you hear from the Consul when *Oyinbo* come, you tell him. Ologboshere."

Elle rose, and had the sudden inspiration to kiss Ologboshere rather chastely on the lips again. She smiled knowingly at him, the heat and the fecund musky smell of him mingling with her own rather rank odor—she had been formulating the theory that in Africa, one began to smell like whatever one ate. And Ologboshere had clearly been eating crocodile. "*O khui-khui vbee ason, orhienrhien vbee owon*," she breathed next to his ear. *As black as the night, as sweet as honey.*

Ologboshere uttered something she hoped was approval, and she backed out of the room, bowing.

~ ⋘ ~

Several days later when Elle returned to the guest house from the market, Rip was lounging in the front courtyard with his feet on a mud bench. He did a comical vaudeville leap when he saw Elle, a cup of *tombo* flying into the air, something like a cheroot crashing in a clay ashtray to the ground.

"Elle!" he cried, smoothing out his denim pants.

Elle frowned. "You seem to have been expecting Oscar Wilde. What is that sm—*Cannabis!* Rip, don't tell me you've been smoking hemp!"

Indeed, Rip's bloodshot watery eyes seemed unable to focus

on Elle, and it struck her he'd looked that way for some time now. "Ah, honey, there ain't no harm to a little hemp once in awhile. It's completely natural, it's not near as toxic to the blood as, say, opium or morphine."

Elle continued on into the house. "So you decided not to go back to New York."

"Without you?" Rip followed her. "Are you fooling around? Honey, you're my entire life. Besides, Pulitzer would pop me off if he knew I left you behind in some savage jungle."

"Yes, he would miss the income from my sensational articles."

"Aw, come now, honey. You know he's been sick, holed up in that yacht in Maine. He loved you as well he could. Who wouldn't love you? You're the most lovable woman I've ever laid eyes on."

Elle was not impressed. Along with losing trust in Brendan, she had lost faith in her partner as well. She felt so dead inside, sometimes she actually thought Mateus was the most trustworthy man on the planet. Everything was upside-down. "I'll have you know. I told Ologboshere that you're a big liar, that you completely invented that bilgewater about Brendan siding with the British, that it was due to your rampant jealousy, and that it would never be repeated again."

With raised eyebrows, Rip rubbed his bare belly. "Well. What did the old boy have to say?"

Elle swept off to her bed room, uncaring if Rip followed, though of course he did. "He says I am to tell him the second I hear of *Oyinbo* heading our—I mean, this way."

"I'll keep that in mind. What are you doing tonight?"

"Right now I am bathing at the *Oyinbo* pool. I haven't bathed in three days and I feel like a cane rat."

"Any special occasion?"

Elle rolled her soap and eau de toilette inside her towel. "Yes. *I* am dining with Evin. He's a dear sweet man, and I think very highly of him."

"Aw, honey! Ain't I invited?"

"No." Elle set her jaw grimly. "I doubt that Evin appreciated the finer aspects of you telling Ologboshere that Brendan was in cahoots with the British. And just possibly Brendan and I didn't get the joke, either."

Elle was thoroughly grateful to be allowed to wander alone down the path by the beach, through the creamy wooly "smokes" that hovered about the rivers, sometimes all day during the dry season. Satisfied nobody was following her, she made a hurried cut off to the side path that led up under the giant looming silk-cotton trees. Soon she could hear the waterfalls that created the pool, clouds of grey parrots swarming high above, and it pained her afresh to have to clamber over the silk-cotton root where she had sat with Brendan, when he had recited the frog poem into her ear.

What had happened to him? For he had turned remote even before he had discovered her true identity.

Elle tossed her towel over the root and hoisted herself over it. She was midway into the short leap down to grab her towel and continue on the path when she saw movement, a flash of white in the black adamantine pool. Holding her breath, she slid her Derringer from her thigh holster, then froze, gripped with an emotion she wasn't able to identify, something between terror and joy.

It was him.

Like a glorious white heron against the bottomless black water, the only other color the overhanging pastel blooms of hibiscus and orchid, Brendan bathed in the shallows of the pool. His sun-browned shoulders flickered under the dappled sunbeams through the jungle canopy, and his gloriously well-made rear was almost blindingly white against the glassy water. Elle managed to duck behind a tree trunk before Brendan turned around to grab a cake of soap from the bank and lather his hair. He piled his hair up in a mound and rubbed it around, then bent headfirst into the pool to rinse it out.

Merely the sight of the man, bending backward now into the pool, then emerging to stand erect, pressing the water from his head like a seal, was enough to render Elle immobile. A ball of heat between her thighs began spreading through her loins; her heart accelerated so rapidly she was afraid she might faint. He was such a thoroughly masculine animal, looking up blankly at the mossy twining jungle covering above him when he bent back to squeeze his hair out. Elle could even see the twinkling in his eyes from her distance of ten yards or so. *How has Osanobua made such a man? And how has he driven us apart?*

He turned to again take up the soap, and Elle saw it: the tattoo she had only dreamed of, back in New York. A stylized leopard baring its fangs, claws outstretched in attack, the leopard curved around the agonizingly exquisite lower swell of his behind, a savage leopard in indigo ink about five inches in length, the same leopard of her dream.

She was so rigid with shock and fear she completely forgot to breathe. She went dizzy when Brendan soaped his chest slowly, almost salaciously, reaming the lengths of his fingers inside his armpits and lingering over the gloriously well-developed pectorals, the mat of hair creating a field of bubbles. When his long thick penis engorged and started rising, without him ever touching it, Elle gulped a sudden lungful of air. Brendan didn't appear to hear as he cocked his hips forward and ran his lathered hand down over the mound of his pubic bone, cupping it, squeezing it with the thickness of his fine well-made thumb, his other hand sliding between his clenched thighs to grip his balls in his broad, strong hand. Elle sucked in air like a beached catfish.

His penis leaped tight to attention before Brendan had even touched it, the full length and breadth of it shiny as brass. He ran his hand down over the root of his cock, pleasuring himself with an overhand stroke. He slithered the thick length of muscle between various fingers, snaking and squeezing his fingers around the shiny mushroom head, languorously, as though in no hurry to meet his climax. With his head thrown back to reveal his full throat, his glossy wet hair playing a chiaroscuro pattern with the sunbeams, he was the most incredible man Elle had ever seen. Utterly naked save for his leopard hip ornament, religious medal around his neck, and the bracelets that played up and down his forearms, Brendan brazenly fondled his balls and massaged the breadth of his stupendous erection, as though to further torture her with the most erotic sight of her life.

Brendan's eyes suddenly flew open. *He was staring directly at her.*

His hands stilled on his member, he drew himself up to his full height in the water, his eyes violently assessing the jungle, his nostrils flaring. He was for all the world a leopard scenting out his prey, and it was as though an icy python had strangled all the life and breath out of Elle. Her hand that still held the Derringer twitched and shook, but she didn't heft it. She knew she was doomed, for to have such a man set his sights on you was a certain death sentence. A tornado would be the only thing to distract him from his prey now.

It seemed to take him only three seconds to spring from the water, leaving a shimmering curtain of glass behind him, and cover the distance to her. One moment he was an achingly gorgeous Roman statue in a fountain, now he was a heartless predator. Elle did not bother to flee. The jig was up. Fact, she even backed up against the mahogany tree to display to him her submission.

He came around the back of the tree, suddenly boneless as he curved with utter fluidity around the trunk, clamping her hips between his powerful thighs, and pressing his Bowie knife blade into her Adam's apple. His eyes flashed with rapacious malignancy, his upper lip curled back from clenched teeth.

Did he not recognize her? "Brendan," she breathed.

"Why are you here," he snarled.

Apparently he did recognize her. That was even more

disheartening. With his free hand he had cinched both of her wrists high above her against the tree trunk. She found she could only move her legs, should she choose to fight him. "To bathe. Please let me go."

His savage tone changed to lascivious, and with his mouth not three inches from hers, he growled in an unfamiliar voice, "Why should I? You have taken me with your eyes when I was unawares. Now I shall take you." He lowered the Bowie knife to trace a pattern down her bare chest to the top of her sarong, for she was clad in Edo style.

"I'm sorry, Brendan. I just came here to bathe, and I happened upon the most . . . amazing sight . . . of my entire life. The sight of you overcame me, I was petrified to the core. I have never . . . seen . . . a man pleasuring himself before. Please forgive me."

"Aye," he growled, and Elle felt the thick head of his penis pressing like a wooden beam between her thighs. "And you liked what you saw."

"Oh, yes." She was able to relax now, though he still slightly pressed the tip of the knife against the swell of her breast. She felt her eyes become limpid, and another trickle of moisture rolled down her inner thigh. "You imagine you are scaring me, but the proximity of your body is having the opposite effect on me . . . sir." She added that "sir" to be polite, for she didn't know how he felt about her now.

He uttered a low, "Ah," as though taken unawares by her response. She was nearly blinded by the sparkly furor of his turquoise eyes, the way they fluttered over her face, the heat from his chest pressed up against hers; it was enough to drive a woman crazy. "I don't scare you?"

Elle smiled. "No. You make me hot."

Brendan smiled, too, looking at every angle of her face as though searching for the feature that would tell him she did not have a screw loose. "Aye. . . . you're a sensual seeming woman,

Elle, and you bring out the randy beast in me."

Rubbing her spine against the trunk of the mahogany, Elle cocked her head coquettishly. "I like the randy beast in you. I like everything about you."

Brendan lunged forward with his hips, pinning her more firmly to the tree. "You're a woman to bring out the best and worst in a man. I could take you right here," he breathed into her mouth. His eyelids slid shut then, and bringing the knife point down so he could grip her waist, he kissed her.

His kiss was soft and sweet, laden with ephemeral moans, and all the tenderness Elle knew Brendan contained in his soul. He still gripped her wrists above her head, but it was a gentle and almost loving way of covering her now, as he swiveled his hips to grind against her, the bursting head of his penis smashed directly on her clitoris. She squirmed her hands to be free, to touch his shoulders, and he let one of her hands go.

His shoulder was like a stretch of sun-warmed velvet. Gasping into his mouth, she gave a little hop, allowing him to back her up the tree trunk, so that her toes were barely brushing the ground. *Oh, how glorious, to be in his arms.* But was it only sexual . . . again?

"Brendan, I . . ."

"Is this what you want . . . my eager strapping cock?" And he took her free hand and led it to his enormous penis that was straining against her lap, bidding her wrap her fingers around it by the root. It was like gripping her own wrist, and her inner canal quivered up and down its length to feel such a prodigious member in her hand.

She was still able to find words to protest, though her caressing, admiring hand was clearly stating otherwise. "Brendan, I don't want . . ."

His voice was kind now, syrupy. "What don't you want?"

"I just don't want to be . . . a hunk of meat to you."

There was a brief silence during which Brendan latched onto

her with his dazzling eyes. Then a smile began at the corners of his mouth. "And just what do you think you're doing to *me* right now?"

Elle's jaw dropped. He allowed her imprisoned hand to go free, and she stepped clear of the tree, smoothing down the mussed lap of her skirt. Breathlessly, she said, "Yes, you're right. It's very improper of me. I'm sorry, you're just so desirable."

Brendan didn't seem to mind that he stood almost completely naked, his penis not having taken Elle's rebuff to heart at all, for it throbbed in its tight purplish state. "And if you're not a hunk of meat?"

"I'm a woman, and I have emotions other than lust! Brendan. If you hate me so much for being an investigative reporter instead of an anthropologist, then I don't think I can bear having your hands and body this close to me."

His voice was plaintive. "I don't hate you, Elle. I don't hate you at all. I admire you and respect you. You was just doing your job."

I admire you and respect you. He remembered that was her preference to the dreaded "love" word. "If you don't hate me, why have you avoided me as though I had bilious fever?"

He didn't answer immediately; she could hear him shuffling his bare feet in the detritus on the ground. "I hated you at first. Now I just think you're much too high-class to want a river varmint such as myself."

"Will you let me make that decision for myself?"

"Yes, Mrs. Bowie."

Elle burst out laughing at the conciliatory tone of his voice, and she turned back to face him. She allowed tendrils of happiness to creep into her spirit then, and she felt buoyant, elevated as she hadn't felt in an entire month. "And I admire and respect you . . . more than you'll ever know." She lightened her voice. "Evin invited me for dinner. He's such a dear, sweet man, I think we get along famously. Is that all right by you?"

Again that urchin smile. Elle wanted nothing more than to

reach out, grab him by the ears, fling him on the ground and have her way with him, but she didn't feel it would be appropriate. "Then I'll set the house apart for your especial use, and strike out for the men's *tombo* hut."

Elle's jaw started to drop, but then she saw the devilish glint in his eyes. "You right bastard!" She faced him squarely now, and pointed at the ground. "Don't you get thorns in your feet?"

He shook his head. "No. Tough feet."

"Oh. Well, then. You might get thorns in something else."

That smile was the wiliest yet. "Let me rinse off the soap. Then the pool's yours."

CHAPTER

17

"Then Brendan takes off all his clothes, piece by piece, and throws each piece over the casks of rum."

Elle laughed joyously. "Why, in God's name?"

Evin explained, "That way, he's giving the booze the protection of his own body, according to Egbo law, and nobody can touch it. He knew they'd get oiled if he let them start drinking right away."

Elle looked down the long table, American tapers warmly illuminating her lovely face, her lips tinged lavender by some artifice. The two Irishmen sat, as was their custom, at far opposite ends of the table so as not to be contaminated with the other's microorganisms, and Elle had been compelled to measure her seat directly in between the two. She was a vision in red glass ear drops and the crimson velvet frock Brendan had seen her wear in the canoe, when she had been on Brazza's arm. She directed her question at Brendan. "And just how many casks of rum were there?"

Brendan smiled crookedly. "I'd estimate well nigh twenty."

"Twenty!" Elle turned back to Evin. "I hope he was dressed for a winter snowstorm in St. Petersburg."

Evin stood, taking the bottle of California wine down the table to Elle to refill her glass. "No, he was dressed for the Oil Rivers. We were in Bonny, so it could have been worse. We could have been in Edo. As it was, he had enough clothing to cover only about ten casks, and he sat there nude on his stool waiting for the crowd to become orderly."

"And you didn't offer your own clothing?"

Brendan answered that one. "No. He bounced up on the instant and made himself scarce."

"Evin Jordan does not disrobe for savages," Evin added politely.

Elle laughed melodiously. "But Brendan Donivan does."

It seemed to Brendan she was looking at him rather more warmly than she looked at Evin. He was going to have a difficult time standing with a hard-on that could break a platter, but he was determined to be gentler and sweeter with the beloved woman. After all, that Pulitzer fish probably laid his gnarled old white hands like tissue over her body, so she was not accustomed to a rough tough. "I do, when it'll save my factory from being burned down by a crowd of loafers and rummies."

Evin continued, "Then, of course, a runner came with a message from another nearby town. So-and-so had died, the funeral was in progress, and of course someone had to be responsible for causing the death, and that someone was about to be rubbed out if Brendan didn't intercede, so what does he do? Grabs a big piece of paper and scribbles something on it, takes his sealing-wax and stamps bits of it on the page, and sends the runner back with it."

"What is that for?" asked Elle.

Brendan answered. "To distract them. By the time they've gathered round and had a long palaver about the mysteries of the whiteman, I've had time to settle my own hash." Brendan used that tactic quite often, and he smiled at the memory. "I think I wrote a grocery list, as that was on my mind at the moment. Things like tomatoes, bananas, limes, pawpaws . . ."

"Oh!" Elle cried. "You really *are* a devil! No, Evin, you must let me clear the table."

Evin stacked the china plates on top of each other. "Stay here and amuse my buff naked partner."

Elle remarked, "Oh, and Miriam's not here to help. No, I don't suppose she would prefer to return to Edo after what happened."

Evin vanished down the hallway, and Elle stood and moved her chair closer to Brendan. In a hushed voice, she asked, "What *did* Miriam's husband do that he was crucified for?"

Brendan hated this topic. She had asked directly, and he could not avoid it. "He stole a dog to eat."

He expected the revolted face she made. "Disgusting. However, hardly a crime to be killed for. Was the owner of the dog someone important?"

Brendan inhaled and exhaled. "Yes. Me." He hurried to add, "I was hunting in the jungle nearby with my dog. I came busting into Edo looking for her, and what I found . . .You don't want to know, Elle. The glory ain't mine. I made a big stink 'til they came and got him. I had no idea he'd be crucified. That was my first introduction to the city of Edo; I thought they'd make him pay me a few cowries."

Elle laid a hand on his bare forearm. "Oh, Brendan. I am sorry. But it came out all right because you took Miriam and her son back to Sapele. I am sure Evin will be thanking you forever for that."

"Aye, because she was converted to Christianity." Placing a hand over Elle's, Brendan said, "I have some mail for you that was brought to Sapele."

He led her to the front room where he had stashed the letters postmarked New York in his secretary. "I am sorry not to invite your 'husband' to our dinner tonight," he remarked casually as he handed over the letters. One was from the New York *World*, and one was from a jackass named S. Bozzio.

"I told him he wasn't invited." The sight of the letters already distracted Elle, and she drifted toward the front door. "I told him in no uncertain terms, after what he did . . ."

"Here, *amebo*." Brendan lit a lantern for her to carry out front. He politely waited in the front room, half-heartedly perusing the new Walt Whitman book he had been studying, proud he could read a large percentage of the words now. The past month, without the prospect of any rendezvous with Elle to occupy his mind, he had given a right smart effort to "reading book."

He saw Elle's shadowy profile as she sat on the bench on the front stoop. She was bent over the pages of the letter, reading intently, then she took something from the envelope and gazed at it for a long time. He heard her sob, muffled at first. Then she started sniffling, and put her hand to her mouth.

Brendan went out front. "Darling, darling," he said with what he hoped was a soothing tone. He sat beside her on the bench, and lifted the curtain of hair from her face, making sure to speak into her ear so she didn't think he was looking at the letter.

It was as though she held her breath now. He could feel her shoulders quaking under his palm, but no sound came from her. Brendan gently kissed her wet cheek. "*Amebo* . . . please tell me why you cry. It pains me to see you in distress."

At last she drew a jagged breath, folding the letter with trembling hands. "Oh, dear heart . . . I just . . . miss my family so much!"

Brendan took her by the shoulders, and placed his fingertips under her chin. She didn't want to face him, and only intermittently looked up, the shuddering in her limpid eyes too much for him to bear. "*Amebo* . . ." He lightly licked another rolling tear from her cheekbone. "You'll be back with your family soon. Are they in New York City as well?"

"Yes," she uttered, her lower lip trembling like an adorable child. Sniffing, she brought a piece of paper up right smack in front of his eyes. "See? That is us; Milos had it made before I left to come here."

Brendan had to hold the paper at arm's length to view it. Apparently taken in one of those photo studios where one always looked rigid like cold meat or a banker, it was the most glorious depiction of Elle in her finery. She wore a Persian lamb hat adorned with ostrich feathers, and a lamb jacket with wide lapels. She looked directly into the camera with a face arrogant and prideful of the two men standing bestride her. One was a ridiculous beanpole of a man, haughty for no apparent reason, as his limbs looked to be all put together by a prankster puppet maker, with no regard to shape or form. His large bulbous nose resembled a gourd. The other fellow was an angel with long shimmering locks and round agate eyes. He seemed uncomfortable in his stiff attire, and his gleaming hoop ear-ring, not unlike Brendan's, told that he would rather be a pirate at sea.

"Ah, they are a fine family. Which one is your brother Milos?"

She pointed to the bulbous-nosed fellow. "And this is my dear Sal."

"Which is the older brother?"

"Milos. Sal isn't really our brother. We came upon him in the early eighties, when we were just children ourselves. He was an orphan in a very bad part of town, and we took him in. Not that *we* had much to offer." She giggled then in a very nearly hysterical manner, bringing her hands back up to her face, and Brendan regretted he had no pockets for a handkerchief.

"Elle, Elle . . . " Brendan whispered in her ear, cupping her chin in his palm. "I would never harm the tiniest piece of skin on your beautiful body. I know you miss your family, and if you stay here there's going to be trouble. No," he hushed her, blowing lightly on her forehead and eyes. "It's dangerous to stay in Edo now. I know Phillips is going to mount his own expedition for Edo regardless of what the Oba tells him. I heard Phillips telling Captain Cockburn of the Protectorate Force, 'I have reason to hope that sufficient ivory would be found in the King's house to

pay the expenses incurred in removing the King from his stool.'
He underestimates our army; he thinks we're cowards, and Moor
has nothing to lose if Phillips miscalculates the situation."

"Oh! I am not leaving Edo without you." Elle hurriedly
stuffed the letter back into the envelope, along with the photograph. She patted it firmly into her lap as though it might blow
away, then she flung her arms around Brendan's neck. Pulling
herself up on him until her bosom rubbed erotically against his
chest, Elle touched the tip of her nose to Brendan's, and whispered urgently, "When I go there, I go there with you. That's all
there is to it."

Brendan lifted the woman up and onto his lap. She perched
there lightly like a shorebird, rubbing her nose against his. How
sensual it was, holding her fully clothed like that, with the petals
of her mushy honeypot smashed ardently against the head of his
penis. This lush, exquisite crimson lady, she was too good for a
savvy palm oil ruffian who dwelled in mud huts, performed
bizarre rituals, and captured leopards! "Elle, you must leave
with Rip, go back to New York." Her silky hair spilled over his
fingers when he cradled her skull in his fingertips like that.

She spoke down at him with determination. "I'm not leaving,
dear heart. I'm not going to let you rot and burn when those
lime-juicers come. I'm dragging you out of here with ten horses
if I have to." As if to shut him up, she kissed him deeply then,
sucking his lower lip into her mouth and nibbling it between her
incisors. Just as swiftly she withdrew, a look of terror shading
her features. "I dreamed of your tattoo before, in New York! It
was the same leopard, facing the same way, with the same claws
and teeth, in the dream with the walls, the heads of kings and
queens. I knew I would find it here!" She slid her fingers down
over his bare hip, as if to caress the tattoo she knew was there.

"Yes . . ." Brendan mused. "You've got leopards in your head,
amebo."

But the woman was searching for something with her eyes,

looking, stroking the side of his face with her free hand, touching his lower lip with her forefinger, panting all the while with a look of such utter concentration Brendan felt it a shame to ruin it all by standing.

He lifted her there in the feathery warm air of the garden, and he barged back through the house, through the darkened hallways he knew so well he could navigate blind drunk. She felt light as a heron in his arms, though she was a tall woman, for he was suddenly imbued with Herculean strength, as though preparing to wrestle a leopard.

In his bed room he found his bedstead with his feet, and he laid her lightly on her back. He knew most women preferred the dark, but he stubbornly lit a lamp, and went to kneel between her outspread thighs. His bed room had suddenly taken on a new aura, as though a harem draped with curtains, everything lush and rich, the mosquitoes swarming against his window screen. His penis under the *eruhan* arced obscenely over Elle's flung arms, her hair squiggling out on the woven coverlet like a siren luring mariners to their death, her breasts swelling over her bodice.

Brendan felt for the chain of his Saint Christopher's medal, lifted it over his head, and bent to slip it over Elle's head. He wasn't sure why he was doing it; there wasn't a logical sentence strung together in his mind that told him to do that. She smiled, though, and fingered the warm medal, then he took the letter she had patted into her lap, removed the photograph, and set them both on the night table by the bedstead, with the photograph facing her.

She remonstrated with girlish ire, "I don't know what my family would think, watching me tussle with a stallion such as you." But she smiled, and reached up her hands for him.

He planted his fists on the mattress on either side of her face, looming large above her. "I was hoping you'd gain comfort from the sight of your brothers."

Elle stroked the side of his face. "I find comfort in *you*."

She was too much. She was too much for him to bear.

Wrenching down her velvet bodice, Brendan dove in and licked her breasts until her nipples stood out. She cradled his head to her bosom, purring leonine sounds that brought out the devil in him. Raising himself to his knees, he divested her of the voluminous cardinal skirt. She squirmed with delight, a seductive angel with plum-bitten lips, his medal jostling in the valley between her breasts.

When she lay spread out with only stockings, shoes, and corset on, Brendan gathered her with such force she was lifted up bodily from the bed, and had to grip on with eagle's talons to the back of his neck. Nose to nose, Brendan breathed into her mouth, "I love you, dear Olokun in heaven . . . I have loved you forever, Elle."

Mayhap it was his imagination. But it seemed then that the woman wound her thighs more tightly about his hips, and gripped onto him for dear life. She panted into his mouth, and uttered strangled animal sounds, and frantically clawed away the feeble pieces of cloth at his waist.

He slid into her deeply, easily. Her shoulders felt like the wings of a bird when he crushed her in his arms. He humped her with such ardent force that he scooted her across the slippery sheets, and her head hung over the edge of the bedstead. The look of her throat laid bare to him, her unfettered hair tumbling over the earthen floor, was enough to drive Brendan out of his head. He erupted inside her, dimly aware of a groaning, keening animal sound somewhere in the room, outside of himself.

Gathering her to his chest, Brendan laid her back onto the raft of pillows he kept at the headboard. She twined around him effortlessly, like a rubber doll with no joints. She smiled, her brown eyes glimmering with rich light.

They kissed. The cicadas outside in the dense undergrowth serenaded them crisply. She lifted the hair from his face, and she seemed happy, her features smoothed out.

"I want to stay with you forever."

Was he imagining it? Mayhap he was in a waking dream, such as when one tried to light the lamp, only to find one's hand went through the match box. One could wander through hallways in those dreams, looking for more matches, but whatever one's hand touched only turned into vapor. A man was left feeling he had no impact on the world.

"Stay, Elle. Stay."

They fell asleep like that, nestled in each other's limbs.

18

That year brought the happiest holiday season of Elle's life. As there was no further word from Captain Phillips in regard to his plans, perhaps everyone was hoping he would just forget about Edo, and festivities abounded in Sapele. In order to demonstrate the benefits of Christianity, Charles and Mary Wells threw open the doors of their mission to orphans, mothers of twins, and others in anathema. Elle had never felt an affinity for children, but she spent more and more time at Mary's caring for the afflicted. She was quietly delighted to find how soothing it was to cradle a babe. Mary made a sling for Elle, a sort of papoose she could carry a child in against her breast while going about other tasks, incessantly boiling water, and peeling and pounding yams for the *fufu* that was a staple of life. And, although Elle proclaimed that "when God made me, He must have left out the part that one believes with," Mary continuously told her she was made for His work. Elle replied, "If the aim of life were happiness and pleasure, then Africa would send us missionaries instead of us sending them to her."

And, as Brendan and Evin had promised, they trimmed a wild custard apple situated between the Riverside Quarter and the

Farmland Quarter. They draped it with hippo grass and curtains of lycopodium, then fastened candles with bits of *tie-tie* and ribbons Brendan had appropriated from a crate of men's neckwear. Every evening at six o'clock there was a pilgrimage to the apple tree. The entire town gathered around at this time to see what strange *juju* the *Oyinbo* were up to. Brendan hoisted a child onto his shoulder to light the candles he could reach, and one of Mary's parishioners climbed a ladder to light the rest. The candles were usually extinguished in the harmattan winds, but it was a nice comforting ceremony everyone enjoyed. Evin brought his guitar and Brendan his banjo. Parishioners brought a wild mélange of shakers and rattles decorated with cowries, drums with bells, and the *kora*, a stringed gourd that approximated a harp or lute. Together, they all made enough noise to keep the leopards awake, playing songs Evin had taught them over the years, such as "We Three Kings," and appropriately enough, "Jingle Bells."

They all hushed up for "O Christmas Tree," sung with just the guitar and banjo. Elle shivered with delight to stand next to Brendan, listening to his fine clear tenor that seemed to sail above the trees and roofs. Her own voice was rough from years of disuse, but the memories of singing cowboy songs with her brothers as youths came back swiftly. After the songs around the tree, they would walk through the Farmland Quarter singing the carols. Vince Gainey in particular put his all into it, belting out the tunes at the top of his lungs, enjoining the Africans to match him in volume, which they proceeded to do with gusto. Mary Wells imagined they converted a lot of Africans simply by virtue of their singing, which the Africans could understand, unlike the monogamy, ban against dancing, and staid prissiness of the other aspects of *Oyinbo* religion.

Elle woke up at Brendan's house every morning in his bed under the "naughty" painting. It was only "The Bath of Psyche" by Lord Frederic Leighton, not indecent at all with its Corinthian columns and angry El Greco sky. Brendan was usually out fishing or hunting by that time, and Elle joined Evin in the arboretum for coffee and pancakes with groundnut paste. Evin was in thrall with holiday cheer, giving festive pepper plants and holly bushes to Mary's parishioners, and the townspeople Miriam thought worthy of a Christian plant. Then Elle marched out boldly through Brendan's front door, still wearing yesterday's ensemble, as she would never be so bothersome as to keep a wardrobe at a man's house.

Elle discovered some of Brendan's endearing rituals. Before greeting anyone in the morning, he wet his finger with spit, drew it over a tiny receptacle of chalk, then down his forehead before saying "May every man, woman, and child do good to me." She did not let him know she was watching, and later had Mateus translate what he had said. It was just another one of those super-stitious ceremonies that Elle was beginning to believe in herself.

And the food! Elle knew she should have to stop being a glutton soon, but that day was always around the bend. Every day Brendan brought into the kitchen guinea fowl, antelope, squab, ostrich, partridge, wigeons, and geese (thankfully, never the cane rat). The grandest meal of all was the buffalo. Brendan roped in a dozen townsmen to carry it back, and he gave away the parts he didn't need, which was most everything, as the *Oyinbo* were stuffed near to bursting. There was Nesselrode Pudding made with French chestnuts from a can, dried plums from Evin's farm, and sherry wine. There were macaroons, persimmon bread, Potatoes à'la Maître d'Hôtel, Roman punch, and a sauce tartare with a sort of flaming smelt. Not being much in the way of a cook, and her brothers thinking fine cuisine was pouring beer over mutton, Elle dredged her memory for platters her mother had made. She remembered *sauerbraten*, and in Brendan's kitchen she recreated it with a hunk of the buffalo that had been marinated for days in vinegar, peppercorns, and the leaves of an acacia.

Elle spent one day in Gainey's parlor with Mary, Victoria, and Caroline cutting into bits old lace frocks sent over by the

Christian Missionary Society. This was brazen of Mary, for the mission could have clothed many *grandees* in fine tacky style with the pieces the women glued to their Christmas cards. These cards necessitated some outings to gather foliage, and the women capered about the town after drinking Roman punch, jamming their baskets full of ferns, hart's tongues, and elkshorn. Elle would never have imagined she would enjoy such a sappy and homely activity, and indeed in New York she would not have been seen pasting cut-outs from *Godey's Ladies Book* onto a card destined for Mr. and Mrs. Nigel Appleby of Devonshire. But somehow, in the exotic smokes of the Ethiope River, the air refulgent with the perfume of a thousand brilliant blooms, it imbued Elle with a happiness she'd never known.

She wrote Joseph Pulitzer a cablegram that she sent by the Cross River Transport informing him that STAYING SAPELE STOP. FINISHING TRAVEL STORY STOP. TREES FOOD CUSTOMS NATIVES FRIENDLY STOP.

She was beginning to wonder if there wasn't more than sexual attraction to Brendan. She would catch herself feeling a vast affection for him, sometimes sleeping in bed with her limbs flung around his bare back, her face nuzzled in the nape of his neck. Certainly one didn't kiss a man on the back of his neck like that when he slept, if one did not care more than a little for him. Of course he was a most singular man, the legendary Guinea trader with bones and feathers in his hair, the leopard hunter with the panache of sartorial splendor, the angel with the mellifluous tenor. So even if it was only an evanescent fling, it was good for one's digestion and blood, and he certainly wiped the cobwebs from the recesses of her womanly places.

~ ~ ~

This was supposed to be good for his back, but Brendan felt like the biggest goose.

He reckoned it was Elle's revenge for making her drink a tea made from umbrella tree bark, which he knew to be good for rheumatic pains. Now she was forcing him to sit on a mat on the floor with his legs straight out ahead of him, reaching his arms to the ceiling. Breath and movement should come together exactly, she told him, and this seemed to involve the silly use of all manner of panting and grunting Brendan thought more suited to sexual pleasures.

But it was enjoyable rolling on the floor with Elle in her drawers and chemise, Brendan naked save for his Balbriggan drawers.

"Postures are balanced in yoga," Elle said, on all fours on the mat. "We must follow that back stretch with The Cobra, so stretching and compression are complemented." She unwound her long-limbed body until she was flat on her face, forehead against the floor, hands at her sides. "Feel comfortable and relaxed."

"In that position?"

"You must have the right attitude." Elle's voice was muffled. Lifting her head and shoulders clear off the mat, she then brought her hands around in front of her, raising her upper body into an approximation of a cobra, Brendan supposed. With eyes closed, her nostrils flared with her quiet breathing. She was cherubic, and Brendan felt a swell of tenderness toward her.

When there came a big banging at the front door, Elle's hands slipped on the mat, and her eyes popped open. "Oh! My concentration is ruined."

Brendan moved his hands around her limbs to assist her in sitting. "Ignore them. Probably just some varmints hollering about fish hooks or pomade." For her exercises, Elle had pinned her hair into a loose bun, and Brendan now took pleasure in slipping some pins from her coiffure, and giving her sucking kisses to the side of her neck until he could see the fine little hairs stand out all a-shiver.

"You keep that up," Elle purred, "and you shall be getting

your massage and rubbing *before* you bathe."

The pounding on the door increased in intent, and a beefeater was shouting, "Dash it all, Donivan! The pullaboys told me you're in there!"

"Oh, avast." Brendan kissed Elle's neck several more times before getting to his feet. "That's old John Swainson, he's got a factory next to mine in Warri. I best see what he's a-hollering about."

"Aye," sighed Elle.

Brendan drew on pants and left his bed room shirtless, snapping his suspenders onto his shoulders as he went down the hall to the front door. "Keep your shirt on, Swainson," he shouted, grinning to himself that they were that casual with each other, familiar with each other's shabby attitudes in these "rivers of corruption."

"Donivan." Swainson nearly fell into the room when Brendan opened the door.

"What're you making so much fuss over?" Brendan locked the door behind Swainson again, in case some of the varmints he could already see malingering on the veranda could not read his sign that said, "no admittance except on business."

He led Swainson to the sitting room, and before he could even pour two whiskies Swainson was breathlessly telling him, "It's Captain Phillips. A runner came this morning with the news. He's formed a palaver party in Old Calabar, and they've already left."

"Who's with him?"

"He's got Captain Boisragon of the Protectorate Force, Peter Copland-Crawford, Art Maling of the Sixteenth Lancers . . ." Swainson caught his breath. "And two traders, to demonstrate that it's not an imperial palaver."

"Which two?"

"Harry Powis and Tom Gordon."

"Tom?" Rolling whiskey around in his mouth, Brendan went to a side window where he could look out at the veranda garden without a dozen faces peering at him. "I'm surprised at Tom. Old Powis is always spouting off about Benin being an enclave of dissidence and barbarism, and being plum satisfied with himself. But Tom, I didn't calculate." The local agent for the African Association, Tom had sometimes ventured to the Upper Ethiope to take trade goods to Brendan's beaches there when Brendan was unable to get down to Sapele. "But Tom's been here in town. He's been going with Gainey about the district, witnessing treaties."

"Yes, he's to join up with them here. They're prepared to give them what for, I'd say."

"You're not accompanying them?"

Swainson smiled wryly. "Rheumatism."

"I've noticed loads of reluctant carriers coming forward into town here, gathering for such an event, mostly Itsekiri sent by Chief Dogho."

"And Donivan . . . He's got a drum and fife band."

There was a brief silence at the mention of the drum and fife band. During this lull, Elle flounced into the room in all her glory in her green holiday frock, completely wiping the subject at hand from the brains of the two men.

"Darling." Brendan reached out a hand for her. "This is John Swainson, a right smart man to have on your side in Warri."

Swainson bowed deeply, scraping the Panama hat in his hand against the carpet. Although Elle was roughly the same age as him, he said, "Miss, I am delighted. We have heard so many flattering things about you over at our old decrepit factories."

Elle flickered her eyelashes at Swainson. "And just what news have you brought from Warri?"

Brendan turned to Elle. "Phillips is making his move. He's bringing a marching band as we sit here speaking. John, when did you say they left Old Calabar?"

"The morning of the twenty-sixth, and they're so encumbered on the Protectorate yacht *Ivy* I daresay it will take them another five or six days to reach here."

"And what sort of ordnance do they have?"

"Well, that's the odd part. My man saw nothing being packed, no artillery or Maxims, but he saw revolvers being put into boxes carried by the carriers."

"He has no wish to threaten anyone, yet he brings a humbug drum and fife band!" Brendan marveled. "Well. I'll be striking out for Gainey's then, see what else I can smoke out. Darling, will you stay and be entertained by John?"

"Or perhaps she will entertain *me*," Swainson leered.

Feeling no competition from the weedy Swainson, Brendan donned a shirt and headed for Gainey's. He could hear Gainey's laughter from the parlor even before the majordomo let him in.

Victoria sat at the pianoforte, Rip leaning back on it with one elbow, brandishing a cocktail in one hand, though the sun was only barely over the foreyard. Gainey and Lyon also lounged with cocktails, looking suspiciously as though celebrating something.

"Brendan, m'boy!" Gainey was in another of his inexplicable ebullient moods. "Come and join us with your saintly voice. We're not doing Christmas songs today. This is a zippy new tune, what was the name again, Victoria?"

Victoria looked at her sheet music, not at Brendan. " 'When The Saints Go Marching In.' "

"A saint singing a song about a saint!" cried Gainey, getting to his feet and going to the sideboard, ostensibly to mix Brendan a cocktail as well.

Brendan barreled ahead regardless of who was listening. "Gainey, I'm sure you know about the party Phillips has mounted that is heading our way." He looked to Rip's face when saying this, as Gainey's back was to Brendan. Rip clearly started, taking his elbow off the pianoforte and standing at attention.

Gainey waved an unconcerned hand. "Oh, my, yes. Poor Jim thinks we will make some headway with the Oba if he puts on a grand show."

Victoria had turned around on her stool. "Vince! Does this mean war? Will we have to leave Sapele?"

Gainey came forward to hand Brendan his cocktail. Brendan took it, for it suddenly didn't seem so odd at that time of day. "My dear, have no fear. This is no war party; poor misguided Jim is just making a friendly stab at opening up the kernel trade."

Rip interjected, his shocked eyes full of concern. "But don't you reckon Donivan here is just going to run and warn the Oba? There could be all sorts of savage ambushes awaiting the poor fellow."

Brendan snorted with disgust. "Rip, a group of eight unarmed whitemen with a drum and fife band is hardly the making of a necktie party. What would I warn the Oba about . . . an impending cricket match?"

Brendan had never for one moment thought of Rip as being anything other than pitiful or buffoonish, but he suddenly had the look of a deranged crackpot when he uttered, "Yes, I'm sure you're right." He didn't seem sure at all.

"It will be pleasant to hear the band," Henry Lyon mused.

Brendan polished off his drink, set the tumbler on a side table, and took his leave. "I must get back."

"Are you coming tonight for the Count's party?" Gainey queried.

"Yes, I wouldn't miss it." Brendan smiled.

For the *Comte* was finally getting back on the ship to Algiers, an event that, combined with the holidays, had Brendan in good cheer.

CHAPTER

19

January 1, 1897

Brendan was aboard the *Hindustan* on the orlop deck sampling palm oil from a "Regular Liverpooler" cask. With a hollow dipstick, one had to extract three samples to test for free fatty acid content, impurities, and moisture. He was standing atop the oily keg, and he was annoyed when a fellow slipped through a hatch and fell like a pile of slimy eels to the deck next to him. The fellow was bloviating something about *Oyinbos* coming, and Brendan leaped from the barrel to stand over him, hands on hips, demanding to know what was up.

"He say nah militie ban . . . he got one long tine so so brass, something lib dah go flip flap, dem call am key!"

"Berrah well," sighed Brendan. He got the picture: the arrival of Phillips and his military band had been a sight to scare the witches. Brendan was already heading up the hatch.

"Dah bwoy kin blow!" the fellow shrieked, still in a pile on the deck. "One Boney bwoy lib oberside nah he like blow bugle!"

Brendan could see them already, from the main deck of the *Hindustan*. Captain Maling in his red uniform, and other officers in tropical whites were the hub of attention next to the Consul General's flag, a blue ensign with the Protectorate crest in the corner, while a crowd of a hundred, easily, milled around them near the grassy clearing in front of Gainey's vice-consulate. The band was a somewhat stirring sight in their blue serge uniforms, cummerbunds, and red fezzes. They were winding down a weary rendition of "God Save the Queen" they had probably been playing for days.

In the ferry canoe, Brendan pondered the scene before him. The cacophonous shouting emanating from the grassy clearing was a dull roar. By the time Brendan strode to the Consulate, the officers had gone upstairs, and he had to fight his way through the squalling pack of men who were picking and poking at the hapless musicians, probably because they wanted their smart uniforms.

Gainey's majordomo was hollering up a storm, not having seen such a ruckus in all his years. He grabbed Brendan by the sleeve and yanked him indoors, dramatically barring the door and flinging himself against it.

In Gainey's offices the men were still in the back-slapping jocose stage of the meeting, describing the travails of traveling with a skirling, off-key band, unruly carriers, and ever so rancid quinine. Brendan squeezed into the sweaty room between Tom Gordon and Major Copland-Crawford.

The Major tipped his solar topee to Brendan. "Donivan." The major still carried a limp from the prior expedition against Chief Nana.

They shook hands, but Brendan turned to Gordon.

"Tom, what in God's name has gotten into you? Don't you know this sort of palaver is madness?"

Gordon folded his arms in front of his chest and wouldn't look at Brendan. "It's madness what your bloody Ober is doing to our trade, Donivan. He's a pompous ass and the height of rudeness in his demands, and he's got to learn."

"He's not going to receive you, Tom! It's the *Igue*, greeting the new year, the ritual of head worship. Your palaver isn't going to cut any ice with him."

Tom snorted. "I don't care a hang whether he's celebrating the resurrection of his *balls*, Donivan. He's got to go."

"Then you admit that's the intent of your expedition."

Gordon abruptly shut his trap. He looked eyes front to the center of the room, where Gainey was handing out gin and quinine cocktails, and Phillips was basking in the glamour of being leader of such a mission.

Captain Boisragon of the Constabulary brayed, "Our men are hard to hustle off the ball, Gainey." This caused general merriment and clinking of glasses, as Brendan shut his eyes in disgust.

Copland-Crawford shouted out, "We shall celebrate my birthday in Benin City on January sixth!" More jovial laughter and toasts.

Phillips said, "I should like to have that Mateus chap as guide and interpreter, if he can be found."

Gainey craned his neck around the room. "He's a slippery bloke. More than likely he's off on some booze-up; are you certain you really want . . . *Brendan!* Come here, you larky sod."

Brendan stepped forward at the urging of the patriotic Gainey, who was suddenly chockablock with colloquial fervor. "I can send for Mateus, but I can't stake my affidavit on him agreeing to join up with you."

Phillips removed his solar topee at the sight of Brendan, perhaps the better to impress him with his height and bang-up authority. "Ah, Mr. Donivan. I don't suppose there's any hope in enlisting you? This is, after all, a peaceful mission."

Again, Brendan patiently closed his eyes. "I am smack and smooth out of sympathy for your cause, Phillips. The Oba can't be seen by strangers during *Igue*. You won't be allowed into the city."

Phillips narrowed his already-beady eyes at Brendan. "Ah, yes, the 'yearly head thing.' Well, he has already accepted our gifts. We are bringing many more gifts now. I have much work to do in other parts of the Protectorate, and I'm obliged to come up *now*."

As if on cue, there was a confused ruckus in the hallway, and

Chief Dogho rushed into Gainey's office. Clad in a mish-mash of rags of old military coats that clearly made him feel well nigh to European culture, Dogho frantically saluted Phillips before falling to the floor at his feet on all fours, pleading for something, more than likely to be made Chief of the new order at Benin City.

Gainey looked around in embarrassment. "*Chief*, really, now . . ."

But Dogho stunned Brendan by crying, "You must not go to Edo! *Kpaa hien mwan!* It is the worst *juju* to go there during *Igue*, and I have seen the dead corpses thrown about the road!"

Phillips laughed it off. "Really, Chief Dogho, I hardly expected this sort of thing from you. Why don't you stand up—here, take this gin cocktail—and we can have it out in private?"

Lyon and Boisragon lifted Dogho to his feet by the elbows, as though they were supporting the Oba himself. But Dogho continued blubbering, "There is a big hole in the ground by the Oba's palace . . .That is where they will throw your dead bodies!"

"Well, if this isn't the most balmy sort of omen," Captain Boisragon muttered.

Gainey took things into his hands. "Dinner tonight, Chief? I shall have Cook serve up some of that delicious buffalo Mr. Donivan was kind enough to give us. In fact, I do believe we have enough to serve plenty. How does buffalo sound, Major? We get all manner of beasts of the bush living in town with Mr. Donivan here."

Dogho was being shooed from the room, and Brendan was striking out to follow him, when Phillips addressed him again.

"Donivan! I have just had the pleasure of meeting a most delightful creature, introduced to me as Miss Elle Bowie. She is a *friend* of yours, I was told. Perhaps you would do us the favor of bringing her to dinner tonight. Female presence is a most rare thing around these parts."

"Yes, and any female relations or friends she may have," added Art Maling of the Sixteenth Lancers.

Utterly ignoring the annoying demand, Brendan faced Phillips squarely and said, "I would at least send back the marching corps, Phillips. Their presence might cast doubts over the peaceful intentions of your mission."

Phillips stared at him with his clear empty eyes, saying nothing.

~ ✸ ~

The very next day Phillips sent the drum and fife band back to Old Calabar. The men stayed, making preparations. While the *Oyinbo* bunked in Gainey's consulate and the Wells' mission (Brendan did not invite the two traders to stay in his house), the carriers camped wherever possible, mainly in the Prison Yard in the Farmland Quarter. Two hundred additional bodies swelled the town and pressed its capacities. In particular there was a sudden shortage of liquor, the absorption of which created no end of fisticuffs and dustups, and Brendan wouldn't allow Elle to even go to the orphanage without an armed guard to accompany her. Ordinarily such restrictions would have rankled Elle, but in Sapele, with Brendan as the jailor, it actually caused her to swell with pride.

In the midst of this fervor, the unlikely pair of Rip and Mateus burst through Brendan's front door. Elle, Brendan, and Evin were at the dining table finishing their pepper soup, and Miriam was unable to keep the staggering pair out. They brought a cloud of gin and hemp into the room with them, and when they breathed fumes that wafted over the table, Brendan got to his feet and protested.

"Why don't you go back to your frolics, and disremember which way you come from?" He pointed at the floor angrily.

Elle stood to intervene, but Mateus was bursting with urgent news. "We're going fishing upriver, we just wanted to tell you that."

Rip nodded eagerly. "Yep, fishing. Fishing, Elle."

Elle screwed up her face. "Fishing? Now why on earth

would you—"

Brendan interrupted, shoving Mateus with his fingertips gingerly against his shoulders. "Let them go. Go, go!"

"But . . . " Elle insisted. "This doesn't even make sense. Mateus, you refused to accompany Vince and Phillips because you didn't want to leave town, you said you were expecting some important shipment from Lisbon. Now you're going upriver to get fish that you could easily get here in town?"

"There are no fish in town!" Mateus proclaimed. "Those fired up carriers have eaten every last fish within a ten mile radius!"

Brendan eagerly agreed. "That's true, Elle."

"But Brendan here has given you enough chop to last a month. Besides," she addressed Rip now, "You don't even like Mateus."

Rip flung an arm around Mateus's shoulders. "I like him right enough when he knows his way around these creeks! All right, then! You stay warm, I mean cool, Elle. We'll be back in a few days with plenty of fish, and maybe this expedition will be gone by then and we can get back to some serious peace and quiet."

"Good, good," Brendan encouraged the pair as they turned and staggered back down the hallway. "Good riddance," he told Elle.

They were actually singing as they took their leave. "Where the Rio Grande is flowing, and the starry skies are bright . . . She walks along the river in the quiet summer night!" The three in the dining room listened quietly, each no doubt surprised for their own reasons. "She thinks if I remember when we parted long ago . . . *Hey!* Now as the senior leader here, you're supposed to let *me* go through the door first, shrimp!"

"If you're going to call me names, I'm not going!"

"I'll give you 'going.' Get down there!"

And with a bang the door slammed behind them, ejecting the men into the clamorous street.

Brendan and Elle sat back down. Evin smiled privately to himself, and Elle in her irritation demanded to know, "What's so funny?"

Evin did not bother hiding his mirth. "Those two are going fishing like I am running for Pope."

"You think?" Brendan had the capacity to be dense about certain things.

Elle nodded at Evin. "That's what I thought, too. There's something fishy—"

"Fishy?" Brendan laughed. "That's a good wheeze, Elle."

That irritated her even more. She pointedly addressed her remarks to Evin. "What sort of thing do you think they could be up to?"

Evin only shrugged. "With those two and their heads together, I don't think we have to be concerned about Phillips, as no doubt they'll create a deadlier war somewhere else."

Brendan added, "As oiled as Mateus was, let's hope the 'deadly' part doesn't occur to your erstwhile husband."

Elle looked blankly at Brendan. "What does that mean? Does Mateus become violent when drunk?"

Brendan and Evin shared glances.

"Well? What has he done when drunk?"

At length, Evin said to Brendan, "You tell her."

Exhaling, Brendan looked at his bowl of soup. "About three years ago Mateus went on a big bender, and he killed a fellow."

"With his bare hands," Evin added.

Elle gasped. "What for?"

Brendan exhaled again. "He thought he stole his pocket watch."

"Oh! And the fellow didn't do it?"

The Irishmen shook their heads in tandem, like toy dogs.

"And you tell me this just now!" Elle put her head in her hands and stared at her own soup bowl. "Now they're probably long gone, and there's nothing to be done about it." She poured herself more wine, and gave Brendan the evil eye.

~ ✍ ~

January 4, 1897

Phillips's mission left town the next day. They took the steam launches *Daisy* and *Primrose* and went west toward Ughoton. The *Primrose* came back with Lyon aboard, Captain Gainey and Dr. Elliott having gone on ahead with Phillips. From Ughoton they would march overland to Edo.

While it was a relief to see them go, the destruction and garbage they left in their wake did not lift Elle's spirits. She and Mary set to organizing women to clean the streets. She wore her most threadbare skirt and shirtwaist for the task, and she started in front of Brendan's house. She picked up banana peels, among the more appetizing items, and placed them in a large burlap bag. There was normally no garbage to be found in Sapele, as everything was utilized by the citizens, but apparently the refuse on this day was too much for the town to absorb.

"Mrs. Bowie! Mrs. Bowie!"

Elle dropped her bag at the sound of Mateus's voice. By now she was thoroughly convinced he had murdered Rip, and the sight of him crabbing up the road with his bowlegs and without her partner only assured her of this deed. She hitched her skirt up to withdraw her Derringer from her thigh holster, holding it down at her side. She need not have worried, though, for Mateus was so *loco* with strange *juju* he would not have been able to harm her. His eyes rolled around in his head, and with outstretched talons he came for Elle.

"Stand back!" she barked.

"Mrs. Bowie, I have something terrible to confess! There is no confessional in town, and besides, it would take too much time to tell Father Wells. I am putting my life in danger, but I cannot live with what I know!"

Halfway expecting Mateus to fall to his knees before her, Elle hiked up her skirt to replace the Derringer. "Mateus, what is it?

Does it involve Rip?"

"Yes! And I cannot rest until I have made a clean slate of it." However, instead of confessing, he started in on a fresh round of self-flagellation, roaring, "Whatever will Saint Peter think of me when I apply for entrance into the House of God? No, I will be sent straight to the lake of fire, there to roast with men such as Charlemagne and Napoleon!"

From what little Elle knew of Catholicism, she did not think Mateus was getting his story straight. Furthermore, Mr. Wells was not a priest. She yelled, "Come out of it, Mateus!" She even grasped him by the shoulders and shook him, hard. By this time a crowd had gathered around them in the road, laughing and gawking at Mateus's histrionics. "Mateus, does it involve Brendan? Rip and Brendan?"

"Sim! Eu sou um criminoso . . . "

Taking Mateus by the arm, Elle marched him down past the anchorage. She may as well have been leading a monkey on a chain, for he lagged behind her with hands before his lap as though in invisible handcuffs. All the while he bemoaned, *"Eu roast no inferno . . . eu sou evil . . . "*

Fortunately, Brendan was in his office, going over specifications he had spread out on a map chest with a seedy supercargo. He was telling the fellow, "Now, normally I am accustomed to seeing turpentine for mixing with paint, not swallowing for medicine."

The fellow eagerly insisted, "But this stuff is *pure.*"

"Land's sake!" Brendan's beautiful face took in the sight of his lover dragging a wailing mess of a probable man behind her into his office.

"Brendan, there's an emergency."

"O Mestre, eu fiz o evil!"

Brendan turned to the supercargo, rolled the specifications up, and slapped him on the chest with them. "Sorry, no. Now you'll have to leave." He shoved the fellow out of his office, locked the door, and turned to Elle and Mateus. "Now. Whatever has scared you well nigh into fits, Mateus?"

Elle explained, "All I can get from him is, he's some kind of evil criminal, he's committed some crime, and it involves Rip."

"Aha. Mateus?"

Mateus, who had heretofore been content to huddle in a quaking mass over by a filing cabinet, now erupted with a roar. "*I have assisted Mr. Bowie in committing the most evil deed ever!*"

Brendan looked to the ceiling for assistance, but he was necessarily patient. "Yes. And what did this evil deed consist of?"

More quaking, more tremors that seemed to shake Mateus to the very core. He began pacing, raking his fingers through his greasy hair. "You will forgive me, you must! You see I had no choice! Mr. Bowie insisted I accompany him to Edo, upon threat of death or that he would reveal a most mortifying secret . . . Something it would not do to be known to you. He said he would either kill me or tell you this secret!"

"Yes. I see. That's fine, Mateus, you don't need to tell me the secret. Now, what did Mr. Bowie want you to do in Edo?"

Mateus stopped pacing, holding his claw hands out as though hefting a large pumpkin before him, his mouth turned down at the corners with horror. "He wanted me to lead him to Ologboshere!"

Brendan blinked. "And?"

"He wanted to tell Ologboshere about Phillips's party arriving!"

"Surely that is common knowledge by now. And surely a great war general like Ologboshere was aware before anyone else. Is there something perhaps . . . *new and interesting* that he told Ologboshere?"

Mateus still held the giant pumpkin. "*That they are an armed war party coming to kill the Oba!*"

"Oh, *Jesus!*" Elle exploded, flinging her arms in the air and twirling to face the wall. "Of all the asinine, deceitful, lowdown, nasty, lousy . . ."

She didn't finish her recital, as when she turned back to the room she saw Brendan had already silently leaped into action. He checked the cylinder of his Schofield, jammed it into his hip holster, then checked the Schofield at his other hip. By the time Elle rushed the few paces across the room, Brendan was already slapping his Bowie knife in his boot to make sure it was there, and tearing the silk businessman's tie from his neck.

Elle felt as if there were a burning rock in the pit of her stomach. Too much medicine had seared a hole there, and it acted up when she was shot through with fear. She tried to put her hand on Brendan's shoulder, but he lifted his arms to tie his hair back with the leather strip, and strode to unlock the door so he could poke his head out and shout at his lurking factotum to get the war canoe ready. The entire hallway full of clerks and pullaboys jumped to it, stampeding over each other in their zeal.

Elle placated herself by meekly saying, "Brendan. I don't like this one bit. I cannot say enough, but I don't blame you if you want to kill Rip. That's fine, you can do that later, but—"

He turned to her finally, saying brutally, "That's fine because I *am* going to do that later, Elle! That jackass doesn't realize what sort of deadly games he's playing here, and thanks to him I now have to follow Phillips's party and hope that I reach them in time! And I don't even *like* them very much!" As he ranted, he continued looping various canteens over his shoulders and cartridge belts around his hips. He now withdrew his Schofield, cocked the hammer, and lifted it until the barrel pointed directly at Mateus's quivering head. "And you. You . . . toad. You're coming with me, or I'm scuppering you right here in my office, and I'm going to make you clean your own brains up."

Elle was surprised that Mateus had the wherewithal to moan, "*O mestre, perdoa-me, perdoa-me!*"

Still holding the gun steady to Mateus's head, Brendan swiveled around to face Elle. Though he was still panting with rage, his eyes had that boyish seductive look, and he said gently, "Elle, I will love you forever, I want you to know that."

"But . . ." She was on the very verge of bursting into a torrent of tears. "You're coming back!"

Then he did something that completely erased almost all fear from her stomach. Lifting one eyebrow, he smiled a crooked smile that matched it, and he reached his free arm out to wrap around her waist. He kissed her for so long that Mateus could have easily snuck away, if he was capable of tiptoeing that quietly without his bones clattering. Brendan kissed her gently yet bur-geoning with such lust that Elle was sliding her hands inside his vest and lifting one shoe off the floor.

"*Mestre?*"

Brendan pulled away a few inches in order to tell Elle, "I'm coming back for you."

Then he faced Mateus, grimly determined, his hand that held the pistol not having wavered the smallest fraction of an inch. "Get in the canoe."

Mateus came forward with his hands threaded together on top of his head, feeling free now to continue bawling in Portuguese. Elle felt her ire rising now for the danger Rip and Mateus were raining upon Brendan.

She hissed at Mateus as Brendan marched him out, "Now I am wishing you *had* killed Rip!"

As they stumbled down the beach, Mateus hobbling like a man going to his own execution, Brendan gave Elle instructions. "When Rip comes back, have him arrested by Gainey's men. I don't know quite what you'd call it, what he did—it can't be treason as he's not British. Interfering with affairs of state, or some such thing. Whatever the case, once Lyon gets wind of it, he'll keep him locked up 'til we can get this whole thing sorted out."

Within sight of ten minutes, the war canoe that had come gliding from the boathouse was ready to go, with twenty of Brendan's strongest pullaboys. He did not take his customary stern seat on the Brussels carpet, shut off from the crew by a curtain, where he could glide quietly under the high masses of vegetation while on leisurely cruises down the river. Today he took the captain's bow seat, facing down the canoe, and seated Mateus right between his legs where he could keep an eye on him.

"Mateus," Elle called from the floating dock. "Have you any idea *why* Rip would want to cause all of these problems for the British?"

Mateus called back in a dead, flat tone. "He thinks the Edo will win. He thinks he'll be a big chief in Edo, and Brendan will be booted out."

Brendan, apparently unable to bring himself to look at either Mateus or Elle, smeared his hair back from his forehead and shouted unfeeling commands down the canoe's length. Men poled the huge canoe away from the anchorage, and Brendan took his seat with his own oars. However, Elle had to ask her question.

"And why does he hate Brendan that badly?"

"Because Brendan likes you."

"And why"—The pullaboys were so strong that the canoe glided as though it merely hovered over the glassy water—"why does Rip care whether or not Brendan likes me?"

Elle had to skip to the end of the dock to hear Mateus's monotone reply before Brendan and the others whisked him away. "Because he's in love with you." Mateus stood then, but a boot in the shin from Brendan, and he was flat on his behind once more. Mateus called through cupped hands. "He wants to marry you!"

20

January 4, 1897

Brendan marched out of Ughoton at full chisel with his four most barbarous men, all heavily armed with weapons he'd loaned them, as well as cutlasses of their own. He weighed the relative benefits of giving Mateus a weapon, and in the end decided it would be inhumane to not allow him to defend himself.

"I have always much preferred you to Mr. Bowie," Mateus proclaimed as they jogged along the flat path, only occasionally deterred by the pendulous roots of the silk-cotton trees.

"That's darned convenient."

"It's the truth, *mestre*. I have always said 'you cannot swim against the stream.' " He had to shout over his shoulder, as Brendan would not allow him to walk behind him. "Why do you think I told you of Mr. Bowie's evil deed? I only went with him under duress."

"Now, why is it . . . I was always *camarada*, and now I am *mestre*?"

"You see, Boss, I have a way of changing my attitude when a gun is directed at my brain."

"Well, then, *escravo* . . . What makes you say Mr. Bowie wants to marry Mrs. Bowie? Did he tell you, in so many words?"

"That he did. He was smoking hemp, and drinking my gin, and he was *feko gha guan*, you know, speaking very quietly." Mateus had to slow to a walk, for he was out of breath with the rapid jogging. Brendan nearly banged into him, and so took a walking break next to him, both men facing down the path. The four warriors ran on past them. When Mateus could speak again, his face red and dripping sweat, he panted out, "He said 'Mateus, I am going to marry Elle. All these years . . . I have been pretending to be her husband . . . She will not turn me down when I ask her!' "

Brendan wasn't short-winded at all. "Did he actually think she'd say yes?"

Nodding, Mateus finally gasped, "He seems . . . to be somewhat . . . *louco*."

"Mighty strange." Brendan waved Mateus back into the jog. "And what of this old goat Joseph Pulitzer?"

"Joseph Pulitzer was a *bastardo casado*, and she really did love the . . . mean old man. He was kind to her . . . at first. That geezer . . . should have been praying to Olokun for the privilege of having such a treasure for a wife! But he could not divorce his old wife . . . For I am somewhat in love with Elle myself, though I do not fool myself with delusions . . ."

"*Hush up!*" Brendan held his pistol high, crossdrew one Schofield from his holster, and aimed at where he'd seen leaves move. "*Sike mwen!*" *Come closer.* "*Vbe ore ni rue? Lare 'mwan.*" *What is your name? Come here.*

The Itsekiri carrier had frozen solid, but wasn't responding to Brendan's questioning, so Brendan stalked cautiously closer. He could hear Mateus following, cocking his own pistol. Brendan hissed, "Please don't shoot when you're behind me!"

Brendan shouted the same things in Itsekiri, and the fellow uncurled his spine and got to his feet, hands up as though surrendering. The poor man's knees were knocking with fright, and he blubbered out, "Many men . . . Edo . . . They come from everywhere."

This wasn't terribly helpful, but it gave Brendan a creepy feeling in his stomach. He told the unarmed frightened man to get back to his war canoe waiting in Ughoton, and urged Mateus back to the full chisel. He instructed Mateus to keep an eye out to the left and right in the jungle, either for Itsekiri carriers running like a thousand of brick, or greasy Edo warriors in leopard skin loincloths.

They were almost to Ugbini, a small village between Edo and Ughoton. They took a detour around a fallen silk-cotton, and Mateus stumbled over the first body. The carrier had been shot clean through the forehead, and he sprawled directly in the path with a face as though he'd seen a witch. Although probably only dead an hour, the chest he had been hoisting was already pillaged and thoroughly empty, his former partner nowhere to be found.

"Olokun . . ." shuddered Mateus, crossing himself in the Catholic manner.

Tossing his head to indicate they must move forward, they discovered more dead carriers, some shot, some hacked with cutlasses. One fellow sat up stock still in the path, lacking a head. Out of the hundred and fifty carriers (Phillips had sent back thirty with the marching band, and twenty had vanished from attrition), Brendan accounted for forty bodies without even leaving the path, most lying with heads or torsos facing west, as though polished off while retreating. The rest had either been taken prisoner or had cut out into the bush. Ologboshere had a tactic of attacking the front of a line, not the center where he would do the most damage, and it was quite possible many carriers had escaped.

There were a few items still strewn about in the bright broad-leafed foliage: a malacca walking cane, a bottle of gin, a lamp. Most ominous was a solar topee, still jammy with splotches of cranial matter. The carnivorous buzzing of the flies became louder, a sickening near-roar.

Brendan's four warriors stood at the head of the line, one leaning on his own walking stick in mute regard, gesturing half-heartedly at Brendan to come over. Brendan saw the headless body of Major Crawford, denuded of his uniform. The same fate had befallen Art Maling, and no doubt more *Oyinbo* who had tried to escape into the bush. Brendan found the beheaded Dr. Elliott, whose right hand gripped a defensive stick of wood.

Brendan knew why Phillips had gone unarmed, and left all of his revolvers in a locked trunk hoisted by carriers. During Brendan's last visit to Consular Hill in Old Calabar, he had glimpsed a letter on Phillips's desk in Ralph Moor's characteristically spiked handwriting, telling Phillips: "And do go unarmed, old boy. The first sign of so much as a revolver and those bloodthirsty savages will have your head."

As Brendan surveyed the field of gore and destruction, he instantly knew why Moor had told Phillips that. Moor had a keen idea there would be some sort of altercation that he could use as the excuse for immediate punitive reprisal, his lusty goal for the region since taking control.

There was nothing to speak of to remove from the bodies, to take back to their wives or relations. Everything vital had already been removed.

"Do you think Phillips got away?" Mateus asked quietly.

Brendan shook his head. "He decided the order of march, and insisted on being at the lead. See, the fellows that're dressed like they're going cycling?" Indeed, there were two corpses splayed across the foliage, oddly dressed in blue knickerbockers, stockings, and white tennis shoes. "That was the guide and the interpreter." *In other words, you, if you hadn't of gone off with Rip*, thought Brendan.

Mateus blanched another shade of pale. He looked like a Mohawk red Indian wailing his death song with his mouth all akimbo like that.

Brendan sighed heavily for about the twentieth time in ten

minutes. "Well," he said at last. "I reckon we could dig some graves."

Mateus nodded. He was still crossing himself. "Some of the bodies are now small enough to fit into those empty chests."

With a gun in each hand, Brendan leaped into bent-kneed combat position, aiming at where he'd heard the rustling of some plants beneath an umbrella tree, shouting, "*Mudia!*" *Wait, stand.*

"Ighiwiyisi!" The laughing form of Ologboshere emerged from under the copse of plants, his own helmet made of crocodile skin. He had a smooth-bore flintlock dane-gun slung over his shoulder, his broad hand firmly around the stock. It wasn't aimed at Brendan, but then neither did Brendan lower his revolvers. "I see you have come to visit with your friends."

"They were no friends of mine, Ologboshere. I have told you that many times. But it was wrong of you to kill them."

Ologboshere kept coming, jovially. So jovial, in fact, that Brendan dared to look swiftly from side to side to see if there were other men hiding in the bush. The buzzing of the flies as they swarmed over the mutilated body parts was enough to drone out all but the most fatheaded stumblings of the biggest dodo.

"I see, Ighiwiyisi, that although you sent this war party, you were much too cowardly to join it. Now you come to loot from the dead and beg our forgiveness for being a traitor."

Ologboshere was maybe twenty feet from the barrels of Brendan's guns. Why was he so jolly and cocksure?

Brendan said, "And I have chanced to notice that you have slaughtered a party that was not carrying weapons of any sort."

Ologboshere shrugged. "We found weapons. In a box."

Brendan shouted louder. "Why would I trade you cannons and ammunition if I was on the side of the English? I did not send this war party, and I refused to join because I knew it was foolish. That white-haired man from Boston has filled your head with lies because he wants the fair maiden Elle for himself."

The smile vanished from Ologboshere's face at the mention of

Elle. He grasped his rifle and now pointed it at Brendan, growling, "The fair maiden Elle is meant for Ologboshere and no one else!"

"*Drop the gun*," Brendan hollered about as loud and mean as he could.

Ologboshere insisted on screeching, "I am going to find Elle, and take her! Nobody will have her but me! I will steal her from her bed—"

"*Drop the gun!* You are under arrest, Ologboshere, for murdering these *Oyinbo*, and—"

Ologboshere's face looked amazingly blank suddenly, as though he did not predict or see that massive solid tree trunk that crashed on Brendan from a great height. His ugly contorted face was the last thing Brendan saw. For an entire minute Brendan could not breathe, and he thought he would die of asphyxiation. All was a deep, velvety black, although he heard a cacophonous crescendo as though an entire band were banging drums and rattles right behind his head. He thought he was face first in the dirt, though he could not be sure, as he had no idea where the sky was.

"*Son of a bitch! Olokun! Olokun!*"

Mateus's hollering flashed through Brendan's fried head. It was with the utmost tidings to Olokun that Brendan felt himself swoop out of the body below and ascend up toward the jungle canopy. He sailed past a monkey, and he flew with a group of grey parrots. He had one brief glimpse of his own white-shirted back sprawled against the blanket of vegetation below, splashed with a red so overwhelming that it sucked the life from the rest of the scene, all else appearing in muted sepia tones.

~ ✵ ~

January 7, 1897

Elle lived in an edgy state of panic all of that day, night, and into the next day's twilight. She had not slept, but sat up with Evin drinking brandy around the table. He tried to distract her with a game of *parchisi*, but they both did poorly at it, mixing up their camels and elephants, throwing the dice when it wasn't their turn, or capturing themselves. Her rheumatism pained her something fierce, mostly in her hands and feet, leading her to think nerves affected it, but she turned down all Evin's offers of various nerve tonics.

For the next two days she felt worse than after a night of imbibing at one of Pulitzer's all-night soirees at Delmonico's. She took up a post at the porthole in Brendan's office, gazing upriver like a mariner's widow, although even if Brendan whistled up and back, he would still not get home for two days. When Evin was out of the office, she dared to look through the drawers of Brendan's desk. If she were caught she planned to say it was idle curiousity and boredom, but knew that at some point she had developed an unforgiveable and sappy crush on the man, much to her chagrin. She wanted to know every detail about him, his favorite mode of music, favorite flower, what sort of breakfast *fufu* he preferred, plantain, yam, or manioc.

She found all the typically masculine items: coins of about fifteen different nations, broken gewgaws, cowries, and bits of the brass *manillas* that passed for currency here. There were three broken pocket watches, money clips, and pages torn from note-books where he had scribbled lines of poetry, Olokun only knew how long ago. Some with bigger words were copied in Evin's admirable penmanship, other simpler ones in Brendan's adorably waifish and blocky letters. How she wished she knew how old the pages were! But she could not ask Evin, for that would mean admitting she snooped. She gathered up the papers in her fist, reading them openly as though Brendan had given them to her, lines like:

I want to stand in the night's imperfect shadow,

And

Whether to elevate deep promises to fact
Or run to the river and walk like a doomed man
With a rock on his head,

And

Whirling, turning with desire
Out of the frying pan, into the fryer

That last bit made Elle smile, though as it was in Brendan's handwriting she wasn't sure if he had mispelled "fire" or was making a statement on the futility of longing. She concluded he was such a quirky and ironic man, he had probably meant "fryer."

Elle was one of the first to see the canoes full of terrorized carriers paddling for their lives coming back on the neap tides of the Ethiope River. She ran up to the main deck of the *Hindustan*, and saw that they paddled going like sixty until the waters were frothy in their wake, and they didn't slow down as they headed for the beach. They ran the canoes up on the sand, as though they wanted to paddle clear through to the River Niger. By this time every soul on the *Hindustan* was clamoring for a canoe ferry, everyone without exception desirous of hearing the carrier's tales. Many men just swam the short channel. Elle quickly scrunched herself onto a canoe.

She didn't know much of the carriers' language of Itsekiri, so she rudely shoved people aside to gain entrance to Gainey's vice-consulate. From the men's faces, gestures, and tones, she was getting a panicked feeling. The carriers were making chopping motions, signing that heads and limbs had been lopped off, re-enacting dramas of hand-to-hand combat.

"My dear, my dear Elle!" Lieutenant Lyon shouted from the top of the stairs. He could not move forward through the crowd on his veranda, though he reached a futile arm down to her.

"Henry, what has happened?" Elle shrieked.

Lyon shaped his hand into a megaphone and shouted back, "Ambush! The brave humanitarian fellows have been massacred due to African treachery and barbarity!"

Squashed in the mass of flailing limbs, Elle shut her eyes, glad for the smelly bodies that propped her up on all sides, otherwise she would have fallen to the ground.

Then she was lifted, and raised up the steps until she was deposited next to Lyon. He was more worked up than she'd ever seen, apoplectic and bug-eyed with rage. "It is the depredation and dissipation of that blasted Fetish Priest King that has done it!"

Or the lies and machinations of a blond-haired cowboy . . .

"They will pay! Oh, they will pay brutally for this attack on a peaceful unarmed mission!"

Elle was finally able to ask, "Was . . . *everyone* murdered?"

"We don't know, my dear. These carriers—wait." More shouting in a melange of real or imaginary dialects. A few carriers were selected as being the most reliable or fluent of the lot, and were shoved through the front door, Elle with them. They flowed down the hall to Gainey's office. Suddenly Victoria was at Elle's side, clutching her arm.

"Elle," she cried, chummy in her anguish. "Have you heard of Brendan? Was he among the murdered?"

"Not yet. Henry is trying to get the story from the carriers."

"Oh, God!" Victoria squealed. "Why did he decide to join up with Phillips's party? What was he thinking?"

"I am hoping he got there too late."

After many long minutes of loud palaver, Lyon held up his hands and demanded silence. "Everyone. At three in the afternoon on January the fourth, Phillips's expedition was ambushed by a war party of Bini warriors, apparently acting on the King's orders. Major Copland-Crawford went toward them, making the Benin salutation, and was instantly shot and beheaded. Phillips, Maling, and Dr. Elliott were dealt the same treacherous hand."

Victoria remembered herself enough to cry, "And Vince?"

Lyon cleared his throat. "There is some confusion about

Captain Gainey. Some men may not be dead."

Elle and Victoria squeezed each other. "Vince . . . " they murmered in tandem.

"What of Brendan Donivan?" shouted Brad Forshaw.

"I have reason to hope he did not make it in time to join their mission." There was a hushed exhalation of relief as thirty people in unison relaxed. "Not a one of these men has seen him, or Mateus Barbosa, and many of them are quite familiar with them."

Victoria let go her claw-like grip on Elle's arm. She rested her forehead against Elle's shoulder and whispered, "Thank God."

For the first time feeling a kinship with Victoria, Elle hugged her back. "Thank God."

Lyon went on, "I am composing a cablegram to the Marquis of Salisbury; Ralph Moor must return from leave immediately, and I am certain there will be a punitive reprisal. Now, if you'd all let me have a few moments . . ."

Out front, Evin was on his way up the front steps. "Evin!" called Elle. "I don't think any harm has come to Brendan!"

"I've heard." Evin gestured for her to come his way. "I'm taking one of the launches and going upriver looking for him. Come with me." He did not need to add that last part.

Elle ran home to get a few supplies and better boat shoes. When she returned to the *Primrose* at the anchorage, she saw Evin's group consisted of Brad Forshaw, John Swainson, Charlie Wells, and Dr. D'Arcy Irvine, who had traveled from Brass to cover for Dr. Elliott. They were pulling out of the anchorage when Lieutenant Lyon came barreling out waving, asking to come along. Nobody could think of a reason why not, so the Niger Coast Protectorate soldiers hauled him aboard, and they were on their way.

Elle and Evin huddled together at the port bow, trying to stay out of the acrid black smoke spewing from the stack.

"I'm certain he's all right," Evin opined.

"I'm not that certain. If he's all right, why didn't he come tearing back here with those carriers? After all, there is no reason to go warn dead, headless men about the danger."

"Brendan is very wily. He's an accomplished shootist and fighter, much more so than me. Besides, no upstanding man of Edo would dare touch a hair on his head. The Oba would be flinging them up the *Iroko* tree in nothing flat."

"Perhaps. But if they think he betrayed them . . . *Oh!* I am so mortified and embarrassed for my former partner, please understand that, Evin. I cannot even live with the thought that I was indirectly responsible, for not having noticed he was smitten by me! Those are the pitfalls of being a bitter, old, lonely spinster such as I."

Evin put a comforting arm around Elle's shoulders. It was quite a show of emotion from such a reserved man. "You are hardly old, bitter, or a spinster."

Elle noticed he did not deny she was lonely.

Lyon became embroiled in an altercation with Brad Forshaw. Lyon was expounding,

"When the Oba signed that treaty with Gallwey in ninety-two, he agreed to place himself and his country under Her Majesty's Protectorate. It's a perfect disgrace that in our Protectorate, such a terrible state of affairs has continued, and this is why Benin City is known as the City of Blood."

Forshaw snorted. "The Oba thought the Gallwey treaty was for protection, not that he was giving up any power or native customs. And for the record, the treaties, as you well know, are always pro forma documents printed in England. By the time they get translated into Russian or whatever insane language and back into the local one, everybody is most thoroughly confused."

Evin piped up, "Yes, and when you have a rat like Mateus translating for you . . . "

Lyon continued to stubbornly assert, "The objective of Phillips's mission was to persuade the King to let whitemen come up to his city whenever they wanted to. We knew we couldn't put down all of their horrible customs at once, but we thought we could stamp them out gradually by officials continually going up."

In only a few hours, the launch rounded a bend and was greeted by a canoe of waving Itsekiri tribesmen. "British! British!" they cried.

When they steamed closer to the canoe, they had the horrifyingly happy sight of Captain Boisragon and the District Commissioner of Warri, Ralph Locke, bloody and battered, but alive and waving for salvation. Men hoisted Boisragon and Locke aboard while Evin handsomely paid the canoe men for saving the British. Champagne and whiskey bottles were opened, and as Dr. Irvine tended to their wounds, the men told their story.

They had escaped into the bush, crawling like animals through brambles with barbs like fish hooks. For four days they lived on plantains and dew from leaves. Boisragon had been shot in the right arm, which had started to smell horrible.

"It made me very nearly sick," Locke said. "I wanted to be as far from you as possible."

Boisragon nodded. "And I wish I could do the same."

They insisted that Vince Gainey had been killed at once.

Boisragon told how the Itsekiri had hidden them under mats in their canoe to get around the Edo patrols. It was a grand story of survival, and of course Boisragon and Locke hadn't seen hide nor hair of Brendan, and Elle understood when they turned the launch around to deliver the wounded survivors back to Sapele.

"I doubled back to get my revolver from the chest," Boisragon told everyone, "and Phillips was standing there in the middle of the path in his pith helmet, shouting 'No revolvers, gentlemen.' Incredible. Next time I saw him, he was missing his head. It was almost as though Phillips wanted to be a martyr, to stir up feelings for a cause."

Elle and Evin agreed the Oba had not sanctioned the ambush.

They decided to return downriver at daybreak on the morrow, perhaps only with fellow traders Forshaw and Swainson, as the doctor and missionary were needed in Sapele in preparation for the forthcoming counteroffensive.

Lyon sent an ultimatum to the Oba. The Oba replied that "no whiteman was alive," and he sent two rings of Major Copland-Crawford's as evidence. There was also some talk that the African Association at New Benin had received Tom Gordon's rings, complete with severed fingers.

21

Brendan languished for days in a vortex of semi-consciousness. His wounded brain imagined he was in Sapele, hovering over the dining table as Elle and Evin fretted. At one point he distinctly heard Elle say, "I'm in love with him, you know. I regret that I never told him that."

To which Evin replied, "Don't you think he knows?"

Elle shook her head, staring downcast at the table. "I told him I hated the word 'love' and refused to use it." And then, gripping her skull in her hands, she cried in anguish, "Oh, it is so true what they say! Life is too short! How I want to kill myself now!"

The entire scene was so absurd, Brendan knew it was the product of an addled brain.

At another point he saw them on the steam launch *Primrose*. Improbably, Evin was telling Elle, "When the two of you marry, remember, I promised to come and live in a dog house in your backyard." This made Elle laugh, but strangely, her eyes glistened with moisture.

At length, though, these absurd delusions began to give way to a more horrifying reality, that Brendan was back in the earthen cell in Edo that was so familiar to him. He'd spent a few days here years before during that dog-eating episode, before it was determined that the true culprit in the affair was Miriam's husband. Evin was also interred in a different cell for his idol-bashing display, but when it was found they were huntsmen of the dreaded buffalo of America, they were turned loose to demonstrate their skills with leopards.

Brendan doubted there would be any such manumission now, for he had been arrested for treason, the offense most often punished by death, along with murder and dog-eating.

It took him days to figure out what had happened. Someone—Ologboshere's bellicose lieutenant Ugiagbe, no doubt—had been up in a tree above, and had jumped him. As Brendan didn't seem to be bleeding anywhere, he concluded the pains in his head, back, arms and legs were just bruises from having a heavy brute fall from such a great height atop him. He became able to move with difficulty, and he went to the iron gate and yelled for the guard, who was apparently under orders not to speak, for he wouldn't even open his mouth. Brendan was churning with rage on so many fronts it was impossible to separate them all. As barely anyone in the town could understand English, Brendan felt free to hobble in circles in the cell, ranting to himself.

"This is all thanks to that miserable old rat, Rip. As if Elle would marry him! But Ologboshere, now, he didn't have to believe Rip. He did that of his own free will. And the Oba! Why on earth would I trade him cannons, ammunition, guns, corrugated sheets of metal, *a talking machine?* Why would I keep giving him leopards *of my own free will* that I could have very well kept for myself and used the skins for impressive uniforms, drums, shields? Ah, those traitorous bastards!"

And then, overwhelmed with the tyranny of those he had trusted, he would sit in a corner of the cell, head in hands. He still had his leopard hip ornament as nobody had even come to see him to take anything away, and he spent hours rubbing it with his thumbs, uttering oaths and prayers.

He could tell they were whistling through the corpses on the *Iroko* tree and elsewhere. The jail was quite close to the tree, and several times a day he heard the frenzied frolics of excitement as they executed some new sucker. Too, a few days ago there had been eight other people in the jail, all Itsekiri carriers from Phillips' party, and now the supply had dwindled to just Brendan. There had been the four warriors Brendan had taken to Ughoton. All four were in the same cell adjacent to Brendan, and all four disappeared yesterday. Their only crime was being kind enough to help Brendan attempt to warn the British.

He had been able to have a shouted conversation with one of the Itsekiri prisoners. The man told him the day after the ambush there had been four whitemen sitting bound in the Oba's sacrificial compound. The following day their heads were brought around with stick-gags in their mouths.

Brendan reckoned he had bad *ehi*. His *ehi* had allowed him to find Elle and now it was taking her away from him. His beloved Edo was going to fall, and he with it, and in a way that was fitting. It was the way he had to go.

There was no hint as to where Mateus was.

~ ~ ~

There was a marked display of corpses hanging in trees in the "Field of Death" on the outskirts of Edo. Elle and Evin traveled alone, not wishing to further risk anyone else's lives, but there was apparently no gripe against Evin, as guards, farmers, and warriors greeted him with "*vbee oyo he?*" and smiled and waved. The language proficiency of Elle and Evin being about equal, they received equally perplexing answers to their presumed queries of "Have you seen Ighiwiyisi?" But the general gist was a shaking of heads. They advanced to the tactic of looking for Mateus, or Rip.

There was more success with this. The mention of the yellow-haired *Oyinbo* brought enthusiastic and happy responses of "*evbani*" and "*evba*," yonder and there, while pointing to Edo. The pair plunged ahead, past the heads of Phillips, Gainey, and their cohorts that were jammed in the branches of the *Iroko* tree, to the house of Brendan and Evin.

The house was surprisingly unmolested. Elle was awash with a fresh surge of grief when she saw the skull on the turkey platter, the brass bas-relief plaques on the walls. She was in the grips of an insidious heartbreak, and she collapsed into a chair, sobbing into her hands. It was that wretched sort of anguish where one could not breathe, and when one finally took a ragged breath, one bawled like an infant.

Evin left the room, presumably to let her grieve in private, but when he returned he pressed two small objects into Elle's wet and snotty hands. It took awhile for her eyes to clear enough to see they were mother-o'-pearl cufflinks, monogrammed BD. She laughed hysterically, while Evin helped pin them to the cuffs of her shirtwaist, and she felt better.

"We'll go check your guesthouse," Evin said gently.

But of course Rip wouldn't be stupid enough to be at the guesthouse, so the next destination was Ologboshere's.

Not surprisingly, Ologboshere wasn't there. But a few of the women Elle had befriended led them into the catacombs of the house, to a courtyard adjacent to Ologboshere's private quarters. And there she found Rip in all his glory.

"Well, hello, girlie. You're looking mighty splendid today."

Clad in an *eruhan* and not much else, Elle supposed he had found his element. Evin started roaring, "You right bastard . . ."

But Elle marched over and belted him one upside the head. The smile was quite literally knocked off his handsome dimpled face. It was such a satisfying feeling that Elle repeated it, this time aiming her fist at Rip's nose.

"Ow!" Rip cried, bringing up one hand to grasp Elle's wrist, the other cupping his nose. His eyes turned ugly, and he shouted,

"What's gotten into you . . . *Colleen*?"

Whap! She knocked him into the middle of next week with her weaker left hand. "Where's Brendan?"

Blood dripped down Rip's upper lip, under his fingers. "Well now, honey, if you'd stop hitting me, maybe I could tell you." Two fawning women came forward with towels to blot the blood from Rip's face.

Elle could not keep quiet long enough to hear Rip's ostensible answer. "I see you are the chosen one here, for your treachery and deceit against Brendan and the British."

Rip grinned crookedly. "Ologboshere said I could become a chief for my assistance."

Elle gawked at him. "A chief of what? Laziness and scandal? There'll be nothing left in Edo but a pile of bones once the British are through with their reprisal."

"Partner, could you put that piece down?" Rip shouted at Evin. Elle hadn't realized Evin was pointing his own Colt at him.

Evin seethed, "Once you tell us where Brendan is."

Rip gathered himself up to his full height as he sat upon his stool. "Well, now. That isn't too difficult to figure out, is it? Just *mayhap*"—and Elle wanted to belt him again for using a term of Brendan's with such derision—"he is in the same place he stuck us months ago when he tried to have us strangled and crucified!"

"The jail," Evin breathed, and as promised, angled his Colt to the dirt floor. "Come, Elle, let's get out of here."

Brendan was alive! Elle allowed herself to be led away.

~ ✦ ~

"Onaiwu!"

It was Brendan's old friend. Someone had finally come to see him. Onaiwu clung to the iron grating, gazing at the pitiful sight Brendan had no doubt become, in his filthy tattered *Oyinbo* clothes.

"Iwi . . . I cannot believe these charges of treason."

"Good. For they aren't true, Onaiwu. It is all Mr. Bowie's fault; he is the one who should be jailed for causing that ambush. What can you do about getting me out of here?"

Onaiwu shook his head with great import. "You know treason is the most serious offense. But it might help you that now the Oba is very angry with Ologboshere."

"Yes, that's very good news. I did not think the Oba would send men to ambush the British."

"No, indeed. You know there are many disagreements in the internal workings of the Oba's court, and Ologboshere and Ugiagbe are rebels seeking to weaken him. They did the massacre to bring trouble on the Oba. It did not look good that they attacked an unarmed party. The Oba said, 'Since I have been born, no whiteman has died in Edo.' He said, 'The whiteman is bringing war, now if you go you must not fight them. Let them come, perhaps they are coming to pay a friendly visit. You must let them come, and if it is war, we will find out.' The Oba is very displeased, and that could help you."

"Yes, since it diminishes Ologboshere's position. Have you seen Mateus?"

Onaiwu looked down at the dirt floor. "Yes. He is living at Ologboshere's also, along with Mr. Bowie."

"That rat!" Brendan appealed to Olokun above to spare him, but he really was not surprised at Mateus's treachery. Mateus would always take care of himself first, and that was why he was one of the few survivors in the "graveyard of Europeans." "And . . . Ikponmwosa? And . . . Mrs. Bowie?"

"I have heard they have just arrived in town. And—what is that?" Onaiwu leaned back into the darkness of the passageway.

Oyinbo! Brendan heard excited voices getting closer; the guard who was always seated outside his gate got to his feet to assert his authority. Evin and Elle! While Evin tussled with the guard, Elle slipped past him and slammed her body against the gate.

They twined fingers through the grate, and were able to kiss for many long moments. Brendan was sure his mouth tasted like a privy, but at the moment he didn't much care.

"Ah, Brendan . . ." Elle breathed moisture onto his face. She untwined one of her hands in order to stick it through a lower grate, and she grasped his hip and held him to her. "This is the happiest I have ever been in my life, touching you."

Brendan was beyond delirious with joy, but he had to say, "I can think of more ecstatic times, Old Man." It seemed that Evin was drawing out his argument with the guard to give Brendan more time with Elle. "I'm to be killed for treason."

Elle's face fell, became bitter. "I've just come from seeing Rip. I knocked him into the middle of next week."

"Good." Brendan drew her into a kiss again. He nibbled at her soft luscious lips, not at all surprised that even under such mortal circumstances, his penis was stiffening. He murmured against her mouth, "I love you, Elle. I love you more than any woman I've known; I love you so much it hurts. I know you don't care for that word, but it's the only one that fits how I feel."

"I know, dear heart. I have been in such pain since you disappeared, I didn't think such agony was possible to bear and still be alive! We will get you out, the Oba will set you free—"

Perhaps at hearing the word "Oba," Onaiwu respectfully interrupted. "Iwi, the Oba has sent me to tell you . . . he would like to see you for an audience."

"Good! Is he willing to listen to what I have to say?"

"It seems that way. And he wants Mr. Bowie at the audience too."

"Good, good." Brendan turned to Elle and explained in English, "I have an audience with the Oba. This had better work. For I am the last victim they have left, after those three fellows who just came in this morning."

Evin, having broken free of the guard, came over to shake Brendan's hand mightily. "We had better start rustling up some more prisoners, then."

Elle held tight onto Brendan's other hand. "There is one naked cowboy in particular I can think of."

Brendan turned to Evin and said, "I want you and Elle to get out of Edo. Those beefeaters aren't going to just swat us like a fly when they come marching in here."

"No!" cried Elle. "We are staying to do anything we can to help! I will *never* leave here without you!"

"Besides," Evin interrupted, "those beefeaters are a few weeks away at least. They can't just mobilize an army overnight."

"Ev," said Brendan, on a new tack. "Why in the name of Olokun would you want to come and live in our backyard, if Elle and I married?"

To his surprise, Evin smiled sheepishly, as though he knew what Brendan meant. "That's a joke between me and Elle."

"He was trying to demonstrate what a faithful and loyal partner he is to you," Elle explained.

So the conversation he'd seen had actually taken place, as well as the part where Elle professed her love for Brendan. This idea threw Brendan into a quandary.

Elle purred, "Come to me, my Alabamy dear heart." Her eyes were full of smiles, and she put her hands through the grate to scratch him behind the ears. Touching her nose to his, she said, "We'll get you out soon. Then I'll wear you into a frazzle." When she drew back, he found she had slipped his Saint Christopher medal back over his head.

"No! This is yours!"

Elle became serious, but she never lost her sly seductive look. "You need it more than I do."

Brendan said soberly to Evin, "Bring me Mateus. He's at Ologboshere's house."

— 🐜 —

"No, we don't want to go that way."

The *okhuo*, wives of Ologboshere, were attempting to steer Elle and Evin back through the galleries that led to Rip.

"No, we want Mateus. Mateus Barbosa."

"Mateus," Evin obediently echoed.

"Ah!" Enlightenment spread over their faces, and they returned to the hall near the front door where Iden had appeared to them before. They motioned for the *Oyinbo* to wait, and they ducked into the darkness.

Elle looked at Evin. "Is all of this giving you a creepy feeling?"

Evin nodded. "In a bad way."

Indeed, Iden herself preceded Mateus out of the dark chamber. Bowing obsequiously, with hands folded in front of her lap, she submitted to the superior presence of Mateus who, with matted Mohawk coiffure apparently greased with palm oil, and shirtless save for the slimy vest, suddenly appeared brutish, even manly.

"*Camaradas,*" Mateus greeted them cheerfully. "I know what this looks like. Let me explain . . . out in the front courtyard, where cowboy ears can't hear."

They obediently followed the bandy-legged man into the front garden area, pausing under a wild custard apple tree. It reminded Elle of trimming the custard apple tree in Sapele. It was impossible to believe that was only a few weeks ago.

"I have only the best of feelings for Brendan Donivan. He may be an antagonistic and hostile bastard at times, but we have become *camaradas* over the many years." Mateus spoke formally, with a sober face. "But I cannot stand by and see him throw Iden to the leopards. He comes and uses her when he pleases, then leaves without any thought as to what she is thinking, how she feels."

Elle closed her eyes patiently. "Mateus . . .We don't care what you do with Iden. Is this the big secret Rip threatened to reveal if you didn't go along with his jackass plan?"

Mateus nodded gravely. "Yes. As she belongs to him, I could have been arrested for adultery. Adultery is punished by selling the wife into slavery and executing the seducer."

"Still can, I reckon," Evin inserted. "We just came from the jail, and there's a big shortage of available victims for the *Iroko* tree."

Elle put a calming hand on Evin's shoulder. "But instead of doing that . . . Brendan needs your help. Fact, in return for your help, I will stake my affidavit that Brendan will be lenient about Iden."

Evin looked surprised, as though such a bargain hadn't occurred to him. "Yes," he said, sounding eager to propound this theory. "He's asking for you, you have to go there immediately."

Mateus saluted smartly. "That I shall do!"

"Another thing, Mateus," said Elle. "If you loathe Rip that much, don't you think it would look better if you lived elsewhere and not at Ologboshere's?"

Mateus's eyes became veiled, as though a second set of saurian eyelids had closed on them. "Iden was already here. Ologboshere took her here. I do not consort with that rabble-rouser Mr. Bowie, and indeed become quite ill to my stomach when I see him prancing about."

"Come to our house," Evin said on the instant.

Standing alert like a rabbit, a slow and seemingly genuine smile oozed forth on Mateus's face. It wasn't the gleeful teeth-gnashing grimace of old, but a new, more human sort of expression. "I would be honored."

22

On his way to the Oba's council house, Brendan kicked up something that suspiciously resembled a man's eye.

As he hefted his iron chains, he wondered at the meaning behind the eyeball. Was it that the dead were watching him, calling him to join them? Or that he could stomp on those watchers, and damn them all to the bottomless pit? It was probably the dichotomy between his mother and father, his Catholic and Protestant upbringing—he could always see both sides of any story.

It was wonderful to feel the light on his face and skin, though he squinted painfully without his blue lens spectacles, his eyes unaccustomed to the brightness. Of particular pain was the glare from the galvanized iron roofs Brendan had supplied for the Oba.

The audience atrium was crowded with peasants, ranged around three walls tightly packed, leaving the lower end clear for Brendan. Guards removed his chains, and pressed him onto a polished wooden bench facing a similar one at the upper end.

"How is the family, Imhonde?" Brendan queried the guard.

The man beamed proudly that Brendan recalled him. "Very well, Ighiwiyisi."

A heavy shower of rain burst over the palace, deluging the

impluvium and threatening to delay the proceedings. A door at the top of the room opened, and Mr. Bowie entered.

It looked as though he were shoved, from the stumbling manner in which he entered. However, Rip quickly corrected his gait, and made as though he had meant to stagger into the room, swaggering confidently in his *eruhan* and cowboy boots.

Rip drawled casually, "You got nerve to think you can win Elle."

"*Oba o gha gb-ue*." *May the Oba kill you*. This oath showed that the Oba was feared more than any god. Brendan had to chuckle at the shallow fool. Unable to speak Edo, how could the jackass possibly think he could take him?

So Brendan looked ahead serenely.

A door opened, and in crowded some thirty fellows of stalwart proportions and huge forms, entirely nude. The *emada* wore no dress until the Oba deigned to give them clothes and wives. This naked throng took its place on the right hand of the stool, crowding into the corner, and the man nearest the royal seat carried upright in both hands a huge *eben*.

Ominously, the *emada* were followed by six *uzama*, elder statesmen and kingmakers who only attended judicial councils for the most critical occasions. Brendan began to sweat a little upon seeing the men, who ranged themselves in line along a raised step perpendicular to the royal stool. All were old men with senile figures, skeletally thin or hideously pot-bellied. Naked to the waist, they wore immense white muslin petticoats extending to the calf, and puffed out to a balloon shape by *eruhan* acting as crinoline. Each had a collar of coral so tightly strung it formed a cone about a foot in diameter. Lastly came the king, supported by two *emada* who led him to the wooden bench upon which a mat had been placed.

The Oba was a vigorous and finely-made man of forty years. His expression was uncommonly intelligent, mild and good-humored. He smiled graciously. He was covered with masses of coral, and his headdress, in the shape of a leghorn straw hat, was composed completely of coral. Meshed closely together, it must have weighed very heavily on his head, for it was constantly being temporarily removed by an attendant. His wrists up to his elbows were covered with coral bangles, as were his ankles. He only wore the usual white *eruhan* of a chief, and underneath, a pair of embroidered and brocaded trousers. His chest was completely covered by the mantle of coral beads encircling his neck.

Brendan stood when an *emada* bade them go forward. He objected to walking through the center of the muddy and watery impluvium, so the peasants were expelled, making a partial clearing of the step running along the left side of the room. As they approached the corner where the *emada* crowded, there were some murmurs and signs to stand back and even to kneel.

"What do they want?" Rip mumbled.

Brendan placed himself standing in front of the Oba, and after a low bow, addressed him as "Death, Great One."

The Oba acknowledged him with a nod and a smile.

Emada spread a mat on the step below the Oba's stool. Mateus was admitted into the room, and when he addressed the king, he knelt upon a step below the stool. Each of Mateus's translated messages began with a "King he send you service."

The Oba said, "Ighiwiyisi, you've been a good slave, bringing me leopards and things from America."

Mateus translated for Rip, "King he send you service. Brendan Donivan is a good slave."

"However, you are both *Oyinbo*, who have lately been troubling Edo. This *Oyinbo* says that Ighiwiyisi my slave has been on the side of the British."

"The King send you service. But you are both whitemen. Brendan Donivan is in cahoots with the British."

"However, this *Oyinbo* has not brought me leopards. He is a friend of Ologboshere, who has been also troubling me lately, by massacring British without my consent."

"King he send you service. Rip Bowie might also bring leopards, because he is a friend of Ologboshere."

"You have both behaved badly, as all *Oyinbo* do. I do not like to imprison my slave Ighiwiyisi; how will I get leopards then? But this one has accused you of treason."

Brendan had the grit to interrupt. Again bowing low, he intoned, "Child of the Sky whom we pray not to fall and cover us." The Oba smiled gratefully, as though glad of a chance to remain silent. "This *Oyinbo* is a traitor to Edo, Liverpool, and Boston. He falsely accuses me of siding with the British, when it is a famous fact that I do not care for them. He is in love with the woman I love, the *Oyinbo* Elle."

"Yes, I have heard," said Oba Ovonranmwen. "This is why you leave Iden alone."

"What are you saying, you beefeating lover?" snarled Rip.

Mateus translated, "Big man in sky, do not fall down on us. Rip is a great man who loves women."

Unsure what the Oba's gist was, Brendan continued, "As I am confident I will be proven innocent, I propose that both me and this evil, vile, crocodile-loving *Oyinbo* take the sasswood ordeal. It will be proven that this lousy slave is lying to the Oba, and he will owe me one life . . . and he has none to give."

"I am a lowdown louse who lies to the Oba."

The Oba's smile grew wider. "Yes, I propose you take the sasswood ordeal. That will show the truth."

Brendan bowed. "Death, Great One. You must imprison this *Oyinbo* until the ordeal takes place. Otherwise he could send spirits to change the poison bark into cocoa beans or kola nuts."

The Oba nodded. Motioning to the naked *emada*, they leaped forward to grab Rip's arms. They took Brendan's chains to bind Rip's hands behind his back. "Mateus, what's going on?" Rip cried in a tremolo. "What did this bastard say?"

Mayhap it was Brendan's imagination, but he thought Mateus grinned even wider, looking over his shoulder as he kneeled on the step. "He said you must take the sasswood ordeal."

Brendan smiled. "Thank you, Death, Great One."

The Oba said, "I am sure you will come out victorious, Ighiwiyisi. Then you can get me more leopards. One has escaped, and another has died of loneliness, and I need more."

The *emada* took Rip away, but Brendan remained for a few moments, just looking at the stool after the Oba was supported out of the room.

~ ⚞ ~

As arranged, Brad Forshaw and John Swainson were allowed into Edo. It was an extremely brave trek for the traders, as Ologboshere had already sent out guerrilla parties to make surprise raids against the British, and the British were sending Hausa scouts with Snider rifles and spies into Benin territory.

They brought the news that twelve hundred bluejackets and Marines from London, Cape Town, and Malta had steamed up to Brass under the command of Rear Admiral Rawson. The brunt of the fighting was to fall on the well-seasoned men of the Niger Coast Protectorate Force, the unit of armed constabulary raised by Moor years before. Boisragon had commanded; they were now commanded by Major Hamilton.

In addition, there were hundreds of African carriers brought from Sierra Leone, Opobo, and Bonny. Ralph Moor, having been mobilized with alacrity back from London, was already en route to Sapele to inspect the Cape Squadron with Rear Admiral Rawson. Ominously, they were equipped with seven-pounder artillery for bombardment, rocket tubes, and Maxim guns that spewed out six hundred rounds a minute. John and Brad returned to Sapele the next day, never to visit again.

~ ⚞ ~

Elle was able to get inside the brig and actually be with Brendan, inside his cell. The guards had much sympathy for him, in particular when Brendan's *ekhen* brought them many gifts of American cloth, cigarettes, rum, and silverware. Elle gained this privilege by telling them, through Mateus, that in America a man condemned to death was given special rights, something she hoped Mateus translated as a conjugal palaver. In particular, the woman must clean and dress the man, being strangled in dirty and shoddy clothes being the most ignominious death of all.

Rip had no such briberies readily at hand. He languished, thankfully, in the cell farthest from Brendan, visited by no one.

It was with the greatest exhilaration that Elle was finally able to sit next to Brendan on the dusty floor of the cell. She had forced the guards to unlock the chains that fettered Brendan's wrists and ankles, and as Evin, *ekhen* and guards did boisterous business in the passageway, Elle and Brendan sat on their tails with legs dovetailed over each other's hips, kissing languidly and sloppily, Brendan's weeks-old beard scratching her face. They had not allowed her to bring her razor in, but the guard had promised to supervise Brendan with many loaded guns while he shaved himself (Edo men not being very adept at it), as Elle detested that scraggly mountaineer look.

She hiked up her skirts brazenly, ignoring the leering guffaws of the guards and hangers-on who had suddenly jammed the passageway. She wrapped her arms so tightly around Brendan's torso she could touch her own elbows with her fingertips, dizzy with love and adoration, and a contentment she had never known. Her love for Brendan was absolute and unlimited. It was accepting of everything he stood for, and anything that might befall him. She had decided that to love completely meant that one would inevitably have to suffer, as one put oneself so fully into the beloved's shoes that there was no turning back, no stepping back onto the cliff.

She forced Brendan to detach, as he had developed the

proclivity to smell like an African. She scooted him to the center of the impluvium, easily stripping him of his musty shirt, the tie of which had long ago had become a pigtail-holder for his oily hair. In a sort of blessed silence, she removed his pants and *Oyinbo* drawers, tossing them in a pile where they would become valued additions to an *Ivbiedo* ensemble. She left off her shirt-waist, and worked with only her camisole covering her.

With her bucket and Edo soap, she poured several calabashes of water over Brendan's head, the water sluicing over his shoulders that had paled a few shades of brown after being in the dark for many weeks. Taking the cake of Edo soap to Brendan's head as he leaned back on his palms, Elle deliciously soaped his hair, holding the tip of his archly sexy nose to her breastplate. She took her time, and she massaged his cranium with the rapture of a Madonna. Most of the leering onlookers turned away out of respect.

"Dear heart . . .What idea have you concocted with Mateus?" For she knew there was a plan of sorts when Mateus had come home gleefully gnashing his teeth, full of himself and some vague plot that he seemed to think would stand Brendan in good stead.

"Didn't he tell you?" Brendan drawled against her chest. He sounded happy, as though he were at a picnic on the shores of the Chattahoochee, not the killing cells of the City of Blood.

Elle pushed him away so she could pour calabashes of fresh water over his head. "No, he refused to tell me." She squeezed the water from his long locks, his ravishing face with closed eyes pointed to the ceiling. She gave him a chaste yet open-mouthed kiss, merely for being who he was. She could think of no better reason.

Sitting up erect, balancing back on his palms, Brendan fixed her with his glittering turquoise eyes. "Ah. Then I can tell you."

Elle soaped his neck and chest nonchalantly, as though the plan made no difference to her. She even shrugged.

"I've demanded to take the sasswood ordeal."

Her hand stilled with a calabash of water held over his clavicle. She spoke in a hushed voice. *"The sasswood ordeal?* Dear heart . . . you can't!"

He beamed with a confident smile that seemed to enliven the very room with its eminence. "Yes, and nobody has calculated how this is going to free me."

"Are you staking your affidavit on it?" She let loose the gourd of water, smearing her hand over the warm mush of his chest hair, delighting in the play of fingertips against muscle, rubbing his erect nipples with her rough fingertips. "You know that thing is bogus, Brendan. Though I am sure that you know more than I."

He looked ethereal, sublime, as though nothing could touch him. "You'll see, *amebo.*" His penis was up like a hard log of wood between Elle's thighs, and it was perversely sexual to squirm atop it while she performed the ablutions to his naked body. She moved her hands down to wash his groin, as he splayed himself out on the muddy floor for her pleasure. "Please trust me to know what I'm doing."

Elle reached for her own bodice, and displayed a breast to him. He looked inviting all laid back like that, and if there was one last memory she wanted to have, it was of him all wide open like the sky above the impluvium, a clean blue slate upon which she could write her most mad desires. Above the festive clamoring of the crowd outside the jail, there was the singular melodious chirping of one bird. "Clockbirds are like drummers who have to keep vigil while others are asleep."

He touched her bared breast lightly, as though amazed by its presence. "Please," he whispered. "Don't keep a vigil for me."

In answer, Elle put more ferocity into soaping the small of his back. Plunging her hand deep between his buttocks like a harsh nursemaid, she laved his ballsac with the palm of her hand. She was furious, and wanted to purge him of any small sign of evil.

"Avast," Brendan yelped, when she took to slathering his calf muscles with her punitive mitts. "I rather need salvation from you, Elle. What's wrong?"

She dismounted him, rotating his hip to splash fresh water over his backside, over the leopard tattoo. He was a gorgeous male animal all unfurled like that, and it was impossible to be angry with him. She snorted and huffed, but at last it was the divine sight of that well-marbled butt that got to her, and she confessed, "How can you be so certain that you'll puke?" For vomiting up the sasswood drink was a sign of innocence.

Brendan twisted his clean wet hair into a rope, grinning seductively. "I cannot say, my darling jungle flower." He touched a finger to his lips in the hushing manner. Then, turning serious, he held Elle by the back of her neck, massaging the sore muscles there. "*Amebo*. Will you tell me about Pulitzer?"

Sighing deeply, Elle dropped her gaze, but as she only wound up staring at the stiff column of his erection that grazed his navel . . . the avoidance didn't help. Since her back was to the iron gate and covered Brendan from the gaping eyes in the hall, she dared to take the bar of soap directly to that stupendous penis, holding it in her palm and stroking the delicious length. It was purple, and angry, and jutted out arrogantly. She saw his eyes quiver as he gasped, but he was resolute.

He whispered, "Tell me, Elle. I need to know who I must go kill."

"Pulitzer is nobody you must concern yourself with. I should have known a married man never divorces." How she wanted to dip her head down and lap up the big soapy prick she was stroking! But she didn't dare, for if the guards thought anything untoward or pleasurable was occurring, they would yank her from there. "I did not mention him because he is not important to me anymore."

Brendan caressed the underside of her chin. "He insults you by keeping you as a mistress."

Her hand stilled. "Mistress? Oh! God!" Her abrupt cry must

have startled Brendan, for he jumped, and lowered his hand to cover hers, to indicate she must not stop her ministrations. She laughed with relief when she told him, "I have not been Pulitzer's mistress for two years. I don't allow him to insult me anymore."

She poured a calabash of water over his tumid penis, to make her ablutions look more medical in case anyone was looking. "I do not wish to discuss such an unappetizing subject while I am"—she had to lower her voice, though it was unlikely any of their audience understood English—"frigging your delectable penis." Sweeping her hand over his full balls, she massaged the sensitive bulge beneath them, Brendan obligingly parting his thighs for her. She slid her middle finger up between the cleft of his stupendous behind, tickling the rim of his asshole in order to distract him, while her other hand moved in to caress the silky knob of his penis.

Brendan was struggling to keep his eyes from sliding shut. "You said you were celibate for four years."

Elle had been expecting that. "I was, dear heart. We were not intimate for two years before I stopped seeing him."

That leonine grin killed her every time! "Ah, that is impossible to imagine, from such a seductive jungle flower as you." He sighed and groaned at the same time. "When I first knew you, knowing you had been . . . unsatisfied for so long, it scared me well nigh into fits, Elle." Her hands stilled, and he opened his eyes, blessing her with their brilliant cerulean intensity. "I thought I'd become too important to you."

Elle nodded. "I was afraid you would be too important to me, too. I do not like that."

"But now I *want* to be important to you. I know all your splendor and grand caring for the downtrodden, your sweet temperament, your wit, your sharp mind"—Elle had to giggle at that—"much sharper than mine, naturally, and I . . . I *want* to be too important to you. I want to be so important that you place me first in your heart, as I have placed you first in mine."

Elle was overwhelmed with gratitude and joy. She knew that Brendan referred to her litany that she had never been first in importance to any man, that something or someone had always had priority. "You must be very certain of the outcome of your sasswood ordeal, dear heart, to take such liberty in assuring I would be devastated by your death." They both laughed quietly, but Elle added, "I have been very frightened of caring too much for anyone, but . . . you have already assumed the foremost import in my heart."

She made the mistake then of kissing his forehead, the bridge and the tip of his nose, and when she placed her mouth on his, a guard behind them, apparently tiring of haggling over a silver teapot, shouted out, *"Hey! Mudia!"* Elle heard him jangling his keys as he cut a figure with his authority, so she hurriedly completed the kiss, mashing Brendan to her breast as they opened their mouths, licking and sucking on each other with voracity.

She heard the gate open. She asked breathlessly, "When will your sasswood ordeal take place?"

Brendan whispered, "They are saving us for the big finale, the most powerful fetish of all to keep the British at bay at the last moment, so it depends how fast Hamilton or Rawson can get here. Ebeikinmwin has posted himself and his troops at Ughoton, and the first word of their arrival should come from there, unless they go up the Ologbo creek."

"There are men hiding in tree platforms at every entrance to the city."

"But we cannot win, Elle, men with bows and arrows and spears and a few breech-loading rifles with iron bolts and potlegs for ammunition are no match for the Maxims and artillery."

The fellow was hauling Elle to her feet, as Brendan grasped her hands in his, standing too. Elle was aware she was sappily pleading now. "Can you tell me how you're so certain of the ordeal working out well?"

His enigmatic smile made him too beautiful for this earth. "I am going to have a whopping breakfast of cane rat and grubs, while Rip is being served milk and honey to coat his stomach."

"*What*?" Elle gasped. "That's *it*? What if he doesn't drink the milk and honey?"

The guard had hauled Elle past the gate and as he was now locking it again after throwing Brendan his fresh Edo clothing, there could be no more private whispers. Brendan called out to Elle, "I have given Iden to Mateus, but I do not want you to feel dismay at having to live under the same roof as her, so let Ologboshere keep her for now. And when the British come, hide, my love. That is the best. *Ivbiedo* might mistake you for a beefeater or you might get in the crossfire, so hide in my armory room which is the most secluded and safest."

"We will come for you."

Wanting his one slim opportunity to talk to his partner, Evin was gently crowding Elle at the gate. "Bren. This *ekhen* says there's already been an altercation out at Ughoton. They claim we routed the British and they evacuated the town, but you know how exaggerated these things can get, and allegedly there's a head of whoever was commanding on its way into Edo now."

Brendan nodded. "Most people here don't think the Oba can be captured; they think he can transform himself into a spirit."

The guard was now shrieking "*Gha khian! Khiamwun!*" that they should make tracks. The stunningly naked Brendan, his imposing penis at half-mast, now grasped the back of Elle's neck through the grate and pulled her face to his. "Stay safe, no matter what."

He didn't kiss her, merely released her and told Evin, "Ev, I am relying on you and Mateus."

Elle was stunned he had let her go with nothing more heartening. As the guard wrenched her by the arm she cried out, "I love you, Brendan, with all my heart and spirit. We will not let you die!"

Crossing his ankles and leaning against the cold iron of the gate, Brendan looked her levelly in the face, as a sober and sad Evin said, "I'm with Elle here, partner. You've got a whole raft of people who won't let you die."

Brendan looked at Elle, amused, a sly smile beginning at the corners of his mouth. He only broke his gaze in order to yell something at the guard that apparently told him to take his hands off Elle, for Evin was allowed to escort her back down the hall.

February 16, 1897

Those were the most maddening days of Elle's life, waiting for the two men to face each other off with a bit of bark from a tree.

Evin could not go out to the fields, everyone having been warned to stay within the city walls. Instead, they had target practice in a field near their house, or Evin held his usual music classes in his courtyard. With that many people unable to get to the fields or markets, and needing the uplifting vigor of music more than usual, the courtyard was jammed. As she was almost entirely unmusical, Elle could only shake a rattle decorated with cowries, but some of the music Evin had woven from Alabama and Edo strains was decidedly beatific. Some tunes resembled church spirituals, with angelic harmonizing that lifted above the tree canopy. Some tunes Evin and Mateus on banjo merely chugged along in American swamp style, and Evin sang in English such melodies as "Don't Nothing Hurt Me But My Back and Side." Yet Evin was very serious these days. Elle knew he was not as confident as Brendan in his exculpation, that he had some doubts about the sasswood bark, and Elle did not want to ask him to elaborate.

And of course Elle sent more than one messenger to

Ologboshere with verbal dispatches begging for Brendan's life. Edo was not a written language, and in the learning Elle had done with Mary Wells and the Edo *ekhen*, she had written down what she believed the sounds to look like phonetically on paper. Elle did not have much confidence in the ability of the runners to effectively convey the messages; indeed, if they did not tell Ologboshere she was a man.

She was not allowed back in to see Brendan.

Onaiwu came by several times a day to give them reports from the various fronts. As a Town Chief he was assigned to protect the inner city if the British got through, an event thought unlikely by any *Ovbiedo*. A group of fifty Edo warriors had attacked bluejackets on what Elle and Evin knew to be the right flank, an approach up the Jamieson River to Sapoba that was intended to capture escaping fugitives. The Edo shot up many bluejackets who were building a zareba of thorns. Though the *Oyinbo* volley-fired into the bush and killed ten Edo, they nevertheless abandoned the zareba.

There were skirmishes all along the Ologbo Creek approach, and more warriors than usual trotted about with white British helmets, swords, and revolvers for which they had no ammunition.

Onaiwu told them the sixty cannons Brendan had traded to Ologboshere were still at Obadan. A few of the ancient Portuguese cannons that had been half-buried for centuries were dug up, put in working order, and mounted on a stockade outside the south gates of the city.

And then, all through the morning, Elle could hear the booming of artillery shells. It sounded like the rumblings of a displeased god in the muffling humidity of the jungle. Elle, Evin, and Mateus, huddling in the courtyard to better hear the war advancing, drank brandy and gin and gave look-sees to the weapons they had checked and cleaned a hundred times.

"I expect they are only interested in sacking the palace, more than likely," Elle said uncertainly.

"Yes, but knowing the British, they'll make sure to rape and pillage everything in their path." Mateus was not a heartening hope in times like this.

"Oh, shut up already!" Evin shouted

Elle persisted in talking. It seemed to calm her nerves, if only a tad. "What I'm saying is, I doubt they'll have much interest in running into every mud hut in the town."

Evin agreed. "Right, and we'll shoot them the minute they do. They're not expecting anyone to be inside a mud hut, armed."

"Yes," Elle agreed vaguely.

Mateus snorted with derision. "We should put a British flag up on our outer wall."

"Oh, that's brilliant!" yelled Evin. "Let's just put big targets on our backs, why not, so the *Ivbiedo* will be certain not to miss?"

"They already know we're here, Jordan!" Mateus hollered. There was no more "sir" or "*mestre*," merely the derogatory use of Evin's surname. "Every *Ivbiedo* in town knows who we are and where we live. I'm just banking on them not shooting us, not a logical assumption after Mr. Bowie cast aspersions on our loyalties with the British!"

Evin half-rose from his bench. "You helped that cowboy go *loco* and try to take Brendan down with him!"

Elle grasped Evin's forearm, lowering him back to the bench next to her. "Mateus knows that, Evin. He's just edgy like we are, because we're under siege."

There was a brief silence at the thought of the siege. There had been a lull in the artillery fire, and now the courtyard gate burst open, causing an explosion of flurries as the three *Oyinbo* leaped to their feet, their weapons drawn in an almost balletic display of military readiness. However, it was only Onaiwu, with two fellows scurrying behind him, carrying, of all things, a large wooden carved chair.

He knew to speak in rudimentary terms to Elle and Evin. "There is not an *Oyinbo* in sight, yet there are messages from the sky!"

Elle put what she hoped was a calming hand on Onaiwu's arm as she returned her Derringer to her skirt pocket; she didn't keep it in her garter anymore. "Those are—oh, what are they?—big guns, Onaiwu."

"They are making big holes in the city walls." With bugged-out eyes, Onaiwu was the most spooked she had seen him yet. "They have guns that spray hundreds of bullets."

"Maxim guns." Elle and Evin nodded to each other.

Mateus inserted in English, "I heard they put the African troops and scouts up front with the Maxims, while they crawl back in the grass."

Elle shook her head with disgust. "As expected. Why do you bring me a chair, Onaiwu?"

Onaiwu looked at the chair with distracted irritation. "Oh. That is from Ologboshere, for you, Elle."

Elle frowned. "Ologboshere sends me a *chair*?"

"It is a special chair, see? Ologboshere had it made just for you, that's why it is in the *Oyinbo* style. There is not a chair like that in Edo."

Indeed, it would look like a regular armchair, were it not for the carvings along the back and legs of mudfish, leopards, and on one spot, an *Oyinbo* in a boat holding an oar.

"This is a strange omen!" Evin cried in Edo. "What is this supposed to mean?"

"I don't know, my friend," said Onaiwu, "but I cannot stay here, I must attend to my men." The two men who had carried the chair had already skedaddled out the gate, as there was a renewed artillery pounding along the south Ologbo walls. As he ran to the gate, Onaiwu yelled, "You should go to the jail; they may be letting Iwi out for his ordeal."

The three *Oyinbo* followed Onaiwu to the gate. They could not see the jail from there, but there was a general chaos of humanity flowing toward the plain in front of the *Iroko* tree. At least four gagged men were being hauled in that direction, along with the crowing and braying that went along with animals tussling against their will on their way to be slaughtered.

An even stranger sight then was Evin exhorting Mateus, "Run!"

Mateus tore away crab-like, darting through the flowing river of people.

"What's he doing?" Elle cried, as Evin tightly gripped her arm in his and led her to join the queue heading for the palace.

"He's going to see the witch doctor, the fellow who prepares the sasswood. We want to make sure the fellow doesn't get drunk, or mess up the sasswood."

It seemed everyone in Edo who didn't have to fight was surging toward the palace. Elle had her first glimpse of the Oba then as he sat thirty feet up on the tower of the palace, laden with coral. There were henchmen up there with him who seemed to be arguing with him, perhaps telling him to get down, as would seem to be the sanest thing to do, but he seemed to want to make a stand.

Elle and Evin stood on a bench and climbed onto a roof to get a view of the altar. There were twelve gagged men who were hurriedly led to a wall where they were decapitated. Following suit were twelve cows and a like number of sheep, goats, and chickens. It was the most rapid-fire series of sacrifices ever, and Elle and Evin gripped both of each other's forearms like iron puncheon hoops as the executioners sloppily swung the severed heads over the altar-pieces. The most glorious of the Oba's brass work had been hauled out for this occasion, busts of the Oba and Queen Mother that supported giant elephants' teeth of the most intricate carvings. Blood was now splashed willy-nilly across all of these idols. There being no room for the dead in the pile of a few dozen bodies already stacked up under the *Iroko* tree, they were thrown into a pit. Elle could see arms and legs already inhabiting the hole, some of them creepily moving.

"They're in a frenzy of homicide," Evin stated needlessly. A bit later he said, "And this is Brendan's beloved city!"

Elle was too stricken to even remark. Still the Oba stayed on his tower. She knew the twelve men and animals had been the pinnacles of the circus, and from here there was only one option. But when Brendan appeared on the bloody ground, cold steel that stopped her heart ran through her veins, and she swooned for a moment against Evin. He gripped her hands so tightly there was no blood in them.

" 'Let him go'? Are they saying 'let him go'?" Elle asked Evin. For she thought she could make out a common chant in the crowd.

He shook his head; there seemed to be nobody inside of his eyes. "I don't know." He squeezed his vacant eyes shut, and Elle distinctly heard him recite through clenched teeth, "For the life of the flesh is in the blood, and I have given it to you upon the altar to make atonement for your souls. For it is the blood that maketh atonement by reason of the life."

In his *eruhan* with his leopard hip ornament, Brendan was barefoot and bareheaded, though he'd been allowed to don the "ceremonial" jewelry Elle had brought him, his leopard tooth necklace, bracelets, vest with the medals. It struck her with a morbid shudder that Brendan looked the picture of a man about to become a human sacrifice, with his handcuffed wrists bound before his lap, dragging the chains through the bloody mud. After four weeks eating nothing but a few plantains, his hip bones stuck out sharply, and his chest was frighteningly sunken.

"Where is Mateus with the witch doctor? Does he live all the way in Ughoton?"

"No, just on the other side of *Eghaebho n'Ore*, a stone's throw from our house."

Then why aren't they here? Elle wanted to scream, but she was shutting her eyes so tightly she had a blinding headache.

Evin shook her arm. "There's Rip."

Rip had shriveled and become sallow. No more glimmering

muscles, he looked sinewy and disoriented. Wearing only his *eruhan* and cowboy boots, he too was shackled as two guards shoved him to stand next to Brendan, about ten feet away. The men didn't look at each other. Elle felt pain beyond tears, because for almost all of her life she had known Rip as a sweet, humorous man, always prepared to assist her—not this vindictive and evil bastard.

Near the *Oyinbo* were two men dressed in the white of Palace Chiefs who were orating and gesticulating, but of course Elle couldn't hear a word they said, especially as the crowd was now chanting something so cacophonous she couldn't make it out.

"I think those fellows are lawyers of a sort," Evin told her.

"Lawyers? Then why weren't we allowed to—*Mateus*!"

~ ✦ ~

For there the little hulk rat was, gently supporting the *Ewaise* by the elbow as though he were the Oba. Brendan exhaled the large gale of anxiety he had been holding in his lungs, for no matter how you shaped it, Mateus was a dubious, shady character from the get-go, and he wasn't entirely sure he'd pull it off with the *Ewaise*. The old man solemnly carried two calabashes that he placed on a tall narrow table before the two litigants. Brendan smiled to share a look of knowledge with Mateus as the crowd (those that hadn't already pulled up stakes, fleeing to the four corners) formed a recognizable chant.

"If they are wizards, let it kill them! If they are innocent, let it go forth!"

All test poisons were sensitive and rational beings that searched the accused's stomach to find the dark hidden sin. As much as he followed other Edo beliefs and practices, Brendan knew such ideas were bilgewater. The sassy bark from the large ordeal tree was a poison, and many innocent people had died during the ordeal. However, he was going to use his more advanced scientific knowledge to his own advantage. He already felt fairly nauseous from wolfing down a cane rat, tail and all, and as many live slugs as the guards would bring him. He imagined he could feel them still squiggling around in his stomach now, as the *Ewaise* orated.

The Oba, up on his tower roof, shouted to the *Ewaise* to shake it, as there was a renewed fusillade of shelling over by the Ologbo gates. For the first time Brendan looked to Rip, miserable critter that he was, and Rip couldn't stand still, kept hopping from foot to foot, eyes darting about. He looked about to burst forth with "the holy laugh," that hysterical condition in which the muscles are ungovernable.

As though Brendan's thoughts enslaved him, Rip bleated out toward the tower, "I take it back! He is not guilty of treason!"

Grand enlightenment came over Mateus's face, and he came forward from behind the narrow table. "We all know that; why do you tell us that now?"

Brendan joined in. "Aye—traitor! I demand you take the sasswood ordeal to clear my name and the dishonor you have brought upon me!"

Rip was nearly hysterical now. Shaking the chains that held his wrists, he cried, "I can't swallow the damn poison! I'm not the guilty one. Why should I be forced to drink poison?"

The crowd hushed as they strained to hear the *Oyinbo* words.

"You are guilty of false accusations and perjury!" Brendan roared. Pivoting to face the Oba, Brendan shouted up to him, "He recants! He says I am not guilty of treason, but I demand he take the ordeal!"

"Yes, yes!" the Oba shouted down. He was not so much supported by his assistants now as being shaken to pieces by them in their nerves and trembling to hustle to safety. "Drink the *iyin*!"

Brendan stepped up to the table. "Give me that fucking stuff!" Brendan told the *Ewaise* in English.

The calabash was held aloft and recited over, accompanied by the eager cheers of the crowd. In Brendan's agitation it sounded as though they shrieked, "He is innocent! Let it go forth!"

Closing his eyes, Brendan imagined scenes of gore and destruction. It wasn't a difficult task, with the blood of twelve decapitated men splashed about the brass heads of Obas and Iyobas, the sublimely carved tusks protruding from the crowns. From where he stood he could see the pit of bodies, several of the limbs still twitching, a hand scrabbling to the top of the pit. The fact of the business was, the entire soil of the judicial courtyard was covered with bones and decaying headless bodies nobody had thought to throw in the pit that was already chockablock with their futile sacrifices.

Brendan accepted the calabash, holding it as high as his chains would allow. "*Ehemwen wÿÿ iren te gua so ihuan, ren te vbe gua ku* ," he intoned. *A cockroach knows how to sing and dance.* "I wish to see face and back. Face and back meet and talk." He had to shout louder in order to hear his own words. "Man looks only on the outside of things; Osanobua looks into the very heart."

"What's this mumbo jumbo?" shrieked Rip.

Brendan frowned. "Can you please get that fellow to shut up?" he asked the guards.

"I'm not drinking any! I'm not swallowing a drop!" Rip continued to scream.

Brendan gulped with gusto every last speck of the reddish-brown astringent brew that was jammed with the bark pieces. He set the calabash down, and waited.

Rip was grinding his teeth closed, and several guards struggled with him.

"Take it like a man, Mr. Bowie!" Mateus shouted.

It didn't bother Brendan any what Rip chose to do, for he was confident he himself would vomit, and the sooner the better. He shut his eyes against Rip's pageant and thought of gore. His eyes were already burning, his breathing was becoming labored and shaky, and he dizzily dropped to his knees.

"You won't drink it? You're going to die like a woman anyway, Mr. Bowie! *Drink it*!"

He didn't even need to rub the back of his tongue with his fingers as he had planned on doing. That was a good old seaman's trick to get the bile out of one's system as fast as possible, so one could continue imbibing with gusto. No, Brendan's stomach just heaved upwards, as though it wanted to explode through his lungs, and he puked. His stomach convulsed violently as it disgorged the poison and, he saw when he chanced to open his pained eyes a tiny fissure, the bones of the cane rat, the long squiggly tail nearly intact, and the lemon yellow slugs that were, indeed, still slithering about. An inane rhyme from his childhood leaped unbidden to his mind:

What are little boys made of?
Snips and snails, and puppy dog tails
That's what little boys are made of!

For a moment, he thought he might die of the poison anyway, that enough had soaked into his entrails already. While the guards jabbered excitedly and released him from his chains, Brendan remained ignominiously kneeling over his lake of fresh offal, stomach heaving, but nothing remaining to be disgorged. For of course they had arranged with the *Ewaise* to fix the drink by stewing so much *iyin*, and adding some poison bean to boot, that his stomach would immediately reject it. Brendan did not know if this was widely known, but he had known for years that witch doctors did this to obtain the best results deemed desirable depending upon the case. Hell, he had seen an *Ewaise* tell the afflicted to go away, he needed to work in peace, eat their offerings to the spirits, and later tell how the spirit came, made an uproar, ate the yams, and left.

There was a whistling, and two resounding crashes in the compound that Brendan felt shake the killing ground beneath his knees. He might have remained doubled over and been trampled to death for all his troubles, as now the crowd commenced a general scramble in promiscuous heaps. He forced his burning eyes open in time to see the Oba in his tower being carried off by the *Iyase*, the *Osodin,* and Chief Obaseki

Brendan could barely see into the sun, but he surmised some chance rockets had landed that had finally scared the Oba away.

"Truly the whitemen are gods!" someone shrieked.

There were hands helping him to his feet, and he felt a bit better.

"Run, Ighiwiyisi, run!" the men exhorted him.

"Stay inside your houses," Brendan advised. "They won't kill anyone who isn't fighting. Where is Elle? Where is my *Oyinbo* woman?"

"We will give you your food later, Ighiwiyisi. Right now we must leave!"

For it was a tradition for the community at large to reward those proven innocent with extreme gifts of food, perhaps to recompense them for losing their last meal. "Yes, run!" Brendan urged them. "Elle!" he shouted. "Evin! Mateus!"

"*Capitão*! Let us run for your house!" Mateus was there, shaking Brendan by the arm.

"Yes, yes, but where's Elle and Evin?"

"I don't know, I saw them minutes ago sitting on that roof yonder, but as they are lifting Mr. Bowie into the *Iroko* tree as of now, I recommend we disappear, lest we begin to look like the next victims regardless of how many slugs you *vomito.*"

"What? But enough time hasn't passed!" As the guilty party, Rip had to give a life, and he had no slaves to give in his stead. Traditionally, there would be an hour's wait, during which often-times the guilty one expired anyway from the poison. With his burning vision reducing most bodies to mere outlines like ginger-bread men, Brendan could see they were lifting someone in chains onto the dreaded tree, using ladders and rope pulleys to get at the highest branches. Rip must have been gagged, as Brendan couldn't hear him screaming above the uproar of the rapidly emptying plain.

Mateus explained, "I think there is some urgency, as this is not your normal everyday human sacrifice, what with rockets exploding, and the enemy at the gates."

"But they can't—" Brendan had what little feeble wind remained knocked out of him by the glorious slamming of the woman's divine body against his.

"Oh, Lord!" Elle cried, her face glued to his neck, her arms in a stranglehold. In her zest she had even wrapped one thigh around his hip, the tips of her toes edging down the already tenuous hold his Edo kilt had around his waist. She held him too tightly to even kiss him, and she whispered, "My love . . . my love . . . "

Cradling the woman's precious skull, Brendan had never been happier to be among the living. Inhaling her jessamine and Edo soap scent, Brendan reveled in the feel of her silken hair, her panting full bosom pressed against his naked chest, and he slid a hand slowly down over her bird-like shoulders, the small of her back, merely to feel every cell of skin and fabric, because *it was her*. And anything that was *her* was vitally holy and sacred to Brendan.

He felt Evin by his side, squeezing the back of his neck, saying "Good job, Bren, good job."

Mateus pulled on his other arm. "*Capitão*, we must remove ourselves."

But the sheer joy of holding Elle overwhelmed all other matters, the least of which was the hoisting of her former partner onto the *Iroko* tree.

"My love . . ." Elle kept whispering.

Elle kissed him tenderly and tremulously. Instantly thoughts of the rat's tail and slugs flooded Brendan's mind.

Evin said, "Bren, I don't know what was said or done down here, but this ain't right." He pointed to the *Iroko* tree. Rip thrashed and kicked against his captors and was clearly so far unharmed as they lashed him with *tie-tie* to the scaffolding.

Brendan looked to Elle for direction. She stared ahead serenely at the vicious scene unfolding as though watching a particularly passionate biblical drama. It appeared to give her an elevated viewpoint, for she said calmly, "Let's get back to your house, Brendan."

Brendan tore his gaze from the morbidly fascinating sight and allowed himself to be borne away from the square, back into the pandemonium of evacuating townspeople, warriors in their leopard skins and shields ominously running *away* from the Ologbo gates, toward the palace to defend it. They scattered to all sides wherever vegetation was found, to take up hiding places.

"Elle!" Evin shouted from behind. "I don't believe you! You cannot condemn a man to a fate worse than death because of a false accusation!"

While Elle had appeared serene until then, she now stopped dead in her tracks and spun around on her heels. She faced Evin with an anger Brendan had never seen in her before, and she seethed, "Rip would have condemned Brendan to the same fate, for doing nothing worse than daring to care for me."

Brendan was prouder than ever of her in that moment. But Evin persisted, pointing to the *Iroko* tree behind them, where men were now smashing Rip's knees with a pikestaff. "But it's barbaric and un-Christian! It's one thing to watch them doing it to themselves, for they are all savages! But when it's a whiteman I absolutely must put a stop to it!"

Elle was silent for a few short moments. They stared each other down, huffing through their nostrils. At last Elle oozed, "Oh, you will, will you?"

"Yes! And I'm going back to repair this situation right now." Withdrawing his own revolver from his hip holster, Evin marched off purposefully toward the square.

Brendan shouted, "Ev, don't! We can't waste a second more; we have to get back to the house!" He had sighted his first beefeater, a red-jacketed Royal Marine running hunched over toward the palace, a battalion not far behind him.

There was a shot, like many other shots from the advancing

troops. But Brendan saw Rip's struggling body suddenly slump on the tree, the men who had been torturing him dispersing like a passel of parrots, and he realized he didn't grasp Elle's hands in his any longer. Evin froze in his furious march; Brendan could tell, from the character of the back of his head, that he realized it was too late for Rip. Slowly swiveling his head, Brendan gazed upon his beloved, her arm still holding his Schofield out at full length, one eye still squinting, though her aim had been true. Slowly, she lowered the gun, without looking replacing it in her hip holster, as all concentration and anger evaporated from her face. She turned to Brendan, beatific now, and said evenly, "Little pea-shooter."

Mateus stood on the other side of her, empty hands at his sides, jaw askew.

Brendan had no time to marvel. "Evin!" he hollered at the top of his lungs. Evin didn't need any more reminders now, as a beefeater was pointing his rifle directly at his head, and he had to throw his arms up in the surrender pose before the nervous fellow noticed he wasn't an African.

～ ✦ ～

She led Brendan as best as she could, hugging his forearm tight to her, lurching ahead. It was not a good sign that frantic women dragging children by the hands were fleeing in the opposite direction, toward them, toward the palace. One woman pulled a squealing child through the mud, let go of him to race forward, thought better of it, and returned to scoop him in her arms. Elle steered Brendan around the corner onto the broad avenue that separated the town from the palace, and instantly flattened him against a mud wall.

"Land's sake!" Evin whispered hoarsely, flattening Elle too.

From both sides of the shadowy bush path that lined the opposite side of the road, Edo men were pouring heavy fire from the protection of tree perches, buildings, and an embankment. About a hundred yards down the wide street, British redcoats were shoving their Maxim machine guns into position.

"Perhaps we should find an alternate route to our house!" Mateus said in a feminine wavering tone.

"What is it?" Brendan demanded.

"It appears we're suddenly on the wrong side of the war!" Mateus shrieked.

"Ighiwiyisi!" A man shouted from somewhere above their heads, and all turned to look at the roof of the building they hugged. The man appeared as a black cookie cutter shape, waving his dane-gun. "You have come to fight with us!"

"Asoro!" Apparently Brendan knew the man. "Get down from there right now! Your stupid gun is no match for the big guns of the whitemen!"

"I have already killed four!" Asoro proclaimed.

"You might kill five with your ammunition of broken metal and iron bolts, but you can't stop the whitemen from coming! Do you see what they have?" He looked to Elle. "What do they have?"

"Maxims and rockets."

Brendan returned to shouting at the roof. "They have big guns! And—"

A huge explosion not thirty feet behind them sent the *Oyinbo* group hurtling to their faces in the dirt, Brendan and Evin both covering half of Elle. It was the unearthed ancient Portuguese cannon that had been hauled to a stockade commanding the entrance to the bush path, and Elle heard the hail of nails and stones peppering the ground, a few pebbles landing on them with plopping sounds.

"Avast," gasped Brendan. "It's just that old dog-eared cannon."

"Why don't we take the back way, through everyone's gardens?" Elle panted when the two men allowed her to move.

She saw that no one had been injured by the cannon shot, but now, coming around the same corner they had just turned down, well nigh onto fifty Edo warriors, advancing plain and bold down the center of the avenue. Not only was there no escape now, the brave marching of the men, who were after all armed only with hunting bows and arrows and dane-guns, swept the *Oyinbo* along in their wake, and toward the redcoats.

Elle felt a weak swooning in her legs that angered her all the more because she needed to fight! She needed to claw her way out from the entombment of these warriors, who were obviously of a suicidal mind, striding toward Maxim guns armed with bows and arrows. "Brendan!"

Brendan flailed away at the men, finally taking one glassy-eyed fellow out with a punch to the nose, but the other men marched right over the fallen warrior. Creamy smoke engulfed them when the warriors fired their pieces packed with banana leaf wadding, and the acrid smell of sulphur stung Elle's nose. Brendan grabbed Elle by the arms. "We'll duck inside that door-way, see right there? Get ready to go when—"

A rapid tattooing of Maxim fire scythed through the men near them. The Maxim bullets were so fast they weren't visible, and they made no sound, but suddenly holes were appearing in men. A muscular warrior standing near Elle twisted sideways like a screw, great ropes of intestines spurting from his back. Another bullet seemed to go through three men at once, leaving the third man toppling at an odd angle, one leg liquefied to mush. This time Brendan and Elle hit the dirt alongside the Edo warriors, and there commenced a confused mangling of limbs as Elle tried to discern which ones were living+ and which were dead.

"Elle!"

She heard Brendan, but her face was smashed in a fellow's armpit. "Brendan!"

"Are you hit?"

"I don't think so. We'd better stay right here."

"Yes; the warriors are going for another round. Don't move."

There was another barrage of Maxim fire, and warriors thudded to the ground. Elle's ears rang from the report of the gun, and bullets pinged when they ricocheted off the Portuguese cannon.

"Elle!" More body parts muffled Brendan's voice. "As soon as it quiets down, I'll stand up waving this *eruhan*, and walk slowly towards the beefeaters."

As Elle was wondering whose *eruhan* Brendan planned on waving, there was a giant crack that made the ground shudder, and clods of soil came raining down on her back. That must have been the seven-pounder artillery. Elle turned her head out from the warrior's armpit to see that one of the clods now balanced precariously on her elbow was a severed hand, still clasping a rusty dane-gun.

The avenue was now relatively calm, as though all the bold warriors had been mown down. Elle shook some more heavy weights off her back and raised herself on her hands, peeking over a body to see Brendan doing the same, squinting down the avenue. The seven-pounder projectile had torn a trough up the middle of the street, piling men and limbs on either side of it like morbid topiaries.

But then there was a baffling interruption.

"*You god damned idiots! Will you just stop shooting? Can't you see we're fucking whitemen?*"

"Evin!" shouted Brendan, thrashing around in the pile of limbs in his attempts to get to his feet. "Avast! What the hell are you doing? Get the hell down!"

For Evin was standing to one side of the trough, waving his arms about like a paddlewheel steamer, his piece firmly in its holster at his hip. "If you'd just stop long enough for us to leave this god damned street, maybe your next casualties won't be fellow whitemen, you bodacious morons!"

The beefeaters appeared to be forming a square. Elle saw that they predictably put the native Protectorate troops at the front of the square, bluejackets and marines forming the other more sheltered flanks. The Protectorate men made a formidable picture in their blue serge uniforms and red fezzes, shouldering their smart Martini-Henry rifles.

"Ev, knock it off!" Brendan tore Evin away by the sleeve, and as he dragged the stumbling man to the side of the road, Elle saw Evin's entire right arm was awash with a coat of blood.

Then, from the roofs above them and the trees across from them, fresh gunfire down the avenue. Elle saw, from behind her breastwork of a dead warrior's back, at least three Protectorate men collapse on the ground. Then more—three of the redcoated Marines, who made brilliant targets there in the dusty smoky street, went jerking to the ground. British troops scampered about, pulling their casualties behind the trunk of an enormous silk-cotton tree. They shrieked curses and cried for water. One bluejacket, leaning against the tree holding a bloody comrade, took enraged shots at roofs and into the jungle, before a man who seemed to be a doctor dragged them both behind the tree trunk.

Elle felt herself lifted in the air, sailing along between Brendan and Evin, blood from Evin's arm plastering the entire front of her shirtwaist.

She was behind the mud gate, in the safety of a jungle garden.

As rapid beefeater volley-firing made a thunderous commotion out in the street, Brendan wrapped his arms round Elle and pressed her back into the mud wall. But oddly, Evin was trying to tear them apart.

"Elle! Come here, look!"

Was Evin going crazy with *juju*? Perhaps he was afflicted with the sort of combat hysteria Elle had heard tell of. To her utter horror, he shoved her back to the garden gate. "Evin! What's wrong? Let's just strike through this house, and out the—"

Evin shook her, and pointed a stiff arm urgently at some trees. Elle didn't see. Evin shook her some more. She then saw brown limbs in a mahogany tree—she could see where the sniper sat, as the leaves trembled on the branch. Fact, as they watched, the gunner popped off another marine, one so close Elle could see his bushy red beard. But it was an awfully thin branch for a warrior to sit on—how did he not slip off it, and hit the ground?

"Yes!" Elle whispered loudly. "A sniper! Now, let's get—"

"No!" Evin's eyes flashed. "Don't you see who it is?"

Brendan was now pressing them from behind, although he could not have seen that far, with his sasswood eyes still bleary from the poison. "Who is it, Ev?"

Evin looked meaningfully at Elle, and she knew he didn't want Brendan knowing who it was. Onaiwu?

"Nobody," Elle breathed.

The beefeaters were now so close the seven-pounder projectiles were smashing to the left of them, up the street toward the palace. But the street was clear of living warriors, and it was the few remaining snipers in the trees that harassed the soldiers.

Another marine went twirling back shot, flinging his rifle aloft and slamming into his fellows. When Elle heard the high-pitched laughter emanating from the leafy bower, she exhaled till her lungs nearly collapsed, and she had to clasp the mud wall. But Brendan was swifter, pushing past her and jogging across the wide avenue, nimbly using the downed warriors as stepping-stones.

"Brendan! Stop! Come back!"

There was no use, and Elle and Evin stepped back into the street with their hands at their sides just in time to see three Protectorate men, whom Elle had known to practice at shooting squirrels out of trees, sprint to the front of the column and take aim at Ode with their rifles.

"*Ode!*" hollered Brendan, then he was gone in the bushes.

Now taking Brendan's Schofield in her hand, Elle joined Evin in racing across the street, heedless of any gunfire, for they had seen Ode tumble to the shrubbery below.

"*Oyinbo!*" a Protectorate soldier said with a slack jaw.

Before they could reach the bushes, Brendan emerged, cradling the loose pile of limbs that was Ode—his rifle must have fallen to the ground, for his arm dangled inertly in the air. Brendan's face was a barely contained mask of rage. Elle touched Ode's forehead, and thought she saw his eyelids flicker. A part of one shoulder had been torn away, and blood from somewhere near his hip trickled over Brendan's fingers.

"Let's run back," Evin suggested. "If we go right now, we'll make it before the troops."

They raced toward the Protectorate men who had shot Ode, and were now jamming themselves against the mud wall in preparation for more volley-firing, as the three-sided square moved up the avenue. But Brendan stopped in front of the men with his bare feet spread wide apart on the dirt, and hollered in a bone-chilling voice, *"This is my son, you right bastards!"*

The men were apparently so cowed at the sight of the murderous *Oyinbo* they huddled against the wall with quaking knees. Hefting Ode onto one powerful arm, Brendan's fingers grappled for something at Elle's side, and she knew he wanted his Schofield.

"Now, men! Before they load again—charge!"

As the bugler played his chipper tune and the queues of men roared a cacophonous cheer, their tromping boots shook the ground, and Elle furiously yanked Brendan back inside the garden gate.

This time they didn't stop. They charged through the house and out the back door, taking back alleys and garden gates till they reached home.

24

After locking the front door not only with the usual iron bar but with carved walking sticks and other iron implements jammed underneath, Brendan and Evin joined the others in the armory room. Elle tended to Evin's arm, while Brendan and Mateus (who had appeared unscathed as though transported to the house by *juju*) looked over Ode. A Maxim bullet had sliced through a vein in Evin's upper arm. Elle cleaned the wound with witch hazel extract, and wrapped it tightly in rags of a ripped *eruhan*. Iden fetched laudanum where directed from Evin's bed room, and Evin chugged freely of the treacly concoction, but Ode was another story.

A large chunk of Ode's shoulder had been torn away by the Protectorate bullets. They placed him on a clean mattress in an alcove off the armory, and the little squirt went in and out of consciousness, eyeballs rolling back in his head, as Brendan and Mateus worked on him. After determining no bone had been taken with the bullet, they cleaned and bandaged the shoulder. The other bullet had pierced his waist just under the ribcage, exiting with a loss of flesh and leaving a horrendous wound, but all his vitals seemed intact, so they cleaned him and rolled him up like a mummy in bandages.

The survivors now sprawled in the armory, listening to the occasional tattoo of the Maxim guns from the palace compound.

"I suppose the British could always just jump down one of our impluviums," Mateus helpfully pointed out.

Elle perched on the only stool in the room, and she now pulled Brendan to sit on the floor between her knees. "I really doubt they have much interest in harming the common man—unless you've heard otherwise, Brendan." With her sea sponge she began lathering and massaging the back of his neck.

"*Ahhhh*," Brendan sighed deeply. Almost as an afterthought, he said, "I agree with you, Elle. I've just been on a long journey. I'm waiting for my soul to catch up with me."

Everyone nodded and fell silent then, in appreciation of Brendan's long journey.

Elle washed Brendan, her fingers following the contours of his long muscles, massaging him in the manner of the masseur from her gymnasium in New York. She paid particular attention to his wrists, blackened by the manacles he had worn for so long, and his beautifully expressive, tapered hands, the stroking of which excited her beyond bounds of propriety for their situation. Brendan breathed deeply, rapidly, his head leaned back against her inner thigh, eyes closed.

Mateus stood, holding aloft one of the lamps. "We're holing up in my chambers. I'll be taking this rifle, if you don't mind."

Brendan didn't flicker an eyelid, so Evin nodded at Mateus.

"And this cutlass."

Evin said tiredly, "Give Iden a weapon too."

Mateus and Iden left, Iden stroking Elle's arm with the back of her hand and gazing fondly at Brendan, but he didn't budge.

"Are you all right?" Elle whispered in his ear. With a towel she dried the black from his wrists.

"*Mmmmm*," Brendan uttered bearishly. Evin, sitting on his

behind with his hands clasped between his knees, jumped visibly. As if sensing this, Brendan finally opened his eyes and said to Evin, "I'm composing a poem in my mind. Listen.

Gentle hunter
His tail plays on the ground
While he crushes the skull.
Beautiful death
Who puts on a spotted robe
When he goes to his victim.
Playful killer
Whose loving embrace
Splits the leopard's heart."

Evin smiled warmly, as though he were at a picnic, and not huddled in an armory while the city fell around him. "One of your leopard praise poems."

"Aye," Brendan continued in his lazy, syrupy voice, but then he leaped with such muscular brawn, Elle was compelled to enwrap his chest in her forearms and hold tight. "*The leopards!* What're they going to do to the leopards?"

Evin was up in a half-crouch, putting out a soothing hand toward Brendan. "Sit tight, Bren. We're not going anywhere just yet."

"Yes, dear heart, wait. We can't go running over there right now; wait 'til they get all of their . . . rampaging and pillaging out of the way."

"Aye, let them plunder!" Evin's Irish accent had never come through before, as Brendan's did when agitated. Evin had always sounded just like an Alabaman.

Elle hugged Brendan tight, and licked the helix of his ear. "If we go out now, they're just going to be crazed, and it's near dark, someone might shoot us by mistake." He ceased to struggle, and deflated into a luscious pile of limbs between her thighs. She spread a fresh sponge of soapy water across his bare chest, basking in the firm tautness of his pectorals.

"Aye, and I can see about as well as a blind mole-rat."

As Elle continued to press sucking kisses to the archly sexy side of Brendan's throat, Evin stood. "I've seen that happen with sasswood. But it goes away within a day or so."

Brendan raised himself to an imperial height between Elle's legs. "Aye, and it were well nigh the *only* thing preventing me from plugging that traitorous worm squirming on the *Iroko* tree."

"Oh, my," breathed Elle. It had not occurred to her that she had stolen Brendan's thunder. It all whistled by in such a snap, and it was her natural reaction, something done without thinking, such as a story she had heard of a mother leaping over an impossibly tall boulder to snatch her infant from the jaws of a wolf. To placate him, she said, "I would have given you the gun, but I knew your eyes were ailing you."

"Mmmph," mumbled Brendan with a dissatisfied air.

"Mmmph," Elle echoed, and to shut him up, she twined clear around his shoulders and planted a ravenous kiss on his mouth. Her hands lingered and slid down farther on his belly, concave from weeks of little food.

Evin gruffly said, "I'll strike for the front room and keep a watch." With a tenderness and humor that was distinctly uncharacteristic of him, he bent down and said quietly to Elle, "Go easy on him."

She looked up, saw the twinkling in his eyes, and knew it was just his love for his partner that spoke. She smiled back.

Alone with only one lamp casting sinister shadows on the mud walls, Elle tossed aside Brendan's *eruhan* with one hand. She had to bend her torso clean over him to lovingly soap his pubic bone, and he took advantage to lean in and growl into her cleavage. "Aye, my little minx. You don't know how many times I wanted to shout for you at the top of my lungs in that bottomless pit."

"Oh," gasped Elle, shocked at the sudden hardness of the thick, hot root of his penis. Leaning farther over him like a washerwoman scrubbing the floor, she swept the sea sponge around his heavy balls in one prodigious motion, pumping his penis with an overhand stroke that filled her entire palm. "I never want to lose you again."

Brendan yanked down her bodice with abandon, and she was glad she had dressed with care that morning as a symbol of her hope for Brendan's survival. She had secured herself in her best mauve corset that he loved. Now he muttered into her bosom, "Ah, my darling minx, you don't know how much you roused me when you masturbated me in the cell. I was well nigh fit to rupture in your hand, then they took you away . . . And for my load of sin, how loud and clanky it is frigging myself with my arms in chains."

That was so unexpected it provoked a peal of delighted laughter from Elle. "Then I can finish what I started . . . " she purred. She cast aside the sponge and proceeded to pump his penis in earnest, her palm worrying the shiny, taut head, her fist admiring the length and breadth of him that brushed up clear against his navel.

"Ah, no! Don't!"

His piercing gasp startled her. Was it wrong to be rutting when outside the city fell? For they could hear intermittent crowds of lime-juicers tramping past their house; apparently all *Ivbiedo* were gone, in hiding, or rounded up. But Brendan reached over his shoulder and vaulted her over him; she tumbled in a rush of striped fabric, the wind knocked out of her.

She stood on her knees between his naked thighs. While his nimble fingers unbuttoned her skirt, he looked her in the eyes. "Nay, my love. I want to take you straight up, like the man I haven't been. I couldn't help you when I rotted in the jail. You wouldn't even be stuck in Edo right now if you weren't waiting for me."

She was rife with distress that Brendan should think in this manner. "No! You wouldn't have been in jail if it weren't for Rip, that's what it is! It's all my fault!" Naked to her drawers now, she climbed atop Brendan and straddled him lustily, pressing his face into her breasts.

Brendan's fingertips limned the outer lips of her quim, flicking against her full stiff button. He lifted his face to hers. "Aye, then it is the fault of us both—"

"—and the virtue of us both—" She jumped with the sudden electrical spasms that shot up her spine. She mashed her honeypot directly down over his erect penis, sliding up and down the length of it without letting him enter her, as though riding a slippery horse.

Brendan gasped. "Nevertheless not . . . withstanding, I am taking you *right now* because if I wait"—he maneuvered her hips with his hands, sliding her in ever longer and more strident gallops against the hulking mass of him—"one more minute"—with each thrust he came centimeters closer to capturing her on the head— "I'm going to come off against your face."

That got to her, that *come off against your face* with his direct, innocent gaze as though he were an uncorrupt youth who had never taken a woman before. She paused on the head of his penis and hovered there, for one half a moment taking in the sight of this ravishing man that she loved so utterly she would kill to protect him, and she knew then she was the most blessed of all women to have found him again, to have found what she was looking for in the Oil Rivers.

And then all his youthful naïveté vanished when he thrust her down to impale her on his penis. She was so unaccustomed to it in recent weeks that a sharp pain knifed through her womb, but as she felt the heat of his pelvis slapping against hers, she melted into a boneless feminine vessel. The more masculine she allowed him to be, humping her from the floor with such abandoned animal thrusts, the more she relaxed until her insides felt like hot candle wax molded around him. She had always scoffed at those customs and conventions that pigeonholed the sexes into categories, but she now felt that Brendan had to take her like this, had to take her like a Cro-Magnon, with pure bestial passion.

She thrilled with such heightened lust she thought she might come off just from the sheer pleasure of him, but only a few more delicious strokes and he was arching into her, crying out with his head thrown back, and she felt him erupting with force against her womb. She sucked on his penis with her female muscles, crouching hunched over him, and she felt in his virile spending he had gained back most of the strength that had drained from him in recent weeks.

He gasped and jerked inside of her for many long moments, his hand wrapped around the back of her neck. Slowly his face ironed out, his mouth began to turn up at the edges, and he was able to open his eyes. They glittered up at Elle, the black dilated pupils no longer obfuscating the turquoise, and he said, clear as a bell, "My love."

Elle wanted to weep then. To hide it she flung herself against his chest, and kissed him sweetly, sucking on his mouth, laughing that she could still make him jump by flexing her inner muscles.

Brendan made a mattress of blankets he pulled from his bedstead. They drank brandy, and he allowed her to feed him some fruit. Although he said his stomach was still queasy, she insisted he needed nutrition, an idea he scoffed at.

There was hollering in the close night air, and the occasional rampaging of troops down the street outside. They lay entwined in each other's limbs. Brendan drifted off, and Elle cradled him in her arms, bestowing butterfly kisses on his sweet upturned face. At length she, too, faded away, and dreamed of headless bodies, carnage, and fire.

～ ✐ ～

"Get up! The city's on fire!"

Brendan heard Evin all right; he just did not much feel like getting up. He felt like he had slept a week—though they had only lounged indoors for another entire day—and he could easily sleep another week, comfortably in his cocoon of blankets and Elle. But now Elle was shaking him, too, saying,

"Brendan, love, get up! Can't you smell the smoke? We have to get out of here!"

Indeed his nose twitched, full of acrid pungent fumes, even in the cavernous seclusion of his armory. Leaping to his feet, Brendan threw on his Edo clothes.

Evin exhorted, "Some women from my music class are here—they saw British soldiers setting fire to roofs with their torches. They want to come with us and leave town."

Brendan did not even bother that Evin had an eyeful of Elle's naked body before she clothed herself. "It's just looting and pillaging, that's all there is to it!"

Elle cried, "How do you burn down mud huts?"

Brendan grabbed from a hook on the wall one of his quilted ponchos, a body armor of sorts the *Ivbiedo* wore, and tossed it over Elle. He yanked until her little head popped out through the opening in the center. "The wattle roofs will burn sure enough, and huts are close enough together to spread from roof to roof. Buddy, I only have one more of these armors; take one of the leopard skins." Brendan took another quilted poncho for himself, draping Elle with an additional leopard skin, and there was a smaller leopard skin for Ode, the one he liked to use when hunting.

Ode had been waking and sleeping for two days. The music class women now fabricated a papoose so one of them could carry the thin boy. Brendan tried to argue that, as the strongest person there, he should carry Ode, but the women insisted, saying they were accustomed to carrying all manner of loads on their backs and heads.

Brendan crammed a knapsack full of essential items that he gave to Elle to sling over her shoulder; he took an additional one containing his poems and "slim volumes." He saw Evin had already festooned himself with similar bags that no doubt contained cuttings and seeds. The last thing Brendan took was his blue lens spectacles, and he faced an entirely fresh world.

He took a veritable arsenal of weapons from the walls, handing whatever seemed reasonable to the other two, regretting he could not take more, and they hustled down the honeycomb of hallways until they burst into the courtyard. One could see layers of smoke settling before the garden wall that was only twenty feet away, and a mantle of ashes fell upon them. Brendan jostled Elle toward the front gate, but Evin wanted to pause, to give a silent panegyric to the gardens he had lovingly crafted.

Brendan twinged with pain to think he didn't get to say goodbye to his *ikegobo*. "What's that chair doing?"

Elle shrugged. "Oh, that. Ologboshere sent it to me two days ago. I have no idea why."

Brendan shook his head as if to rid it of cobwebs. "You don't know what it is? It's a throne."

Trying to giggle foolishly, Elle wound her arms through his. "Aren't most thrones just like stools?"

Brendan was serious under the faded buckskin color of his face. "I've never seen a throne like that either. But that's what it is."

"Now, why would he . . .?"

They had only just stepped onto the road when a trio of blue-jackets ran toward them, rifles at the ready.

"Crikey!" said one, motioning to the other two to lower their weapons. "Eh, what're you doing dressed up like a savage?" Behind him, another youth whispered, "*She's a woman!*"

Brendan shook his pike at the three young men. "Because I *am* a savage. Who's in charge here and where can I find him?"

The youth looked uncertain. "Lieutenant Colonel Hamilton, and I daresay you can find him over by what used to be the palace."

"And why did you start these fires?"

For the first time, the three men relaxed. They well nigh started slapping each other with jocosity as the midshipman said, "Oh, *we* didn't start no fires, sir! It were some carriers, playing with gunpowder, like."

"No, sir," piped up another. "We wouldn't start no fires. Carriers."

"Playing with gunpowder," Brendan echoed.

Evin emerged from the garden then, and it was difficult to tell if his eyes watered from melancholy or from the smoke. The three soldiers were galvanized to attention afresh at the sight of another *Oyinbo* savage, and they turned to escort Brendan to where they presumed he didn't know the palace was.

Brendan shared looks with Elle and Evin to see a brass Portuguese horseman pendant sticking out from the back pocket of the corporal's trousers. Around his rifle stock, one private had a brass altar ring that he probably didn't know depicted bound and severed heads, and decapitated bodies with vultures feasting upon them. Indeed, the closer they got to the palace, more soldiers dashed hither and yon carrying all manner of spoils of war. Some of the carved tusks were so big and heavy it took two or more men to hoist one of them, and there was barely a beefeater who did not cradle an altar tableau or a head of the Oba under his arm.

"I say." Brendan fell easily into the beefeater lingo. "Would it be possible to get some colors to accompany us back to Sapele?"

"Oh," said the corporal merrily, "I daresay you could take a whole regiment back with you. Everyone's blooming eager to get out of here. It's been a larky expedition, but we've seen enough human sacrifices to last us all month."

"Do we really want to accompany a regiment, Brendan?" Elle asked. "Is that wise?"

"I'd say whatever saves our hides right now is wise, *amebo*." Brendan turned to Evin, who walked a bit behind him in a daze, gazing up at the firmament as though he had been smoking hemp.

"By the way, where's Mateus?"

"I don't know," Evin answered vaguely. "When I woke this morning, Iden and him were gone."

The wind blew toward them as they entered the main palace compound. The fires engulfed the wattle roofs of buildings almost as fast as they walked, but the road was broad enough to walk down the center in safety. Sobbing women shouted oaths in the front gardens of burning houses; people threw valued objects into the street, where most were stomped on or scooped up by soldiers before being deemed worthless and smashed.

"Camps," murmured Elle.

About twenty encampments were indeed already erected in neat rows in the square of the Oba's market, soldiers bivouacking under temporary tarpaulins. The *Oyinbo* marched slowly through the spectacle, wordless at seeing soldiers seated on folding chairs, shaving in brass Neptunes, writing dispatches, cleaning guns. On the perimeter soldiers of the Niger Coast Protectorate Force had set up their own cooking fires, and it was a gruesome juxtaposition to see them grilling something as yet unidentified on sticks while not twenty yards away human remains lay decomposing.

The bluejackets led them to an operation on the grand scale. In one of the Oba's storehouses, the corrugated iron roof was smoldering, smoke poured out the doors, and bluejackets dashed in and out carrying off the heaviest tusks and brass plaques. Some of them had already decorated themselves with the absurd finery Brendan had traded the Oba: satin umbrellas, glass walking sticks, and comic opera gold-braided jackets. Brendan did not mistake the irony that these items had come all the way from America and Liverpool, only to wind up on *Oyinbo* soldiers.

A primped-up fellow sat behind a table near the door, apparently attempting to take an inventory of the items being looted, but it seemed he was only getting about half of them written down. He was oblivious that directly behind him, soldiers who had tied cloths around their faces were piling headless bodies, and in some cases only limbs, into a mound. At the nearby body pit, a few of the more hale Protectorate Force men were being lowered on ropes to discern the life behind some of the moving limbs.

"Lieutenant Colonel Hamilton?" The strange old bird regarded the *Oyinbo* with more distaste than anything else around him. "You'll find him directly there, wearing leopard skin. What are you Yankees doing here?"

Brendan ignored the fellow. *"Leopard skin!"* That was the ultimate in sacrilege, for an outsider to wear leopard skin.

They had only to walk on the other side of the corpse mound to find a robust man a few years senior of Brendan, shaven head nearly bald, striding around in flag-waving zeal. He had blue lens spectacles on such as Brendan, Brendan noted with distaste.

"As to the parts you're not sure of, Groper, throw them in there as well! We've no need for random body parts without any brains attached to them!" Hamilton was bellowing with mirth, holding an unlit cigar that he incessantly jabbed between his teeth.

"Sir!" Brendan saluted. "Request to be allowed to accompany a regiment back to Sapele, where we hail from."

"Hoo, hoo!" Hamilton's face almost split in half with glee to see the *Oyinbo*. "Yankees! Hailing from—what's the name of that bloody town?" he asked his Lieutenant. "Sapooboo? Ookinfuk?"

Brendan willed his face to remain impassive. "And sir, I am requesting . . . have you seen any *live* leopards around the palace in your . . . travels?"

Hamilton posed with his cigar in mid-air. "Why, yes, indeed, how did you come to know that, young Yankee? Are you in need of some more uniforms for your party of women, boys, and niggers?"

Brendan shut his eyes briefly. "Actually, sir . . . I caught the leopards. For the Oba. And I'd appreciate taking what's left of them. If Moor is around here anywhere, he can give you the whaling big story."

"Moor, eh? Yes, he's here somewhere. Where'd you see him

last, Cowan?"

The Captain said, "He's over by the . . . *that tree*, dictating the terms of surrender."

"May I ask . . ." Brendan tried to make the weapons in his hands seem small by casually hefting them at his side. "What *are* the terms of surrender? Will you allow the Oba to continue to rule?"

Hamilton threw his head back and laughed boldly, poking his cigar at Brendan. His face behind the dark spectacles took on a cadaver's cast, as though it were full of skin powders. "No, young Yankee, he made the mistake of running! I have proclaimed the independence of all dukedoms and fiefs, or whatever bloody thing you want to call these hamlets. We have freed the Benin populace from a most appalling yoke of pagan Ju-juism." Abruptly he changed his mood, and he leaned in confidentially to Brendan. "This city deadened every feeling of right and crushed out all desire for improvement, you know, old bloke. No worse state has ever existed in any country or at any time."

Brendan blinked. "Sir. The fact of the business is, it would stand everyone in good stead if instead of looting treasure, you'd send a few bucket brigades to the Ikpoba River, for you're torching the houses of good common people. There'll be well nigh nothing left to rule over if you don't."

This idea sent Hamilton into greater paroxysms of laughter. His Lieutenant handed him a can of kerosene that he grabbed without even looking, after sticking his cigar into his mouth. He spewed in sibilant joy, "These bronze pieces of Egyptian and Chinese casting? Hoo, hoo!" He backed up to the pile of bodies. "These are Bini curios, blooming pieces of junk that we'll use to defray the costs of the expedition."

Hamilton turned, and sloshed great gallons of fuel onto the stiff limbs. He made an entire round of the pile that now stacked up as high as the men could throw, assisted by great carved wooden pillars torn from the palace roofs. He then tossed the empty can onto the ground and resumed his palaver with Brendan, accepting a match safe from his Lieutenant. Above them, the sky was a deadly rust brown. Brendan imagined he could see the spirits of those recently departed swirling up to enter *erinmwin*, the world across the sea and the private home of Osanobua.

"I am telling you, young Yankee." Hamilton threw a match over his shoulder without looking. The entire pyre exploded into a revolting and oddly poignant sphere of flame. Brendan felt Elle, beneath his arm, twitch at the sudden eruption, and they backed off from the pyre as Hamilton advanced on them. "This is goodbye, Benin. Your character must indeed be bad if the longing of seven hundred men to see you is in two days changed to a fervent desire never to look upon your red walls again."

Brendan clasped Elle to his chest. "It's a mighty grave thing, sir."

Brendan led his party toward the compound where he knew the leopards were kept. His friends corralled some men who yearned to leave Edo, along with their attendant straggling women and children. Soon they had a party that approximated a regiment of their own. It was simple to capture the leopards, tamed after years in their pen. Brendan and two fellows latched tethers onto the animals, and they walked them calmly in a sober group to the Ologbo road, where they met up with a similarly ragtag assemblage of beefeaters, all nauseous regarding their expedition.

They passed by a strange party that was headed into Edo. The supply column of bluejackets looked harmless at first, but a jolly fat man attired in khaki was creating a ruckus.

"What would you say the mood of the soldiers is?" he queried the blasé soldiers of Brendan's regiment. When they did not reply, the fat man insisted, "Would you say they are ebullient? Shocked? Filled with angst?"

A few men draped with photographic equipment scrambled behind the fat man who took scribbled notes as he trudged.

Brendan shared an empty glance with him, but the man moved on to the next soldier. Oddly enough, he handed the soldier a cigar. "There's a lot more where that came from! England needs to know the truth from you world-weary men." His donkeys were laden with deck-chairs, what looked like hams, and a champagne bottle he now proffered to Lieutenant Harrold. "What's up with this human sacrifice? How many bodies would you say they sacrifice every day?"

It took Brendan's group another five minutes just to pass the long column of servants associated with the jovial reporter.

Rain fell just after they passed Agagi. Elle stumbled quite a bit, and Brendan was glad when Evin brought out a flask of her special brandy. There was a twinge of jealousy inside him for the time Elle and Evin had shared together, but he knew he was being ridiculous.

"Are you going to come live in our backyard?" *When we're married*, Brendan added in his mind.

Evin appropriately walked on the other side of Brendan, away from Elle, sliding over his own set of silk-cotton roots that lay in their path.

"Even if it rained tadpoles and periwinkles."

Brendan snorted skeptically, merely to do it. "That sounds like a Lee County saying."

Evin snorted back. His lupine face didn't look exhausted in the slightest. "No, it's from Marengo County, as you might recall."

Brendan saw one of his Edo friends carrying an umbrella. He approached the fellow and palavered to borrow it. Brendan opened it, and held it over Elle's head as they walked.

She looked up with refulgent beauty. "You know, Mick," she said with a mellow sort of dignity that was quite flattering to her. "I was worried about Ode, but I think he'll do just fine."

"Aye," Brendan averred. He felt caught between two immense emotions. "It's the *Akpo r'Oyinbo* coming to take over the *Akpo r'Oba*."

They were silent for a long time, trying to walk abreast of each other on the narrow footpath. Every once in awhile they'd come to a glade where smoke from the burning city hovered before them, like witches planning evil.

"Do you know," Elle said suddenly, as bright as a bell. "If a woman dies childless with no one to bury her correctly, she will be stuck here as a ghost."

Brendan didn't know how that pertained to her at that very moment. "Yes . . . " he said uncertainly.

Elle was silent for another hundred feet or so. Then she seemed to clear her throat. "But if I have Ode . . . do you think that counts?"

"Oh, aye! It counts most assuredly!" Brendan was glad for a chance to make Elle happy for once. Fact, it emboldened him enough to say, "I had a vision, Elle, back in August when I was hunting with Ode. I envisioned you, with your luxuriant auburn hair, only I hadn't met you yet. And you were sitting in that . . . *throne* that Ologboshere caused to be carved for you."

Elle tilted her head. It seemed that he could see the reflection of green leaves in her face. "Is that so?"

His vision seemed to make her happy, for she clasped his arm even tighter, and walked beside him all the way to Ologbo.

25

August 17, 1897

"Ighiwiyisi is back!"

Ode scooted to a stop, made his proclamation, and raced out of the room.

Elle rose slowly. She had a squalling young one in a papoose beneath her breast, and was cleaning the behind of another. She needed something to do in Sapele, and mission work was the closest thing to her former New York job of helping the afflicted.

Mary Wells looked on Elle with mild surprise. "Aren't you going down to the anchorage?"

Elle gazed at the open door. "I'm just so . . . happy."

There was a brief pause, then both women broke out in laughter. Mary untied the sling from Elle's shoulder and exhorted her to run.

Brendan had been gone over a month. On the sixth of August, runners had come from Edo, telling that the Oba had finally surrendered. He "went for bush" for six months with those of his wives he had not sent to his mother's house, and seven hundred of his subjects. They had entered the city by the Sapoba Road, unarmed, holding aloft a white flag. The runners told that the twenty wives were of a different sort from those seen before, with chignons in the European style, and splendid hair pins, necklaces, and ornaments.

Brendan had made tracks for Edo. He desired to testify that the Oba was one of the last to leave Edo before it fell, and was blameless in the Phillips affair. He wanted to further express that it would make for a cool transition if the Oba were allowed to continue to rule as a de facto head of state, without any connection or tribute from outside towns. The British had done away with central authority and rule through the provinces, chasing out Edo officials resident there. In any case, the British had been unable to appoint a new Oba, for as long as Ovonranmwen continued to live, a new Oba could not be anointed.

Now Elle met Brendan in the middle of the road. He had already pushed himself through the surging bevy of people who, regardless of the fact that it was pouring rain so forcefully the air was nearly solid water, were eager with intent to discover news of the Oba. Although Brendan had many people clinging to his person, he grasped Elle's body with fervor as he attempted to extricate himself from the native limbs. She squeezed him for a long time before he freed himself, and she was able to pull back and regard him.

He had grown darker, thinner, stronger, if such a thing were possible in a man of such "advanced years" as a full forty. Elle was gratified to see him in his *eruhan* that he had not worn for the entire rain season, though of course he still wore his river boots and a new blue silk vest encrusted with his medals and pins.

"You're home," Elle breathed.

"I would never leave you." His words were such syrup for Elle's ears, an enticing shiver ran up her arms. He finally freed his arms from the mélange of limbs, and instantly grabbed Elle behind the neck, kissing her deeply and profoundly.

They were accustomed to being in the thick of Africans, and would not have released each other had not Evin appeared to shake Brendan by the arm.

"Buddy! Let's get back to the house!"

They had brandies, and Evin showed Brendan the cuttings of his new cherry tree. Evin had been busy the past month chopping down the silk-cottons, palms, and *Iroko* trees that populated the jungle at the back of their house. He needed to make room for the leopards, and he wanted to build a new farm with some Edo trees he had created by grafting. This idea was a big sensation with townspeople, mostly women who were accustomed to farming and had all manner of ideas for the location of various fruits and vegetables, none of them involving anything that looked like a straight line. The soil was so fertile, the problem was not how to make things grow, but how to prevent them growing.

For Evin had given his Edo farm to Onaiwu's sons. After their Edo house had burned down to the mud pipes under the impluviums, Brendan had not wished to give *Ivbiedo* the impression he was in the good books of the British, so they had abandoned their *Akpo r'Oba*.

They sat now in the unmitigated sun of their back veranda, Brendan, Elle and Ode on a settee from Liverpool. Ode had been the "big dog of the courtyard" since coming to Sapele, a popular bossy child who liked to regale others with stories of Edo. The dog Pequod, who now resembled a lion with her rippling sienna fur and curious blonde topknot, lay panting at attention with her eyes fixed on her master. In the distance, lovely wine and raffia palms struck poses against the dove-colored sky as though they had been grown under glass. Evin was teaching Elle to care for the arboretum, and she particularly excelled at developing a new strain of daisy that could be planted in any climate.

Brendan swirled the brandy in his snifter. "Mayhap with all this new sun we could get some kind of cloth to cover one side of the veranda."

Evin leaped back into his chair, aghast at Brendan's trivial remark. "Forget about the cloth, Bren! Tell us about Edo."

Brendan squiggled in his seat, the better to prepare himself for the tale. "They've laid out a nine-hole golf course. The first hole is on the exact spot of the *Iroko* tree they cut down. Ah, well. The Resident, that bastard Captain Roupell you know, forced the Oba to kneel before him and rub his forehead against the ground three times."

"*No*," breathed Elle and Evin.

The other ten chiefs with the Oba had been forced to do the same, after which Roupell explained to the King that he was deposed. The Oba retired to the Obaseki's house—he had returned to Edo in April to take a position on a council of chiefs— and they had to wait for three weeks for Ralph Moor to arrive. At last the trial showed that Ologboshere along with five other chiefs was responsible for the slaughter of the Phillips mission, and had acted without the Oba's knowledge. In the interregnum, one chief had committed suicide, Ugiagbe died from fear of punishment, and another was deemed a boy so was passed over. There remained only Ologboshere at large, who was condemned to be hung in absentia, along with two remaining chiefs in Edo.

"So," Brendan explained, "this left five more chiefs needed to bring to account the seven white chiefs killed in Phillips's party. Moor said"— and here Brendan drew himself up and imitated the proper British accent—" 'This is no idle threat, and I solemnly promise to do what I say.' I struck a bargain for the Oba that if they could produce Ologboshere, all other *Ivbiedo* would go free."

"Oh, that's very smart of you, giving everyone the incentive to find Ologboshere," Elle said gently.

"Aye, they altered their tune mighty sudden," Brendan agreed. "But as you know, they've been harrying the hinterlands for six months trying to find him." He leaned over to bridge the gap between himself and Evin, and whispered loudly, "Am I affected with imaginary perceptions, or is Miriam in a family way?"

For Miriam had been wandering in and out of the veranda smiling and humming, bringing them unnecessary foodstuffs that nobody touched. Right now they could hear her clattering in the kitchen as she dragged something from the back of the pantry.

There ensued a big tense silence. Evin merely looked wolfish, but did not shy away from Brendan's stare. Elle opened her mouth, but shut it again when she realized it was Evin's place to speak.

At last Brendan lost the Mexican standoff. "I will interpret that in the affirmative." He turned to Elle. "Who might the father be?"

Again, Elle opened and shut her mouth. She looked to Evin for assistance. Evin took a couple of deep breaths and reluctantly opened his mouth wide enough to utter, "Me."

This new silence was awkward in the strained unspoken emotions running between the two partners. Elle longed to break the silence by referring to her daisies, the oilcloth that could shade part of the veranda, or somebody's gout. Miriam obliviously came wandering in just then, face still wreathed in smiles, to offer Brendan a tray of stuffed snails.

Elle cleared her throat. Brendan did not even appear to notice the juicy crustaceans Miriam proffered beneath his very nose. Elle massaged his bare bicep with what she hoped was a distracted air of unimportance, but Brendan only shuddered a little, as though trying to shake off an annoying fly. The relief in the air was palpable when Brendan finally opened his creaky jaw and said, "So. How long has this been going on?"

Evin exhaled all in a rush. "For a long time, Bren; sometimes you're just too obtuse or distracted by other things."

There was another brief Mexican standoff, but Brendan broke it by looking up at Miriam, smiling, and patted her hand. "I'll tell you one thing," he said affably, "I ain't forcing you to sleep in our backyard."

Elle laughed with relief. "Well, the backyard's a lot bigger now."

Brendan stood and went to gaze at their newly enlarged yard. "Do you love her?"

Evin took a long time about answering. "It's impossible to tell, Bren. Things are so different here in Africa. It's not the same sort of . . . whimsical flowery thing it is in America."

Brendan twirled around, fire in his face. "And this, from a fellow who looks down upon fraternizing with Africans!"

Evin leaped to his feet and pointed at the ground. "I've been a hypocrite, I'm well aware of that, Donivan! But Miriam is . . . different."

"And that's why you kept this a secret from me for so long?"

Evin shouted, "I kept it a secret from you because . . ." He stopped. "Because . . ." At last Evin's arms deflated, falling to his sides where they hung like wet towels. "Because I was ashamed."

Brendan nodded minutely, as Elle stood and took Miriam by the hand. "It's all right," Elle whispered to Miriam in English. "Evin is very happy that you will have his baby."

A most provident interruption occurred then. The thunderous clattering that echoed down the central hallway of the house came to a standstill at the back veranda door. The door exploded open. Miriam jumped several inches in the air, and Elle had to put a calming arm around her.

"Land's sake," Brendan whispered, and headed toward Elle.

But he need not have bothered protecting her, for there was Mateus in all his glory, Red Indian tonsure, the same dog-eared oily vest dangling from his wiry torso. "The Cross River Transport just arrived!" he proclaimed.

Elle's thoughts were of a more personal nature as she rushed the man, flinging her arms around him, ecstatic to breathe his gelatinous fishy odor, surprised to discover he was as dirty as he looked. "Oh, Mateus! Brendan didn't tell us you were found!"

Mateus didn't try much to extricate himself from Elle's grip, but he squirmed uncomfortably. "Maybe because I didn't *want* to be found! I was traveling with the Oba, you know. *Ikeja Orisa*, second in command to the gods. Well, we had to surrender after a while, as he got very tired of the unaccustomed roaming bush life. But, as the *Capitao* here probably told you, he made the dire mistake of trying to run again when he became nervous." Edgy at the female propinquity, Mateus shoved some things that resembled letters into Elle's hands.

"Aye," said Brendan, who was protectively squeezing the back of Elle's neck. "I didn't get to tell them that part."

Evin asked, "What's this, old buddy? What happened when he ran?"

Mateus stepped back several feet and described a whopping scenario with his talon hands. "Moor told him he couldn't order people about as before, but he'd still probably be the biggest chief depending on how he could govern. Moor said he'd take him and a few chiefs and servants on a tour for a year to Old Calabar, Lagos, and Yoruba country to show them how other towns were governed."

Elle nodded rapidly. "Yes, yes, that sounds like a humane idea."

"That was your fiancé's idea. But the Oba fled! He got scared and ran into the bush, without my knowledge, I might add. He was captured the next day, but Moor was so worked up by that time that he had him clapped in chains, and he's going to exile him to Old Calabar." Mateus paused for dramatic effect. "Forever. He told the Oba, 'Now this is whiteman's country. There is only one king in this country and that is the whiteman.' "

Elle's hand touched her mouth. "And the Oba is here, on the steamer?"

Brendan took over the story. "He's out there on deck! He shouted, 'I appeal to Olokun and the spirits of the departed Obas of Benin, my fathers, to judge between me and the Edo, who cunningly sold me into the hands of the British troops in search of their own liberty and benefit! Oh Edo, merciless and wicked, farewell!' "

Elle said to Brendan, "Come; we must go see the great man before he goes."

Instantly Brendan was hustling Elle to the door, Evin and Mateus hot on their heels. The gang of *Oyinbo* clattered down the wooden front steps to the silent tribute of the accumulated crowd of their clerks, factotums, converted, and music students. They fell into a lively pace down the road to the anchorage.

Brendan said flippantly, "*Amebo* . . .What were those letters Mateus dropped you?"

"Oh!" Elle had forgotten she clutched some papers. "Let me see. Oh, lovely! A letter from my brother Milos. And then . . . *oh, my!*"

"What?"

"A letter from Pulitzer. He . . ." Elle's voice trailed off as she opened the missive. "My!" she said, in an entirely new tone. "He has agreed to my proposal to make the trek to Tombouctou." For Elle had suggested to Pulitzer some articles might come from a trip to the fabled camp of Tuaregs and gold.

She looked out over the Ethiope River, where the bright white steamer *Daffodil* was at berth, flying Her Majesty's colors. Enlightenment dawned on Brendan's face, and he sucked Elle up into his embrace, his warm face against her pallid neck. He held her in his grip for many long moments before he gasped, "My *amebo* . . . that is the best news ever." He drew back to regard her, and his striking brilliant eyes warmed her heart. "I'm coming with you to Tombouctou."

"*What?*"

"There are many trade items I can pick up from those camel-lovers. Aside from . . . who else is going to protect you?"

They struck for the steamer, but Elle continued the argument. "But who will run your trade? You said Evin isn't the best at bargaining."

"Will the trade suffer if I leave for three months?"

"Well! Maybe in Marengo County they do things that way."

"No *amebo*, you've got it backward. It's Lee County where they are stunted."

"If you insist on coming along, you could make yourself useful by killing animals for our meals."

"Yes, see? I am handy to have around."

Elle wound her hand around Brendan's bicep, and looked into his serene face. She saw then that he was not joking about coming to Tombouctou with her. She had never loved a man who wanted to travel anywhere with her. They had always preferred to meet her for an hour, or to do business in the financial district. There was nobody who had wished to take a train to Queens with her, much less go overland to a godforsaken desert outpost.

"Let's get to the steamer." Still clutching his arm warmly, Elle resumed her walk in a light skip. "Do you want to hear something? I now feel that I know myself. But now I don't mind if the world knows me."

"Aye, you see, *amebo?* The ways of *Akpo r'Oba* are rubbing off on you."

"I think it is more the ways of *Akpo r'Ighiwiyisi.*"

CHAPTER

26

Brendan couldn't sleep.

Olokun knew he had expended enough tireless vim to have laid out flat thirty men by now. Since he'd returned to Sapele three days ago, there had been a mass of action—business on the *Hindustan*, every man jack accosting him as though he'd just canoed to *erinmwin* and returned to tell about it. Everyone wanted to know what had happened in Edo, what the Oba's last words were, when the Liverpool men were coming to sack Sapele, too. Then, Evin had been asking him for advice on proper crop rituals in the newly-cleared fields behind the house. Odd thing, Evin interested in how to form yam heaps and correctly align the cutlasses and hoes next to the calabash of *tombo*. Brendan showed him how to sacrifice a snail, and call upon the yams to come and feast on it.

And then, of course, he hadn't wanted to attend any dinners at Lyon's Consulate, even though Major Gallwey was in town, and Brendan was partial to the "Old Coaster" Gallwey, with his penchant for cricket and lawn tennis. For when the day's work was done, and Evin and Miriam had swept the table clear of all the dishes, Brendan just wanted to be with Elle either sitting on the sofa "reading book" or tangling with her for hours in his bed.

He'd just done that, for well nigh onto four hours. He still couldn't sleep.

He heard the baby crying somewhere in the house, and Evin's low voice shushing it as he quietly paced barefoot, Miriam usually being too exhausted to tend to it at night. Brendan went to his armory room to visit his *ikegobo*.

Onaiwu's son had unearthed his *ikegobo* in the ashes of his former house in Edo and had personally carried it back to Sapele to present to Brendan, along with many weapons and plaques he'd left behind, and some humorous items Onaiwu's son thought he might want, such as a smoking jacket (now suitably smoky), some zither picks, and a hog tamer.

Brendan felt an unease, but he was unable to figure out where it resided. It could be someone's bush soul harassing him, or a witch that was flying about at night as a bird. Perhaps he was hearing the crying of the Oba, who had by now probably reached his jail in Old Calabar. This last image filled Brendan with the most dread, so as a sort of catchall insurance against anything evil in general, he opened and held out a small calabash of *uxumu* and whispered, "Help me find the way." This would let him figure out whose spirit was sassing him at the moment.

"*Kóyo.*"

Brendan was so startled that he dropped the calabash.

Elle stood in the doorway, erotically wrapped in only a colorful length of cloth. Brendan rose to enfold her in his arms, nuzzling his face into her mass of tumbling hair. "Why are you awake?" he whispered against her neck.

She rubbed her lips on his face. "I woke up, and you weren't there."

Brendan smiled that she should mind him being gone. "Come, let's go back."

Leading the way to the bed room, he carried the lamp above their heads, setting it on the night table by Elle's side of the bed.

He saw the letters from three days ago brought by the Cross River Transport. He'd been so busy he'd forgotten to be curious about them.

He put Elle to bed like a child, loosening the dyed fabric about her body as a coverlet. "What was in those letters Mateus dropped you?"

With an arm flung above her head on the pillows and her hair spread out, Elle looked to be posing for a pre-Raphaelite painting. She even had that eerily illuminated skin, as though a celestial body behind her glowed. "One is from my dear Sal. He writes better than Milos. And one is from Pulitzer."

The back of Brendan's neck bristled to think of that old fish Pulitzer. He knew the old crock was still her boss, and he knew that after sampling the glories of such as himself Elle would never want another, but it still irked him, especially as Pulitzer was powerful, and richer than him. He wished Elle would go work for another reputable sheet. "What does Pulitzer want."

"Oh . . . " Elle stretched as though she hadn't stretched in years. She finally answered lightly, "Remember my idea to go to Timbuctoo and write a series of articles about it? Well . . . he approves of it, and wants me to get up an expedition." As a casual afterthought, she added, "The *World* will pay all expenses." She wiggled her toes at the end of the bed, and looked at them.

Brendan felt sick. He stood and went to the window, where all manner of fireflies were clamoring to be let in beyond the mosquito-netting. "When do you propose to leave?"

Getting to her feet, Elle came to stand behind him. He could see her in the reflection of the glass, wrapping the fabric around her body again. "Surely you can come along, as well? You've always been a world traveler. It will be nice for you to get out of the Oil Rivers, to see the fabled camp of Tuaregs and gold. And I certainly need you to skin and quarter all the animals we shoot!"

Brendan's jaw was so grimly set he could barely creak out the words. "You know I can't do that. I can't just let Evin take care of all the upcountry trade, the waterside trade, especially now that he's so busy with that nipper."

For Miriam had not been doing well since birthing the little Osahon. She'd been having a profound stretch of the blues and didn't have much zest for anything, as Elle well knew, having had to assist Miriam at all hours of the day herself. "Miriam will get better soon. The expedition isn't planned 'til next April when it rains again. We need the high water to get the steamer over many of the rocky rapids. You can come!"

Brendan tried to shake off her clinging hands. "No. If I up and abandon all my business for what—six months?—I leave it wide open for any man jack to come in and take over, take all my contracts away from me. And between Miriam and his farms, Ev has well nigh given up all commerce." At last he turned to her. "He's not a businessman at heart, Elle."

Gripping his shoulders, Elle moved against him sinuously. "But you must, Brendan! I've only just . . . found you, I can't lose you for six months or more!"

Brendan shrugged. "It's your business, Elle. Sapele is *my* business." Moving to Elle's dressing table, Brendan helped himself to some medicinal brandy. Elle's rheumatism had been much better these past months, so she hadn't drank much medicine, and he hoped the guiacum hadn't gone rancid.

"But . . ." Her voice was a waifish whisper. "I can't . . ."

The three large gulps of brandy made Brendan's eyes water. He exhaled acridly and almost retched. "Who do you aim taking with you, then? Mateus would be a good man, but he's pretty ensconced with Iden these days. I can loan you several of my Kroomen, and as many strapping Itsekiri warriors as you want, as long as Pulitzer pays them the going rate in *manillas*."

Exhaling hotly through her nostrils, Elle stalked to the brandy and poured herself some as well. With her back to Brendan, she said calmly, "Perhaps my brothers. Yes, since I send them money anyway, and goodness only knows they're capable of getting into enough trouble on their own in New York, it might be best if they came along." She walked in an oblique angle back to the window, so she wouldn't have to look at Brendan. "They're both very good with guns."

"I'm sure." Brendan felt terrible. This wasn't what he wanted, to be feeling such ire toward Elle, merely for having the grit to have a newspaper job. Her job meant she had to leave—his job meant he had to stay. Suddenly he felt riddled with uncertainty. This was no doubt the unease he'd felt earlier crawling up his spine.

They both stepped toward each other at the same time.

"*Amebo*—"

"Mick—"

He held her tight around the waist. "*Ma khia du ugie oron-mwen.*" *We want to perform the festival of marriage.*

Her eyes were eager, yet confused. "We want to—what is *oronmwen*?"

"Marriage." Bending at the knees, Brendan wrapped his arms around Elle and stood with her over his shoulder like a sack. Tossing her onto her back on the mattress, Brendan jumped down too, and covered her with his body. "We have to get married as soon as possible, Miss Bowie. That way, I'll believe that you're coming back to me."

"Oh!" cried Elle, and he saw her eyes mist over. "But . . . don't you think it's just . . . plain lunkheaded to marry before I go to Timbuctoo? What if I don't come back, and you become a widower?"

Brendan roared. "Avast, woman! Stop sending yourself to the bone-orchard before your time!"

"Ah." Elle seemed to agree. "I wanted to wait for that fancy wedding ensemble from New York."

Brendan growled some more into her neck. "I will find you the fanciest Edo ensemble ever created."

Elle stroked his back. "But when I do not bleed on the marriage bed spread . . ."

She referred to the ritual of the bride taking her bed spread to her mother-in-law to demonstrate she was a virgin. If there was no blood, all wasn't lost, however. "You just tell her of the other men in your life, and take an oath of fidelity, faithfulness, trustworthiness, and honesty. Besides, who is your mother-in-law?"

"Oh, my. Mary Wells?" Elle giggled. "And who will be my father? Whose lap will I sit on during the wedding?"

"No one! You're not sitting on anyone's lap! Except mayhap . . . let's see . . ." Who was old or unattractive enough for the job?

"Ralph Moor?" Elle giggled, as though she had heard his thoughts.

"No! All right, then—Major Gallwey."

"OK. Henry. He's the most like a father, anyway." Propping herself up on her elbow, Elle seemed to be warming to the idea of a quick wedding. "And where shall you find me the fanciest Edo ensemble?"

"Ah. It's already taken care of, *amebo*. Iden's family in Edo is sewing it as we lie here. And when you come along the road toward my house, me, Evin, Onaiwu, Brad, Charlie, Mateus, Henry, we will all shout, *"Ovbioha gha mien aro-aro!"*

Elle screwed up her pretty face. "Bride, be embarrassed? The bride is embarrassed?"

Roaring louder, Brendan leaped upon the woman, and they rolled over and over each other on the bed. Brendan wound up on top, pinning her motionless to the mattress with his thighs. He brushed his mouth against hers. "The bride is proud."

Elle sighed, locking her thighs around his hips. "Oh, aye. This bride is proud."

He slid inside her, and she sighed like the harmattan winds through the sails, as she did when she was particularly pleased.

EPILOGUE

April 15, 1898
Sapele

"Milos, darling. Have they loaded the paraffin tins yet?"

An uncoordinated and adorable crashing of metalware came from the kitchen. "You bet your bones," Elle's brother hollered back. "That Lugard guy sent me an entire list of stuff the West African Field Force took with them on some march. He said he didn't want anyone dying of starvation, like when they went to Egypt." Milos's large booted feet tromped down the hallway to Elle's bed room, where she was languidly pressing womanly items into her gripsack, but mostly gazing at Brendan's "naughty painting" with a terrible sense of foreboding.

She was making an awful mistake.

She was too hard, too determined for her own good.

"But what in hell is a cholera belt?"

Elle was numb for a fraction of a second. When Milos's query sank in, she exhaled with a smile and turned to face him. "I do believe Evin knows what that is."

Milos lounged against the doorjamb, his awkward limbs all in disarray, a tin of curry powder in his hand. "Lugard said that everyone should wear one, and carry a spare one."

Elle's sense of right was renewed by the sight of her beloved brother, attired as he thought was proper. The only khaki suit for his towering height looked to have been made for a sea cow, so he'd dyed a white tropical uniform with brown Condy's Fluid. His black eye erupting into shades of yellow gave him a rugged Oil Rivers look. "Did he also tell you that sitting out at night in your flannels was a 'fruitful cause of illness'?"

"Yep, and to rub your feet with soap before marching."

Elle rolled her eyes. "Milos. I've been in the Oil Rivers for well nigh onto a year and a half now. I've never had to rub my feet with soap or wear a crappy cholera belt. But I do like his advice about rum. Do we have enough on board?"

Milos shrugged. "Depends. What's a 'tot'?"

"A tot? Oh, that's British for the biggest barrel you can find."

Cheering visibly, Milos retorted, "Then I think we have enough."

"And now." Elle turned to gaze at the open gripsack that sat on the bed. She'd been stroking and petting the silk bathrobe, drawers, and toiletries in an effort to avoid leaving. "One last thing."

She strode into the hallway, knowing Milos would follow her, and turned into the bath room. She loved this bath room, with a skylight so one could bathe during a full moon without a lamp, and lined with hanging pots of greenery so lush one could imagine they grew from the very roof. With confidence she went to the mirrored cabinet on the wall and took from it a half-full decanter of brandy.

"Why you stowing your medicine in the bath room?" Milos asked casually, leaning now against the wall.

Elle felt devilish as an *ehinoha*, a bush soul that led man to do evil things. She didn't answer Milos, only took the decanter to the blue bath tub and whispered, *"Degh' igbina ugha gbina, daghi'ko ughaku, tama mwen n'ighe hon." Whether you want to fight, or whether you want to play, let me hear it clearly.*

She bent down and lowered the decanter into the four inches

of cold sludge, tipping it so that some water flowed into the decanter. Happily stoppering it, she marched back to her bed room, feeling even more confident now at the sight of Milos's aghast face. Of course Milos wouldn't know Edo *juju*, the incomprehensible mysterious forces of nature. He'd come directly from New York only three weeks ago, and was still disgusted at fetish shrines with kola nut and chalk offerings.

Snapping her gripsack shut, Elle took one last look at the naughty painting, inhaled deeply, and turned to Milos. "OK! Let's go." She meant to stride coolly past her brother, but he reached out and grabbed her arm so forcefully her neck snapped back and her feet nearly cleared the floor. "What?"

"Colleen. I know there're some strange spirits at work in this part of the jungle. You've told me, and I believe you—about some of them, anyway. But even the most discombobulated voodoo looks good next to you drinking Sal's dirty bathwater with your brandy."

All vim and zest drained from Elle in an instant, as though someone had opened up a hatch beneath her feet. Her lifeless fingers dropped the gripsack and the decanter, which thudded to the floor and rolled without opening. Her shocked eyes regarded her brother's calm face. "Sal...?"

He let go of her arm and shrugged. "Yeah, sure. He took a bath this morning, when you were aboard the *Mick* with Gallwey and Lyons going over those maps." She must have continued staring at her brother in utter disbelief, for his face became shaded with a slight concern. "Whose bathwater did you think it was?"

Raising a hand to her open mouth, Elle looked at the floor, for she needed to see the path to take to the bedstead. She could not have made it there any other way. Collapsing, she sank into the down mattress, and discovered she was wailing like an infant. Here, Brendan and she had made untrammeled love for so long last night, she had finally fallen asleep from exhaustion.

Great irrepressible sobs came from the pit of her stomach and wracked her entire torso. While she knew in some part of her brain she was being absurd in her fetish belief in drinking bathwater, she was completely incapable of stopping the childish sobs that bubbled out of her.

Now she couldn't give Brendan the love potion. Now Brendan wouldn't love her forever.

Showing an uncharacteristic gentleness, Milos sat next to her on the bed, and even stooped to putting a hand on her shoulder. "Colleen, Colleen . . . I take it that was supposed to be some voodoo . . . Don't worry about it. You know it's all bogus anyway."

With her hands to her face, Elle drooled long strings of spit and snot between her fingers. "I have..." she sobbed.

Milos scrunched her shoulder with his fingers. "Colleen, don't cry. You know . . . I don't really think your husband is the rattiest out-and-out big stiff I've ever known. I just said that because . . ." He had to remove his hand from her person in order to admit anything that might show he had an emotion somewhere. "Because he married you, and as your only brother, I don't think anyone should be allowed to do that."

"I have . . . bad *ehi*!" Elle finally managed to gasp.

Milos ignored her outburst. "I actually think Donivan's a good man. A good man who has made a good career in a hellhole like this, you've got to hand that to him, and boy, he sure does pack a wallop. Don't worry, Colleen, you'll come back here, and you'll be able to have kids, and—"

"*Ehi* is the way a person has to go!" Elle shrieked.

Milos was finally stupefied into silence.

She lowered her hands from her face and beseeched Milos. "I don't *hi* well, and my prayers and offerings haven't been heard! Milos, I just don't have the best of feelings about this!"

Milos frowned. "You *hi* perfectly well; I don't want to hear you saying that again!" He stood and tried to pull her to her feet. "Now let's go."

"Why am I going to Timbuctoo?"

"Because you're Elle Bowie, the Daredevil Female Journalist, that's why! Because they made thousands of Elle Bowie travel caps and everyone copies your hairstyle!"

Just as it seemed Milos might really be angry with her, there came the padding of bare feet down the hall, and Elle knew she had to compose herself.

"Mum, mum!"

Mary Wells had taught Ode to call Elle "mum," and it pleased her. She quickly stood, wiping her face with the back of her hand, prepared to hug the little urchin who ran in.

"Mum. Ighiwiyisi is waiting for you."

Milos held the umbrella over Elle's head as they walked down to the anchorage. The light-draught steamer had been loaned them by the Niger Coast Protectorate, as Moor hoped to gain a shred of glory when the expedition proved that the Bussa rapids, where Mungo Park had drowned, could be navigated in such a vessel during the rain season. At Lokoja they were to take on some troops of Lugard's West African Field Force to show that the Protectorate was not really in competition with the Royal Niger Company, to keep the Niger clear of pirates, and because the Company had some good flat-bottomed canoes that could navigate around the flint rocks at Asongo.

It would be a glorious expedition, and Pulitzer cabled almost weekly wanting to know their status.

How Elle wished she could photograph the sight—Brendan, Evin, Sal, Gallwey, Brad Forshaw, Charlie Wells, Dr. Irvine, and Lyons all standing on the deck of the *Mick* heedless of the pleasant rain that was no doubt soaking them, manfully folding their arms before their chests. Scores of townspeople milled about merely to give themselves something to stand next to, perhaps hoping the excitement would rub off on them. *"C'est l'Afrique,"* as Brazza had told Elle. *That's Africa.*

Mary Wells stepped out of the throng to hug Elle. She gave her a crucifix pendant without a neck chain, and Elle didn't know what to do with it, so she stuffed it between her shirtwaist buttons, between her breasts. "My sister," cried Mary. "I'll pray for your safe return. Do not fall victim to the evil of *Ur-immendess*."

He hears it not. Timbuctoo was purportedly the land of marauding Tuaregs, a country forsaken by God.

Elle didn't want to see these people. She didn't want to see anyone. She wanted to be gone, on her way to Lokoja and thence to Bussa, because she had to.

She did not want to see Evin come forward to robustly shake Milos's hand, and ask him if he had a cholera belt. Ode slipped her gripsack from her hand to take it to her cabin, and she was left stupidly holding the brandy decanter. Soon everyone was shaking everyone's hands, even if the two men doing so weren't even leaving Sapele.

Brendan shook Milos's hand, too. They had not got on well together from the start. Elle knew Milos had an obnoxious manner of confronting people, in particular men that Milos imagined were treating his sister badly. That included everyone Elle had ever known, spoken to, or sat next to on a train.

"Take care of her," Brendan advised Milos. Brendan cast a sly sideways glance at Elle, and Elle felt her innards melting.

"You bet your bones, pal," Milos assured him valiantly. "I'm keeping a sharp eye out for any Johnny Turk that comes near her."

How handsome Brendan looked in his Irish linen suit, with his lush silk four-in-hand tie showing off his splendidly strong throat. Elle did not want to see him, but when she looked to his cordovan shoes, he was so exquisite she cringed even more, and had to step away to the rail, turning a shoulder on Captain Gallwey, who was blathering something about a "hopeless labyrinth of rocks and rapids," somewhere on the Niger, Elle presumed.

"Aye, and remember, Milos Voljacek," Elle heard Brendan instructing Milos. "My wife's life is in your hands. She's a precious bit of ripe beauty, so use that Schofield wisely."

He'd given Milos his Schofield!

Elle felt Brendan's presence at her back, felt the emanating warmth of him, his sun-browned skin, the exquisitely pointed tip of his nose, his powerful chest, the freckles sprinkled across his high cheekbones. Gooseflesh rose on her shoulder blades, quickly running down the sides of her calves. There was a sudden hushing of the mens' voices on deck, as though they all saw Brendan approach her, and politely moved off.

Elle turned to look at the *Hindustan*. The new rains had washed it clean of the "Coast Smell," and its corrugated iron roof flashed under the lowering corundum sky.

His voice was syrupy and rich, as though someone had spilled molasses over it. "I see you brought me some brandy."

She had to face him. "Yes." She gave it to him anyway. In the very worst possible instance, it would make him love Sal, and Sal would be with her, so she'd still have that connection to Brendan.

He put the decanter down on a deck chair. He looked at her with glittering turquoise eyes that had never before seemed to hold such pain. "*Amebo*." He nearly whispered, but Elle would have been able to hear him clear on the other side of the Ethiope. "I told you I'm not one for saying goodbye."

He paused for an eternal moment during which Elle knew she had never loved a man so fully and completely. The love that she had thought so profound with Pulitzer now seemed the childish folly of an unformed mind. Now she was afraid to even touch Brendan's hand lest her determined will, always her strongest trait, would be annihilated.

He moved close and their noses nearly touched. "You'll be back," he told her in a choked voice, then stunned her by suddenly dropping to his knees.

The other men on deck moved away in horror, perhaps afraid at being contaminated by such a display of complete love, evanescing on the fringes of Elle's awareness, like trivial people on the edges of a dream. Elle gasped, and couldn't prevent her fingers from threading through Brendan's chestnut hair that blew loose about his shoulders. He clutched her to his chest, breathed hot breaths against her lap, and held her in such complete reverence that the tears did start to drip from her eyes, burning tears that had been boiling unshed until now.

For many long minutes they remained, melded to each other by passion.

The pilot idled the steam engine, the Kroomen lackadaisically set to polishing brass fittings with their filthy cloths, the *Oyinbo* on deck left one by one.

Brendan rose slowly, running his face against her entire front. He kissed her mouth so profoundly it felt he was pouring into her his *ehi*, his spiritual double. Elle grasped him fervently, and she knew she couldn't let him go. She was making a terrible mistake! How could she go up a godforsaken river without him? What was the point, when everything she'd ever wanted was right here, in the rivers of corruption, the whiteman's grave?

He released her, but kept his mouth close to hers, and whispered, "*Amadin, ai yan agbon.*" *Without courage, one cannot live.*

And then he was gone.

Elle was left grabbing the steamer's rail with trembling fingers, her chest shuddering with each tenuous breath she tried to take.

She didn't even notice they had pulled out of the anchorage. Canoes, Chief Dogho's grand ceremonial one among them with its proud Niger Coast Protectorate flag, accompanied them with a waving joy that normally would have swept Elle right along in their cheerful wake. Now she merely gazed at them with eyes drained of tears.

Sal came to hold her. Sal had always been an affectionate boy, and the two had grown up in each other's arms, often for no other apparent reason than the sheer calm in holding each other, much to Milos's disgust.

Elle put her head on Sal's shoulder and caressed his silky

angelic curls.

At length he said, "Hey. What's this medal Brendan was putting over your head? Ah, Saint Christopher."

"Mmmm?" Elle felt the neck chain that Brendan must have slipped over her head before he went to his knees. "Oh! Oh Lord, that man!" And her face went all rubbery and emotional again, but there were no tears left to cry. With two fingers, she withdrew Mary's crucifix from her bosom. "Now I have some-where to put this."

Sal's eyes were round with innocent wonder. "Wow. If that isn't providential, I don't know what is. Here. Let me unhook the chain, and I can add the cross to it."

Elle felt happier now, with Sal's fingers patting the medal and cross on her chest, ensuring they both had equal weight and prominence on her bosom. He drew back a little to regard his handiwork, shaking his head in awe.

"You know, that husband of yours is so wonderful. Sometimes, I halfway feel like I'm in love with him myself."

END NOTE

The Benin "Punitive Expedition" was one of the most successful, and least known, of the Victorian "little wars."

Between 1897 and 1914, the Igue festival was not celebrated in Edo. Oba Ovonranmwen was imprisoned in a security force of the British agent Ralph Moor at Old Calabar. When Ovonranmwen passed in 1914 a new Oba was appointed, his son, Eweka II, and the Edo were once again allowed to celebrate Igue.

General Ologboshere was captured and hung by British soldiers in 1899 after leading a guerrilla war from the hinterlands.

A decade later, the German Africanist Leo Frobenius attributed Edo "bronze" (in reality brass) plaques to the heritage of Atlantis, the "lost continent."

Sir (he was knighted for his part in the Benin Punitive Expedition) Ralph Moor committed suicide in 1909 by drinking potassium cyanide.

EDO GLOSSARY

Akpo r'Oba	*The Oba's world*
Akpo r'Oyinbo	*The whiteman's world*
Amebo	*Favorite wife*
Amufi	*Tree top acrobats*
Eben	*Ceremonial leaf-shaped swords*
Edion	*Elders*
Eghaebho n'Ore	*Town Chiefs, commoners, who their enterprise and the Oba's favor, have risen to positions of power.*
Ehi	*Personal guardian spirits. Spirit counterpart or double.*
Ehinoha	*Bush soul. Evil genius that lesds men to do evil things.*
Ekhen	*Traders*
Emada (sing. Omada)	*Sword-bearers*
Erinwin	*The world across the sea; heaven. Home of supreme God Osanobua. The invisible world.*
Eruhan	*Men's kilt*
Esere	*A poison bean, the ordeal of which was a favorite of Calabar*

Ewaise	*Medicine men; guild of physicians*
Fufu	*Porridge indeigenous to West Africa, it can be made with plantains, yams, or manioc*
Idiogbo	*Three sticks planted upright in ground representing ancestors who first farmed along the path.*
Idjere ro Oyinbo	*Wide, paved, white men's roads*
Igbesanmwan	*Ivory carver's guild of Edo*
Ighele	*Mature adult men from 30 to 50, they serve as police officers and soldiers*
Ighiwiyisi (Iwi)	*The hunter who shall not get lost in a foreign land*
Igue	*Palace festival to revitalize Oba's spiritual powers and thereby strengthen all of Edo*
Ikegobo	*Altar to one's Hand*
Iroghae	*Youths & men from early teens to 30, they clear paths and repair shrines*
Isikuo	*Festival to honor Ogun, god of iron and war*
Ivbiedo (sing., Ovbiedo)	*Citizen of Edo*
Iwebo	*The most senior palace society*
Iyase	*Head of the nobles; the highest dignitary. Leader of town chiefs, often in opposition to the Oba.*
Iyin	*Sassword, a poison bark that was favored in Edo*

Kora	*Stringed instrument to similar to lute or guitar.*
Kóyò	*Hello*
Manilla	*Large rings of brass first traded by Portuguese. Currency of Benin*
Ób'ávàn	*Good afternoon*
Ofoe	*Messenger of death*
Òkhíen òwie	*Until tomorrow morning; good night*
Okhuo	*Wives of Ologboshere*
Olokun	*God of the sea. Worship of Olokun increased with arrival of whiteman, as he came from the sea*
Osanobua	*Creator of everything in the universe*
Oyinbo	*Whiteman*
Òy' èsé	*It is fine, OK*
Tie-tie	*Raffia twine*
Tombo	*Palm wine*
Uxumu	*Medicinal objects that protect people and property*
Uzama	*Elder statesmen and hereditary kingmakers*
Vbèè óye hé	*How are you?*
Vbo yé hé	*How is it?*

Alphabet: Á B D É È F G H Í K L M N Ó Ò P R S T Ú V W Y Z